ALWAYS
REMEMBER HIM:
JESUS CHRIST

THE WAY, THE TRUTH, AND THE
ETERNAL LIFE OF MAN

Gordonhurd)t/
6)12)12
Toledo, OH,

ALWAYS REMEMBER HIM:
JESUS CHRIST

THE WAY, THE TRUTH, AND THE ETERNAL LIFE OF MAN

Brett D. Benson

CFI
Springville, Utah

ISBN 13: 978-1-59955-300-9
Published by CFI, an imprint of Cedar Fort, Inc., 2373 W. 700 S., Springville, UT 84663
Distributed by Cedar Fort, Inc., www.cedarfort.com

LIBRARY OF CONGRESS CATALOGING-IN-PUBLICATION DATA

Benson, Brett D.
  Always remember him : Jesus Christ, the way, the truth, and the eternal
life of man / Brett D. Benson.
    p. cm.
  ISBN 978-1-59955-300-9 (acid-free paper)
  1. Jesus Christ. 2. Church of Jesus Christ of Latter-day
Saints--Doctrines. 3. Mormon Church--Doctrines. I. Title.

  BX8643.J4B45 2009
  232--dc22

          2009015849

Cover design by Angela D. Olsen
Cover design © 2009 by Lyle Mortimer
Edited and typeset by Heidi Doxey

Printed in the United States of America

10 9 8 7 6 5 4 3 2 1

Printed on acid-free paper

Acknowledgments

This book would not be possible without those men called as special witnesses of Jesus Christ, both ancient and modern—those who have established through revelation what Jesus accomplished with His perfect life. Their words are preserved for the blessing of our lives through the Holy Scriptures, as well as those revelations currently given through modern-day prophets and apostles.

I am also grateful for many other students and disciples of the Lord Jesus Christ, who provided valuable insights and understanding of so many aspects of the Master's great life. I pay particular tribute to those men and women of faith whose writings express their love of the Lord in their every teaching.

A special thanks goes to the following for the generous assistance and contributions to this work: first, to my parents, Randy and Elaine Benson, and my father-in-law, Michael Murdock. I also wish to thank David Larsen, Tom Borg, Monty Cochell, Val Lambson, Claire Allen, Scott Hogan, Scott Peterson, Scott Wilde, Michael and Jolene Allphin, and many family members for their generous counsel and encouragement.

Finally, I express my appreciation to the publishers at Cedar Fort for their belief and assistance in this work. I am particularly grateful for the work of the designers, editors, and publishers who brought this work to completion.

❧ CONTENTS ❧

AND ALWAYS REMEMBER HIM

The very thought of the Savior is often what men and women need to hold faithful to His wonderful paths, especially when challenges surmount to entice them away to different and significantly lesser destinations. Jesus came to earth for this purpose. He came to show the right way that His followers must live to be worthy of the same kingdom into which He has already entered. His perfect life and teachings show his followers the manner of men they ought to be, what to do in every circumstance, and whom to rely upon for strength to overcome temptation and sin. Through the glorious Atonement, He provided the means to overcome the world.

This project began about ten years ago. As a young seminary instructor, our faculty challenged the students to memorize "The Living Christ: The Testimony of the Apostles." Students who could recite the document from memory would have their names printed on the main wall of the seminary building. Of course, the teachers wanted to lead the way in this, and so I decided to memorize it immediately.

I began working on it during a family trip to St. George, Utah. I had a ten-year-old son and an eight-year-old daughter who sat next to me as I drove and helped me to read and recite the the document out loud, one line at a time. Before long, they caught on and were doing the same thing, telling me what I missed. Soon we were all able to do a paragraph, then a second, and then a column. Before we were home, having worked on it only when we were driving in the car, the three of us had the entire document memorized.

What I did not know when I began is that I would be doing more than just memorizing a document. I did not realize that the words of this testimony would draw me into the life of the Savior. But as I proceeded along with my children, trying simply to memorize the words, I found I wanted to be there with the Savior, and not just to know about Him but to know Him. Something within me created a desire to know more than the fact that Jesus had lived a sinless, perfect life—I wanted to understand how He had done it. I wanted to walk the roads of Palestine and watch Him heal the sick, cause the blind to see, and raise the dead. I wished to sit with Him in that upper room where He instituted the sacrament. I longed to be with Him when He walked alone into the Garden of Gethsemane, and from there follow Him through the events that led to the cross. I wanted more than anything else to see Him emerge triumphant from the tomb to show His resurrected body to those who loved Him.

As these things settled into my mind and heart, this desire moved me into a personal journey of searching out the details and reliving with Him Jesus' great life. I began what became the project of my life. In my mind's eye, I saw His coming from the premortal life into mortality. I accompanied the seeking wise men into Bethlehem to see for myself. I continued from there into Nazareth to watch Him grow and prepare so carefully for that special purpose for which He was sent. I watched as He was baptized. I saw how He was tempted in the wilderness. I followed Him from there, imagining every circumstance of His ministry. My heart thrilled as I watched Him perform miracles, provide the teachings of eternity, and perfectly handle every challenge that arose to hedge up His way. I wrote as I went along, carefully recording every moment and scriptural detail up to and including the marvelous Atonement and then beyond.

During this journey, I discovered something wonderful. As it turned out, the true project in which I was immersing myself was not what I was writing, but what I was living as I wrote. When confronted with challenges and temptations during the normal routines of daily living, I thought to remember Him. I contemplated what He had done in similar situations, and I found myself trying to act accordingly. Whenever I was mistreated by someone close to me, I remembered what He experienced at the hands of His enemies and even His friends. I discovered that as teacher, none of my classes were more difficult than the teaching situations Jesus faced in Jerusalem, the challenges of which He handled appropriately without ever losing the Spirit. I found that I too could render good for evil when I faced difficult challenges, and that such situations were an opportunity for me to learn to become more like my Savior.

Through these experiences I discovered that I understood better the sacramental promise: If we are willing to take upon ourselves the name of Jesus Christ, "and always remember him and keep his commandments which he has given [us]; that [we] may always have his Spirit to be with [us]" (D&C 20:77). It happened for me personally when I started remembering. And it became much easier to remember the Savior when I knew the details of His perfect life. Of course, I could not withstand every temptation with similar perfection. But I began to rely more heavily on the Lord and His Atonement. I found that a simple prayer in times of need made me more able to follow His perfect example. I learned how making and keeping covenants in sacred places could help me far beyond what I could myself. I came to appreciate that significant tool for spiritual survival in this difficult world—always remembering Him.

My son and my daughter learned to perfectly recite "The Living Christ" from start to finish, as did many of the seminary students that year. Their names were placed on the display wall under the name of Christ for this accomplishment. But more important than this reward, if their experience was anything like mine, they felt the Spirit of Christ enter into their lives, causing something about Him to work within their own spirits. It became an incredible project for all who participated and taught many to remember Him.

Of course the ability to remember Him can come through many ways—scripture study, church and temple attendance, personal prayer, and so on. We should be better able to remember Him because of the covenants we have made in holy places. And we should make a special effort to remember Him because of our unique need for spiritual survival in a fallen world.

For any who desire to better remember the Savior through the details of His perfect life, His story is retold in the pages that follow. Having experienced such a wonderful journey, I invite you to read His life story as I have organized it in this book, and I hope that you will experience the same outcome that I discovered in the process of writing it. I pray that we may come together into a more perfect remembrance of that which was offered in our behalf as we relive His story. I invite you to ponder the Savior's great life so that you can say, like Nephi of old, "Behold, my soul delighteth in the things of the Lord; and my heart pondereth continually upon the things which I have seen and heard" (2 Nephi 4:16).

In this book we will follow the story line of Jesus' life as described in the Harmony of the Gospels contained in the Bible Dictionary. The chapters are also organized alphabetically under various scriptural titles of the Lord as they coincide with the particular functions He performed as the Messiah. Remembering the offering of His sinless life gives us the courage we need to remain positive, through the strength of His glorious Atonement, in whatever circumstances may befall us.

⋙ INTRODUCTION ⋘

JESUS CHRIST

The name of Jesus Christ is the only name given under heaven by which men can come unto God the Father and be saved. Jesus said, "I am the way, the truth, and the life: no man cometh unto the Father, but by me" (John 14:6). Only through the teachings and Atonement of Jesus Christ can we return to our Father in Heaven and have eternal life with our families in the celestial kingdom. Such is the importance of this one life to all mankind.

Most modern calendars count the year of Jesus' birth as their starting point. (Scripturally, we refer to this era as the "meridian of time, the time in which Jesus Christ was born in Bethlehem of Judea.") Jesus Christ was born in Bethlehem of Judea. Based on the time of Jesus' birth, as marked across the world by the apperance of a new star, the world's time was "adjusted and systematized with reference to the time of the Savior's birth; and this method of reckoning is in use among all Christian nations."[1] Even the history of modern time has established the significance of this one life to every life throughout the world—from those who lived in the era designated Before Christ (BC) to those who came in the years after His birth, Anno Domini (AD).

The holy scriptures best establish the importance of the Lord Jesus Christ. They hold the prophecies that preceded His birth; the fulfillment of those prophecies in His life and works; and the teachings, laws, required covenants and ordinances, and doctrines of salvation that constitute His gospel. They outline the plan of happiness established in heaven from the foundation of the world. They teach the need for a Savior, and they show the fulfillment of that need in Jesus of Nazareth who was crucified and died to save those who would follow Him in faith. They testify of the resurrected Christ who accomplished what He was sent forth to do. They prophesy of the manner in which His message will go forth unto all men.

But even with everything the scriptures have given us there are many who simply do not understand. There are those who slip away from the true path of life and find themselves struggling along through the deceitful ways of the world. Others substitute the fashionable whims of the day, which bring momentary satisfaction, for the eternal salvation that only heaven offers. And still others find themselves completely distracted by the various activities of life, thinking, somehow, that they have found themselves.

Yet Jesus came to show the way, teach the truth, and provide the life. He came to take for man the burden of sin, which could not be removed in any other way. He came to provide us with the teachings, commandments, ordinances, and the Atonement—the door through which we can enter to find life and peace. Jesus Christ of Nazareth, the Only Begotten Son of God, was born of Mary in the meridian of time, fulfilling the prophecies that foretold His coming.

Jesus' earthly life covered a short thirty-three years—and His ministry an amazingly short three—yet in that small space of time, Jesus accomplished more than any other man or all other men that ever lived on the face of this planet combined. He established His gospel; taught the truths of eternity; exemplified the way in which to live; performed many miracles; established His Church, built upon a foundation of His chosen revelators; atoned for the sins of all men; broke the bands of death and hell; and arose triumphantly to His Father's throne to prepare a place in the mansions in heaven for those who would follow Him. He brought about His Father's plan, doing all that was necessary so that mankind might obtain eternal happiness.

Many authors consider the life of the Lord from the perspective of what happened from His birth to His death. But the work which He inaugurated in Israel was just that crucial piece of mortality for which He needed a mortal body. A complete testimony of Christ encompasses all that occurred before His birth, through His perfect life, and after His Resurrection. A complete testimony of Him also includes a belief that His word would be sent to all mankind through the workings of prophets, apostles, and the servants ordained under their direction and authority. This work will also consider Jesus' current doings in our modern day through His chosen prophets on earth.

In this book, you will find a recounting of Jesus' life that is designed to help fulfill the very purpose for which He lived. He lived His life for the blessing of all humanity. He truly is the way, the truth, and the life. The way of salvation was demonstrated by the Lord Himself through His own words and works, and that is why we continue to retell His story as often as men will hear it.

Notes

1. James E. Talmage, *Jesus the Christ* (Salt Lake City: Deseret Book, 1977), 54–55.

1

⤜ ALPHA AND OMEGA ⤛

FROM BEFORE THE WORLD BEGAN

Alpha and Omega: A title given of the Lord, indicating His all-encompassing power, according to the scripture: "I am Alpha and Omega, the beginning and the ending, saith the Lord, which is, and which was, and which is to come, the Almighty" (Revelation 1:8). The name is derived from the first and last letters of the Greek alphabet, indicating that this is the Almighty Jehovah, whose influence spans time and space. The Lord also used this title in His self-introduction to the people of the New World when He declared: I am the light and life of the world. I am Alpha and Omega, the beginning and the end (3 Nephi 9:18). He is Adonai, whose life and teachings would establish the blessings of eternity for all mankind. He is the Firstborn of the Father, whose influence would touch all and penetrate every heart (see D&C 1:2). He would come to earth as the Anointed, the Advocate, the Atoning One, the Author and Finisher of our faith (see Hebrews 12:2), the great Amen.

The story of the Son of God began long before His mortal doings. The Apostle John taught concerning Him: "The same was in the beginning with God" (John 1:2). In the premortal world, the Savior prepared with His Father to help mankind obtain the kind of life God had in store for His faithful sons and daughters. The Firstborn did all things necessary for His ordained mission. He progressed unto Godhood in every capacity of intelligence and power, not forgetting that such influence must be perfectly governed through love and humility.

Before coming to earth, Jehovah was foreordained the Savior and

Redeemer of mankind. The same Being who said to Jeremiah, "Before I formed thee in the belly I knew thee; and before thou camest forth out of the womb I sanctified thee, and I ordained thee a prophet unto the nations" (Jeremiah 1:5) also received His own foreordination in heaven.

Also known in premortal realms as the Word (see John 1:1), Jesus magnified His Father's will in the creation of worlds, including the earth upon which His subjects would dwell. John taught that "the Word was with God, and the Word was God. . . . All things were made by him; and without him was not any thing made that was made" (John 1:1–3). The Apostle John would reveal how this same "Word was made flesh, and dwelt among us" (John 1:14).

But long before Jesus' advent into mortality, Heavenly Father presented a great plan to all of His spirit sons and daughters. This plan, He announced, would require a Savior. Upon learning of this plan, the hosts of heaven rejoiced and the "morning stars sang together, and all the sons of God shouted for joy" (see Job 38:4–7). Heavenly Father's children acknowledged the need for a glorious Savior to make it possible that "the spirit shall return unto God who gave it" (Ecclesiastes 12:7).

When Heavenly Father presented His plan, Jesus stood forth and accepted His role as Savior and Redeemer: "And one answered like unto the Son of Man: Here am I, send me" (Abraham 3:27), saying also, "Father, thy will be done, and the glory be thine forever" (Moses 4:2). The results that followed such willingness and humility would one day bring the Son of God to declare on earth, "And now, O Father, glorify thou me with thine own self with the glory which I had with thee before the world was" (John 17:5).

In those great events that followed this primeval council in heaven, the way of salvation was established and the Lord was chosen and set apart from all others to do His great work. It was then that Lucifer rebelled. Jesus obtained further glory by way of His perfect preparation and victory in the war that ensued after Lucifer eagerly attempted to accept that special role of Savior in Jesus' place. This "son of the morning" soon became the devil, seeking only to destroy the plan of God.

While Lucifer insisted on compelling the souls of men, Jesus offered to fulfill His Father's will by going personally among the sons of men as their Teacher and Exemplar, allowing them to choose which path they would follow. It was upon this point that the great contention resulted, "And there was war in heaven, Michael and his angels fought against the dragon;

and the dragon fought and his angels, And prevailed not; neither was their place found any more in heaven. And the great dragon was cast out, that old serpent, called the Devil, and Satan, which deceiveth the whole world: he was cast out into the earth, and his angels were cast out with him" (Revelation 12:7–9).

As a result of this war in heaven, Lucifer, the very one who insisted that even one soul would not be lost, caused the destruction of a third of the host of heaven. "Wherefore, because that Satan rebelled against me, and sought to destroy the agency of man, which I, the Lord God, had given him, and also, that I should give unto him mine own power; by the power of mine Only Begotten, I caused that he should be cast down; And he became Satan, yea, even the devil, the father of all lies, to deceive and to blind men, and to lead them captive at his will, even as many as would not hearken unto my voice" (Moses 4:3–4).

This terrible war erupted in the heavens according to the scriptures, wherein the warring hosts of heaven, known figuratively as the dragon and his angels—being literally Lucifer and his band of followers—were overcome and cast out.

> And I heard a loud voice saying in heaven, Now is come salvation, and strength, and the kingdom of our God, and the power of his Christ: for the accuser of our brethren is cast down, which accused them before our God day and night. And they overcame him by the blood of the Lamb, and by the word of their testimony; and they loved not their lives unto the death. Therefore, rejoice, ye heavens, and ye that dwell in them. Woe to the inhabiters of the earth and of the sea! for the devil is come down unto you, having great wrath, because he knoweth that he hath but a short time. (Revelation 12:10–12)

In contrast to the love and life made possible through the Savior of the World, came this hateful and dead branch. Lucifer opposed the Father's plan and brought a third part of the host of heaven with him. In so doing, he fell and influenced many others to follow away with him from God to perdition. Having failed to keep their first estate, they became a disembodied host. They lost the opportunity to progress into mortality and the possibility of immortality and eternal life.

Seeing this in vision, Isaiah asked, "How art thou fallen from heaven, O Lucifer, son of the morning! how art thou cut down to the ground, which didst weaken the nations! For thou hast said in thine heart, I will ascend into heaven, I will exalt my throne above the stars of God: I will sit also upon the mount of the congregation, in the sides of the north: I will ascend above the heights of the clouds; I will be like the most High. . . . But thou art cast out of thy grave like an abominable branch" (Isaiah 14:12–14, 19).

From that trying period in premortality that developed the righteous character of Heavenly Father's faithful sons and daughters, the Savior of mankind has served in His place beside His Father. The One anointed as Christ then established His testimony on earth from the premortal realms through revelations to prophets, who were sent forth to declare it among those already in the flesh. Jesus later fulfilled those prophecies by personally coming forth from His throne above to stand upon His footstool below.

From before the beginning of time, Jesus Christ thus demonstrated the way that men should be, and many chose to follow and become like their perfect Leader. The Firstborn among Heavenly Father's children was willingly obedient, humble, and faithful, seeking only the glory and will of the Father. Jesus established the way and provided the power of salvation. A testimony of Christ was of pre-eminent importance for man, even before the dawning of mortality on the earth. Having a testimony of Jesus Christ was an essential step in overcoming the dragon, and holding to that testimony while on earth determines the level of righteousness a man obtains. It is only through a steadfast reliance upon the Lamb that the valiant can ever be victorious in the battle for the souls of men.

ADDITIONAL COMMENTARY

Another Reference to the Premortal Life of Man:

> The doctrine of man's premortal state as spirit children of God was broadly defended by Jewish tradition, specifically through the Pharisees, and was also widely taught by Origen . . . The (Jewish) Talmud itself teaches the premortal existence of the soul: "In the seventh heaven, Araboth, are stored the spirits and the souls which have still to be created (Chag. 12b), i.e., the unborn souls which have yet to be united to bodies . . . The Guph [is] the celestial store-house where these souls await their time to inhabit a human body."[1]

Men Became Blessed in the Premortal Realms: The scriptures and the prophets tell of what occurred in heaven before the earth was formed. Our efforts there justify our varying conditions on earth. This principle negates the idea of men being placed into situations of "unjust favoritism."[2] John confirms that some warred valiantly and overcame the dragon Lucifer. The Joseph Smith translation of Revelation 12:11 renders the scripture thus: "For they have overcome him by the blood of the Lamb, and by the word of their testimony; for they loved not their own lives, but kept the testimony even unto death."

Premortal Versus Mortal Progression: President Joseph Fielding Smith explained:

> In the former life we were spirits. In order that we should advance and eventually gain the goal of perfection, it was made known that we would receive tabernacles of flesh and bones and have to pass through mortality where we would be tried and proved to see if we, by trial, would prepare ourselves for exaltation. We were made to realize, in the presence of our glorious Father, who had a tangible body of flesh and bones which shone like the sun, that we were, as spirits, far inferior in our station to him.[3]

First Estate Versus Second Estate: Abraham saw through revelation the spiritual rewards that result from keeping the first and second estate. "And they who keep their first estate shall be added upon; and they who keep not their first estate shall not have glory in the same kingdom with those who keep their first estate; and they who keep their second estate shall have glory added upon their heads forever and ever" (Abraham 3:26).

The Importance of Eternal Laws First Given in that Premortal World: The Prophet Joseph Smith instructed,

> The organization of the spiritual and heavenly worlds, and of spiritual and heavenly beings, was agreeable to the most perfect order and harmony: their limits and bounds were fixed irrevocably, and voluntarily subscribed to in their heavenly estate by themselves, and were by our first parents subscribed to upon the earth. Hence the importance of embracing and subscribing to principles of eternal truth by all men upon the earth that expect eternal life.[4]

He Sent Me Here to Earth: "He sent me here to earth, by faith to live his plan. The Spirit whispers this to me and tells me that I can, And tells me that I can."[5]

Glad Tidings on Earth: The Prophet Joseph explained the manner in which this testimony first went forth upon the earth when he said, "God . . . prepared a sacrifice in the gift of His own Son, who should be sent in due time, to prepare a way, or open a door through which man might enter into the Lord's presence, whence he had been cast out for disobedience. From time to time these glad tidings were sounded in the ears of men in different ages of the world down to the time of Messiah's coming."[6]

Notes

1. Abraham Cohen, *Everyman's Talmud* (New York: Schocken Books, 1995), 78, as quoted by Scott R. Petersen in *Where Have All The Prophet's Gone?* (Springville, Utah: Cedar Fort, 2005), 86–87.
2. Ibid.
3. Joseph Fielding Smith, *Doctrines of Salvation*, comp. Bruce R. McConkie (Salt Lake City: Bookcraft, 1954), 1:57.
4. Joseph Smith, *History of The Church of Jesus Christ of Latter-day Saints* (Salt Lake City: The Church of Jesus Christ of Latter-day Saints, 1932–51), 6:51.
5. Reid N. Nibley, "I Know My Father Lives," *Hymns of The Church of Jesus Christ of Latter-day Saints* (Salt Lake City: The Church of Jesus Christ of Latter-day Saints, 1985), no. 302.
6. *History of the Church*, 2:15.

2

✦ BREAD OF LIFE ✦

THE BIRTH IN BETHLEHEM

Bread of Life: Bethlehem means "house of bread," a fit title for the place in which the blessed Bread of Life would be born on earth. The Lord declared: "I am the bread of life: he that cometh to me shall never hunger; and he that believeth on me shall never thirst" (John 6:35). The comparison to the manna that came down from heaven to temporarily save the ancient Israelites was thus made with that greater "living bread which came down from heaven: if any man eat of this bread, he shall live for ever: and the bread that I will give is my flesh, which I will give for the life of the world" (John 6:51). Through the sacramental emblems of bread and wine, the symbolic flesh and the blood, Christ would dwell in man. The covenants they make bind men to Him through the sacrifice given in their behalf. Jesus was thus the elder Brother, the Only Begotten, the Blessed, the Beloved Son of God who, as the Bread of Life, would sustain His children in their journey home.

When the young carpenter Joseph and the choice virgin Mary were betrothed, they did not know they were to be the parents of the Holy One. But Jesus would come through Mary as rightful heir to the scepter that bore the title King of the Jews. Under the conditions of the day, with Herod in power, Joseph remained in obscurity as a carpenter. Neither did Mary walk in the castle halls of a princess, but along the rugged stone lanes of Nazareth, carrying jars of the water she retrieved from the local well. Under such circumstances, Mary became "espoused to a man whose name was Joseph, of the house of David" (Luke 1:27).

A short time after this espousal, the angel made its annunciation of the coming Christ to Mary. Gabriel went to meet her where she dwelt in Nazareth and announced that she would be the mother of the Son of God. The angel declared to this most precious vessel, choice among all women: "And, behold, thou shalt conceive in thy womb, and bring forth a son, and shalt call his name JESUS. He shall be great, and shall be called the Son of the Highest: and the Lord God shall give unto him the throne of his father David: And he shall reign over the house of Jacob for ever; and of his kingdom there shall be no end" (Luke 1:31–33).

The angel further testified, "The Holy Ghost shall come upon thee, and the power of the Highest shall overshadow thee: therefore also that holy thing which shall be born of thee shall be called the Son of God" (Luke 1:35).

After such glorious announcements from heaven, "Mary arose in those days, and went into the hill country with haste, into a city of Juda" (Luke 1:39). Surely she needed the support and wisdom of her trusted confidant, her elderly cousin Elisabeth, from whom she could receive strength. Elisabeth rejoiced upon Mary's arrival and gave her the encouragement she needed. Through the power of the Holy Ghost, this special cousin of Mary knew beforehand, even as the young maiden approached, the importance of Mary's coming. She declared as she greeted her with joy:

"Blessed art thou among women, and blessed is the fruit of thy womb. And whence is this to me, that the mother of my Lord should come to me?" (Luke 1:42–43). Mary in turn bore her own witness as both of these favored women were filled with the Spirit of the Lord. She declared in response: "My soul doth magnify the Lord, And my spirit hath rejoiced in God my Saviour. For he hath regarded the low estate of his handmaiden: for, behold, from henceforth all generations shall call me blessed. For he that is mighty hath done to me great things; and holy is his name" (Luke 1:46–49).

Being the Son of the Immortal Father, Jesus could fulfill the mission for which the Father sent Him. Yet as the Son of a mortal mother, He would experience the pains and infirmities of mankind in the process. With these special mortal and immortal characteristics combined, Jesus alone would hold the power over life and death while perfectly understanding how to succor His children (see Alma 7:11–12). Jesus would have power to do many things through the increased capabilities inherent in a God. The Resurrection would be His greatest miracle; only a God could raise Himself from the tomb and thereby provide deliverance for mankind. In this special manner, Jesus inherited life from His Father who is eternal and immortal. Having God-given capacity, Jesus would valiantly seize all power and the keys over death and hell after personally passing from death to life. By this He would open the graves of all men and thus make possible both physical and spiritual deliverance even as He succored His children with perfect understanding.

Mary returned to Nazareth a short time after her visit with Elisabeth, ready to share the good news with those who needed to know. Joseph discovered to his dismay that his betrothed was carrying someone else's child in her womb. He could not yet understand how Mary remained a virgin in fulfillment of Isaiah's prophecy: "Behold, a virgin shall conceive, and bear a son, and shall call his name Immanuel" (Isaiah 7:14). Joseph's disappointment and grief were overwhelming. "Then Joseph her husband, being a just man, and not willing to make her a publick example, was minded to put her away privily" (Matthew 1:19).

The next angelic annunciation of the Son of God came at this time to Joseph, even as he "thought on these things" (Matthew 1:20). He loved Mary and did not want to lose her. He respected her and wanted to preserve her dignity. While being "minded to put her away," as custom would deem necessary, he was still "[thinking] on these things." Perhaps he was looking for any other possible solution. In the merciful and tutorial timing of the Lord, "the angel . . . appeared unto him in a dream, saying, Joseph, thou son of David, fear not to take unto thee Mary thy wife: for that which is conceived in her is of the Holy Ghost. And she shall bring forth a son, and thou shalt call his name JESUS: for he shall save his people from their sins" (Matthew 1:20–21).

Joseph and his wife, Mary, would be the earthly guardians of the only perfect mortal. Their boy would be the Son of the Highest, as well as the fulfillment of the prophecy concerning the Son of David. Joseph then did as the angel had commanded him and took Mary as wife, but "knew her not till she had brought forth her firstborn son" (Matthew 1:25).

As the time of the birth approached, Rome declared that "all the world should be taxed" (see Luke 2:1) and ordered the Jews to the home of their fathers for the census. Joseph and Mary would have to journey to Bethlehem from Nazareth, a distance of over eighty miles. The city of King David's upbringing lay on the trade route between Jerusalem and Hebron and was always busy with travelers journeying to and from the holy city.

On the eve of the Savior's birth, the inns were not just crowded but completely filled. Joseph and Mary discovered this upon their arrival, and as the time of her child's delivery neared, they found shelter with animals in the only place that was left.

The Messiah arrived in the world as silently as the night upon which He came. Those who were not looking, searching, and seeking for this Light, missed the meaning of the great signs that indicated His coming. The prophecies had already declared Bethlehem as the place of the Messiah's coming: "But thou, Beth-lehem Ephratah, though thou be little among the thousands of Judah, yet out of thee shall he come forth unto me that is to be ruler in Israel; whose goings forth have been from of old, from everlasting" (Micah 5:2).

Jesus would thus come out of Bethlehem, a place that was little among the dwellings of men. And in Bethlehem, He would come forth from the lowest of all places there. His birth in Bethlehem provided a type of what the Savior would receive from the world He came to bless. While He came to prepare mansions in heaven for His Father's children, there would be no room in their inns for Him. Coming with an infinite offering of eternal life for all mankind, the Son of God would not find place in the habitations of man, but only in a stable for animals. The Creator who came to His own footstool as the Bread of Life and the Light of the World would find Herod's decree of death and darkness. But still He came. The Messiah arrived to fill the world with light and goodness beyond the comprehension of those He came to bless.

The scripture record tells of wonderful signs that would accompany the Messiah's birth. For example, a new star. The Bible had long prophesied of this star. The Book of Mormon also told of this star and of the blessings that would be given to those who believed. A prophet was sent to the ancient inhabitants of the Americas just prior to the Lord's coming into the world; Samuel the Lamanite went forth and gave the specifics of a "new star" among the seed of Joseph. He said, "And behold, there shall a new star arise, such an one as ye never have beheld; and this also shall be a sign unto you. . . . And it shall come to pass that ye shall all be amazed, and wonder, insomuch that ye shall fall to the earth. And it shall come to pass that whosoever shall believe on the son of God, the same shall have everlasting life" (Helaman 14:5, 7–8).

In Bethlehem on the holy night of the Savior's birth, shepherds were abiding in their fields, when "lo, the angel of the Lord came upon them, and the glory of the Lord shone round about them: and they were sore afraid. And the angel said unto them, Fear not: for, behold, I bring you good tidings of great joy, which shall be to all people. For unto you is born this day in the city of David a Saviour, which is Christ the Lord" (Luke 2:9–1). Suddenly there was with this angel a multitude of angels who said, "Glory to God in the highest, and on earth peace, good will toward men" (Luke 2:14). The shepherds spoke to each other at the departure of the angels, and said, "Let us now go even unto Bethlehem, and see this thing which is come to pass, which the Lord hath made known unto us" (Luke 2:15).

Another significant response to the sign of the new star was the coming of the wise men. These men were truly wise in the manner in which they sought for the Son of God. They were among the few who came to receive the Son of God after having properly searched. When the sign came, the magi reacted with faith. They went forth in response to their preparations and study regarding the coming of the Messiah. But unlike the shepherds of Bethlehem's fields, who were told: "Ye shall find the babe wrapped in swaddling clothes, lying in a manger" (Luke 2:12), the magi were not given specific directions. Though they had come to the right location as quickly as they could, they did not reach the Christ Child on the night of His birth. So instead, when they arrived some time later, they began to ask among the people, "Where is the child that is born, the Messiah of the Jews?" (JST Matthew 2:2).

This greatly troubled King Herod, "and all Jerusalem with him" (Matthew 2:3). The unexpected arrival of such faithful witnesses brought fear to the king and his people.

> And when [Herod] had gathered all the chief priests, and scribes of the people together, he demanded of them, saying, Where is the place that is written of by the prophets, in which Christ should be born? For he greatly feared, yet he believed not the prophets. And they said unto him, It is written by the prophets, that he should be born in Bethlehem of Judea, for thus have they said, The word of the Lord came unto us, saying, And thou, Bethlehem, which lieth in the land of Judea, in thee shall be born a prince, which art not the least among the princes of Judea; for out of thee shall come the Messiah, who shall save my people Israel. (JST Matthew 2:4–6)

Herod then asked the wise men concerning the time the new star had appeared. Then Herod "sent them to Bethlehem, and said, Go and search diligently for the young child; and when ye have found him, bring me word again, that I may come and worship him also" (Matthew 2:8). The magi departed and sought for Jesus until they found Him. They worshipped Him, offering their gifts of gold, frankincense, and myrrh (see Matthew 2:11). These special gifts witnessed their understanding. The wise men knew the true position of the Son of Mary, the rightful King of the Jews.

Being warned in a dream that they should not return to Herod who only sought to destroy the Christ, the wise men "departed into their own country another way" (Matthew 2:12). Joseph was also informed of Herod's intentions by an angel in a dream. In response, Joseph "took the young child and his mother by night, and departed into Egypt: And was there until the death of Herod: that it might be fulfilled which was spoken of the Lord by the prophet, saying, Out of Egypt have I called my son" (Matthew 2:14–15).

Herod waited for their return, but when they did not come, he was filled with wrath. "When he saw that he was mocked of the wise men, [he] was exceeding wroth, and sent forth, and slew all the children that were in Bethlehem, and in all the coasts thereof, from two years old and under, according to the time which he had diligently enquired of the wise men" (Matthew 2:16). King Herod thus fulfilled the prophecy of Jeremiah who predicted the terrible calamity that would follow among Israel's children at the coming of Christ: "In Rama was there a voice heard, lamentation, and weeping, and great mourning, Rachel weeping for her children, and would not be comforted, because they are not" (Matthew 2:18; see also Jeremiah 31:15).

King Herod jealously attempted to retain the throne of David from the rightful Heir who had come, a foreshadowing of the general disrespect or outright rejection the prideful world would offer its great redeeming King. And yet, even in a world that would largely reject its Creator, there were wise men who did seek Him. The shepherds and the magi who came as the first witnesses of Christ arrived with understanding. They knew the signs of the Messiah's birth. Their coming required a personal sacrifice of their own comforts, leisure, and good fortunes in life. Both shepherds and magi came, the humble and the honorable, after carefully searching the prophecies, signs, and their own hearts. Only then was the greatest gift given to them. It was given freely from the Living Christ, whom they had found, like manna from heaven, after they had successfully sought the Bread of Life.

ADDITIONAL COMMENTARY

The Star of Bethlehem: Some have speculated concerning both the manner and timing of the new star, which signified the Messiah's coming. However it occurred, we know it happened under God's direction to fulfill prophecy. Some interpretations are as follows:

> "A . . . clue to the date of the Nativity is the star of Bethlehem. Chinese sources record a comet in 12 B.C. and a stellar explosion, or nova, in 5 B.C., either of which could have been the celestial guide to the three wise men seeking Jesus. Another explanation was proposed early in the 17th century when the German astronomer and mathematician Johannes Kepler observed the conjunction of the two planets Saturn and Jupiter within the constellation Pisces. Kepler remembered an ancient Hebrew tradition that the Messiah would appear when these two planets moved so close to one another that they appeared to be a single large star. Checking astronomical tables, Kepler found that Saturn and Jupiter had three such space rendezvous in the year 7 B.C. on May 29, September 29, and December 4."[1]

Clues from Modern Revelation: The Book of Mormon records the specifics of the new star:

> And it came to pass that the words which came unto Nephi were fulfilled, according as they had been spoken; for behold, at the going down of the sun there was no darkness; and the people began to be astonished because there was no darkness when the night came. . . . And it came to pass that there was no darkness in all that night, but it was as light as though it was mid-day. And it came to pass that the sun did rise in the morning again, according to its proper order; and they knew that it was the day that the Lord should be born, because of the sign which had been given" (3 Nephi 1:15,19).

A Star in the East: The Wise Men came according to prophecy. Edersheim notes that the ancient Jews knew of the star. One ancient writing says: "'A star shall come out of Jacob. . . . The star shall shine forth from the East, and this is the Star of the Messiah.' Another said that 'a Star in the East was to appear two years before the birth of the Messiah.' "[2]

Hidden to the World: A modern prophet declared: "The treasures of both secular and spiritual knowledge are hidden ones—but hidden from those who do not properly search and strive to find them."

Notes

1. *Atlas of the Bible: An Illustrated Guide to the Holy Land,* ed. Joseph L. Gardner (Pleasantville, New York: The Reader's Digest Association, 1982), 172.

2. Alfred Edersheim, *The Life and Times of Jesus the Messiah,* 1:211–12, as quoted with commentary by Ed J. Pinegar, K. Douglas Bassett, and Ted L. Earl in *Latter-Day Commentary on the New Testament* (American Fork, Utah: Covenant Communications, 2002), 26.

3. Spencer W. Kimball, *The Teachings of Spencer W. Kimball,* ed. Edward L. Kimball (Salt Lake City: Bookcraft, 1982), 389.

3

❧ CARPENTER ❧

PERIOD OF PREPARATION

Carpenter: This title of Christ came from men, based on His occupation under His earthly guardian, Joseph. People knew Jesus as a carpenter. When He first declared His true position among His neighbors in Nazareth, they said, "Is not this the carpenter, the son of Mary, the brother of James, and Joses, and of Juda, and Simon? and are not his sisters here with us? And they were offended at him" (Mark 6:3). Others would ask, "Is not this the carpenter's son?" (Matthew 13:55). He, the same Being who would one day be known as the Chief Cornerstone, was initially known as a carpenter. But Jesus had come to serve mankind, not only as a carpenter of homes, but as the very Creator of the world. In fact Jesus had come to do more than construct a world. He had come to build men. He would be the Christ, the Captain of Man's Salvation, the Counsellor spoken of by Isaiah, the Commander, the Consolation of Israel, the Chosen of God who would help men to perfect themselves. He knew the worth of every soul as an integral part of the house of God, fitly framed under His direction. And yet, after all that He did to build men, under their hands He would also come to be known as the Crucified.

Jesus grew into a man of perfect knowledge and understanding in Nazareth, an environment where men were not just devoid of the Spirit of enlightenment but were also pridefully resistant to it. Isaiah saw the developing Messiah in revelation: "For he shall grow up before him as a tender plant, and as a root out of a dry ground: he hath no form nor comeliness; and when we shall see him, there is no beauty that we should desire him"

15

(Isaiah 53:2). Like a tender plant growing out of dry ground, Jesus thrived in the spiritually arid environment of His upbringing. As the Living Water, even "a well of water springing up into everlasting life" (see John 4:10, 14), this tender and thriving plant grew to perfection amidst a spiritually desolate people.

After King Herod's death, Joseph returned with his family from Egypt to the city from whence he had originally come. Joseph, a rightful heir to the throne of David, would hide the Savior in obscurity as a carpenter in Nazareth. Surely no one could have suspected that village to be a sanctuary to the child Messiah. Knowing eyes were upon Bethlehem and its surrounding regions. It was there that even Zacharias was slain and his family driven into seclusion. Joseph and Mary knew they would have to hide their family from searching eyes until the prophesying star was all but forgotten.

As He grew, Jesus became familiar with the synagogue, the well, the narrow streets, and Nazareth's surroundings. In Nazareth, Jesus would receive acceptance and rejection. He would grow up as the carpenter's son, working under Joseph's instruction. While there is so little recorded about Jesus in His youth, the crucial information of His preparations are scattered throughout the scriptural record. Much more was going on in Jesus' upbringing than could ever be comprehended by His Nazarene neighbors.

Although little is written about the youthful Christ's preparation to preach, heaven's established pattern is apparent in the records of the training various other prophets received. If the God of Heaven made careful provision for teaching His holy prophets who headed each dispensation, what kind of tutorials would He give His developing Son in preparation for His special mission? John the Revelator indicated the way in which the Savior learned: "And I, John, saw that he received not of the fulness at the first, but received grace for grace; And he received not of the fulness at first, but continued from grace to grace, until he received a fulness" (D&C 93:12–13).

Jesus Himself later alluded to the lessons He received from His Father: "Verily, verily, I say unto you, The Son can do nothing of himself, but what he seeth the Father do: for what things soever he doeth, these also doeth the Son likewise. For the Father loveth the Son, and sheweth him all things that himself doeth" (John 5:19–20).

Later the Jews questioned Jesus' ability to teach; they "marvelled, saying, How knoweth this man letters, having never learned? Jesus answered them, and said, My doctrine is not mine, but his that sent me" (John 7:15–16). In a later sermon, Jesus revealed this important fact from His preparatory period: "I have many things to say and to judge of you: but he that sent me is true; and I speak to the world those things which I have heard of him. . . . Then said Jesus unto them, When ye have lifted up the Son of man, then shall ye know that I am he, and that I do nothing of myself; but as my Father hath taught me, I speak these things. . . . I speak that which I have seen with my Father" (John 8:26, 28, 38).

Throughout Jesus' ministry, the disciples noticed their Master continually praying, at times all night, seeking the will of His Father. Surely it was no different in His youth. Whenever Jesus acted, He did so under His Father's direction. "For," said He, "I have not spoken of myself; but the Father which sent me, he gave me a commandment, what I should say, and what I should speak" (John 12:49).

In this manner, Jesus learned. "And it came to pass that Jesus grew up with his brethren, and waxed strong, and waited upon the Lord for the time of his ministry to come. And he served under his father, and he spake not as other men, neither could he be taught; for he needed not that any man should teach him" (JST Matthew 3:24–26). Jesus did not need men to teach Him, considering His special mode of instruction from Heaven as he grew from "grace to grace."

As always, the boy Jesus did His Father's will. He learned what His Father intended for Him by that quiet and gentle instruction of the Spirit, through the word of the Lord, and from life's experience. "And the child grew, and waxed strong in spirit, filled with wisdom: and the grace of God was upon him. . . . And Jesus increased in wisdom and stature, and in favour with God and man" (Luke 2:40, 52).

Jesus' preparations in Nazareth became apparent when He went up to the temple at the young age of twelve. During the Feast of Passover, Joseph and his family, with the other faithful and able citizens of their village, traveled up to Jerusalem to observe the religious feast.

> Now his parents went to Jerusalem every year at the feast of the passover. And when he was twelve years old, they went up to Jerusalem after the custom of the feast. And when they had fulfilled the days, as they returned, the child Jesus tarried behind in Jerusalem; and Joseph and his mother knew not that he tarried. But they, supposing him to have been in the company, went a day's journey; and they sought him

among their kinsfolk and acquaintance. And when they found him not, they turned back again to Jerusalem, seeking him. And it came to pass, that after three days they found him in the temple, sitting in the midst of the doctors, and they were hearing him, and asking him questions. And all that heard him were astonished at his understanding and answers. And when they saw him, they were amazed; and his mother said unto him, Son, why hast thou thus dealt with us? behold, thy father and I have sought thee sorrowing. And he said unto them, Why is it that ye sought me? Knew ye not that I must be about my Father's business? (JST Luke 2:41–49)

Joseph and Mary noticed the absence of their Son. They returned to Jerusalem and searched for three days before they found Him in the temple, teaching those who generally gave instruction themselves. His parents recognized the astonishment of those present, who reacted to Jesus' unique understanding. Joseph and Mary were equally amazed to find their Son in such circumstances when they expected Him to be with them on the caravan back to Nazareth.

Joseph and Mary spoke in words of reprimand, indicating the sorrow and fear which Jesus' actions had brought them. Jesus' response was spoken in simplicity and gentle reproof from the Master of all men to the two wonderful parents chosen to care for Him. He asked, "How is it that ye sought me? wist ye not that I must be about my Father's business?" (Luke 2:49) His first recorded words thus bespoke His innocence in doing first what His Heavenly Father required. His words also served a gentle reminder of whom He had heeded by staying behind. His actions were not willful rebellion but obedience. Jesus' words reminded His parents of the mission for which He had come, a call far greater than anything that would bring Him prematurely back to Nazareth for the tasks associated with daily living. Such was the profound, first-recorded statement of the young Jesus.

Having accomplished the work for which He had purposely lingered, Jesus complied with His parent's wishes: "And he went down with them, and came to Nazareth, and was subject unto them: but his mother kept all these sayings in her heart" (Luke 2:51). Jesus continued in Nazareth, working with Joseph. He did so "that it might be fulfilled which was spoken by the prophets, He shall be called a Nazarene" (Matthew 2:23).

At a young age, Jesus was well advanced and getting ready for that which was to come. The specific instructions that came to Him during this period of mortal development can readily be seen in all that He did and said in His later ministry. The work he did later required those crucial teachings of the Spirit which only come through revelation—principles such as faith, prayer, and keeping the commandments of God. This is what Jesus exemplified in Nazareth from the days of His youth; he was able to continue working under Joseph the carpenter while simultaneously doing His Heavenly Father's will. His preparation was exactly the kind required for the life he later lived, and it was this preparation that led Jesus to the ultimate way of happiness and fulfillment.

The world would never comprehend the kind of joy that followed the Lord as He, with knowledge obtained from heaven, went about doing good, even as others around Him wasted their time in the frivolity of endless and empty forms of entertainment. While being known as the son of Joseph among the neighbors, Jesus was the Son of God. With remarkable restraint, Mary kept this knowledge in her heart. The good news that one would want to shout from the rooftops was kept a secret until the proper time, so that it could be shared in the way the Lord Himself had ordained.

ADDITIONAL COMMENTARY

Who Taught Jesus? "As I look at the hills around Nazareth and across the valley to Mt. Tabor, I wonder how many times Jesus climbed their summits or knelt in the woods that clothe their sides, and sought His Father's will and wisdom. If it took multiple visits and teaching from Moroni to train the prophet of the last dispensation, what kind of intense schooling would be demanded of the Savior of worlds, and who could best impart those sensitive lessons?"[1]

Labor Enthroned and Idleness Abhorred:

> Our knowledge of Jewish life in that age justifies the inference that the Boy was well taught in the law and the scriptures, for such was the rule. He garnered knowledge by study, and gained wisdom by prayer, thought, and effort. Beyond question He was trained to labor, for idleness was abhorred then as it is now; and every Jewish boy, whether carpenter's son, peasant's child, or rabbi's heir, was required to learn and follow a practical and productive vocation. Jesus was all that a boy should be, for His development was unretarded by the dragging weight

of sin; He loved and obeyed the truth and therefore was free.[2]

Upon Finding Their Boy Teaching in the Temple:

> Yet it is Mary, not Joseph, who alone ventures to address Him in the language of tender reproach. "My child, why dost Thou treat us thus? see, thy father and I were seeking Thee with aching hearts." And then follows His answer, so touching in its innocent simplicity, so unfathomable in its depth of consciousness, so infinitely memorable as furnishing us with the first recorded words of the Lord Jesus: "Why is it that ye were seeking me? Did ye not know that I must be about my Father's business?" This answer, so divinely natural, so sublimely noble, bears upon itself the certain stamp of authenticity. The conflict of thoughts which it implies; the half-vexed astonishment which it expresses that they should so little understand Him; the perfect dignity, and yet the perfect humility which it combines, lie wholly beyond the possibility of invention. . . . Mary had said unto Him, "Thy father," but in His reply He recognizes, and henceforth He knows, no father except His Father in heaven. In the "Did ye not *know*," He delicately recalls to them the fading memory of all that they *did* know; and in that "*I must*," He lays down the sacred law of self-sacrifice by which He was to walk even unto the death upon the cross.[3]

Spiritual Preparation Compared with Other Kinds of Learning: As with all that Jesus did, there is a pattern established in this part of Jesus' story. And yet it seems that some miss this critical point of the need for spiritual development. Instead they devote their efforts to other things. When it comes to physical or mental preparation in things such as athletics, school, or career, it is easy to understand the kind of work that is required. Somehow when it comes to spiritual performance, many people leave that to chance, thinking somehow it will come without any effort whatsoever. A wise man declared: "It is a paradox that men will gladly devote time every day for many years to learn a science or an art; yet will expect to win a knowledge of the gospel, which comprehends all sciences and arts, through perfunctory glances at books or occasional listening to sermons. The gospel should be studied more intensively than any school or college subject. They who pass opinion on the gospel without having given it intimate and careful study are not lovers of truth, and their opinions are worthless."[4]

All the Intelligence Necessary to Rule and Govern: The Prophet Joseph explained Jesus' knowledge and the wisdom that He held at such a young age: "When still a boy [Jesus Christ] had all the intelligence necessary to enable Him to rule and govern the kingdom of the Jews, and could reason with the wisest and most profound doctors of law and divinity, and make their theories and practice to appear like folly compared with the wisdom he possessed."[5]

The Knowledge Obtained by the Lord: By revelation, Joseph Smith also received the Lord's word concerning His eternal preparations: "And the Lord said unto me: These two facts do exist, that there are two spirits, one being more intelligent than the other; there shall be another more intelligent than they; I am the Lord thy God, I am more intelligent than they all" (Abraham 3:19).

Necessary Preparations as Directed in Scripture: As for the time that men have, how many people fill it with fun, leisure, entertainment, or pleasure? Some think that they must mirror their environment, however lacking it is in terms of its spiritual condition. These people remain happily in their comfort zone, forgetting the more important responsibility of pleasing the Lord and growing up in His light. The Lord carefully prepared His spiritual development with the time that He had and set the pattern for how a man should prepare, even when the world around is focused on other things.

The proper way was demonstrated by the Lord and His spiritually thriving servants. It comes with both fasting and prayer, as demonstrated by the sons of Mosiah in the Book of Mormon, who "had given themselves to much prayer, and fasting; therefore they had the spirit of prophecy, and the spirit of revelation, and when they taught, they taught with power and authority of God" (Alma 17:3). It comes with "study and also by faith" (D&C 88:118), which means learning His words and putting those words into action through faith, by which those words become knowledge. Jesus did this, and through His teachings and example He recommended this way of learning to all of His followers. Finally, it comes by going about doing good (Acts 10:38), as demonstrated in the life of the Master who went forth with a life of service, teaching, helping, and edifying mankind, literally leading everyone he could into the ways of the Lord.

Notes

1. S. Michael Wilcox, "The Youth of a Redeemer," *The Way, the Truth,*

and the Life (American Fork, Utah: Covenant Communications, 2002), 4–5.

2. Talmage, *Jesus the Christ*, 105–6.

3. Frederic W. Farrar, *The Life of Christ* (Salt Lake City: Bookcraft, 1995), 84–85.

4. Elder John A. Widtsoe, *Evidences and Reconciliations* (Salt Lake City: Bookcraft, 1960), 16–17.

5. Joseph Smith, *History of The Church of Jesus Christ of Latter-day Saints*, edited by B. H. Roberts, 2d ed. rev., 7 vols. (Salt Lake City: The Church of Jesus Christ of Latter-day Saints, 1932–51), 6:608.

4

⇥ DAVID'S SON ⇤

PROPHECIES TO PREPARE THE WAY

David's Son: According to prophecy, the Deliverer, known also as the Door of the Sheep, would come as the Son of David, the famous Jewish king who slew Goliath. When Jesus performed mighty miracles in His role as Defender of the poor and fatherless (see Psalms 82:3) and as the fulfillment of other known prophecies, the people would ask: "Is not this the son of David?" (Matthew 12:23). Jesus Himself would ask the people, "What think ye of Christ? whose son is he? They say unto him, The Son of David" (Matthew 22:42). Of all of the points which the people used to discredit Jesus of Nazareth as the Son of God, they never argued against His known lineage. Both Joseph and Mary were descendants of the king.

Prophecies were given to prepare the way of the Lord. They were provided in scripture so that all men could have the opportunity to search and discover the Messiah at His coming. In addition to what was written, a living prophet was also sent so that the prophecies could be interpreted correctly. For this reason, John the Baptist went forth among the people just prior to the coming of Jesus, for "Surely the Lord God will do nothing, but he revealeth his secret unto his servants the prophets" (Amos 3:7).

After many prophecies, the annunciation of the coming Christ was given to Zacharias in Jerusalem by an angel. The angel that appeared to this chosen priest in the temple announced that Zacharias and his wife Elisabeth, would have a son who would go before the Messiah to prepare the way of the Lord. For a sign as to the veracity and importance of the angel's message, Zacharias was struck dumb, which amazed the people. This happened to him while he was fulfilling his role in the temple. He went into the sacred edifice to prepare the incense for burning, and while he was there, the angel appeared to him to declare the birth of his son. Zacharias departed from the temple unable to speak.

The miraculous manner in which the angel made this thing known to Zacharias helped in establishing John the Baptist's important mission. As the angel declared to his father, this prophet's work would be sharing his witness of Christ and preparing the people to receive Him. "Many of the children of Israel shall he turn to the Lord their God. And he shall go before him in the spirit and power of Elias . . . to make ready a people prepared for the Lord" (Luke 1:16–17).

In fulfillment of the angel's promise, Zacharias and Elisabeth conceived a child in their advanced age. The events surrounding John's miraculous birth brought a great reaction from those who knew of them. For Elisabeth, "her neighbors and her cousins heard how the Lord had shewed great mercy upon her; and they rejoiced with her" (Luke 1:58). As for Zacharias, his tongue was loosed at the naming of John. "And fear came on all that dwelt round about them: and all these sayings were noised abroad. . . . And all they that heard them laid them up in their hearts, saying, What manner of child shall this be!" (Luke 1:65–66).

Zacharias declared many things through the power of the Holy Ghost at the birth of his son. He prophesied that the time of the Messiah's coming had drawn nigh and many would be turned to the Lord as a result. Among the most important things Zacharias proclaimed was this: "Blessed be the Lord God of Israel; for he hath visited and redeemed his people . . . As he spake by the mouth of his holy prophets, which have been since the world began. . . . And thou, child, shalt be called the prophet of the Highest; for thou shalt go before the face of the Lord to prepare his ways" (Luke 1:68, 70, 76).

John's ministry of preparing the way for the Messiah was so important that it was foretold by prophets. Each Gospel writer specifically mentions Isaiah's prophecy regarding John: "For this is he that was spoken of by the prophet Esaias, saying, The voice of one crying in the wilderness, Prepare ye the way of the Lord, make his paths straight" (Matthew 3:3; see also Mark 1:3, Luke 3:4, and John 1:23 quoting Isaiah 40:3).

The prophet then came forth as predicted with a special mission to prepare the way before the Savior. When he was ready to go before the people,

John dressed in camel's hair with a leathern girdle and began to preach in the wilderness of Judaea, saying, "Repent ye: for the kingdom of heaven is at hand" (Matthew 3:2). Many people went forth to hear his words, from "Jerusalem, and all Judaea, and all the region round about Jordan" (Matthew 3:5). John baptized those who believed and confessed their sins, but many wondered in their hearts of John, "whether he be the Christ, or not." John answered their musings, "saying unto them all, I indeed baptize you with water; but one mightier than I cometh, the latchet of whose shoes I am not worthy to unloose: he shall baptize you with the Holy Ghost and with fire" (Luke 3:16).

Thus began John the Baptist's ministry. His was a mission that would send forth the testimony of the Son of God who had come. Of this, he would prophesy fearlessly. For the Messiah, John would testify boldly before men and kings. For Him, John would in fact give all things, including his life.

ADDITIONAL COMMENTARY

Not Done in a Corner: In the establishment of the Lord's kingdom, the Lord worked through a prophet. In all that Jesus did, He brought along witnesses to verify His works. In the restoration of the gospel in the latter days, it was the same. Joseph Smith the Prophet never worked alone. In the translation of the Book of Mormon, the witnessing of the plates, the vision of the angels and the reception of sealing keys, Joseph was not alone. He was even instructed to have eyewitnesses of the work, who could bear testimony of what had occurred.

Preparing the Way for the Kingdom of God: Modern revelation gives additional understanding of how John would be fit for this ministry through the help of the Spirit of the Lord. John, "whom God raised up," was "filled with the Holy Ghost from his mother's womb. For he was baptized while he was yet in his childhood, and was ordained by the angel of God at the time he was eight days old unto this power, to overthrow the kingdom of the Jews, and to make straight the way of the Lord before the face of his people, to prepare them for the coming of the Lord, in whose hand is given all power" (D&C 84:27–28).

Herod's Edict and the Affect on a Good Family: The Prophet Joseph

Smith also explained the severity of the times surrounding Jesus' birth. He taught: "When Herod's edict went forth to destroy the young children, John was about six months older than Jesus, and came under this hellish edict, and Zacharias caused his mother to take him into the mountains, where he was raised on locusts and wild honey. When his father refused to disclose his hiding place, and being the officiating high priest at the temple that year, was slain by Herod's order, between the porch and the altar, as Jesus said (see Matthew 23:35)."[1]

Behold, the Lamb of God: The prophet Lehi saw the sharing of John's testimony in vision long before John the Baptist stood in the flesh to declare the Son of God. Lehi said, "And after he had baptized the Messiah with water, he should behold and bear record that he had baptized the Lamb of God, who should take away the sins of the world" (1 Nephi 10:10).

Lessons from the Faithful: Like John and the other faithful witnesses of Christ during his lifetime, anyone who loves the Lord can stand valiantly behind Him after searching the scriptures and obtaining a knowledge of the Lord. John demonstrated this by seeking knowledge in the wilderness and then coming forth to share his witness of the Lord. Elisabeth and Mary did the same, and both women stood firm in their knowledge until the end of their lives. Joseph and Zacharias also proved their devotion. Zacharias showed that his life was not precious compared to that which he would stand to protect. Anna and Simeon demonstrated the way to endure patiently in faith. They knew that all that was necessary for life and salvation would be granted to the faithful in the due time of the Lord. Men and women of faith can testify boldly, standing as witnesses of Christ in all that they do and say, withholding nothing from the Lord whom they love above all else—even above their reputations, opportunities, or the luxuries of life.

Prophecies predicting the coming of the Son of God as Established in Holy Scripture at the Time of Jesus' Coming: See the following scriptures: Gen. 49:10; Gen. 49:24; Num. 24:17; Deut. 18:15; Job 19:25; Psalms 2:1–7; Psalms 22:1; Psalms 22:16; Psalms 24:10; Psalms 34:20; Psalms 69:9; Psalms 69:21; Psalms 110:4; Psalms 118:22–23; Psalms 118:24–26; Psalms 132:17; Isaiah 7:14; Isaiah 8:14; Isaiah 9:1–2; Isaiah 9:6–7; Isaiah 11:1–5; Isaiah 25:9; Isaiah 28:16; Isaiah 40:3; Isaiah 42:7; Isaiah 49:7; Isaiah 50:6; Isaiah 53:2–12; Isaiah 59:20; Isaiah 61:1; Jer. 23:5–6 (33:15);

Jer. 31:15; Ezek. 37:12; Hosea 11:1; Hosea 13:14; Jonah 2:1–10; Micah 5:2; Zechariah 3:8 (6:12); Zechariah 9:9; Zechariah 11:12–13; Zechariah 12:10; Zech 13:6; and Mal. 3:1.

Another prophecy has been lost and does not appear in our current canon, but its fulfilment is mentioned in Matthew: "And he came and dwelt in a city called Nazareth: that it might be fulfilled which was spoken by the prophets, He shall be called a Nazarene" (Matthew 2:23).

Notes

1. *Scriptural Teachings of the Prophet Joseph Smith,* sel. and arr. by Joseph Fielding Smith (Salt Lake City: Deseret Book, 1993), 294.

5

✦ EXEMPLAR ✦

THE BAPTISM AND TEMPTATIONS OF JESUS

Exemplar: He who came in the express image of His Father demonstrated the way His disciples ought to serve one another. The Savior said, "For if I have given you an example, that ye should do as I have done to you" (John 13:15). Nephi taught of the Savior's exemplifying actions beginning with baptism, "And again, it showeth unto the children of men the straitness of the path, and the narrowness of the gate, by which they should enter, he having set the example before them. And he said unto the children of men: Follow thou me. Wherefore, my beloved brethren, can we follow Jesus save we shall be willing to keep the commandments of the Father?" (2 Nephi 31:9–10). For this purpose we study the life of Christ, the same who is also called Emmanuel, the ETERNAL GOD (see the Book of Mormon title page), the Expiator, the Everlasting Father and Prince of Peace. We do so that we might know what He did and thereby have a guide to follow unto life eternal. "Therefore," said Jesus, "what manner of men ought ye to be? Verily I say unto you, even as I am" (3 Nephi 27:27).

When Jesus went to John the Baptist in Judea, He went for the purpose of keeping His Father's commandment to be baptized. He found John baptizing in the River Jordan, "because there was much water there" (John 3:23). When John learned the Savior's purpose, he expressed his feelings of unworthiness, for he thought it should be him going to the Christ. Jesus answered, "Suffer it to be so now: for it becometh us to fulfil all righteousness" (Matthew 3:15). Jesus entered into the water and was baptized by immersion, demonstrating the way for men to follow if they were interested in the path to salvation.

At the completion of the ordinance, something marvelous occurred. Jesus came "up straightway out of the water: and, lo, the heavens were opened unto him, and he saw the Spirit of God descending like a dove, and lighting upon him: And lo a voice from heaven saying, This is my beloved Son, in whom I am well pleased" (Matthew 3:16–17). For everyone who wants to overcome the world like the Master did, it is of utmost importance to know what the Savior did to show the way. He provided the perfect example in all things, including the way to salvation. What better commendation can there be of the ordinance of baptism than that which came from all three members of the Godhead on this special occasion?

The only way to enter into the kingdom of God was demonstrated by the One called "The Way;" Christ personally showed the way that men should follow in order to gain life eternal. Jesus taught the true path into heaven by walking it first. His true disciples follow along that same pathway so they can eventually go to the same place where He has worthily gone before them. Jesus testified in a way stronger than words. As Nephi said, "according to the flesh he humbleth himself before the Father, and witnesseth unto the Father that he would be obedient unto him in keeping his commandments" (2 Nephi 31:7).

After He was baptized, but before He went forth to perform His great redeeming mission, Jesus went into the wilderness, seeking the direction and strength of His Father. "And when he had fasted forty days and forty nights . . . the tempter came to him" (Matthew 4:2–3). Through every temptation which followed, Jesus retained all power "even to the destroying of Satan and his works at the end of the world" (D&C 19:3). Jesus demonstrated complete mastery over all things. He exemplified the way to overcome temptation.

What was it that made Jesus Christ able to perfectly withstand the temptations which came to remove Him from His incredible purpose? Being the Son of God, Jesus had power to do great things, but more important, he was continually focused on the things that made it possible for Him to overcome temptation. With each succeeding challenge, He held to His Father's words, quoting the scripture which told Him what to do (see Matthew 4:1–11). The fact that He focused on His purpose is evident throughout His temptations and ministry. When he was berated by His enemies or even His friends, He reminded them, "The cup which my father hath given me, shall I not drink it?" (John 18:11).

It was no different when Satan arrived to attack the Holy One. The adversary began with what a man would desire most. Ironically, Satan offered bread to Him who came as the Bread of Life for mankind. The devil thus tempted the Holy One at the time of His physical deprivation. Jesus knew what to do. He remained steadfast as Lucifer approached, even though He had been fasting for forty days and forty nights and He was hungry.

The scriptural account reveals the manner of the Savior's triumphant mastery over sin:

> And when the tempter came to him, he said, If thou be the Son of God, command that these stones be made bread. But he answered and said, It is written, Man shall not live by bread alone, but by every word that proceedeth out of the mouth of God. Then Jesus was taken up into the holy city, and the Spirit setteth him on the pinnacle of the temple. Then the devil came unto him and said, If thou be the Son of God, cast thyself down: for it is written, He shall give his angels charge concerning thee: and in their hands they shall bear thee up, lest at any time thou dash thy foot against a stone. Jesus said unto him, It is written again, Thou shalt not tempt the Lord thy God. And again, Jesus was in the Spirit, and it taketh him up into an exceeding high mountain, and showeth him all the kingdoms of the world, and the glory of them; And the devil came unto him again, and said, All these things will I give thee, if thou wilt fall down and worship me. Then saith Jesus unto him, Get thee hence, Satan: for it is written, Thou shalt worship the Lord thy God, and him only shalt thou serve. (JST Matthew 4:3–10)

Jesus stood unshaken. In every case, He held strictly to the word of His Father. Any one of these temptations, had Jesus succumbed to them, would have been sufficient to destroy His great purpose. The sacrifice for sin required an unblemished Lamb. After a single transgression, Adam immediately heard the words, "thou shalt surely die" (Moses 4:25). Death is the wage of sin (see Romans 6:23). Overcoming death required One for whom such a consequence was not due. It took a Being whom the adversary had never dominated. Jesus of Nazareth had to conquer every temptation so that He could kneel in Gethsemane and take upon Himself the sins of the world. He retained the power to drink the bitter cup completely and provide, through His Infinite Atonement, a way for man to repent. Having conquered all sin, only Jesus could personally break the bands of death and Hell and thus become the given instrument for the salvation of all.

The temptations that Jesus withstood can be matched to the offerings Satan used anciently on Eve.

Christ		**Eve**
Bread to Satisfy Hunger	*Physical Appetites*	Fruit: "good for food."
Prove: "If thou be the Son of God"	*Pride*	"It will make one wise."
Kingdoms and Glory	*Power and Worldliness*	Things "pleasant to the eyes."

Jesus overcame each of these temptations, as well as every other conceivable type of temptation that preceded and followed throughout His life. He perfectly fulfilled the prophecy: "And he shall go forth, suffering pains and afflictions and temptations of every kind . . . and he will take upon him their infirmities, that his bowels may be filled with mercy, according to the flesh, that he may know according to the flesh how to succor his people according to their infirmities" (Alma 7:11–12).

It should be noted that only Christ knew the full extent of the power of the adversary, never having given in. God is faithful, not allowing the devil to tempt a man above that which he can bear (see 1 Cor. 10:13). This means that since we all come short of the glory of God, "We may not know," and so surely, "we cannot tell, what pains He had to bear, but we believe it was for us He hung and suffered there."[1]

The Savior of mankind held true to His course from His birth to His death on the cross. When the sins of all men hung in the balance, only the guiltless Son of God could offer His great life as an equal payment. He did not shrink beneath the weight He carried. Even as He was being delivered to death by those He came to save, He declared: "Father, forgive them; for they know not what they do" (Luke 23:34). He remained upon the cross in sinless purity just as He had existed throughout His life, whether he was being spat upon, scourged, ridiculed, or rebuked by those for whom He had come to provide life and salvation.

Jesus later said of this offering, "I have trodden in the wine-press alone, and have brought judgment upon all people; and none were with me" (D&C 133:50). Only Christ can now stand as our ideal, the perfect example, the Rock of our safety, the Judge and Mediator. Only He can say in every way, "Come, follow me."

This is what Jesus truly taught in dealing with His own temptations. As He relied on the word of His Father, even so men and women must rely upon Him. Jesus Christ is the Word that was prepared before the foundation of the world (see John 1:1). In his vision of the Tree of Life, Lehi saw how the word of God was the one solution to make it past the great obstacles along the way. John also saw this: "And the Word was made flesh, and dwelt among us, (and we beheld his glory, the glory as of the only begotten of the Father,) full of grace and truth" (see John 1:1, 14). When there are trials in our lives that are beyond our capacity and strength, we must rely on Him. That is why He came among us. His testimony and example remains as a permanent source of strength, like a great rod of iron along the pathway of life. He is the only permanent support. We obtain His assistance through faith and obedience.

This is why the Father, who so loved the world, sent His Only Begotten Son. This is the testimony confirmed personally to all who seek to know, "that Jesus was crucified by sinful men for the sins of the world, yea, for the remission of sins unto the contrite heart" (D&C 21:9). The Atonement is what men must remember and hold to by keeping His word. It was the culmination of His efforts to truly overcome the world. It was, in fact, the most important lesson for man that was given through Jesus' perfect life.

ADDITIONAL COMMENTARY

The Example that Men Should Follow: President Ezra Taft Benson explained: "To be like the Savior—what a challenge for any person! He is a member of the Godhead. He is the Savior and Redeemer. He was perfect in every aspect of His life. There was no flaw or failing in Him. Is it possible for us . . . to be ever as He is? The answer is yes. Not only can we, but that is our charge. (3 Nephi 27:27.) He would not give us that commandment if He did not mean for us to do it."[2]

The Same Areas in Which Men Will Also Be Tempted: President David O. McKay taught:

> When Satan said, "If thou be the Son of God, command that these stones be made bread" (Matthew 4:3), he was appealing to the appetite. He knew that Jesus was hungry, that he was physically weak, and thought that by pointing to those little stones which resembled somewhat a Jewish loaf of bread, he could awaken a desire to eat. . . . Satan

then tried him in another way. He dared him—an appeal to his pride, to his vanity, quoted scripture to support his temptation for remember the devil can find scripture for his purpose. . . . What was the third? An appeal to his love of power, domain, wealth. "All these things [the kingdoms of the world and the glory thereof] will I give thee," said the tempter, "if thou wilt fall down and worship me." Nearly every temptation that comes to you and me comes in one of those forms. . . . (1) a temptation of the appetite, (2) a yielding to the pride and fashion and vanity of those alienated from the things of God, or (3) a gratifying of the passion, or a desire for the riches of the world, or power among men.[3]

Jesus Chose to Prevail in Every Instance: President Howard W. Hunter affirmed that Jesus voluntarily overcame the temptations that came to Him. President Hunter said,

> It is important to remember that Jesus was capable of sinning, that he could have succumbed, that the plan of life and salvation could have been foiled, but that he remained true. Had there been no possibility of his yielding to the enticement of Satan, there would have been no real test, no genuine victory in the result. If he had been stripped of the faculty to sin, he would have been stripped of his very agency. It was he who had come to safeguard and ensure the agency of man. He had to retain the capacity and ability to sin had he willed so to do.[4]

Sinlessness and the Resulting Capacities: Elder James E. Talmage taught of Jesus' sinlessness and the capacities that He alone held as a result:

> What other man has been without sin, and therefore wholly exempt from the dominion of Satan, and to whom death, the wage of sin is not naturally due? . . . Christ's absolute sinlessness made Him eligible, His humility and willingness rendered Him acceptable to the Father, as the atoning sacrifice . . . What other man has lived with power to withstand death, over whom death could not prevail except through his own submission? . . . Only such a One could conquer death; in none but Jesus the Christ was realized this requisite condition of a Redeemer of the world.[5]

In the Footsteps of the Master: Like grasping onto an immovable rod of iron, those who love the Lord will find a support in Christ that cannot be moved by any adversity that may mount against them. This is what Jesus taught through example, so that men might also obtain as He did. Because the Savior held true to His great purpose, mankind now has something to use for support against the railing adversary—the teachings and Atonement of Jesus Christ and the knowledge of the blessings that flow from them. Keeping a focus on these things places disciples of Christ on the same ground upon which Jesus walked for continual safety. Jesus' example needs to be remembered for the spiritual survival of man in a fallen world. Jesus is the Living Christ. As His help is sought, and His commandments lived, His Spirit is amply sent and His grace provided to enable the seeking soul to manage every difficulty. Through the Atonement, Christ provided a way for all mankind to be given the strength and power to deal with things that would otherwise be beyond their ability to handle.

A Book of Mormon Example: Many years before Jesus Christ was born in Bethlehem, Lehi had an experience in which he learned an all-important truth from the Eternal Messiah. It happened after Lehi had become overwhelmed with the great wickedness of the people in Jerusalem, not to mention the devastating effects that wickedness was certainly having on his two eldest sons. Seeking assistance for the problems he knew had grown out of anyone's control, he prayed with all of his heart in behalf of his people. The Lord then revealed the solution to Lehi. He personally appeared to Lehi and demonstrated His power, causing the prophet to exclaim: "Great and marvelous are thy works, O Lord God Almighty! Thy throne is high in the heavens, and thy power, and goodness, and mercy are over all the inhabitants of the earth; and, because thou art merciful, thou wilt not suffer those who come unto thee that they shall perish!" (1 Nephi 1:14).

Lehi was comforted, and with renewed faith He went forth among the people and testified of Jesus Christ. He offered his people the key he had obtained for their salvation. In this way, the prophet Lehi began to learn and teach about the only source of salvation. Thus began the journey of this great man, which would continue until the end of his days with the Lord as his support through many challenging trials.

Notes

1. Cecil Frances Alexander, "There Is a Green Hill Far Away," *Hymns*, no. 194.
2. Ezra Taft Benson, *The Teachings of Ezra Taft Benson* (Salt Lake City: Bookcraft, 1988), 13.
3. David O. McKay, "Unspotted from the World," *Ensign*, August 2009, 24–29.

4. Howard W. Hunter, *The Teachings of Howard W. Hunter* (Bookcraft: Salt Lake City, 1997), 4.

5. Talmage, *Jesus the Christ*, 21–22.

6

⟫ FAITHFUL WITNESS ⟪

THE MINISTRY OF THE MESSIAH BEGINS

Faithful Witness: "Jesus Christ, who is the faithful witness" (Revelation 1:5), is the perfect Friend unto all. He is faithful and true, the Father and the Son, the Firstfruits of them that slept, the Foundation Rock, and the Fountain of Living Waters. This is all possible because of what He provided, both in His teachings and in the great sacrifice of His own life. For this reason, the Firstborn of the Father is the Faithful Witness unto all mankind. "Greater love hath no man than this, that a man lay down his life for his friends. Ye are my friends, if ye do whatsoever I command you. Henceforth I call you not servants; for the servant knoweth not what his lord doeth: but I have called you friends; for all things that I have heard of my Father I have made known unto you" (John 15:13–15).

The time for Jesus' ministry had come. Every preparation was in place, from the foreordination and the prophecies, to the knowledge and the power. Jesus had grown from grace to grace in all understanding and ability. Coming from a forty-day fast, and having overcome the temptations of the adversary, Jesus moved forward into His ministry with authority, humility, and perfect unselfish love. His goodness, proved through the fiery furnace of temptation, would now be felt by all of Israel. That Jesus came forth in such a quiet way provides a tribute to Him. He did not come for worldly honors, but to save men; not to receive, but to give. As He said, "Even as the Son of man came not to be ministered unto, but to minister, and to give his life a ransom for many" (Matthew 20:28).

37

How did mankind receive the One who had come as their only hope, the Deliverer of men? John the Baptist had personally declared Jesus' true identity, and Jesus Himself went forth boldly in as the Lord and Savior. What did men do with that testimony? What effort did God's children make to search the truth of the matter? Did they seek answers? Did they strive to know? Some did indeed search to know the truth. Others thought they somehow already knew the answer to the question of Jesus' identity without any personal effort whatsoever. They would argue the point just for the sake of demonstrating their greater wisdom. Still others would find greater interest in the things of the world and demonstrate indifference when it came to matters of eternal salvation.

When Jesus traveled from the wilderness of His final ministerial preparations back toward Galilee, He passed near the place where John was baptizing. As Jesus approached, "John bare witness of him, and cried, saying, This was he of whom I spake, He that cometh after me is preferred before me: for he was before me" (John 1:15). "Again the next day after John stood, and two of his disciples; And looking upon Jesus as he walked, he saith, Behold the Lamb of God!" (John 1:35–36).

John knew his Master. Through the spirit of prophecy, he imparted his knowledge to those who would listen. His testimony would go forth from John and these first believers to become a witness to the entire world. These early disciples would never let the prevailing persuasions of the day influence them before they determined what was truth. They exemplified the need to seek and obtain a personal witness from the source. They sought after, listened to, and wisely followed the prophet of the day, John the Baptist. By so doing, they were led to the promised Messiah who had come. When John's accompanying disciples first heard this testimony, they instantly turned and followed Jesus. "Then Jesus turned, and saw them following, and saith unto them, What seek ye?" (John 1:38).

In response to that question, "They said unto him, Rabbi, (which is to say, being interpreted, Master,) where dwellest thou? He saith unto them, Come and see. They came and saw where he dwelt, and abode with him that day" (John 1:38, 39).

One of the two disciples who followed Jesus, a man by the name of Andrew, went immediately from that experience to tell his brother Peter what he had discovered: "We have found the Messias" (John 1:41), he announced upon his arrival. Considering that the sign of the Messiah's birth, the star, had appeared only thirty years before (see Helaman 14:5–6), surely there were some who were still thinking about these things. There must have been some who were seeking diligently for the Christ. With a living prophet declaring the good news, there were surely some who were prepared, after long years of waiting, searching, hearing, and now finding. "And he [Andrew] brought him [Peter] to Jesus" (John 1:42).

Peter then went forth seeking the same knowledge that his brother now had. Andrew had born his witness to Peter in both his own words and also by the sharing the more sure word that came from the Prophet John the Baptist. Andrew explained that he indeed found the Messias, the very One they had long been seeking, and Peter responded by going to see for himself. Upon Peter's arrival, Jesus beheld him and said, "Thou art Simon the son of Jona: thou shalt be called Cephas, which is by interpretation, A stone" (John 1:42).

As with Andrew to Peter, so with Philip to Nathanael—the witness was shared. These first disciples carried the crucial message of the Christ to those closest to them first. When Philip approached Nathanael with this testimony, his friend responded, "Can there any good thing come out of Nazareth? Philip saith unto him, Come and see" (John 1:46). Philip had come to know the Messiah through personal experience. He had responded to the Savior's call to follow. He knew what his friend Nathanael needed.

But instead of responding as Peter did, by going immediately to discover the Savior for himself, Nathanael questioned the Master's origin. He spoke as he felt, questioning how such a place could be the origin point for the Messiah. Perhaps it is no wonder that Nathanael would question the Master's origins, considering the reaction that followed Jesus' own testimony in Nazareth.

To the questioning Nathanael, Jesus went personally. As He approached, "Jesus saw Nathanael coming to him, and saith of him, Behold an Israelite indeed, in whom is no guile! Nathanael saith unto him, Whence knowest thou me? Jesus answered and said unto him, Before that Philip called thee, when thou wast under the fig tree, I saw thee. Nathanael answered and saith unto him, Rabbi, thou art the Son of God; thou art the King of Israel" (John 1:47–49).

Nathanael's response came of faith in the word given through his friend. At this point Nathanael had left his place where he had rested under the fig tree and had begun to come see for himself. When he found the truth, as Philip had told him he would, Nathanael declared his own understanding. In response to this, "Jesus answered and said unto him,

Because I said unto thee, I saw thee under the fig tree, believest thou? thou shalt see greater things than these. And he saith unto him, Verily, verily, I say unto you, Hereafter ye shall see heaven open, and the angels of God ascending and descending upon the Son of man" (John 1:50–51).

It was in this setting of Galilee that the Messiah began His personal ministry. His word of testimony in the fertile regions around the Sea of Galilee would go forth from there into all the world. After the preparatory testimony from His servant, John, and the reaction of His first faithful disciples, an important miracle followed to validate the given word: "There was a marriage in Cana of Galilee. . . . And both Jesus was called, and his disciples, to the marriage" (John 2:1–2). Together they arrived in Cana where Mary had some responsibility over the festivities. "And when they wanted wine, the mother of Jesus saith unto him, They have no wine" (John 2:3). When Mary felt the pressure to fill the needs of such a gathering, she turned to Jesus. Her holy Son's response came immediately in words of respect. "Jesus saith unto her, Woman, what wilt thou have me to do for thee? that will I do; for mine hour is not yet come" (JST John 2:4).

Jesus' thoughtful response demonstrated a perfect attitude. Adding to the question the answer: "That will I do," completed His example. In this example we can see the ever-present attitude of contrition in the Savior's life. He said, "I seek not mine own will, but the will of the Father which hath sent me" (John 5:30). His next statement, "for mine hour is not yet come," was a gentle reminder to Mary of who her Son really was, a foreshadowing statement of the special sacrifice for which He had really come.

As in the beginning when he said, "Father, thy will be done, and the glory be thine forever" (Moses 4:2), Jesus' attitude in this example again showed his willingness. As ever, it was, "the will of the Son being swallowed up in the will of the Father" (Mosiah 15:7). In honoring His earthly father and mother, Jesus exemplified the way of heaven. He was subject to his earthly guardians even when the work which He had come to perform was far greater than that which they usually required.

The miracle followed as Jesus acted to fulfill His mother's desires. He ordered the pots to be filled with water and then to be instantly drawn out with wine. At that moment Jesus gave His disciples a lesson in that which follows perfect obedience—perfect faith. As for those who looked unto Him after "this beginning of miracles . . . his disciples believed on him" (John 2:11). Jesus' disciples received the testimony, validated through His works. How interesting that by accomplishing the will of His Father, Jesus strengthened the faith of His disciples.

As Jesus prepared to honor his mother's request, Mary directed the servants, saying,

> Whatsoever he saith unto you, do it. And there were set there six waterpots of stone, after the manner of the purifying of the Jews, containing two or three firkins apiece. Jesus saith unto them, Fill the waterpots with water. And they filled them up to the brim. And he saith unto them, Draw out now, and bear unto the governor of the feast. And they bare it. When the ruler of the feast had tasted the water that was made wine, and knew not whence it was: (but the servants which drew the water knew;) the governor of the feast called the bridegroom, And saith unto him, Every man at the beginning doth set forth good wine; and when men have well drunk, then that which is worse: but thou hast kept the good wine until now. (John 2:5–10)

Mary's understanding of her Son was not lacking. Somehow she knew that only He could fulfill her request as needed at that very moment. She knew that it was not a small favor she was asking for since this was a great gathering. But the size of the task did not matter to the Creator of the world, the same who had once turned the Nile into blood according to the faith of His servant Moses. Even so, through this impressive miracle at a wedding in the small village of Cana, Jesus accomplished the will of His Father. By so doing, He lost none of His individuality as the Son of God. By losing Himself in the service of God, or in the service of His fellow beings (see Mosiah 2:17), He sent forth the testimony of who He really was. Jesus revealed Himself through such actions as the One in whom His disciples might trust implicitly. In Him, they would need to place their faith, hope, and love.

ADDITIONAL COMMENTARY

Only God Would Thus Begin His Kingdom:

> The proclamation and inauguration of the "Kingdom of Heaven" at such a time, and under such circumstances, was one of the great *antithesis* of history. With reverence be it said, it is only God Who would thus begin His Kingdom. A similar, even greater antithesis, was the commencement of the Ministry of Christ. From the Jordan to the wilderness with its wild beasts; from the devout acknowledgment of the Baptist, the

consecration and filial prayer of Jesus, the descent of the Holy spirit and the heard testimony of Heaven, to the utter forsakenness, the felt want and weakness of Jesus, and the assaults of the Devil—no contrast more startling could be conceived. And yet, as we think of it, what followed upon the Baptism, and that it so followed, was necessary, as regarded the Person of Jesus, His Work, and that which was to result from it.[1]

What Seek Ye? President David O. McKay taught, concerning such searching: "Suppose the Son of Man said to mankind in the present age, 'What seek ye?' What would be the answer? Many would say: We seek pleasure; some, wealth, others, fame and power; but the most thoughtful would answer: We are seeking the light of the ages."[2]

Notes

1. Alfred Edersheim, *The Life and Times of Jesus the Messiah* (Grand Rapids, Michigan: Wm. B. Eerdmans Publishing Co., 1980), 291.
2. David O. McKay, *The Improvement Era*, Oct. 1966, 860–61, as quoted with commentary by Pinegar, Bassett, and Earl in *Latter-Day Commentary* (American Fork, Utah: Covenant Communications, 2002), 48.

7

☞ GOD OF ALL THE EARTH ☜

WITNESS IN JERUSALEM

God of All the Earth: The Jews did not know when they took offense at Jesus casting out the moneychangers from the temple that they were responding to the Lord Himself. He who was derided as a Galilaean was the God of Abraham, Isaac, and Jacob, the Governor who had come suddenly to His temple to cleanse His Father's House. After the prophets of God were first rejected, last of all He sent unto them his son, saying, "They will reverence my son" (Matthew 21:37). But the wicked would only plot Jesus' death for the things he said in His Father's name while at the temple. Though rejected, the Lord would yet work among the people, for He was the Good Shepherd who would give His life for the sheep, the true and living God, and the Stone of Israel who came for the support of men. "And he shall be for a sanctuary; but for a stone of stumbling and for a rock of offence to both the houses of Israel, for a gin and for a snare to the inhabitants of Jerusalem" (Isaiah 8:14).

After a brief stay in Capernaum following the marriage in Cana, Jesus proceeded into Jerusalem where He would proclaim His true position to the children of Israel. Jesus came to His temple in the prophesied manner: "Behold, I will send my messenger, and he shall prepare the way before me: and the Lord, whom ye seek, shall suddenly come to his temple, even the messenger of the covenant, whom ye delight in: behold, he shall come, saith the Lord of hosts" (Malachi 3:1). With the coming of the Lord to Jerusalem, the Jews faced a decision about what they should do with the Messiah.

The time was during the Feast of Passover when Jesus first went to the temple. He went there for the specific purpose of revealing to the Jews that the Messiah had come—and it was He. The people heard His testimony but called His words blasphemous. This self-introduction in Jerusalem would eventually be used as evidence against Him when He was brought to be crucified, for when Jesus cast out the money-changers from His Father's house the Jews demanded a sign and Jesus answered, "Destroy this temple, and in three days I will raise it up. Then said the Jews, Forty and six years was this temple in building, and wilt thou rear it up in three days? But he spake of the temple of his body" (John 2:19–21). On the fateful day when Jesus was judged by men, the people remembered this; witnesses declared: "This fellow said, I am able to destroy the temple of God, and to build it in three days" (Matthew 26:61).

Jesus' first public reference to His true identity captured the attention of the Jews because of the comparison with their temple—the object of their devotion and zeal to God. And yet there was One greater than the temple (see Matthew 12:6) who stood before them. From that moment until the end, the people were forced to choose one side or the other. Some considered Jesus' testimony and the works which backed His word, but others violently rejected Him without any honest consideration of the matter. There was little room for indecision when it came to the bold and forthright testimony of the Son of Man.

Ever since Moses's time, the children of Israel had been celebrating the Feast of the Passover. Each year, they offered up animal sacrifices, looking forward to the great and last sacrifice of the Son of God. When "the Jew's Passover was at hand . . . Jesus went up to Jerusalem" (John 2:13). Jesus and His disciples probably entered the city through the Sheep Gate, leading onto Solomon's Porch, which surrounded the temple. Coming from this direction, Jesus would have instantly seen the happenings at the temple. He would have quickly observed the "den of thieves" that had overtaken His Father's House.

The fact that there were moneychangers at the temple would not have come as a surprise to the knowing Son of the Father. Jesus knew His Father had sent Him to help the children of Israel. He had come to bless through divine correction the lives of those who erred. Accordingly, Jesus made "a scourge of small cords" (John 2:15) and then, with the authority of His Father, He took charge of the House of the Lord. He "drove them all out of the temple" (John 2:15) and restored the place to its correct condition.

Some men were strongly offended by this action, but Jesus did not care what they thought. He sought only to do His Father's will. "I am come in my Father's name," Jesus would later teach them, "and ye receive me not: if another shall come in his own name, him ye will receive. How can ye believe, which receive honour one of another, and seek not the honour that cometh from God only?" (John 5:43–44).

During the Passover, the Jews gathered for a seven-day celebration called the feast of unleavened bread. Families traveled from all over Israel to gather near the temple. They came principally to offer up a sacrificial lamb, a figure of the Lamb of God who would come to bring redemption. They had done this since that first ancient Passover feast when Moses commanded that a male lamb without blemish be taken and slain by each household of the congregation and its blood sprinkled on the lintel and two side posts of the door of their houses. The lamb was then roasted on a fire, with none of its bones broken. The meat of the lamb was eaten while standing up, as if the people were ready for a journey. Further signifying their haste, they ate unleavened loaves and bitter herbs. Anything left over after the meal was burned (see Bible Dictionary, Feasts).

Since that first symbolic feast, the tradition had continued but it had been modified to become a sanctuary feast, including a seven days' feast of unleavened bread near the temple in Jerusalem. Little did the Jews know that this year, the Lord would suddenly come to His temple to accept the sacrifices that had been made, but to reject other traditional practices at the temple that had come to be associated with the sacred feast. Many would fail to recognize the Messiah when He came in such a manner.

When Jesus appeared at the temple, He declared to the money-changers, "Take these things hence; make not my Father's house an house of merchandise" (John 2:16). When the Jews heard this, they did not miss its intended meaning: "Therefore the Jews sought the more to kill him, because . . . [He] said also that God was his Father, making himself equal with God" (John 5:18).

The people's reaction to Jesus' testimony roused the attention of the ruler Nicodemus from the Sanhedrin. He also came because of the miracles. He said, "Rabbi, we know that thou art a teacher come from God: for no man can do these miracles that thou doest, except God be with him" (John 3:2). The use of the word "we" in this sentence indicates that Nicodemus was not alone in his estimation of Jesus. "Nevertheless among the chief rulers also many believed on him; but because of the Pharisees they did not confess him, lest they should be put out of the synagogue: For they loved the praise of men more than the praise of God" (John 12:42–43). Others had earlier approached the Messiah in disbelief and asked for a sign. Jesus' answer, comparing Himself to the temple, testified of His power and divinity. Under such bold Messianic declarations, Nicodemus "came to Jesus by night" (see John 3:2).

Being a member of the ruling Sanhedrin would have meant much for a man such as Nicodemus. The Sanhedrin held the authority, so far as Rome allowed, to be the Jewish senate. It had power over both the civil and ecclesiastical issues facing Israel in those days. The high priest governed the Sanhedrin and its seventy-one members, who were mainly Pharisees, with some elders and scribes (see Bible Dictionary, Sanhedrin). Later in his life, Jesus denounced the Sanhedrin as hypocrites, saying that they acted in all apparent holiness while inwardly they were "full of dead men's bones, and of all uncleanness" (Matthew 23:27).

Nicodemus ruled over the people daily, but he came to Jesus secretly. He came for himself to see if Jesus was indeed the One he had long awaited. He wanted to see if Jesus really was the promised Messiah. The pressures associated with going against the tide of sentiment that his Pharisee colleagues had for Jesus, make it surprising that Nicodemus came at all. Even more interesting, his first words were a declaration of his testimony: "Rabbi, we know that thou art a teacher come from God" (John 3:2). As stated previously, Nicodemus based this statement upon the fact that no man could do such miracles without being of God.

Then Jesus answered Nicodemus, "Verily, verily, I say unto thee, Except a man be born of water and of the Spirit, he cannot enter into the kingdom of God" (John 3:5). Nicodemus must have failed to grasp the meaning or importance of the saving ordinance, for Jesus then said, "Marvel not that I said unto thee, Ye must be born again" (John 3:7).

To understand why entering the waters of baptism and receiving the Spirit was so important, Nicodemus would first need to recognize what the ordinance meant; entering into the watery grave symbolizes accepting the Savior's sacrifice for man because the Savior also entered a tomb in His offering; coming forth out of the water symbolizes the Lord's Resurrection into the renewal of life, being thus spiritually and figuratively born again in Christ. In order to help Nicodemus understand the importance of being born again through baptism, Jesus bore testimony of Himself. His words were unique in that they were given by the same person who would ultimately fulfill them. This witness eventually brought Nicodemus to an understanding regarding the ordinance that Jesus required His followers to receive.

The next step in bringing Nicodemus to a knowledge of the only true and living God, was teaching him how to receive spiritual knowledge. Such understanding can only be received through the Spirit. Therefore, Jesus took the time to teach of the Holy Ghost. "The wind bloweth where it listeth, and thou hearest the sound thereof, but canst not tell whence it cometh, and whither it goeth: so is every one that is born of the Spirit" (John 3:8). Nicodemus could not understand the comparison and asked how these things could be. But Jesus was not speaking of the wind; he was likening something from the physical world to something in the spiritual world.

Nicodemus had a physical understanding of the wind that could aid him in his spiritual understanding of the Holy Ghost. You cannot see the wind, but you can see its effects. The fact that it cannot be seen does not mean that the wind does not exist. You can feel it. You can hear it. You can see the way it sways the branches and moves the leaves. It is real. Jesus was simply comparing the Holy Spirit to the wind. While invisible to the physical world, the Spirit can be felt. It has observable effects upon the world and its people. The Spirit can be discerned by men who listen to the still, small voice.

Until this point, Nicodemus had based his understanding only on things he had seen, such as the miracles Jesus performed. Jesus wanted him to realize that an even greater and more complete knowledge could come through the quiet impressions of the Holy Spirit. Concerning such learning, the apostle Paul would later instruct:

> But God hath revealed them unto us by his Spirit: for the Spirit searcheth all things, yea, the deep things of God. For what man knoweth the things of a man, save the spirit of man which is in him? even so the things of God knoweth no man, but the Spirit of God. Now we have received, not the spirit of the world, but the spirit which is of God; that we might know the things that are freely given to us of God. Which things also we speak, not in the words which man's wisdom teacheth, but which the Holy Ghost teacheth; comparing spiritual things with spiritual. But the natural man receiveth not the things of the Spirit of God: for they are foolishness unto him: neither can he know them, because they are spiritually discerned. (1 Corinthians 2:10–14)

47

After their discussion, Jesus asked Nicodemus, "Art thou a master of Israel, and knowest not these things? Verily, verily, I say unto thee, We speak that we do know, and testify that we have seen; and ye receive not our witness. If I have told you earthly things, and ye believe not, how shall ye believe, if I tell you of heavenly things? And no man hath ascended up to heaven, but he that came down from heaven, even the Son of man which is in heaven" (John 3:9–13).

Now that Nicodemus was prepared to receive spiritual knowledge, the Savior proceeded with a solemn witness that would also help Nicodemus understand the need for baptism by water and the sanctification of the Holy Ghost: "And as Moses lifted up the serpent in the wilderness, even so must the Son of man be lifted up: That whosoever believeth in him should not perish, but have eternal life. For God so loved the world, that he gave his only begotten Son, that whosoever believeth in him should not perish, but have everlasting life" (John 3:14–16).

And so it transpired. The people witnessed Jesus' personal testimony through his words and workings at the temple, and at least one responded by coming in person to find out for himself. Even for a man such as Nicodemus, the Lord had much to give. When Nicodemus came to discover if Jesus was indeed the One for whom he had waited, the Savior provided the evidence. Would Nicodemus understand spiritual things after the Savior instructed him about the source of this knowledge? Would the man follow the Master when he came to realize what was required: a manifestation of his personal acceptance of the Savior's sacrifice (namely baptism)?

At this point, Nicodemus faced the same decision that exists for the entire world. In order to accept the message of the living Christ who had come, he would need to let everything else fall behind. He would have to consider anything else in comparison as dross and filth. He would have to put everything else on the list below his first priority: the One who had come to provide eternal life and salvation.

Additional Commentary

God Must Come First: "We must put God in the forefront of everything else in our lives. He must come first, just as He declares in the first of His Ten Commandments: 'Thou shalt have no other gods before me' (Ex. 20:3). When we put God first, all other things fall into their proper place or drop out of our lives. Our love of the Lord will govern the claims for our affection, the demands on our time, the interests we pursue, and the order of our priorities."[1]

Knowest Thou Not These Things?

"Art thou the teacher of Israel," asked our Lord, "and knowest not these things?" Art thou the third member of the Sanhedrin . . . and yet knowest not the earliest, simplest lesson of the initiation into the kingdom of heaven? If thy knowledge be thus carnal, thus limited—if thus thou stumblest on the threshhold, how canst thou understand those deeper truths which He only who came down from heaven can make known? The question was half sorrowful, half reproachful; but He proceeded to reveal to this Master in Israel things greater and stranger than these; even the salvation of man rendered possible by the sufferings and exaltation of the Son of Man; the love of God manifested in sending His only-begotten Son, not to judge but to save; the deliverance for all through faith in Him; the condemnation which must fall on those who wilfully reject the truths He came to teach.[2]

The Key to Knowledge for Nicodemus and All Learned Men: "And whoso knocketh, to him will he open; and the wise, and the learned, and they that are rich, who are puffed up because of their learning, and their wisdom, and their riches—yea, they are they whom he despiseth; and save they shall cast these things away, and consider themselves fools before God, and come down in the depths of humility, he will not open unto them. But the things of the wise and the prudent shall be hid from them forever—yea, that happiness which is prepared for the saints" (2 Nephi 9:42–43).

The Only True God and Jesus Christ Whom He hath Sent: President Marion G. Romney spoke of how to obtain the knowledge of God: "This knowledge of 'the only true God, and Jesus Christ' (see John 17:3) is the most important knowledge in the universe; it is the knowledge without which the Prophet Joseph Smith said no man could be saved. The lack of it is the ignorance referred to in the revelation wherein it is written: 'It is impossible for a man to be saved in ignorance.' (D&C 131:6). . . . Everyone who would know God the Eternal Father and Jesus Christ, whom he has sent, must receive such knowledge by the Spirit."[3]

The Kingdom of God is Spiritually Discerned: President Romney also explained why Jesus taught Nicodemus in such a manner before presenting the witness:

> Jesus promptly pointed to the truth that without the aid of a superior learning process, a process sensitive to the infinite world of reality above and beyond the world of sensory perception, the kingdom of God could not be discovered, seen, or entered. . . . As I have contemplated this text, I am persuaded that the Master was here affirming that the knowledge to be obtained through the gift of the Holy Ghost . . . is just as sure and certain to us as the wind that blows, even though we cannot see it. The Lord was teaching Nicodemus that the process of learning about things from the Spirit is real, even though the Spirit's workings cannot be understood by those who have not been born again.[4]

Baptism Essential: Said the Prophet Joseph Smith:

> I contend that baptism is a sign ordained of God, for the believer in Christ to take upon himself in order to enter into the kingdom of God, 'for except ye are born of water and of the Spirit ye cannot enter into the Kingdom of God,' said the Savior. It is a sign and a commandment which God has set for man to enter into His kingdom. Those who seek to enter in any other way will seek in vain; for God will not receive them, neither will the angels acknowledge their works as accepted, for they have not obeyed the ordinances, nor attended to the signs which God ordained for the salvation of man, to prepare him for, and give him a title to, a celestial glory; and God had decreed that all who will not obey His voice shall not escape the damnation of hell. What is the damnation of hell? To go with that society who have not obeyed His commands. Baptism is a sign to God, to angels, and to heaven that we do the will of God, and there is no other way beneath the heavens whereby God hath ordained for man to come to Him to be saved, and enter into the Kingdom of God, except faith in Jesus Christ, repentance, and baptism for the remission of sins, and any other course is in vain; then you have the promise of the gift of the Holy Ghost.[5]

Following the Lord into the Watery Grave: "As an emblem of thy passion And thy vict'ry o'er the grave, We, who know thy great salvation, Are baptized beneath the wave. Fearless of the world's despising, We the ancient path pursue, Buried with the Lord and rising To a life divinely new."[6]

Notes

1. President Ezra Taft Benson, "The Great Commandment—Love the Lord," *Ensign*, May 1988, 4.
2. Farrar, *The Life of Christ*, 168–69.
3. Marion G. Romney, "Except a Man Be Born Again," *Ensign*, Nov. 1981, 14.
4. Marion G. Romney, "Receiving and Applying Spiritual Truth," *Ensign*, Feb. 1984, 3.
5. Joseph Fielding Smith and Richard C. Galbraith, *Scriptural Teachings of the Prophet Joseph Smith* (Salt Lake City: Deseret Book, 1993), 225.
6. John Fellows, "Jesus, Mighty King in Zion," *Hymns*, no. 234.

8

❧ HEAD OF THE CHURCH ❧

RECEIVED BY STRANGERS, REJECTED BY HIS OWN

Head of the Church: The Healer and Holy One of Israel would yet be despised and rejected of men. But "the stone which the builders rejected, the same is become the head of the corner" (see Matthew 21:42). While Jesus would come unto His own and His own would reject His testimony and receive Him not (see John 1:11), yet it would be upon Him that the Church would be built, He Himself being the Chief Cornerstone. The Church of Jesus Christ would thus be established under the Lord's personal direction like a stone being cut out of a mountain without hands, as Daniel prophesied. It would then roll forth through the efforts of those who established themselves upon that Rock. The Master would bless many under His leadership, allowing the Church to grow through individual efforts, every man working in his office. The Holy One of Jacob stands as the head over the entire structure: "But speaking the truth in love, may grow up into him in all things, which is the head, even Christ: From whom the whole body fitly joined together and compacted by that which every joint supplieth, according to the effectual working in the measure of every part, maketh increase of the body unto the edifying of itself in love" (Ephesians 4:16).

Many reacted strongly when word of the events in Jerusalem, and Jesus' claims of authority, became generally known. Only the Lord Himself would so work, letting news of his mission spread in order to prepare the people's minds before He visited them in person. He knew that no prophet is accepted in his own country (see Luke 4:23–27). The Master would eventually return to Galilee where many of the Galileans would receive Him, "having seen all the things that he did at Jerusalem at the feast: for they also went unto the feast" (John 4:45). Some who held positions of influence would become His strongest adversaries, while many of the humble would prove to be Jesus' most faithful disciples. Before long all of Israel would face a decision regarding Jesus of Nazareth. A great number of souls would come to Him because of the miracles. Others would attribute His power to Beelzebub and declare Jesus a deceiver. He who came as the Prince of Peace found such a variety of reactions to the joyful message He had come to proclaim.

When Jesus first left Jerusalem after the Feast of Passover, He went "into the land of Judaea; and there he tarried with them, and baptized" (John 3:22). John was also baptizing at the same time in Judaea, in Aenon near Salim. The Savior's success in the region seemed to worry John's disciples, "And they came unto John, and said unto him, Rabbi, he that was with thee beyond Jordan, to whom thou barest witness, behold, the same baptizeth, and all men come to him" (John 3:26).

John's response to this complaint demonstrated both the method for receiving a witness of Christ and John's loyalty to Him. "John answered and said, A man can receive nothing, except it be given him from heaven. Ye yourselves bear me witness, that I said, I am not the Christ, but that I am sent before him. He that hath the bride is the bridegroom: but the friend of the bridegroom, which standeth and heareth him, rejoiceth greatly because of the bridegroom's voice: this my joy therefore is fulfilled. He must increase, but I must decrease" (John 3:27–30).

John thus taught diligently, but not of himself. His work was about Christ. Everything he did was for the sole purpose of bringing others to Jesus. He worked with his eye single to the glory of God. John's testimony of the Son of God proved the purity of his purpose. His words valiantly indicate his mission:

> He that cometh from above is above all: he that is of the earth is earthly, and speaketh of the earth: he that cometh from heaven is above all. And what he hath seen and heard, that he testifieth; and no man receiveth his testimony. He that hath received his testimony hath set to his seal that God is true. For he whom God hath sent speaketh the words of God: for God giveth him not the Spirit by measure unto him, for he dwelleth in him, even the fulness. The Father loveth the Son, and

hath given all things into his hand. He that believeth on the Son hath everlasting life: and he that believeth not the Son shall not see life; but the wrath of God abideth on him" (John 3:31–36; JST John 3:34).

John testified, but not of himself or of earthly things. He spoke of Him who was above all as the Head of the Church. He testified of the Father and of the Son. And he did so through the power of the Holy Ghost.

It was in this same setting of Judaea that Herod sent guards to take John away. Picture John preaching before the people and the soldiers coming to arrest the prophet and take him to prison. The reason for Herod's action was that "John said unto him [Herod], It is not lawful for thee to have her [Herodias, his brother Philip's wife]" (Matthew 14:4). "For Herod himself had sent forth and laid hold upon John, and bound him in prison for Herodias' sake, his brother Philip's wife: for he had married her" (Mark 6:17). It appears that Herod's initial intention was to make an example of John for speaking against the king's actions. It would be a lesson to his subjects that even a man who was so revered by the people could be punished for speaking against the king.

Before John the Baptist spoke against the king's immoral action, Herod had respected him, for "Herod feared John, knowing that he was a just man and an holy, and observed him; and when he heard him, he did many things, and heard him gladly" (Mark 6:20). By boldly speaking against his sin, John provoked the king's anger. Though he was cast into prison and facing eventual death, John was not forsaken by the Lord for holding to the truth. For "now Jesus knew that John was cast into prison, and he sent angels, and, behold, they came and ministered unto him [John]" (JST Matthew 4:11).

We can also see Jesus' love for John in the fact that Jesus came to Judaea just prior to John's imprisonment. There He personally spent time serving with His chosen servant. What a blessing He provided to His friend. John the Baptist could rejoice until the end in his faithfulness in serving the Bridegroom. John did not fear the false teachings of men, but held to the word of God and Christ.

Having taught in Judea for some time, and with John now being cast into prison, Jesus left on His return journey to Galilee where He would accomplish a great ministry among the people. En route from Judea to the land of His upbringing, Jesus passed through Samaria "near to the parcel of ground that Jacob gave to his son Joseph" (John 4:5). He stopped at Jacob's well, as recorded in the scripture: "Jesus, therefore, being wearied with his journey, sat thus on the well" (John 4:6).

From the scriptures it appears that Jesus stopped to rest while His disciples went into the city to buy meat, yet as the story unfolds, it becomes clear that Jesus paused for anything but rest. He came to Jacob's well to perform an important work in the life of one soul, for when "There cometh a woman of Samaria to draw water: Jesus saith unto her, Give me to drink" (John 4:7).

The Samaritan woman had long devoted her life to filling her emptiness with substitute saviors. She had tried in many ways to fill the gap in her soul, seeking happiness from all the wrong sources. Perhaps she thought at times she had found exactly what she needed, only to realize that she still remained in the same miserable condition.

Jesus, knowing what the woman truly needed, led her toward a new understanding with His simple request for water. His petition brought a negative reaction from the woman. She questioned: "How is that thou, being a Jew, askest drink of me, which am a woman of Samaria? for the Jews have no dealings with the Samaritans" (John 4:9). Jesus answered, "If thou knewest the gift of God, and who it is that saith to thee, Give me to drink; thou wouldst have asked of him, and he would have given thee living water" (John 4:10). The woman could not understand and remarked that Jesus had nothing to draw with. With the well being deep, how would He ever obtain the water He mentioned?

This Samaritan woman, who had long sought her happiness only from worldly sources with no permanent sustaining power, was about to be led into the discovery of truth. Jesus went on to teach her, "Whosoever drinketh of this water shall thirst again: But whosoever drinketh of the water that I shall give him shall never thirst; but the water that I shall give him shall be in him a well of water springing up into everlasting life" (John 4:13–14). As he said, those who come unto Him in the way He prescribes will be filled with living water that quenches thirsty souls.

Not knowing who He was, the Samaritan woman challenged Jesus to fulfill His word: "Sir, give me this water, that I thirst not, neither come hither to draw" (John 4:15).

If Jesus' first declaration seemed strange, then surely His next appeal was also confusing: "Go, call thy husband, and come hither. The woman answered and said, I have no husband. Jesus said unto her, Thou hast well said, I have no husband: For thou hast had five husbands; and he whom thou now hast is not thy husband: in that saidst thou truly" (John 4:16–18).

The woman grew solemn: "Sir," she said, "I perceive that thou art a prophet" (John 4:19). With this change in attitude, the woman began to speak with reverence of spiritual matters according to her understanding. "Our fathers worshipped in this mountain; and ye say, that in Jerusalem is the place where men ought to worship" (John 4:20). Jesus could now share with the woman the important message He had come to deliver. "Woman, believe me, the hour cometh, when ye shall neither in this mountain, nor yet at Jerusalem, worship the Father. Ye worship ye know not what: we know what we worship: for salvation is of the Jews. But the hour cometh, and now is, when the true worshippers shall worship the Father in spirit and in truth: for the Father seeketh such to worship him" (John 4:21–23).

From calling Jesus a Jew to perceiving Him as a prophet, the woman progressed right along with the teaching. She now declared: "I know that Messias cometh, which is called Christ: when he is come, he will tell us all things" (John 4:25).

"Jesus saith unto her, I that speak unto thee am he" (John 4:26).

The woman then left her waterpot and went into the city. Her silence, followed by her immediate departure, tells of her deep emotion. After having tried for years to fill her emptiness with one relationship after another, she suddenly understood what the Savior truly had to give, and that it was above all the temporary offerings of the world. Her dawning understanding led her into the city to impart her knowledge to her neighbors, bringing them at once to come out and hear for themselves.

Jesus taught the woman at the well something eternally significant that day—the importance of remembering and coming unto Him. He is the living water and the source of life.

When Jesus' disciples returned from purchasing meat, Jesus told them he also had meat to eat that they knew not of. "My meat," He explained, "is to do the will of him that sent me, and to finish his work" (John 4:34). The living water (Christ) and meat to eat (doing the Father's will) brings a truly satisfying spiritual feast according to the promise. "For unto such hath God promised his Spirit. And they who worship him, must worship in spirit and in truth" (JST John 4:26).

This doctrine is also central to the sacramental covenant that always remembering Him and keeping the commandments which He has given brings the promise of always having His Spirit to be with us. The Samaritan woman, who had forgotten, was reminded. Though she had placed her heart on empty things to satisfy her despair, she was now brought back to the one thing she truly needed in her life. She needed the Lord. And then so much good could follow when her heart remembered and returned to her Savior. Even though she had stepped away and become lost, He found her. As He did with this woman, Jesus labors to gather all His Father's children into His safety as a hen would gather her chicks under her wings (see Matthew 23:37).

He went on to teach His disciples who had returned with the meat. "Say not ye, There are yet four months, and then cometh the harvest? behold, I say unto you, Lift up your eyes, and look on the fields; for they are white already to harvest. And he that reapeth receiveth wages, and gathereth fruit unto life eternal" (John 4:35–36).

Jesus built the people's trust through His works and prophecies so that they would come and listen with an open heart. He was the perfect teacher. He would carefully prepare the hearts of those He taught before He would give instruction. With such preparations preceding His words, as demonstrated in the situation at the well, Jesus could then open His mouth to reveal the word of God. After boldly sending forth the testimony of who He was by his miracles in Jerusalem, casting out the money-changers from His Father's house, turning water to wine in Cana, and especially with John bearing personal witness to prepare the way before Him, Jesus knew the people were ready to hear the will of heaven. Jesus had so captured the attention of the Galileans. Now that they were ready to hear, what would that critical first message from the Messiah be? "From that time Jesus began to preach, and to say, Repent: for the kingdom of heaven is at hand" (Matthew 4:17).

Coming now to Galilee, a great reception awaited Him, for the people there received Him having seen all the things done in Jerusalem at the feast. They were present at the time of Passover to see and hear the things Jesus had done in Jerusalem. Among those who went forth to receive Him in Galilee, first came a certain nobleman "whose son was sick at Capernaum. When he heard that Jesus was come out of Judea into Galilee, he went unto him, and besought him that he would come down, and heal his son: for he was at the point of death" (John 4:46–47).

Jesus answered the nobleman, "Except ye see signs and wonders, ye will not believe" (John 4:48). Such a response evoked an even greater plea: "Sir, come down ere my child die" (John 4:49). Jesus then told the nobleman to go his way; his son would live. The man believed the word and went home to find his child cured from the very hour the word was given.

When coming into Galilee, Jesus went from those who openly received Him to His own people in Nazareth. This visit to Nazareth gave the Lord Jesus, as the Head of the Church, the opportunity to announce His true identity among His friends and neighbors. Little did those who ruled in the synagogue that day realize that they, who were the least in the kingdom, would be rejecting Him who stood as the Head. With the general introduction of Jesus' Messiahship being already spoken in Jerusalem, the Savior now came home to Galilee to validate the rumors. He went among His own friends to offer salvation to those He loved, with every true fruit bearing witness of the Tree of Life that stood in their midst. Jesus left no room for doubt for any honest seeker of the truth. He fulfilled every prophecy and symbolism that had been established to bear record of the Messiah when He came.

In Nazareth, he preached among the friends and neighbors of His upbringing and revealed His actual identity to them. But the people of Nazareth could not consider receiving one of their own as the fulfillment of the prophecies regarding the Messiah. Instead, as John testified, "He came unto his own, and his own received him not" (John 1:11).

Nazareth was a small town, so the people in the synagogue that day could not have been strangers. Among those who came were those who had known Him from His youth.

> And he came to Nazareth, where he had been brought up: and, as his custom was, he went into the synagogue on the sabbath day, and stood up for to read. And there was delivered unto him the book of the prophet Esaias. And when he had opened the book, he found the place where it was written, The Spirit of the Lord is upon me, because he hath anointed me to preach the gospel to the poor; he hath sent me to heal the broken hearted, to preach deliverance to the captive, and recovering of sight to the blind, to set at liberty them that are bruised. To preach the acceptable year of the Lord. And he closed the book, and he gave it again to the minister, and sat down. And the eyes of all them that were in the synagogue were fastened on him. (Luke 4:16–20)

This well-known Isaiah passage, foretelling the coming of Christ, would not sound at all unusual being quoted in such a setting. The message of a future Messiah was of utmost importance among the Jews. And yet, with all of the rumors, the eyes of the faithful this day were "fastened on him" to hear if He would confirm the unbelievable reports. According to the synagogue's tradition, a commentary would follow from the reader.

And so, after Jesus finished reading, He declared: "This day is this scripture fulfilled in your ears" (Luke 4:21).

These people had heard of Jesus' doings in Jerusalem and among some of the other Galileans. So when Jesus spoke, everyone listened for what He might say about His mission and authority. Now, as the people in the synagogue heard the declaration from Jesus' own mouth, they began to realize the truthfulness of the rumors. "And all bare him witness, and wondered at the gracious words which proceeded out of his mouth. And they said, Is not this Joseph's son?" (Luke 4:22).

This question shows that the people knew He was referring to Himself as the coming Messiah. His words confirmed their fears: Jesus had proclaimed Himself as the fulfillment of the prophecies. At that moment the rejection began, from the ruler to the elder to the neighbor sitting in the front row. Who could ever believe that the long-awaited Messiah, the One in whom they had placed all their hopes and dreams, the One they preached of and hoped for, now stood before them in their own neighbor, Jesus of Nazareth?

They began to feel their faith was under attack. "Is this not Joseph's son?" they asked. He had come before them just the same as ever, a carpenter of no reputation. Now they were asked to accept Jesus of Nazareth as Jehovah in the flesh, the Creator of the universe.

Those present were offended, but Jesus went on,

> "Ye will surely say unto me this proverb, Physician, heal thyself: whatsoever we have heard done in Capernaum, do also here in thy country. And he said, Verily I say unto you, No prophet is accepted in his own country. But I tell you of a truth, many widows were in Israel in the days of Elias, when the heaven was shut up three years and six months, when great famine was throughout all the land; But unto none of them was Elias sent, save unto Sarepta, a city of Sidon, unto a woman that was a widow. And many lepers were in Israel in the time of Eliseus the prophet; and none of them was cleansed, saving Naaman the Syrian" (Luke 4:23–27).

In this Godly rebuke, Jesus elevated the acceptance of "ungodly" Gentiles over His own covenant and "chosen" neighbors who rejected Him. Such a comparison dealt the final blow. "And all they in the synagogue, when they heard these things, were filled with wrath, And rose up, and thrust him out of the city, and led him unto the brow of the hill whereon their city was built, that they might cast him down headlong" (Luke 4:28–29).

The angry crowd took Jesus to the top of Nazareth's hill. The penalty for blasphemy was death by stoning. In this case it appears the people opted to take the blasphemer to the edge of the city and cast the sinner down from the pinnacle of the hill. However they did it, the law required that they execute him. And who could deny the blasphemy? Jesus had pronounced Himself as the very fulfillment of the prophet Isaiah's prediction of the coming Messiah. What more needed to be said unless it was an apology from Jesus or a plea that they spare him? But Jesus spoke forthrightly and without apology. Now the people needed something to disprove His word. They turned immediately to His upbringing. Jesus was Joseph's son. That fact alone should discredit His claims.

Jesus stood at the top of the cliff, without a friend or anything to prevent His demise. What must have passed through the people's minds at that moment of delivering their judgment? They knew nothing could stand between them and their law, "But he passing through the midst of them went his way" (Luke 4:30). That day, the men in Nazareth bowed involuntarily under the authority of the Son of God.

And so the people were unable to do as they had planned, and Jesus continued on His way. "And leaving Nazareth, he came and dwelt in Capernaum, which is upon the sea coast, in the borders of Zabulon and Nephthalim: That it might be fulfilled which was spoken by Esaias the prophet, saying, The Land of Zabulon, and the land of Nephthalim, by the way of the sea, beyond Jordan, Galilee of the Gentiles; The people which sat in darkness saw great light; and to them which sat in the region and shadow of death light is sprung up" (Matthew 4:12–16).

ADDITIONAL COMMENTARY

The Power of the Messiah Was Thus Manifest:

The visit to Nazareth was in many respects decisive. It presented by anticipation an epitome of the history of the Christ. He came to His own, and His own received Him not. The first time He taught in the Synagogue, as the first time He taught in the temple, they cast Him out. On the one and the other occasion, they questioned His authority, and they asked for a "sign." In both instances, the power which they challenged was, indeed, claimed by Christ, but its display, in the manner which they expected, refused. The analogy seems to extend even farther—and if a misrepresentation of what Jesus had said when purifying the temple formed the ground of the final false charge against Him, the taunt of the Nazarenes: "Physician, heal thyself!" found an echo in the mocking cry, as He hung on the Cross: "He saved others, Himself He cannot save."[1]

Nazareth: The village of Nazareth rested in a hollow within the hills of Galilee, above the plain of Esdraelon, and near several main roads of Palestine (see Bible Dictionary, Nazareth). Mary came from this village, as did Joseph. A public cistern, which served the vicinity was located at the base of the valley, near the center of this hillside village, and women carried jars atop their heads to retrieve the precious water. A narrow road passed between the buildings, leading through the center of the village, with craftsmen and other trades working nearby. Outlying houses surrounded the village, and a cliff stood above the town in the hills. A synagogue rested in the center.[2]

Joseph and Mary on the Day of the Messiah's Visitation: With the small size of this village, there is no question that Joseph and Mary were well known in the community. Mary would have drawn water from the well on a daily basis and thus she would have associated closely with all the other women in the village. Joseph worked in an occupation that required a connection with the people as well. There is no doubt that the people knew the holy family, as indicated in their immediate reference to Joseph at the synagogue. And certainly Joseph would have been there to hear the testimony and the response from his friends, as was Mary. What went through their hearts on this day when their Son, who they knew was speaking the truth about His rightful position among men, was so treated? Surely a sword had begun to pierce through Mary's soul, as Simeon prophesied, when Jesus' purpose began to be revealed before the eyes of the people.

Leaving Nazareth:

> And so He left them, never apparently to return again; never, if we are right in the view here taken, to preach again in their little synagogue. Did any feelings of mere human regret weigh down His soul while He was wending His weary steps down the steep hill-slope toward Cana of Galilee? Did any tear start in His eyes unbidden as He stood, perhaps for the last time, to gaze from thence on the rich plain of Esdraelon, and the purple heights of Carmel, and the white sands that fringe the blue waters of the Mediterranean? Were there any from whom He grieved to be severed, in the green secluded valley where His manhood had

labored, and His childhood played? Did He cast one longing, lingering glance at the humble home in which for so many years He had toiled as the village carpenter? Did no companion of His innocent boyhood, no friend of His sinless youth, accompany Him with awe, and pity, and regret?[3]

Nazareth Revisited: We might consider the way we receive the servants of the Lord who are called from our own neighborhoods, whom we know, and whose mortal frailties are observable. We could think about the way we receive the testimonies spoken in our own congregations. These testimonies are given from God, who loves all of His sons and daughters and develops their faith by allowing them to serve other men, in spite of their own weaknesses. Finally, we may consider how it is not the speaker who is being tested when he delivers a message, but the hearer. The listener has an opportunity to choose what to do with the words that are spoken from above. The fact that those words come through men is exactly the way the Lord has ordained it. He works through the weak things of the earth so that the glory remains with the Father. Let no man speak evil of the Lord's anointed.

Notes
1. Edersheim, *The Life and Times of Jesus the Messiah*, 451.
2. O. Preston Robinson and Christine H. Robinson, *The Holy Land* (Salt Lake City: Deseret Book, 1963), 111–12.
3. Farrar, *The Life of Christ*, 188.

9

❖ IMMANUEL ❖

THE CALLING OF THE FISHERMEN

Immanuel: The Great I AM made flesh, the sinless Intercessor whose innocent blood was betrayed (see Matthew 27:4), came according to the prophecy: "Behold, a virgin shall conceive, and bear a son, and shall call his name, Immanuel" (Isaiah 7:14). This scripture is quoted in Matthew, demonstrating its fulfillment in Jesus through Mary, that she was indeed the virgin to conceive and that "they shall call his name Emmanuel, which being interpreted is, God with us" (Matthew 1:23). When Jesus called His disciples from their employ as fishermen to their new mission as "fishers of men" (see Matthew 4:19), He quickly demonstrated that God loves His children. He reaches out to them in this life. Though we are sent away from our home above, God comes to be with us through His own presence or in the sending of His servants.

One of the amazing qualities of the Savior is that no matter what treatment He received, He went on. He did not allow discouragement to prevent His course. He sought only to lift those around Him. After being tempted, rejected, or abused, Jesus simply continued to teach, accept, and to bless. Such was the case in Capernaum. Following that which had occurred in Nazareth, He went forward to Capernaum to teach any who would listen. Though previously tempted with worldly power and riches, Jesus "went about all Galilee, teaching in their synagogues, and preaching the gospel of the kingdom, and healing all manner of sickness and . . . divers diseases and torments, and those which were possessed with devils" (Matthew 4:23–24). Jesus accomplished His important work among the people by overcoming evil with good.

In the days that followed His declaration in Nazareth, Jesus entered the Sabbath service in Capernaum's synagogue. There He taught the people, "And they were astonished at his doctrine: for he taught them as one that had authority, and not as the scribes" (Mark 1:22). There had not been a prophet speaking with such authority for centuries. What a privilege to hear His words!

On one occasion while Jesus was preaching, a man with an "unclean spirit" stood and cried out, "Let us alone; what have we to do with thee, thou Jesus of Nazareth? "Art thou come to destroy us? I know thee who thou art, the Holy One of God" (Mark 1:24). Jesus did not want the witness of His Messiahship to come through any medium other than the Holy Ghost, so he immediately commanded the evil spirit to be silent.

Among the principles associated with this event is the important fact that knowledge alone is insufficient for salvation. Even faith, without the required ordinances, is dead. "The devils also believe, and tremble" (James 2:19) without any hope of glory hereafter. Understanding without conversion is damning. Jesus had nothing else to say to the vanquished devil that recognized the true Messiah it had long rejected.

In contrast to the disobedience of a devil, when Jesus Christ first called His early disciples to leave their chosen professions for something so much greater, they heeded His holy call. They came when He said to them, "Follow me, and I will make you fishers of men" (Matthew 4:19). As fishermen on the Sea of Galilee, these early disciples knew the meaning of work and responsibility. They had toiled under an employer, typically their father or another family member, working in the outside elements. Most of this work was done at night when the catching was best, but the harshness of the experience was greatest. The wind, rain, and cold would often work together to make the fishermen's efforts painstakingly difficult. After a challenging night of rowing, casting, retrieving nets, and taking their haul into the ship, the fishermen would return to the shore to sell their catch, secure the ship and sails, and repair their nets. The effort would pay them according to the harvest they had enjoyed, and this money would provide them with the necessities for survival.

When Jesus called the fishermen, they were busy doing this kind of work. The first disciples chosen were two brothers, Peter and Andrew. They were called while they were casting a net into the Sea of Galilee. Upon hearing the voice of the Lord, whom they already knew through the testimony of John the Baptist as well as their personal experience in following Jesus previously, their witnessing of miracles in Jerusalem and Cana, and surely their hearing His words multiple times in their own synagogue in Capernaum, they immediately left the things that brought them their livelihood. They were seeking first the kingdom of God, somehow knowing that all other things would be added unto them (see Matthew 6:33).

Jesus went on to call others to follow Him. "And going on from thence, he saw other two brethren, James . . . and John his brother, in a ship with Zebedee their father, mending their nets; and he called them" (Matthew 4: 21). These two came as did the first, who "straightway left their nets" (Matthew 4:20), and they also "immediately left the ship and their father, and followed him" (Matthew 4:22). The moment is profound, both in His words: "Follow me," and in the reaction of those who trusted Him. They knew that to follow when called is required of those who believe in order to gain salvation.

From that early calling along the shores of Galilee, "Jesus went about all Galilee, teaching in their synagogues, and preaching the gospel of the kingdom, and healing all manner of sickness and all manner of disease among the people" (Matthew 4:23). Luke relates the following incident, "And it came to pass, that, as the people pressed upon him to hear the word of God, he stood by the lake of Gennesaret, And saw two ships standing by the lake: but the fishermen were gone out of them, and were washing their nets. And he entered into one of the ships, which was Simon's, and prayed him that he would thrust out a little from the land. And he sat down, and taught the people out of the ship" (Luke 5:1–3).

After teaching for a time, Jesus asked Simon Peter to launch out into the deep and to let down his net. Peter complained that he had already toiled all night long without any success. "Nevertheless," he concluded, "at thy word I will let down the net" (Luke 5:5). Heeding that word, Peter immediately discovered his net full to its breaking point. He called to his partners in the second ship to come and help, and working together they filled both ships with the fish until the ships began to sink with the enormity of the haul. "When Simon Peter saw it, he fell down at Jesus' knees, saying, Depart from me; for I am a sinful man, O Lord" (Luke 5:8).

Such a miracle left him completely humbled. Peter might have momentarily hesitated when receiving advice in his own area of expertise from someone who had worked only in Nazareth as a carpenter. But when Peter remembered who it was that spoke, he acted in accordance with Jesus' counsel. Faith always precedes the miracle. James and John, the two partners in the other ship, were equally astonished. Jesus answered, "Fear not; from henceforth thou shalt catch men. And when they had brought their ships to land, they forsook all, and followed him" (Luke 5:10–11).

Jesus then went with these faithful disciples whom He had chosen. They left the ship to go into the city where He was instantly approached by a leper. "And, behold, there came a leper and worshipped him, saying, Lord, if thou wilt, thou canst make me clean. And Jesus put forth his hand, and touched him, saying, I will; be thou clean. And immediately his leprosy was cleansed" (Matthew 8:3). While this story might appear to show the greatest of all men descending to one of lowly circumstances, it is also the account of a man of great faith ascending to the One who could carry him the rest of the way he needed to go.

In the process of serving all men, Jesus went about calling His Twelve Apostles from the body of believers. He ordained and empowered His disciples for their special assignments to preach the gospel, heal the sick, and cast out unclean spirits. They would be, in every sense of their calling, fishers of men. These apostles voluntarily placed their faith in the Lord, and then followed His every call. Their names were Simon (Peter), Andrew, James the brother of John, John, Philip, Bartholomew, Thomas, Matthew the publican, James the son of Alphaeus, Lebbaeus, Simon, and Judas Iscariot. These men were sent forth as special witnesses of Jesus' holy name. According to Mark's record: "And he ordained twelve, that they should be with him, and that he might send them forth to preach" (Mark 3:14).

His charge to the Twelve Apostles demonstrates how Jesus gave power to men to function in His authority and in His name. These special servants of the Messiah would ultimately go forth bearing record of His name among all nations, kindreds, tongues, and people. None could prevent this message of salvation. But for the present, the work of the apostles would be accomplished only in the land of Israel. Working with His chosen disciples, Jesus prepared to teach the people the principles that would help them draw closer to heaven. But would the people follow when this special testimony came from men and not the Son of God? The Lord knew they would, for this was how He had always worked and how He still works today, showing forth His marvelous power through simple means: "The weak things of the world shall come forth and break down the mighty and strong ones, that man should not counsel his fellow man, neither trust in the arm of flesh" (D&C 1:19).

The special lessons for mankind that are apparent in the calling of the apostles is that the Lord calls to every man, and he does so for the same reason—that men may follow Him, for He alone holds the power of salvation. He is the only One who can rightly say, "Come, follow me." As the scriptures declare, "Behold, Jesus Christ is the name which is given of the Father, and there is none other name given whereby man can be saved" (D&C 18:23).

ADDITIONAL COMMENTARY

Follow Me: "In the midst of the noise and seductive voices that compete for our time and interest, a solitary figure stands on the shores of the Sea of Galilee, calling quietly to us, 'Follow me'"[1]

How Often Have I Called You: Elder Bruce R. McConkie described the various callings of the fishermen. He said,

> From these abbreviated and fragmentary gospel accounts, it is difficult to reach a positive conclusion as to whether one or two calls are involved. Clearly Matthew and Mark are recording the same event, but Luke may have reference to a later and different occasion. Added details easily could harmonize the two seemingly different accounts and establish that they are records of one and the same event. Viewing the whole New Testament record as it now stands, however, it is not unreasonable to conclude that some of the disciples received as many as five separate calls to follow Jesus.[2]

Called Many Times: Like Peter, James, and John, many of the Lord's most valiant servants in mortality had to be called several times before they became fully compliant to the will of the Lord. Jonah in the Old Testament is an example of this fact. Amulek in the Book of Mormon is another. Amulek described this process as it happened to him. He said, "I said I never had known much of these things; but behold, I mistake, for I have seen much of his mysteries and his marvelous power; yea, even in the preservation of the lives of this people. Nevertheless, I did harden my heart, for I was called many times and I would not hear; therefore I knew concerning these things, yet I would not know; therefore I went on rebelling against God, in the wickedness of my heart" (Alma 10:5–6).

Testimony by Unembodied Spirits: Elder James E. Talmage described the devilish testimony as unwanted and unneeded by the Savior:

> On these as on other occasions, we find evil spirits voicing through the mouths of their victims their knowledge that Jesus was the Christ; and in all such instances the Lord silenced them with a word; for He wanted no such testimony as theirs to attest the fact of His Godship. Those spirits were of the devil's following, members of the rebellious and defeated hosts that had been cast down through the power of the very Being whose authority and power they now acknowledged in their demoniac frenzy. Together with Satan himself, their vanquished chief, they remained unembodied, for to all of them the privileges of the second or mortal estate had been denied; their remembrance of the scenes that had culminated in their expulsion from heaven was quickened by the presence of the Christ, though He stood in a body of flesh.[3]

Notes

1. Joseph B. Wirthlin, "Follow Me," *Ensign*, May 2002, 15.
2. Bruce R. McConkie, *Doctrinal New Testament Commentary* (Salt Lake City: Bookcraft, 1965), 1:165.
3. Talmage, *Jesus the Christ*, 182.

10

❧ JESUS OF NAZARETH ❧

SERMONS AND MIRACLES NEAR THE SEA OF GALILEE

Jesus of Nazareth: Unbeknownst to the Nazarenes who judged Jesus as a blasphemer when He declared His divinity, Joseph's Son truly was the Just One who had been foretold. Over thirty years earlier, the angel had come to Nazareth and told Mary, "And, behold, thou shalt conceive in thy womb, and bring forth a son, and shalt call his name JESUS" (Luke 1:31). The angel had also spoken to Joseph concerning Mary, "And she shall bring forth a son, and thou shalt call his name JESUS: for he shall save his people from their sins" (Matthew 1:21). All of these things happened in that small village to prepare the way before Jesus of Nazareth. The Book of Mormon prophet Jacob learned from an angel other details about the carpenter's son. "Wherefore, as I said unto you, that Christ—for in the last night the angel spake unto me that this should be his name—should come among the Jews, among those who are the more wicked part of the world; and they shall crucify him—for thus it behooveth our God, and there is none other nation on earth that would crucify their God" (2 Nephi 10:3). Thus the Lord Himself would come, the Judge of all the earth, to be judged by men and crucified to save His people from their sins. Knowing how the people would react to His message, He still came to provide the necessary help for mankind unto salvation. The purpose for which the Lord of men came corresponds directly with the meaning of His name "Jesus," which is the Greek form of the name "Joshua" or "Jesua" meaning "help" or "Savior."

Working with His witnessing disciples, the Lord spread His testimony throughout the regions of Galilee. Many became acquainted with the Master through this effort. In time he had great multitudes of followers. One day Jesus led them into the hills that bordered the Sea of Galilee. There Jesus stood in the midst of the people and began to teach what we now refer to as the Sermon on the Mount. This particular sermon gave the Master an opportunity to declare His pathway of virtue to the multitudes that had responded in faith to His ministry in Galilee.

Those who came were taught how to proceed on the journey of spiritual progression toward the Christlike way of being. In the Sermon on the Mount, each of the Beatitudes was given as a stepping stone leading to Christ. As all men need to know what level they are on to know what step to take next, the Sermon on the Mount provides this step-by-step progression so that all can know what to do to improve and become blessed as Jesus. As it was given so it yet stands: the pathway to Christlike virtue, the heaven-inspired declaration of blessed living. Jesus personally provided this important sermon even as He walked the path to show the way.

The qualities that bring a person to a state of being truly blessed are as follows:

Blessed are the poor in spirit (humble).
Blessed are they that mourn.
Blessed are the meek.
Blessed are they which do hunger and thirst after righteousness.
Blessed are the merciful.
Blessed are the pure in heart.
Blessed are the peacemakers.
Blessed are they which are persecuted for righteousness' sake.

This sermon also warns of things that will assuredly mount up as stumbling blocks to prevent that next step toward the Christ. It provides a sound warning against anger, lust, divorce, swearing out oaths, and other evils.

Jesus taught that for each characteristic there would be a specific blessing. Spiritual inheritances would follow:

Group	Blessing
the poor in spirit (humble)	the kingdom of heaven
they that mourn	being comforted

Group	Blessing
the meek	inheriting the earth
they which do hunger and thirst after righteousness	being filled with the Holy Ghost
the merciful	obtaining mercy
the pure in heart	seeing God
the peacemakers	being called the children of God
they which are persecuted for righteousness' sake	eternal life in the kingdom of heaven.

Those who would receive these teachings were compared to a wise man who built his house upon His rock, even the Rock of Christ, and when the devil would send forth his winds and shafts in the whirlwind, and the rain would descend and the winds would blow, this disciple would never fall. "And it came to pass, when Jesus had ended these sayings, the people were astonished at his doctrine: For he taught them as one having authority, and not as the scribes" (Matthew 7:28–29).

Jesus then left the multitudes to go back to Capernaum. Upon His arrival, the Roman centurion who officiated over that area of Galilee approached Him with the news that his servant at home was "sick of the palsy, grievously tormented" (Matthew 8:6). If Jesus would but speak the word, the servant would be healed. "When Jesus heard it, he marvelled and said to them that followed, Verily I say unto you, I have not found so great faith, no, not in Israel" (Matthew 8:10). As the centurion asked, Jesus spoke the word, and the servant was healed in that very hour.

Of all of the examples of faith from those who sought a blessing, this one received the Savior's highest praise. For the Roman centurion to bow before a Jew would indeed require the utmost faith. The Romans were in command of the Jews at this time, and this centurion was in command of one hundred Romans. The Roman centurion properly demonstrated humility or the quality of being poor in spirit, which is the first step on the pathway to perfection as declared in the Sermon on the Mount. Because of this, he was blessed with the kingdom of heaven (see Matthew 5:3).

The next day Jesus departed from Capernaum and traveled with His disciples to the village of Nain. He arrived just as a funeral procession left through the gate of the city. A widow was mourning the loss of her only son. "And when the Lord saw her, he had compassion on her, and said unto her, Weep not. And he came and touched the bier: and they that bare him stood still. And he said, Young man, I say unto thee, Arise. And he that was dead sat up, and began to speak. And he delivered him to his mother" (Luke 7:13–15).

With the great miracle accomplished in Nain, the people began to realize the special nature of this Man. Jesus of Nazareth knew the thoughts and troubles of all men. The worth of every soul was great to Him. He would go to every effort to help those in need. He loved His people with all of His heart and would never forsake them. "And there came a fear on all: and they glorified God, saying, That a great prophet is risen up among us; and, That God hath visited his people" (Luke 7:16). Another step on the declared pathway to perfection was thus chronologically presented: "Blessed are they that mourn: for they shall be comforted" (Matthew 5:4).

Going immediately back to Capernaum, the Savior entered the city to find that Peter's mother-in-law lay ill. Peter immediately asked for Jesus to come and heal her. Jesus did come for His chief Apostle and for the woman. The family members of those whom Jesus called away from home were not forsaken by the Lord. He responded to their meekness when they were pressured and mocked by the world. The world defines meekness as a weakness in character, but for these early followers, it required great strength to fulfill the will of the Lord when scorning fingers of contempt were pointed at them in derision. Being meek in a world which cried for individualism, selfishness, and prideful vanity took much more fortitude than going along with the crowd. To Peter and his wife's mother, the Savior had rightly spoken: "Blessed are the meek: for they shall inherit the earth" (Matthew 5:5).

In the evening while yet in Capernaum, many gathered at Jesus' door, and they brought all that were sick, diseased, or possessed with devils and Jesus healed them (see Mark 1:33–34). Then, in the morning before the sun came up, the Savior went out and found a solitary place where He could pray alone. When His disciples arose they found Him gone and went to seek for Him. Among the others, Peter approached the Master and said, "All men seek for thee" (Mark 1:37). Certainly Jesus was pleased. One of His foremost teachings at His Sermon on the Mount specifically instructed His disciples to ask, knock, and seek, with the promise that they would thus find (see Matthew 7:7).

Having already accomplished His desire to lead the people of

Capernaum to spiritual self-reliance, Jesus answered Peter: "Let us go into the next towns, that I may preach there also: for therefore came I forth" (see Mark 1:35–38). The Savior departed from the place where He prayed and went down to the edge of the Sea of Galilee. His disciples followed. "Now when Jesus saw great multitudes about him, he gave commandment to depart to the other side. And a certain scribe came, and said unto him, Master, I will follow thee whithersoever thou goest. And Jesus saith unto him, The foxes have holes, and the birds of the air have nests; but the Son of man hath not where to lay his head. And another of his disciples said unto him, Lord, suffer me first to go and bury my father. But Jesus said unto him, Follow me; and let the dead bury their dead" (Matthew 8:18–22).

Both of these men were willing to follow Jesus while things remained convenient and comfortable, but Jesus taught that there was something more important. Faith in the Lord Jesus Christ is of pre-eminent importance in the plan of His Father. Jesus did not try to impress these men with His friendship or keep from offending them by allowing them to do what they wanted to do before following Him. In every case Jesus insisted on faith and devotion to Him over those other things that might have engendered only a superficial allegiance. The "carpenter's son" came to earth to build men. As the great Creator of the Universe, Jesus constructed faith in His disciples. He helped His followers to truly hunger and thirst after righteousness.

Challenging times in a disciple's life were not to be used as an excuse to rest from doing the will of God. Instead they were opportunities to build a man's faith and prove the extent of his devotion. The words "come, follow me" came when Peter's nets were full. The commandment to follow usually comes with a sacrifice. In His call to follow, the Savior insists on faith in His Father's ways over those other things that might seem to excuse some followers.

Jesus next entered a ship to depart from Capernaum and visit the other cities, and "his disciples followed him" (Matthew 8:23). Mark recounted how "there were also with him other little ships" (Mark 4:36). These seeking disciples chose not to be offended at His call to come unto Him when other matters yet pressed upon them. They followed into the sea in their own ships only to find that their faith was soon to be tested by a great storm. How long would they continue to follow when their ways were hedged up before them? That would depend on the strength of their faith and desire to follow Him who could provide the way. Blessed were they which did hunger and thirst after righteousness. According to their desires they were filled (see Matthew 5:6).

As the boat carried Jesus across the Sea of Galilee to its destination, Jesus slept on a pillow in the "hinder part of the ship" (Mark 4:38). His labors with the demanding multitudes seemed to take a toll on the Son of man. Jesus understood the demands of life. He experienced the same hunger, thirst, and fatigue that all men do at times. And so Jesus was asleep when "there arose a great storm of wind, and the waves beat into the ship, so that it was now full" (Mark 4:37).

The disciples hesitated to wake their Master, waiting until they finally saw no other solution. They respected Him so much that they waited until "they were filled with water, and were in jeopardy. And they came to him, and awoke him, saying, Master, Master, we perish. Then he arose, and rebuked the wind and the raging of the water: and they ceased, and there was a calm" (Luke 8:23–24). Mark writes: "And he arose, and rebuked the wind, and said unto the sea, Peace, be still. And the wind ceased, and there was a great calm" (Mark 4:39). "And he said unto them, Where is your faith? And they being afraid wondered, saying one to another, What manner of man is this! For he commandeth even the winds and water, and they obey him" (Luke 8:25).

After calming the waters, Jesus pointed the way to where the ship would rest along the shore of the Gadarenes. With what had happened on the sea, and that which was next to follow in Gadara, Jesus demonstrated the next Beatitude, which declared, "Blessed are the merciful" (see Matthew 5:7). And so Jesus went to Gadara to help a man who was overcome by the adversary and needed the assistance that heaven alone could offer. To rescue this man, Jesus would stand alone against a legion. He would have to vanquish a great enemy to redeem a single soul. "And when he was come out of the ship, immediately there met him out of the tombs a man with an unclean spirit" (Mark 5:2).

The details surrounding this strange man are as bizarre as the event itself. He lived among the tombs. He wore no clothing. No man could bind him, not even with chains. The people once caught him and bound him with fetters, but he tore asunder the chains that confined him. He had returned to his dwelling among the tombs where he remained day and night, crying and cutting himself with stones. No man could rule him, so he remained with none as master, until Jesus came. "But when he saw Jesus afar off, he ran and worshipped him, and cried with a loud voice, and said, What have I to do with thee, Jesus, thou Son of the most high God? I adjure thee by God, that thou torment me not. For he said unto him, Come out of the man, thou unclean spirit" (Mark 5:6–8).

Jesus then asked his name, to which he answered, "Legion: for we are many" (Mark 5:9). The warring spirits inside the man instantly surrendered to the power of the Master, pleading that He would not send them out of the country, but into the bodies of the swine. Apparently even the body of a pig was preferable to the state into which these spirits were normally condemned. After their rebellion, the devil and his angels were "cursed above all cattle, and above every beast of the field" (Genesis 3:14). "And forthwith Jesus gave them leave. And the unclean spirits went out, and entered into the swine: and the herd ran violently down a steep place into the sea, (they were about two thousand;) and were choked in the sea" (Mark 5:13).

The swine herders who witnessed the event fled into the village to tell of such strange doings. "Then they went out to see what was done; and came to Jesus, and found the man, out of whom the devils were departed, sitting at the feet of Jesus, clothed, and in his right mind: and they were afraid" (Luke 8:35). When the Gadarenes asked Jesus to leave, "the man out of whom the devils were departed besought him that he might be with him" (Luke 8:38). This Jesus refused, telling the man instead that now he had a mission to perform: to publish the great things that God had done for him. From that moment the healed man became a powerful witness of Christ in that city.

Jesus had come to the citizens of Gadara with a witness of His authenticity that could not easily be denied. He alone defeated the satanic host that day and then sent his new servant forth to rescue the other captured multitudes in the vicinity. The rescued man was now not only clothed and in his right mind, but he now rested safely in Christ. He would be sent among those who were yet unclean and without knowledge of the ways of the Lord. Ironically, this man who had been filthy under the adversary's hold and fettered by the people's chains would now come forth to provide them with deliverance from the bondage of their own sins. He would lead them from their state of uncleanness to the ways of purity in the Lord, personally demonstrating the way to become pure in heart, no matter what the challenge of life. His scarlet sins were made white through the blood of the Lamb (see Isaiah 1:18), and even so could this people be cleansed. "Blessed are the pure in heart: for they shall see God" (Matthew 5:8).

In the land of Gadara, Jesus performed a miracle that foreshadowed what He would do for all men. Like a faithful, perfect friend He comes. And if men respond, He helps them to eliminate the problems that have kept them in such misery. He comes to all men through the Atonement, a reuniting of man to his God! Though Jesus' death would seem to be the cause of such sadness, in actuality it would become the only thing that could ever bring eternal happiness. Jesus went through the ultimate sorrow to bring mankind the highest joy.

That is how the Master finished His work. The only way for men to also become peacemakers is to provide that same blessing for others by leading them to Christ where they can partake of the Atonement themselves. Such leading will at times require entering a personal Gethsemane of sacrifice. Certainly Jesus demonstrated the pathway to perfection which leads to that ultimate step. Of all men He could be called Peacemaker, even the Prince of Peace. And, after having completed His work, He entered that final state of those who proclaim peace, even when they are persecuted for bringing such peace. "Blessed are they which are persecuted for righteousness' sake: for theirs is the kingdom of heaven" (Matthew 5:10).

ADDITIONAL COMMENTARY

The Prince of Peace Not Spared Grief and Sorrow: President Howard W. Hunter taught: "Jesus was not spared grief and pain and anguish and buffeting. . . . His ship was tossed most of his life, and, at least to mortal eyes, it crashed fatally on the rocky coast of Calvary. We are asked not to look on life with mortal eyes; with spiritual vision we know something quite different was happening upon the cross. Peace was on the lips and in the heart of the Savior no matter how fiercely the tempest was raging. May it so be with us."[1]

Blessed Are They Which are Persecuted for Righteousness' Sake: As Jesus said, great shall be the reward in heaven for those who are persecuted in the name of Christ, for so persecuted they the prophets of old. In the modern dispensation He has spoken again to those who are persecuted for His name. "And all they who suffer persecution for my name, and endure in faith, though they are called to lay down their lives for my sake yet shall they partake of all this glory. Wherefore, fear not even unto death; for in this world your joy is not full, but in me your joy is full. Therefore, care not for the body, neither the life of the body; but care for the soul, and for the life of the soul" (D&C 101:35–37).

He Knows How to Succor His Children: Said Elder Jeffrey R. Holland concerning how the Lord helps mankind: "He knows [how] because He has suffered 'pains and afflictions and temptations of every kind . . . that he may know . . . how to succor his people according to their infirmities' (Alma 7:11–12). To *succor* means 'to run to.' I testify that Christ will run to us, and is running even now, if we will but receive the extended arm of His mercy."[2]

The Peacegiver: A story in the Old Testament exemplifies every characteristic Christlike element taught in the Sermon on the Mount. James Ferrell teaches how the story of David and Abigail is symbolic of Christ and His peacemaking, ultimately made possible only through the Peacemaker Himself (see 1 Samuel 25). The following is a summary of Ferrell's book *The Peacegiver.*

Ferrell teaches that as with Nabal, the character in the story who severely offended David, when someone sins against us we often feel that they owe us and must pay what is due or there will be war between us. Then suddenly a sinless Mediator approaches, typified by Abigail in this story, and offers to repay in full to the offended while at the same time pleading to carry the iniquity which was committed by the offender. "Look upon Me," the Christ figure says, "as the One who has done thee the wrong, and with this payment restored wilt thou forgive the offense?"

Thus the moment of mistreatment is the most important in our lives, for that is when we prove if we will walk the path the Savior walked as Peacemaker in the midst of challenge. At that moment we prove if we will turn to Christ and accept His infinite and innocent offering when made available to others through the simple act of forgiveness, or instead go to war against all that is offered and deliver revenge to our enemy. Remember in the situation with Abigail, it was Abigail as the figure of Christ who came as the peacemaker, not the offender Nabal or the offended David. And it was David who needed to forgive in order to receive that which was given to bring peace to all. This is how we show our faith and acceptance of the Atonement of Jesus Christ—which is sufficient for all sinners—through the simple act of forgiving.

Forgiveness combines many of the Beatitudes into one ultimate offering of peace. Like Abigail who brought peace to David and his men, to be a peacemaker when we are mistreated, we must first be humble. Even when we begin to mourn for that which is dealt us unfairly, we must remain meek, offering mercy in return. To do so, we must have a pure heart, meaning that we, like the Savior, must overcome evil with good. In essence, we hunger and thirst for a righteous outcome in spite of being mistreated, providing forgiveness to the offender, whatever the offense. Christ maintained perfect dignity while being berated by the very ones He came to save; he said, "Father, forgive them" (Luke 23:34) in the midst of His atoning offering and thus showed Himself to be the true Peacemaker. By forgiving others, we accept the Lord's infinite atonement as sufficient for all men who repent and thus become a part of His great offering. By forgiving we become walking peacemakers among men.[3]

How interesting that the name "Abigail," given to the woman who came symbolically representing Christ, literally means "Father of rejoicing."

A Captured Soul: To continue with the summary:

Ferrell teaches that many who are captured by the adversary, like the citizens of Gadara, fail to recognize their state as they continue to live out the comfortable routine of their lives. They may think that they are free and that someone else is more in need of the assistance of heaven. Yet the Savior recognizes the dilemma in all of those who walk without faith and sounds the message of salvation in their ears, offering them deliverance from death and hell. At times He sends a servant to them who might appear to be the least qualified for the job. At other times, like Jonah of old, the deliverer of the message may not realize how much he needs the same blessing that he is telling the others about. The servant may not know that he is really no more worthy than his hearers of that salvation which comes to all who repent.[4]

Blessedness Versus Happiness: "Blessedness is defined as being higher than happiness. 'Happiness comes from without and is dependent on circumstances; blessedness is an inward fountain of joy in the soul itself, which no outward circumstances can seriously affect.' "[5] Thus Jesus is teaching the secret of true happiness, the permanent kind that comes from within and above, in contrast to that which is fleeting and comes from without and below. No wonder that which is highly esteemed by men is an abomination before the Lord (see Luke 16:14–15). It is false happiness and can rob men of true peace.

For a closer look at each of the Beatitudes as steps in the progressive journey to becoming like Christ, see the Appendix at the end of this book.

Notes

1. Howard W. Hunter, "Master, the Tempest is Raging," *Ensign*, Nov. 1984, 33.
2. Jeffrey R. Holland, "Teaching, Preaching, Healing," *Liahona*, Jan. 2003, 13.
3. James Ferrell, *The Peacegiver* (Salt Lake City: Deseret Book, 2005).
4. Ibid.
5. Harold B. Lee, *Decisions for Successful Living* (Salt Lake City: Deseret Book, 1973), 57, as quoted with commentary by Pinegar, Bassett, and Earl in *Latter-Day Commentary*, 85.

11

✤ KING OF KINGS ✤

A NEW COVENANT IN CAPERNAUM

King of Kings: Who knew that when the King of Kings (see Revelation 19:16) first came, He would come so meekly? Only those familiar with the prophecies: "Rejoice greatly, O daughter of Zion; shout, O daughter of Jerusalem: behold, thy King cometh unto thee; he is just, and having salvation; lowly, and riding upon an ass, and upon a colt the foal of an ass" (Zechariah 9:9). Despite being meek and lowly in heart, He came with great power to establish His covenant among His people, even as the Messenger of the Covenant. Though they did not initially know the humble manner in which the King of the Jews would come and serve, even the magi knew He would be King as they indicated when they sought Him in Herod's palace. They knew the many scriptures which prophesied of His reigning position among men, not the least of which specifically said: "For unto us a child is born, unto us a son is given: and the government shall be upon his shoulder: and his name shall be called Wonderful, Counsellor, The mighty God, The everlasting Father, The Prince of Peace. Of the increase of his government and peace there shall be no end, upon the throne of David, and upon his kingdom" (Isaiah 9:6–7). Though King, Jesus walked among men as their servant, bearing the glorious gospel for the benefit of mankind. Only those who had followed could eventually enter where He alone would stand as the Keeper of the Gate, where no servant would be employed in His unique place, and where He could not be deceived (see 2 Nephi 9:41) by those who would try to enter in some other way.

Within the confines of Capernaum, the city Jesus called His own, many responded to the Messiah. Some sought His blessings there. Those who were wise decided in Capernaum to come and follow Jesus. Many would establish their faith in Jesus through the things He came to teach while on the banks of the Sea of Galilee. Others would openly reject the direct manifestations of His divinity. Their pride caused them to miss the mark of the salvation, established by heaven and given only in and through the Son of God. The Book of Mormon prophet Jacob prophesied of this blatant rejection: "But behold, the Jews were a stiffnecked people; and they despised the words of plainness, and killed the prophets, and sought for things that they could not understand. Wherefore, because of their blindness, which blindness came by looking beyond the mark, they must needs fall" (Jacob 4:14).

Many great things happened when Jesus returned to Capernaum from the land of the Gadarenes and "it was noised that he was in the house" (Mark 2:1). After such an eventful journey to and from Gadara, Jesus re-entered Capernaum, and, upon learning of His presence, many came to hear. Some came out of curiosity, others because of their faith, and some wanted to find something against Him. In Capernaum, Jesus spoke to the unbelievers of what they should come to believe in. In this instance, as in so many others, hearts were moved in such a way that the people became accountable before the Lord, whether or not they chose to follow.

With the announcement of Jesus' return so many came to the house, that they could not all enter where the Master taught. During the confusion caused by the great numbers of people, a man was carried to Him "borne of four" (Mark 2:3), and lowered through the rafters of the roof. Nothing would stop this man from getting to the Master, and Jesus "seeing their faith said unto the sick of the palsy; Son, be of good cheer; thy sins be forgiven thee" (Matthew 9:2).

Silent criticism and doubt from certain of the scribes in the group followed this blasphemous talk. Jesus answered them with the words, "Wherefore think ye evil in your hearts?" (Matthew 9:4). "Whether is it easier to say to the sick of the palsy, Thy sins be forgiven thee; or to say, Arise, and take up thy bed, and walk? But that ye may know that the Son of man hath power on earth to forgive sins, (he saith unto the sick of the palsy,) I say unto thee, Arise, and take up thy bed, and go thy way into thine house" (Mark 2:8–11). The palsied man obeyed to the astonishment of all that were present. Jesus' works fulfilled the very words He had promised. This could not be missed by even the most critical observers.

Jesus taught the people of Galilee that they could trust Him as the One the Father had empowered to be the Savior of mankind. He taught His willing disciples the principle of faith. As strong as these new disciples were, they could not succeed on their own. They also needed to learn to trust Him. His lessons on faith were profound as He worked through special circumstances to develop faith in His disciples. From such teachings Jesus left the important lesson that man is not alone. Nor can he succeed alone. God the Father sent His Son as the One sure support and the only way by which men can make it back to heaven.

With these events in Capernaum preceding Matthew's calling to be an apostle, there is little doubt but that the publican Matthew knew who Jesus was before he was called. In fact the whole city was in commotion with Jesus' presence there. We can see from Matthew's calling at this time that Jesus' calling of the Twelve was an ongoing process. And so Jesus met Matthew and asked him to leave the things of this world for those of a better. "And as Jesus passed forth from thence, he saw a man, named Matthew, sitting at the receipt of custom: and he saith unto him, Follow me. And he arose, and followed him" (Matthew 9:9).

That evening Matthew invited Jesus to his house for a feast with his friends. The Pharisees labeled these people as "publicans and sinners." Publicans were despised. They stood before the people as tax collectors and took what belonged to Israel and turned it over to Rome. Matthew worked as a publican. Being part of this group, he would have been considered a traitor to the cause of freedom in Israel by many, but not by Him who would render unto Caesar the things which were Caesar's (see Matthew 22:21). Publicans were living according to the rule of their times. "And when the Pharisees saw it, they said unto his disciples, Why eateth your Master with publicans and sinners? But when Jesus heard that, he said unto them, They that be whole need not a physician, but they that are sick. But go ye and learn what that meaneth, I will have mercy, and not sacrifice: for I am not come to call the righteous, but sinners to repentance" (Matthew 9:11–13).

The Pharisees asked in return why Jesus' disciples would not fast. John's disciples observed this law. Why not Jesus and His disciples? Jesus answered by telling that the Bridegroom presently stood with them. But the days would come when He would be taken from them. And then they would fast. These Pharisees understood well the law of the fast. It was taught in that day, as it had been from the days of Isaiah. "Is not this the fast that I have chosen? "To loose the bands of wickedness, to undo the heavy burdens, and to let the oppressed go free, and that ye break every yoke? . . . Then shalt thou call, and the Lord shall answer; thou shalt cry, and he shall say, Here I am" (Isaiah 58:6, 9). Fasting would always bring Christ to that soul who would so seek Him through this sacrifice. Therefore the days would soon come when they would need to fast, but that time was temporarily postponed among His disciples, for Christ stood among them.

The Pharisees continued to ask about the laws they knew so well because they felt that they had kept the laws to the letter: "Why will ye not receive us with our baptism, seeing we keep the whole law? But Jesus said unto them, Ye keep not the law. If ye had kept the law, ye would have received me, for I am he who gave the law. I receive not you with your baptism, because it profiteth you nothing. For when that which is new is come, the old is ready to be put away" (JST Matthew 9:18–21).

This group of learned Pharisees understood the necessity of baptism. This had been, and forever would be, the ordinance to signify to heaven a man's acceptance of God's laws. These men apparently thought they had kept the law as it had existed even before John, for why else would they be previously baptized? But now they heard that they needed to be baptized again to be accepted of God. Jesus explained how no man puts a piece of new cloth into an old garment or new wine into old bottles. That which was new had come and they yet held to their old ways which did not include accepting the living prophet and the manifested authority. For this purpose Jesus came to perform such ordinances, to make new the covenant.

Modern revelation also speaks of the need to be baptized by authority into a new covenant with Christ in His only true and living Church (see D&C 1:30). In the current dispensation, the Lord, still officiating in His role as messenger, said,

> Behold, I say unto you that all old covenants have I caused to be done away in this thing; and this is a new and an everlasting covenant, even that which was from the beginning. Wherefore, although a man should be baptized an hundred times it availeth him nothing, for you cannot enter in at the strait gate by the law of Moses, neither by your dead works. For it is because of your dead works that I have caused this last covenant and this church to be built up unto me, even as in the days of old. Wherefore, enter ye in at the gate, as I have commanded, and

seek not to counsel your God. (D&C 22:1–4)

In Jesus' day those who were baptized by John yet awaited the time when they would be baptized anew to obtain the new covenant in Christ. For John said, "I indeed baptize you with water unto repentance: but he that cometh after me is mightier than I, whose shoes I am not worthy to bear: he shall baptize you with the Holy Ghost, and with fire" (Matthew 3:11). Such rebaptism is demonstrated in New Testament times when Paul found certain disciples who had become lost.

> He said unto them, Have ye received the Holy Ghost since ye believed? And they said unto him, We have not so much as heard whether there be any Holy Ghost. And he said unto them, Unto what then were ye baptized? And they said, Unto John's baptism. Then said Paul, John verily baptized with the baptism of repentance, saying unto the people, that they should believe on him which should come after him, that is, on Christ Jesus. When they heard this, they were baptized in the name of the Lord Jesus. And when Paul had laid his hands upon them, the Holy Ghost came on them; and they spake with tongues, and prophesied. (Acts 19:2–6)

Shortly after His dialogue with the questioning rulers concerning the important doctrine of baptism, Jesus was approached by Jairus, the ruler over the synagogue in Capernaum. He came for the sake of his little daughter. Jairus would have had to come before the eyes of many of his own synagogue. Consider the challenge:

1. Jairus was the local authority, most likely a Pharisee elevated to the title Rabbi—a master of the scriptures.
2. The traditions of the day told of a forthcoming Messiah that would come in great majesty, not as a humble carpenter.
3. His own position as a ruler and leader of men were threatened if members of his congregation became followers of Jesus. Many others rejected the Messiah in order to preserve their own power. The temptation of priestcraft was very real when One with authority spoke and thousands turned their ears to the true Teacher. As Jacob prophesied, "But because of priestcrafts and iniquities, they at Jerusalem will stiffen their necks against him, that he be crucified" (2 Nephi 10:5).

Jesus' rank and understanding of the law could have stood between this ruler and his Master, as with the other Pharisees who frequently questioned Jesus. For this reason, his story becomes one of surmounting faith. It should not be too difficult to imagine the inward struggle as the ruler from Capernaum's synagogue approached Jesus in the midst of the multitude. How difficult for a ruler over a synagogue to banish the local traditions, his reputation, his role, and ultimately his standing by bowing before Jesus of Nazareth. All that Jairus stood for and waited upon would have to be offered to the Man before whom Jairus now bowed, a Man who stood as the self-declared fulfillment of Messianic prophecy.

But there was one thing that Jairus loved more than himself and his position: this one "little daughter." For her he would do all things, even bow himself before the eyes of all people to the Christ who could save. "And, behold, there came a man named Jairus, and he was a ruler of the synagogue: and he fell down at Jesus' feet, and besought him that he would come into his house: For he had one only daughter, about twelve years of age, and she lay a dying" (Luke 8:41–42).

Considering the critical Pharisees who observed Jesus' every move, this story of the ruler of Capernaum's synagogue coming unto Christ through such pointing fingers becomes especially poignant. "And [Jairus] besought him greatly, saying, My little daughter lieth at the point of death" (Mark 5:23). We hear in the petition that which helped this man to seek the Lord over all other considerations—his desire to help his daughter. Jairus had come to Christ for help. His little daughter's circumstance assisted his faith. What great miracles could then follow? For these people who were coming to know Jesus for the first time, the act of faith required coming unto Him against the traditions and rancor of the day.

Jairus' declaration of faith came under trial even before he could receive the witness. "While he yet spake, there came from the ruler of the synagogue's house certain which said, Thy daughter is dead: why troublest thou the Master any further?" (Mark 5:35). Had he failed? Had he chosen incorrectly and now lost his reputation by beseeching a Nazarene carpenter whom he had confused for the great Healer as foretold in the scriptures? Had he waited too long to make the petition? Surely her health had deteriorated to a critical point, finally urging Jairus to this last extreme measure. The fact that she died before Jairus could eventually bring the Master to her tells something of Jairus' timing.

Jesus recognized the doubts that began to arise in Jairus' heart at the announcement of his daughter's death. "Be not afraid," the Lord urged

Jairus, "only believe" (Mark 5:36). Here Jesus spoke again of His own divinity and power over all things, including death. He declared it before the man and all others who now followed with him, whether they came out of curiosity or true faith. Commoners, learned scribes, rabbis, lawyers, elders, rulers, Pharisees, Sadducees, and chief priests all heard and they all waited to see what Jesus' next action would be.

As the Master journeyed with the ruler of the synagogue toward his house, Jesus was stopped along the way. Jairus witnessed Jesus' power as virtue went out of Him in the healing of the "woman having an issue of blood twelve years" (Luke 8:43). Jesus then told Jairus, "Fear not: believe only, and she [thy daughter] shall be made whole" (Luke 8:50), and Jairus had that extra help he needed to base his faith upon. As he had done with others, Jesus carefully constructed the man's faith in order to prepare him for that which was to follow, fully knowing of the temptations and doubts that would arise.

Arriving at the house to find how his friends and family members wept at his daughter's death, Jairus continued through the crowd to hear the Master say, "Weep not; she is not dead, but sleepeth. And they laughed him to scorn, knowing that she was dead" (Luke 8:52–53). Then Jesus put them all out of the house, inviting only the maiden's parents with Peter, James, and John to stay as witnesses. There, in the privacy of the ruler's home, Jesus "took her by the hand, and called, saying, Maid, arise. And the spirit came again, and she arose straightway: and he commanded to give her meat. And her parents were astonished: but he charged them that they should tell no man what was done" (Luke 8:54–56).

Jairus learned for himself how the path to God begins with faith in the Lord Jesus Christ. Jesus is the way, the truth, and the life; no man can come to the Father, but by Him (see John 14:6). How great is the need to first develop faith in the Lord. Such is the example that proceeded through many of Jesus' doings in Capernaum. Jairus, like the centurion, received the Savior's highest praise because his desires moved him past his pride to a point where humility could lead him onward to faith. The Savior worked through trying circumstances to greatly assist these individuals toward salvation in Him.

Concerning the woman who had suffered with an issue of blood for twelve years, whom Jesus and Jairus witnessed along the way, none could heal her infirmity. Although she had spent all that she had on the physicians and healers in the region, she only grew worse with time. As the

Savior crossed through the town of Capernaum with Jairus to heal his daughter, Jesus stopped on the roadway. "Who touched me?" He asked. No one claimed responsibility, and Jesus' own disciples defended the crowd, saying, "Master, the multitude throng thee and press thee, and sayest thou, Who touched me? And Jesus said, Somebody hath touched me: for I perceive that virtue (power) is gone out of me" (Luke 8:45–46).

The woman came forward trembling to confess her action and to tell how she was immediately healed at the touch, for "straightway the fountain of her blood was dried up; and she felt in her body that she was healed of that plague" (Mark 5:29). Jesus knew what was done and He comforted the woman: "Daughter, be of good comfort," He said, "thy faith hath made thee whole; go in peace" (Luke 8:48).

After healing both the woman and Jairus' daughter, Jesus continued on his way when two blind men heard of the Lord's passing on the road. At this point multitudes reacted at Jesus' every action as "the fame hereof went abroad into all that land" (Matthew 9:26). Hearing the reaction as Jesus walked by, these two men cried after Him, saying, "Thou Son of David, have mercy on us" (Matthew 9:27) thus declaring their understanding of Jesus' true position.

Jesus brought them into a house alone for the same reason He brought only Peter, James, and John into Jairus' home. These sacred healings would not be performed before the world. He would command only that they would tell no man what was done. Jesus acted not to be seen of men, for He wanted faith, the "evidence of things not seen," to increase in the earth (Hebrews 11:1). "And when he was come into the house, the blind men came to him: and Jesus saith unto them, Believe ye that I am able to do this? They said unto him, Yea, Lord. Then touched he their eyes, saying, According to your faith be it unto you. And their eyes were opened; and Jesus straitly charged them, saying, See that no man know it. But they, when they were departed, spread abroad his fame in all that country" (Matthew 9:28–31).

While still in Capernaum, Jesus traveled along the slopes that arose from the Sea of Galilee into the seaside village, continuing to bless and heal. As He went along, the people brought to Him one that was dumb, possessed with a devil. "And when the devil was cast out, the dumb spake: and the multitudes marvelled, saying, It was never so seen in Israel" (Matthew 9:33). But the Pharisees said that He had cast out the devil by the power of the devil. After all that the people had witnessed in Capernaum—the blind receiving their sight, the dead being raised, the lame walking, the fever leaving, the sea calming, and the hearts of men changing—certain Pharisees still fought against the Lord. These men attributed Jesus' power to the devil. How else could they explain such things without declaring Jesus the Son of God and losing their own power among men?

But those who were wise and humble would establish their faith in Jesus through the things He taught them. Now numbered among the disciples, Jairus believed. When Jesus raised Jairus' daughter, Jairus was simply astonished. Surely joy followed his surprise. Not far behind that emotion would follow faith. Jesus thus inspired the hearts of people one good deed at a time. The man with the palsy similarly exercised his faith and received so much as a result. Such were among the many blessings that came to those willing to start on the pathway toward their new covenant in Christ.

ADDITIONAL COMMENTARY

Baptism Essential to Entering the Kingdom of God: The Prophet Joseph revealed:

> The ancients who were actually the fathers of the church in the different ages, when the church flourished on the earth, . . . were initiated into the kingdom by baptism, for it is self evident in the scripture—God changes not. . . . Now taking it for granted that the scriptures say what they mean, and mean what they say, we have sufficient grounds to go on and prove from the Bible that the gospel has always been the same; the ordinances to fulfill its requirements, the same . . . Surely, then, if it became John and Jesus Christ, the Saviour, to fulfil all righteousness to be baptised—so surely, then, it will become every other person that seeks the kingdom of heaven to go and do likewise; for he is the door, and if any person climbs up any other way, the same is a thief and a robber! (see John 10:1–2)[1]

To Heal Infirmities but Not to Forgive Sins? Elder Bruce R. McConkie taught the following concerning the healing of the palsied man and the forgiving of his sins:

> Rightly understood, this event in the life of our Lord was visible and irrefutable proof that he was the Messiah; and it was so recognized by those among whom he ministered. He had borne frequent verbal

testimony that God was his Father and had supported that personal witness with an unparalleled ministry of preaching and healing. Now it was his purpose to announce that he had done what no one but God could do and to prove that he had done it by a further manifestation of his Father's power. Both Jesus and the "doctors of the law" who were then present knew that none but God can forgive sins. Accordingly, as a pointed and dramatic witness that the power of God was resident in him, Jesus took (perhaps sought) this appropriate occasion to forgive sins. Being then called in question by the scripturalists who know (and that rightly) that the false assumption of the power to forgive sins was blasphemy, Jesus did what no imposter could have done—he proved his divine power by healing the forgiven man. To his query, "Does it require more power to forgive sins than to make the sick rise up and walk?" there could be only one answer! They are as one; he that can do the one, can do the other.[2]

"My Little Daughter:" President Howard W. Hunter affirms Jairus' priorities in life as demonstrated when he came against all that would prevent him. "The tremor we hear in Jairus' voice as he speaks of 'My little daughter' stirs our souls with sympathy as we think of this man of high position in the synagogue on his knees before the Savior. Then comes a great acknowledgment of faith: 'I pray thee, come and lay thy hands upon her, that she may be healed; and she shall live.' "[3]

Notes
1. Joseph Smith, *Teachings of Presidents of the Church* (Salt Lake City: The Church of Jesus Christ of Latter-day Saints, 2007) 92–94.
2. McConkie, *Doctrinal New Testament Commentary*, 1:177–78.
3. Howard W. Hunter, "Reading the Scriptures," *Ensign*, Nov. 1979, 64.

12

✦ LORD OF THE SABBATH ✦

TRUTH SPRINGING FORTH THROUGH ALL OF GALILEE

Lord of the Sabbath: Jesus proclaimed Himself Lord of the Sabbath and did good on that day. This specific title came from the various times Jesus revealed His true identity to those who criticized the good things He did on the holy Sabbath day. As the Life and Light of the World, the Lion of the Tribe of Judah, and the Lamb of God, the Lawgiver was the One who could define what to do on that day. To those who found fault, He would explain how the priests were allowed in the temple to profane the Sabbath and were blameless because of their service. David himself had also entered on the Sabbath day to eat the showbread when he hungered. "But I say unto you, That in this place is one greater than the temple. For the Son of man is Lord even on the sabbath day" (Matthew 12:6, 8). As the Living Bread and the Living Water, Jesus stood among men as Lord of Hosts to whom all men should give honor.

Based on the scriptural test of a true prophet, "by their fruits ye shall know them" (Matthew 7:20), Jesus of Nazareth proved Himself. He is known by that which he could not hide; for out of the abundance of his heart he spoke and brought forth works "as a very fruitful tree which is planted in a goodly land, by a pure stream, that yieldeth much precious fruit" (D&C 97:9). Many evidences would prove Jesus' Messiahship. From Galilee to Jerusalem, men would be left accountable because of the many witnesses established by the God of Israel and the God of the whole world.

93

At this time the Lord continued His work by taking a teaching tour into the cities of the apostles. He went personally with His chosen twelve to preach in the cities of their upbringing. On one occasion, John the Baptist sent instructions from prison to his own disciples, telling them to ask Jesus if He were indeed the One they waited for. They asked, and Jesus answered: "Go your way, and tell John what things ye have seen and heard; how that the blind see, the lame walk, the lepers are cleansed, the deaf hear, the dead are raised, to the poor the gospel is preached" (Luke 7:22). Of course John knew the answer to the question. He simply wanted them to discover the answer for themselves.

Jesus then spoke of His servant John before the people. What was John to be compared with? A reed shaken with the wind? No, John was immoveable. A man clothed in soft raiment, gorgeously appareled, living delicately in king's courts? No, John lived unto Christ, not unto himself. Then what did they witness through the words and workings of John the Baptist? A prophet of God?

> Yea, I say unto you, and much more than a prophet. This is he, of whom it is written, Behold, I send my messenger before thy face, which shall prepare thy way before thee. For I say unto you, Among those that are born of women there is not a greater prophet than John the Baptist: And all the people that heard him, and the publicans, justified God, being baptized with the baptism of John. But the Pharisees and lawyers rejected the counsel of God against themselves, being not baptized of him. (Luke 7:26–30)

The Pharisees would not be baptized again, even after hearing from the Lord's own mouth that their baptism would not be received when that which was new had come.

After these things, Jesus went up again to Jerusalem for the Passover (see John 5:1). On this second Passover trip, Jesus went forth with a different purpose. He had already announced His Messiahship there during His first visit. This time He came to Jerusalem to serve, uplift, and bless. On the Sabbath day, after arriving in Jerusalem, Jesus went to the pool of Bethesda to heal a man. According to tradition, an angel had once touched these waters. He who touched the water first when it was troubled would supposedly be healed of any affliction. Jesus' compassion is evident in His coming to the man who had an infirmity for thirty-eight years. "When Jesus saw him lie, and knew that he had been now a long time in that case, he saith unto him, Wilt thou be made whole?" (John 5:6).

When the man explained that he had no one to carry him into the water, Jesus told the man to take up his bed and walk; the man obeyed and found in the act the strength that follows heeding the Lord's call. Since the healing took place on the Sabbath day, the man received a fair amount of criticism for carrying his bed. He answered that he was only doing as asked by the One who had healed him. The Pharisees questioned, "What man is that which said unto thee, Take up thy bed, and walk?" (John 5:12). The healed man did not know Jesus, but when he later found Him in the temple, Jesus said to him, "Behold, thou art made whole: sin no more, lest a worse thing come unto thee" (John 5:14).

Going out of the temple, the man "told the Jews that it was Jesus, which had made him whole. And therefore did the Jews persecute Jesus, and sought to slay him, because he had done these things on the sabbath day" (John 5:15–16). "My Father worketh hitherto, and I work," Jesus explained of His doing good on the Sabbath day. "Therefore the Jews sought the more to kill him, because he not only had broken the sabbath, but said also that God was his Father, making himself equal with God" (John 5:17–18). Jesus knew the intentions of these people for He knew their hearts. He told them: "That all men should honour the Son, even as they honour the Father. He that honoureth not the Son honoureth not the Father which hath sent him" (John 5:23).

Many times the people criticized Jesus for bearing record of Himself. He spoke to those who wanted to condemn Him for doing good on the Sabbath day, thus teaching who it was who governed and ruled the very law they tried to use against Him. On this occasion, the testimony from the Master was given from multiple sources in addition to His own word:

1. "Ye sent unto John, and he bare witness of the truth. . . . He was a burning and a shining light: and ye were willing for a season to rejoice in his light."

2. "But I have greater witness than that of John: for the works which the Father hath given me to finish, the same works that I do, bear witness of me, that the Father hath sent me."

3. "And the Father himself, which hath sent me, hath borne witness of me."

4. "Search the scriptures; for in them ye think ye have eternal life: and they are they which testify of me."

5. "For had ye believed Moses, ye would have believed me: for he wrote of me" (see John 5).

The testimony given from the Savior's own mouth witnessed the true Messiah. For them to disbelieve in His testimony now would be to turn against the truth as verified through multiple witnesses in the way the Lord always works. Their own law stated: "In the mouth of two or three witnesses shall every word be established" (2 Corinthians 13:1). After bearing record in this manner during His second visit to Jerusalem, Jesus returned to Galilee and went about all of their cities teaching, preaching, and healing. Multitudes followed Him. "Then saith he unto his disciples, The harvest truly is plenteous, but the labourers are few; Pray ye therefore the Lord of the harvest, that he will send forth labourers into his harvest" (Matthew 9:37–38). "And it came to pass afterward, that he went throughout every city and village, preaching and shewing the glad tidings of the kingdom of God" (Luke 8:1).

The Twelve accompanied Christ on this mission, bearing record of the Son of God. Certain women also came along. The first mentioned is Mary Magdalene; then Joanna, the wife of Chuza, Herod's steward; Susanna; and others "which ministered unto him of their substance" (Luke 8:3). Many others stayed away and even fought against the testimony. Since the Pharisees could not find anything with which to accuse Jesus of Nazareth, they had to turn to the good that He did on the Holy Sabbath.

For this purpose they brought a man to Jesus who had a withered hand. "And they asked him, saying, Is it lawful to heal on the sabbath days? that they might accuse him" (Matthew 12:10). In this case they thought they had the perfect thing with which to trap the Master. If Jesus were to say it was indeed lawful to heal on the Sabbath then they would present the man with the withered hand which no earthly power could heal, and thus prove their case against Jesus as Messiah. And if Jesus did heal the man, then they would say He had sinned by doing so on the Sabbath day. Either way they would destroy this self-proclaimed Christ.

When Jesus responded, "he said unto them, What man shall there be among you, that shall have one sheep, and if it fall into a pit on the sabbath day, will he not lay hold on it, and lift it out? How much then is a man better than a sheep? Wherefore it is lawful to do well on the sabbath days" (Matthew 12:11–12).

The man was thus presented, and Jesus spoke: "Stretch forth thine hand. And he stretched it forth; and it was restored whole, like as the other" (Matthew 12:13). Jesus the Messiah could not be disputed because He backed his sayings up with the very fulfillment of His words. He who knew no sin had spoken, and by the authority given of His Father, His word was accomplished. All of the knowledgeable priests and rulers were confounded in that instant when "the Pharisees went out, and held a council against him, how they might destroy him" (Matthew 12:14). In so doing, the Pharisees provided only evidence of their own wickedness before the One in whom no fault could be found.

Shortly thereafter Jesus went to a man possessed with a devil, that had made him both blind and dumb. Jesus cast out the devil and healed the man. When the people saw it they remarked, "Is not this the son of David?" (Matthew 12:23). Once again having nothing with which to accuse the Holy One, the Pharisees decided that He must be doing good works through the power of the devil. Jesus answered them by saying: "Every kingdom divided against itself is brought to desolation. . . . And if Satan cast out Satan, he is divided against himself; how shall then his kingdom stand? And if I by Beelzebub cast out devils, by whom do your children cast them out. . . . But if I cast out devils by the Spirit of God, then the kingdom of God is come unto you" (Matthew 12:25–28).

While the Pharisees spoke evil against Him, Jesus' words spoke of truth to them. His words and works manifested His divinity. "Either make the tree good, and his fruit good," He would tell them, "or else make the tree corrupt, and his fruit corrupt: for the tree is known by his fruit" (Matthew 12:33). If these men were to judge Jesus by His fruits, what kind of a tree would He be? In contrast, if the Pharisees were judged by their fruits, what kind of a tree would they be? "O generation of vipers," the Savior would go on to say to answer that question, "how can ye, being evil, speak good things? for out of the abundance of the heart the mouth speaketh. A good man out of the good treasure of the heart bringeth forth good things: and an evil man out of the evil treasure bringeth forth evil things" (Matthew 12:34–35).

Much like Jesus' earlier teaching in the Sermon on the Mount, Jesus referred to that which would always prove a true or false prophet: their fruits. Could men gather grapes of thorns, or figs of thistles? Every good tree would bring forth good fruit, but a corrupt tree could only bring forth evil fruit. A good tree would not have the capacity or desire to bring forth evil fruit. Neither would a corrupt tree bring forth good fruit. Wherefore by their fruits they should know them (see Matthew 7:16–20).

According to this test, that which proceeds out of the mouth is indicative of the kind of person that is speaking. If only a wicked and adulterous generation would seek after a sign, the words of the Pharisees quickly established what kind of trees they were. The only sign Jesus would give to these people would be the sign of Jonah. They would understand when the Messiah emerged from the tomb after three days. Then they would remember Jonah and the whale, and how Jonah spent three days in the whale's belly before he emerged into a life renewed with God.

While Jesus instructed these people "his mother and his brethren stood without, desiring to speak to him" (Matthew 12:46). His family had come to see their Son and Brother whom they loved and missed very much since His absence was necessitated by His holy calling. Jesus did not forget His calling, whether speaking at the temple as a boy, at a marriage in Cana, or even now while teaching His followers in Galilee. He remembered what He was doing and to whom He was sent. "But he answered and said unto him that told him, Who is my mother? and who are my brethren? And he stretched forth his hand toward his disciples, and said, Behold my mother and my brethren! For whosoever shall do the will of my Father which is in heaven, the same is my brother, and sister, and mother" (Matthew 12:48–50).

After having made His ministry known in such ways, Jesus found many coming unto Him. Some came seeking knowledge while others had ulterior motives. In order to teach the message the people were ready to receive, Jesus began to teach in parables. The height and depth of His teachings would only be completely received by the honest, while a message could still be provided according to the level of instruction every individual was ready for and in need of.

In each of the following parables—the sower, the wheat and the tares, the grain of mustard seed, the leaven, the treasure hid in the field, the pearl of great price, and the net cast into the sea—Jesus taught the importance of the true fruits that could be found in the kingdom of God. He taught most completely those who truly desired to understand. To such would be given the greatest of all treasures.

The parable of the sower addressed how to receive the word and the blessings that would flow therefrom. This parable particularly taught how men might themselves be found worthy to bear the fruits of the kingdom. The sower planted the seed (the word) in four different kinds of ground. The first fell by the way side and was immediately devoured by birds. The second fell into stony places and sprung up quickly only to wither with the first heat because it had no depth of root. The third fell among thorns, and when the weeds sprung up with the plant, they choked it. The fourth fell into good ground and bore fruit.

The seed by the way side—"When any one heareth the word of the kingdom, and understandeth it not, then cometh the wicked one, and catcheth away that which was sown in his heart" (Matthew 13:19). This is the description of that soul who will not hearken unto the word when it is presented because he lacks understanding.

The seed in stony places—"the same is he that heareth the word, and anon with joy receiveth it; Yet hath he not root in himself, but dureth for a while: for when tribulation or persecution ariseth because of the word, by and by he is offended" (Matthew 13:20–21). This is the soul who will joyfully hear but not live according to the message when faced with any level of difficulty. Thus their roots cannot grow down into that moist soil which contains the living water. Root growth requires work.

The seed among thorns—"the care of the world, and the deceitfulness of riches, choke the word, and he becometh unfruitful" (Matthew 13:22). This soul both heard and followed. That is why the root was growing and the plant developing. Unfortunately, this soul also hearkened unto the voices of the world, allowing weeds also to grow up which would end up choking off the word. This struggling plant proves that no man can serve two masters. Ultimately the voice of the world which is louder will prevail over the still, small voice of the Holy Ghost if sin is simultaneously allowed to have root and nourishment near the growing tree.

The seed into the good ground—"he that heareth the word, and understandeth it; which also beareth fruit, and bringeth forth, some an hundredfold, and some sixty, some thirty" (Matthew 13:23). This soul heard the truth, heeded it, and also shunned the world. No weeds were allowed to choke this growing plant. The word had thus fallen into good ground; these souls received the word with gladness and lived their lives accordingly. For such a reception, the blessing came in that they brought forth much good fruit unto salvation. Even so, the fruit of those who are true can be obtained and shared. Only these souls can become a benefit to their fellow men, thus bearing forth the fruits of the true tree.

After so teaching, Jesus returned to Nazareth where He was rejected only a few months earlier. By now word from Capernaum would have arrived there, telling of His mighty works and the results of the multitudes who believed. Other testimonies from all over Israel would also have preceded this visit. The Nazarenes had been given sufficient time to get over their earlier offenses. Perhaps some had even come to grips with the reality of what had happened when they tried to impose the penalty of death. Who could disbelieve when His authority superseded theirs, One over a multitude? From the ruler of the synagogue who had pronounced the judgment to the common member who had gone along to help carry it out, all had been forced to consider the testimony of Him who had stood forth at the risk of His own life. His words had spoken of blasphemy and the penalty for blasphemy was death. Yet He stood forth to declare it. That kind of courage should have elicited some kind of an examination of the facts. Furthermore, Jesus yet lived after the penalty had been pronounced. None had been able to carry it out, and now, with the multiple testimonies that validated the claim, the Nazarenes were given sufficient opportunity to reconsider Jesus' testimony.

Yet in this second offering, they again questioned their neighbor: "Is not this the carpenter's son? is not his mother called Mary? and his brethren, James, and Joses, and Simon, and Judas? And his sisters, are they not all with us? Whence then hath this man all these things? And they were offended in him" (Matthew 13:55–57).

Herein lay the test of the true Savior. His works stood approved. He had fulfilled every prophecy to the letter and the spirit of the law. The testimony of John the Baptist bore an indisputable witness. The scriptures testified of Him. The Holy Spirit bore record. Faithful men with sound understanding stood forth to testify. Others told how He had personally healed them. Special witnesses preceded Him. Multitudes followed Him. Miracles went forth from Him. His words and works bore witness of the kind of tree that stood among them, but still in Nazareth, the testimony of Jesus remained obscured by the fact of His earthly upbringing.

ADDITIONAL COMMENTARY

The Church of Jesus Christ of Latter-day Saints: As it was with the Master, so it is with His Church. The blessings provided through The Church of Jesus Christ of Latter-day Saints to the world stem from principles as old as the gospel itself. The blessings are so amply granted that there is not "room enough to receive it" (Malachi 3:10). From even before the days of Malachi, the Saints were commanded, "Bring ye all the tithes into the storehouse, that there may be meat in my house" (Malachi 3:10).

The Church has been blessed to lay up in store, and the Lord is abundant in His blessings as He opens up the windows of heaven and pours forth such blessings when His followers abide in Him. But it is not enough to receive such blessings. John the Baptist taught that "Every tree which bringeth not forth good fruit is hewn down and cast into the fire" (Matthew 3:10). While each tree may be receiving a similar amount of rainfall, that does not mean it produces a similar kind or amount of fruit.

A True Tree: A tree is known by the kind of fruit it produces to be shared with others. As the Savior said, "Wherefore by their fruits ye shall know them" (Matthew 7:20). By this test of the fruits which come from a tree, mankind can judge the Church which stems directly from the Lord. He said, "He that abideth in me, and I in him, the same bringeth forth much fruit: for without me ye can do nothing" (John 15:5). The blessings provided through The Church of Jesus Christ of Latter-day Saints are granted from the Lord by His miraculous ability to bear His fruits into all the world, becoming even "a very fruitful tree which is planted in a goodly land, by a pure stream, that yieldeth much precious fruit" (D&C 97:9).

Other Kinds of Fruits: The fruits of the Lord's Church are all wonderful, and they are not always monetary or temporal. When Peter and John went through the gate called Beautiful on the way to the temple, they met a man who needed their help. Being crippled from birth, he was unable to work for his own support. "Peter said, Silver and gold have I none; but such as I have give I thee: In the name of Jesus Christ of Nazareth rise up and walk" (Acts 3:6).

In the Church That Bears His Name: How wonderful it is to be planted near a pure stream, even the stream of revelation. Those who are led by the living prophet of God then go forth bearing the true fruits of the Lord's kingdom under His direction. As a people we stand ready, ably assisting those who need us with what they need. In this manner we share the blessings produced by the glorious tree of life.

13

⇒ MESSIAH ⇐

JOHN THE BAPTIST'S DEATH AND THE GIVER OF LIFE

Messiah: The Anointed. The title Messiah, the Mighty One of Jacob, upon whom the Jewish world waited to restore them from the Romans and make of them a prosperous nation, could hardly apply to the meek and lowly Jesus when He came. Or at least that was what the people thought. The Christ was preached among all people. Even the woman at Jacob's well mentioned how this knowledge existed among the people of Samaria when she said: "I know that Messias cometh, which is called Christ: when he is come, he will tell us all things" (John 4:25). Jesus replied to her: "I that speak unto thee am he" (John 4:26). The true Manna from heaven had come, the Messenger of Salvation, the Master Himself, having been sent with an offering of life to a people under the bondage of spiritual death. Jesus would be their Mediator, for He was their Maker, the Mighty God, the Most High.

The martyrdom of John the Baptist occurred during his imprisonment, even though "Herod feared John, knowing that he was a just man and a holy man, and one who feared God and observed to worship him; and when he heard him he did many things for him" (JST Mark 6:21). After having cast John into prison, Herod was manipulated by the new queen and her daughter to do the unthinkable.

This all came to pass on Herod's birthday when he made a supper for his lords, captains, and chief estates of Galilee. Herod's new wife's daughter had come by invitation and danced for the guests, pleasing the carnal minds of those who sat observing. The king then remarked to the woman, "Whatsoever thou shalt ask of me, I will give it thee, unto the half of my kingdom" (Mark 6:23). She asked for John the Baptist's head in a charger to appease her miserable mother whom the prophet had declared sinful. "The king was exceeding sorry; yet for his oath's sake, and for their sakes which sat with him, he would not reject her" (Mark 6:26).

Herod was easily lured by the enticement which led his heart away from the prophet he had once delighted in. He became trapped by his own word and the pressure to please men. Embracing the sin, Herod rejected the Lord and His servant. "And immediately the king sent an executioner, and commanded his head to be brought: and he went and beheaded him in the prison, And brought his head in a charger, and gave it to the damsel: and the damsel gave it to her mother" (Mark 6:27–28).

Some time shortly thereafter, when the fame of Jesus reached Herod the tetrarch of Galilee, the king "said unto his servants, This is John the Baptist; he is risen from the dead; and therefore mighty works do shew forth themselves in him" (Matthew 14:2). Others said it was Elias or one of the prophets. "But when Herod heard thereof, he said, It is John, whom I beheaded: he is risen from the dead" (Mark 6:16). Herod's words thus spoke of the torment he felt for his actions against the prophet.

After his martyrdom, John's disciples came to ready the prophet's body for burial. And "when Jesus heard of it, he departed thence by ship into a desert place apart" (Matthew 14:13). Jesus mourned the loss of his friend and cousin as well as the prophet who had prepared the way before Him. He went into a desert place to be alone where few would go, "and when the people had heard thereof, they followed him on foot out of the cities" (Matthew 14:13).

How would Jesus respond now? He had lost His friend and helper. How would the Lord react when the people came after Him? "And the people saw them departing, and many knew him, and ran afoot thither out of all cities, and outwent them, and came together unto him" (Mark 6:33). Though he had "departed into a desert place by ship privately" (Mark 6:32), the Savior of men would not be allowed to mourn alone. Instead He would find multitudes chasing after Him. His response reveals the greatness of His heart, the fruit again bearing witness of the tree: "And Jesus went forth, and saw a great multitude, and was moved with compassion toward them, and he healed their sick" (Matthew 14:14).

When the disciples of Jesus noticed the inconvenience imposed on the Master by so great a multitude, they "came to him, saying, This is a desert place, and the time is now past; send the multitude away, that they may go into the villages, and buy themselves victuals. But Jesus said unto them, They need not depart; give ye them to eat" (Matthew 14:15–16). To Philip He spoke particularly: "Philip, Whence shall we buy bread, that these may eat? And this he said to prove him: for he himself knew what he would do. Philip answered him, Two hundred pennyworth of bread is not sufficient for them, that every one of them may take a little" (John 6:5–7).

With only five loaves and two fishes among them, Jesus commanded the people to sit down upon the grass. Taking the fishes and loaves and "looking up to heaven, he blessed, and brake, and gave the loaves to his disciples, and the disciples to the multitude. And they did all eat, and were filled: and they took up of the fragments that remained twelve baskets full. And they that had eaten were about five thousand men, beside women and children" (Matthew 14:19–21). When the chosen disciples gave all of what little they had to offer, their own twelve baskets were returned overflowing. Truly, as the Savior instructed "that nothing be lost" (John 6:12), those who give all know that nothing is ever lost when given to Jesus.

Then they who had received remarked, "This is of a truth that prophet that should come into the world. When Jesus therefore perceived that they would come and take him by force, to make him a king, he departed again into a mountain himself alone" (John 6:14–15). Jesus came as the King of Kings. He wouldn't let the world make Him a king of men. As He would later tell Pilate: "My kingdom is not of this world" (John 18:36). Though the true King of the Jews completely denied Himself the empty offerings of the world, His fame would go forth unrestrained from this day, reaching even unto Herod.

In the meantime, the Lord's faithful Twelve responded to His call to enter into a ship to go to the other side of the Sea of Galilee. In contrast to previous times when the chosen disciples traveled with their Master, on this occasion they traversed the Sea of Galilee alone, leaving Jesus as He had gone into the mountains.

As they sailed, they were met by a storm, which tossed them in the waves and drove them with its wind. They fought against the tempest until in the fourth watch of the night, sometime in the early morning hours, being wearied and worn from the struggle, "Jesus went unto them, walking on the sea" (Matthew 14:25).

When Jesus walked on the water to His disciples who were in peril, He showed Himself as their One sure support. He answers every prayer in His own time and way. He who could walk on water and ascend into heaven needed nothing temporal for His support.

And so it happened that the Lord appeared when his servants had rowed until the fourth watch of the night, when they had been praying for deliverance, and after all they could do (see 2 Nephi 25:23). As the Savior approached, Peter asked if he could do as the Master was doing, that is, to walk to Him on the water. Peter would need to rely on his faith in the Lord Jesus Christ to accomplish what the Master exemplified. The man of faith stepped from the boat, and with his trust in the Lord, walked on the water to Jesus. In typical fashion, opposition mounted immediately as the disciple sought to approach the Lord. Peter feared when he saw the wind and the waves, shifting his focus away from Him who could have yet sustained his efforts. Peter then sank into the water and cried out, "Lord, save me. And immediately Jesus stretched forth his hand, and caught him" (Matthew 14:30–31).

Those who witnessed the event "came and worshipped him, saying, Of a truth thou art the Son of God" (Matthew 14:33). "Then they willingly received him into the ship: and immediately the ship was at the land whither they went" (John 6:21).

In all of this, Jesus received the praise and the glory. His disciples knew that He alone held such power and that this power could only be granted to another through faith. The fact that Peter also walked on the water that night is often forgotten when recalling instead how he ultimately sank and earned the Savior's words, "O thou of little faith, wherefore didst thou doubt?" (Matthew 14:31). Though the apostles were troubled at first seeing Jesus, thinking it was a spirit that came to them, they heard the Master's words: "Be of good cheer; it is I; be not afraid" (Matthew 14:27). It was then that Peter replied, "Lord, if it be thou, bid me come unto thee on the water. And he said, Come. And when Peter was come down out of the ship, he walked on the water, to go to Jesus" (Matthew 14:28–29).

Throughout Peter's life he went to Jesus in a variety of challenging circumstances. He forsook all after his nets were first filled; he came in response to the question, "Whom do men say that I the Son of man am?" (Matthew 16:13); he ran to the tomb at the announcement that Jesus had been taken away out of the sepulchre; he was there when Jesus appeared on the shore of the Sea of Galilee following His Resurrection and even leaped from the boat, not waiting for his fellows to row to shore; and finally Peter was there to bear his testimony when arrested and interrogated with the question "By what power, or by what name, have ye done this?" And Peter answered, "Be it known unto you all, and to all the people of Israel, that by the name of Jesus Christ of Nazareth, whom ye crucified, whom God raised from the dead, even by him doth this man stand here before you whole" (Acts 4:7, 10). In all of these opportunities that Peter had to prove his faith in the Holy One, there were few more powerful than the one which occurred on the night when Peter asked if he could come unto Him on the water.

Even though he had such a valiant spirit, the chief apostle's flesh remained weak (see Matthew 26:41). He who would proclaim a willingness to go first to death before being offended in Jesus (see Matthew 26:35) would also experience myriad weaknesses. He would fall asleep before witnessing the suffering in the garden. He would thrice deny Jesus at Caiaphas's palace. He would falter in word and in deed in so many ways. On this night, even while being sustained by the Savior upon the water, Peter would shift his focus to the wind and the waves. As a man of testimony, his heart knew, but Peter's true conversion would only come by doing the will of the Father and becoming like his Master.

In the morning when the people found that Jesus had departed with His disciples, they went back to Capernaum to find Him. When they discovered Jesus' whereabouts, they asked Him, "Rabbi, when camest thou hither?" (John 6:25). Instead of telling them of His miraculous crossing over the sea on foot, He answered by telling them what they lacked:

> Verily, verily, I say unto you, Ye seek me, not because ye saw the miracles, but because ye did eat of the loaves, and were filled. Labour not for the meat which perisheth, but for that meat which endureth unto everlasting life, which the Son of man shall give unto you: for him hath God the Father sealed. Then said they unto him, What shall we do, that we might work the works of God? Jesus answered and said unto them, This is the work of God, that ye believe on him whom he hath sent. (John 6:26–29)

The people responded by asking for further evidence that would prove to them that they should believe on Jesus. They argued that their fathers had eaten manna in the wilderness as a sign from God that Moses was the promised deliverer. "Moses gave you not that bread from heaven," Jesus answered, "but my Father giveth you the true bread from heaven. For the bread of God is he which cometh down from heaven, and giveth life unto the world. Then said they unto him, Lord, evermore give us this bread. And Jesus said unto them, I am the bread of life: he that cometh to me shall never hunger; and he that believeth on me shall never thirst" (John 6:32–35).

Jesus went on to teach how He came down from heaven to do the will of Him who governed from above. He taught, "My meat is to do the will of him that sent me, and to finish his work" (John 4:34). "And this is the Father's will which hath sent me, that of all which he hath given me I should lose nothing, but should raise it up again at the last day. And this is the will of him that sent me, that every one which seeth the Son, and believeth on him, may have everlasting life: and I will raise him up at the last day" (John 6:39–40).

The Jews began to murmur, not understanding how Jesus could have come down from heaven when He was known to be the son of Joseph. To this Jesus answered, "Murmur not among yourselves. No man can come to me, except the Father which hath sent me draw him: and I will raise him up at the last day" (John 6:43–44).

If any of the Jews still wondered if Jesus meant that He was the long-prophesied Messiah who should come, He went on to plainly tell them, "Verily, verily, I say unto you, He that believeth on me hath everlasting life. I am that bread of life. Your fathers did eat manna in the wilderness, and are dead. This is the bread which cometh down from heaven, that a man may eat thereof, and not die. I am the living bread which came down from heaven: if any man eat of this bread, he shall live for ever: and the bread that I will give is my flesh, which I will give for the life of the world" (John 6:47–51).

Many of those present could not yet understand these words. They were so focused on the things of the natural man, missing the Spirit, that they could not see the Son of God when He stood in person before them. "How can this man give us his flesh to eat?" they asked. The doctrine is as sure as the rock upon which man can be planted. As the Savior Himself said, "Verily, verily, I say unto you, Except ye eat the flesh of the Son of man, and drinketh his blood, ye have no life in you. Whoso eateth my flesh, and drinketh my blood, hath eternal life; and I will raise him up at the last day" (John 6:53–54).

Jesus now taught the importance of the ordinances of the gospel. Earlier, He had said to Nicodemus, "Verily, verily, I say unto thee, Except a man be born of water and of the Spirit, he cannot enter into the kingdom of God" (John 3:5). Nicodemus had still needed the ordinance of baptism, the acceptance of the sacrifice of the Son, symbolically entering into His tomb and arising into a newness of life in the Lord. With regard to these disciples who now followed, many of them were already baptized, but they would need to renew that covenant once the sacrament was instituted on the eve of the great Atonement. They would need to symbolically receive the flesh and blood of Him who came to offer salvation. Again, they had to accept the sacrifice of the Son and manifest their acceptance through an ordinance. "Therefore, in the ordinances thereof, the power of godliness is manifest. And without the ordinances thereof, and the authority of the priesthood, the power of godliness is not manifest unto men in the flesh" (D&C 84:20–21).

The people could not yet understand this. They had come to be healed and fed. They had come for the physical blessings He offered. But when He said, "He that eateth my flesh, and drinketh my blood, dwelleth in me, and I in him" (John 6:56), they went away. "From that time many of his disciples went back, and walked no more with him" (John 6:66). This experience proved to be a teaching moment for those who remained. To them Jesus asked, "Will ye also go away? Then Simon Peter answered him, Lord, to whom shall we go? thou hast the words of eternal life. And we believe and are sure that thou art that Christ, the Son of the living God" (John 6:67–69). Peter knew and he now began his work of doing the will of the Father by strengthening the other Apostles with his testimony.

Like John the Baptist who withheld nothing from the Lord, those who would follow Jesus through the trial of their faith would receive eternal life. Peter knew this, just as he knew his Master had the words of eternal life. John the Baptist had set an example by living his own life in faithful endurance, no matter what had come against him. And now the disciples had to follow John's example. They had just buried their beloved prophet who had prepared their hearts for the coming of the Lord. And now they would need to remember his example during the difficult times that would also face them.

Alongside his father, Zacharias, who was slain between the altar and the porch of the temple, John the Baptist was taken into that special place reserved for those who withheld nothing from the Lord. He gave his every effort to the work that ultimately also required his life. After Herod's rebellion against the ways of God, John had been called to go forth with that word of rebuke that would ultimately lead him to seal his mission and testimony with his own blood. True disciples are those who are willing to do whatever the Lord requires, whereas those who are only interested in satisfying the demands of the moment, are more apt to shift their focus from the Lord even as He stands right before them, waiting to sustain them.

ADDITIONAL COMMENTARY

The One Sure Support: Through prophecy, the Prophet Lehi taught his struggling sons how to obtain the support they so needed. He taught that "a prophet would the Lord God raise up among the Jews—even a Messiah, or, in other words, a Savior of the world. And he also spake concerning the prophets, how great a number had testified of these things, concerning this Messiah, of whom he had spoken, or this Redeemer of the world. Wherefore, all mankind were in a lost and in a fallen state, and ever would be save they should rely on this Redeemer" (1 Nephi 10:4–6). Jesus taught: "I am the resurrection, and the life: he that believeth in me, though he were dead, yet shall he live: And whosoever liveth and believeth in me shall never die" (John 11:25–26).

The Need to Always Remember Him: As it was with Peter, so it applies to us all. With our focus on Christ, we stand. When we turn our attention away from Him and dwell on temptation and trouble, we sink. That is why it is so important to "always remember Him" (D&C 20:77).

Testimony and Conversion: "Testimony is to know and to feel, conversion is to do and to become."[1]

A Lesson from Abraham and His Brother Lot: When Abraham and Lot arrived at the promised land, Lot "pitched his tent toward Sodom" (Genesis 13:12). But Abraham pitched his tent toward the temple (see Genesis 13:18). With Lot focusing on the wicked city, he eventually moved into that environment to the ultimate destruction of his family. Abraham led his family to the covenants of the Lord, eventually securing for his seed the blessings of eternity because his heart was focused on righteous things.

Our Strength and Redemption: The Master provided this experience for Peter in order to teach him and all His followers. Peter's example is one of strength of spirit. He truly wanted to come unto Christ under every condition. Peter pointed the way to the Master as Jesus' chief apostle. We can also learn from what Peter discovered through his Master at a different time: "Watch and pray, that ye enter not into temptation: the spirit indeed is willing, but the flesh is weak" (Matthew 26:41). Among the lessons taught by Peter comes the instruction to maintain focus upon the Savior and rely upon Him through prayer. Whenever Peter forgot, he sank. When Peter remembered, he stood firmly supported.

When we are tempted and sinking, great strength still comes in remembering Jesus. Turning our minds from the negative things that plague us to the life and sacrifice of Jesus Christ truly holds us on a support that cannot be moved. When we are accomplishing His will as we stand firm, the Rock becomes impenetrable. This is according to the sacramental covenant. For the soul who falters, even with the hand of the Lord extended right before him, the Savior is still the answer. Though many are focused elsewhere during such trying times and so fail to see the Lord, Jesus still stands close by, ready to assist. When Peter failed and sank, he remembered in his desperation and cried out to receive the Lord's redeeming hand. Jesus is both our strength and our redemption. Through Him we can prevent sin or repent of it. He is our salvation and our deliverance.

The Rock of Our Support: Through Peter's walking on the water, Jesus taught that men may stand upon the foundation of the Redeemer, whether upon the waters or against the wiles of the devil. For this reason it is critical to remember Christ and "remember that it is upon the rock of our Redeemer, who is Christ, the Son of God, that [we] must build [our] foundation; that when the devil shall send forth his mighty winds, yea, his shafts in the whirlwind, yea, when all his hail and his mighty storm shall beat upon [us], it shall have no power over [us] to drag [us] down to the gulf of misery and endless wo, because of the rock upon which [we] are built, which is a sure foundation, a foundation whereon if men build they cannot fall" (Helaman 5:12).

The Sacramental Covenant between God and Man: We establish a focus on the Son of God through the promise to take upon ourselves the name of Christ, always remember Him, and keep His commandments. As a result we receive the Holy Ghost. This is what brings the power of God into our lives, or in other words the ability to obtain eternal life.

The prayers that invoke the blessings of this covenant, as read by one with priesthood authority, are as follows:

> O God, the Eternal Father, we ask thee in the name of thy Son, Jesus Christ, to bless and sanctify this bread to the souls of all those who partake of it, that they may eat in remembrance of the body of thy Son, and witness unto thee, O God, the Eternal father, that they are willing to take upon them the name of thy Son, and always remember him and keep his commandments which he has given them; that they may always have his Spirit to be with them. Amen. . . . O God, the Eternal Father, we ask thee in the name of thy Son, Jesus Christ, to bless and sanctify this wine to the souls of all those who drink of it, that they may do it in remembrance of the blood of thy Son, which was shed for them; that they may witness unto thee, O God, the Eternal father, that they do always remember him, that they may have his Spirit to be with them. Amen. (D&C 20:77, 79)

Notes
1. Elder Dallin H. Oaks, as quoted by Allan F. Packer in "Finding Strength in Challenging Times!" *Ensign*, May 2009, 17–19.

14

⇒ NAZARENE ⇐

THE REVELATION OF JESUS AT CAESAREA PHILIPPI

Nazarene: "And he came and dwelt in a city called Nazareth: that it might be fulfilled which was spoken by the prophets, He shall be called a Nazarene" (Matthew 2:23). Somehow this prophecy was lost to those who were much more concerned that the Christ would come out of Bethlehem, thus missing this important piece of the prophetic puzzle. "But some said, Shall Christ come out of Galilee?" (John 7:41). The chief priest himself argued, "Search, and look: for out of Galilee ariseth no prophet" (John 7:52). So interested were the people in disproving Jesus as Messiah that they missed all the things that truly bore witness of Him, particularly the indisputable personal revelation that came from heaven to every honest seeker of the truth.

Peter stood upon the rock of revelation to testify of Christ's divinity when asked, "But whom say ye that I am?" (Matthew 16:15). Like Peter, the man or woman of Christ can knowingly respond that Jesus is the Christ, the Son of the living God. This witness can only be given through the power of the Holy Ghost. All the knowledge that is essential to gain eternal life is spiritually discerned, and hence to be spiritually minded is life and peace. The opposite mind set, which the world teaches is the way to happiness, is to be carnally minded. This blocks the Spirit and leads to spiritual death (see 2 Nephi 9:39 and Galatians 5). This chapter will consider the special revelation that was given at this time to Peter and the other apostles during their visit to Caesarea Philippi.

The Master had just departed with those who had passed the test of faith by remaining with Him after he taught them about the giving of His flesh and blood to His believers. "After these things Jesus walked in Galilee: for he would not walk in Jewry, because the Jews sought to kill him" (John 7:1). Leaving Capernaum, Jesus crossed over into Gennesaret by sea and came into that country. At His arrival there, the people immediately knew who He was and "ran through that whole region round about, and began to carry about in beds those that were sick . . . and besought him that they might touch if it were but the border of his garment: and as many as touched him were made whole" (Mark 6:55–56).

Following this experience, Jesus departed again, going into the regions northward in Israel. Many times when people from the nations outside of Israel besought Jesus for help, as with the Roman centurion, Jesus answered their faith. He did so even though He had not come to personally teach them. He was sent first unto the house of Israel. From there His followers would be organized and sent unto the Gentiles. While "there is no respect of persons with God," there is an order of things (Romans 2:11). In ancient Israel, it was the Levites who carried the priesthood first, though many others would be granted that privilege later when the revelation was given through a prophet.

When Jesus met a woman of Canaan in Tyre and Sidon as He was teaching in the upper regions of Galilee, she came crying to Jesus for her daughter. The Master answered that He was not sent, "but unto the lost sheep of the house of Israel" (Matthew 15:24). This answer did not lower the woman's status; she was still a daughter of God. It simply defined the order in which the Lord worked, the gospel being sent first unto the Jew and then unto the Gentile, as Paul also explained: "For I am not ashamed of the gospel of Christ: for it is the power of God unto salvation to every one that believeth; to the Jew first, and also to the Greek" (Romans 1:16).

Even after this explanation, the woman insisted on the Master's help for that which she felt only He could give. "Then came she and worshipped him, saying, Lord, help me" (Matthew 15:25). Who could refuse such a petition? And yet Jesus knew His priority: "It is not meet to take the children's bread, and cast it to dogs. And she said, Truth, Lord: yet the dogs eat of the crumbs which fall from their master's table" (Matthew 15:26–27).

In the attitude of the Roman centurion who received from the Lord a blessing for his servant, this Canaanite woman sought through her faith the crumbs that fell from the initial feast prepared upon Israel's table. This was not beyond her entitlements. She would also receive the gospel, and her faith could not wait until well-fed Israel in turn presented the feast unto the Gentiles. "Then Jesus answered and said unto her, O woman, great is thy faith: be it unto thee even as thou wilt. And her daughter was made whole from that very hour" (Matthew 15:28). It never had been Jesus' intention to deny her desire, but instead, as with so many others whom he resisted initially, His purpose was to build her faith. He wanted her to seek with all her heart before He would answer. Sometimes an initial refusal carries the seeker to an even higher level of personal effort in seeking for deliverance.

Jesus left Tyre and Sidon and returned near unto the Sea of Galilee where He sat down upon the slope of a mountain. Great multitudes came to Him there, bringing their lame, blind, dumb, maimed, and others, and Jesus healed them. The people glorified God in the event and recognized the Son of God. One of the healings there is of particular mention because of its unique nature. They brought a man with a speech impediment and asked Jesus to heal him.

> And he took him aside from the multitude, and put his fingers into his ears, and he spit, and touched his tongue; And looking up to heaven, he sighed, and saith unto him, Ephphatha, that is, Be opened. And straightway his ears were opened, and the string of his tongue was loosed, and he spake plain. And he charged them that they should tell no man: but the more he charged them, so much the more a great deal they published it; And were beyond measure astonished, saying, He hath done all things well: he maketh both the deaf to hear, and the dumb to speak. (Mark 7:33–37)

Much like the earlier feeding of the five thousand, Jesus again had compassion upon the multitudes. They had now been with Him for three days. Again, He took a small amount of bread and fish that His disciples carried with them and fed four thousand men, with women and children. The lesson was repeated by the Master. After giving all that we can, doing all that lies within our power, however meager the offering, Jesus carries it to success. In every instance the glory goes to the Lord. What man could take credit for feeding the multitudes when all he had was some loaves of bread and a few little fishes?

After feeding the great multitude, Jesus left them. "And he sent away the multitude, and took ship, and came into the coasts of Magdala"

(Matthew 15:39). The small village of Magdala rested along the western bank of the Sea of Galilee, and it was here that Jesus next went to preach. Magdala was where Mary Magdalene came from. We remember how Mary was first healed, for there were "certain women, which had been healed of evil spirits and infirmities, [and] Mary called Magdalene, out of whom went seven devils" (Luke 8:2). On several occasions Mary Magdalene accompanied Jesus to minister unto Him while He did the work of His Father. This Mary would be near the cross at Jesus' crucifixion (see Matthew 27:56; Mark 15:40; John 19:25). She would be at the burial, then at the tomb to be the first to see the stone rolled back "and two angels sitting thereon" (JST John 20:1). Mary of Magdala would be the first to witness Jesus' resurrected body. Mary, who believed and held faithful, saw many signs to confirm her faith.

In contrast, the Pharisees who did not believe would be given signs only to their condemnation. "But, behold, faith cometh not by signs, but signs follow those that believe. Yea, signs come by faith, not by the will of men, nor as they please, but by the will of God" (D&C 63:9–10).

In Magdala opposition mounted from those who came without faith. "The Pharisees also with the Sadducees came, and tempting desired him that he would shew them a sign from heaven" (Matthew 16:1). Had they not seen signs enough? Could they not believe the words of so many witnesses who testified so plainly of the Son of God? Without faith these men wanted to see with their own eyes that which they could not believe or feel with their hearts. To these the Savior answered: "A wicked and adulterous generation seeketh after a sign; and there shall no sign be given unto it, but the sign of the prophet Jonas" (Matthew 16:4). He left these people to wallow in their traditions, which they valued more than the presence of Jesus Christ.

Practices passed from one generation to another are called traditions. But just because a tradition is generally accepted does not make it right. In fact, traditions can defile and lead astray. That which is given by God is correct, and any deviation from Him, no matter how ingrained in tradition, is incorrect. Jesus had earlier taught this to certain Pharisees who came tempting Him to see if they could find fault and have something with which to accuse Him. Having found nothing by the law, they turned to tradition. "And when they saw some of his disciples eat bread with defiled, that is to say, with unwashen, hands, they found fault" (Mark 7:2).

They immediately asked of Jesus, "Why walk not thy disciples according to the tradition of the elders, but eat bread with unwashen hands? He answered and said unto them, Well hath Esaias prophesied of you hypocrites, as it is written, This people honoureth me with their lips, but their heart is far from me. Howbeit in vain do they worship me, teaching for doctrines the commandments of men" (Mark 7:5–7).

The Master went on to teach, giving the example of the commandment to honor father and mother. Their tradition made it acceptable to break this commandment simply by saying, "It is Corban," or "a gift, by whatsoever thou mightest be profited by me" (see Mark 7:11). They could then disrespect their parents and remain free of punishment. Jesus taught how their tradition defiled them, "Making the word of God of none effect through your tradition" (Mark 7:13).

Jesus taught that what truly defiles a man is not the unwashed hands or a particular type of food that they might reject as unclean. Those things would not defile a man, "Because it entereth not into his heart, but into the belly, and goeth out into the draught" (Mark 7:19). But other things that entered the treasure of the heart would be dangerously defiling: evil thoughts, adulteries, fornications, murders, thefts, covetousness, wickedness, deceit, lasciviousness, an evil eye, blasphemy, pride, or foolishness.

Thus, in contradiction to the commandments, certain errant traditions often make the word of God "of none effect." For the Pharisees it was their traditions that made the belief in a future Messiah popular, instead of a present Savior. Similarly, modern traditions still cause men to reject the Living Christ. These traditions include: recreation, certain kinds of entertainment, or shopping on the holy Sabbath; media that plays on the carnal mind; immodesty; improper language; some kinds of dating practices; and certain kinds of music. Indeed, traditions can defile—"And that wicked one cometh and taketh away light and truth, through disobedience, from the children of men, and because of the tradition of their fathers" (D&C 93:39). In contrast to tradition, revelation will keep the faithful disciple on an immoveable Rock—"He that keepeth his commandments receiveth truth and light, until he is glorified in truth and knoweth all things" (D&C 93:28).

Jesus came to give life. He offered an understanding of salvation through personal revelation. Whether revealed by His own mouth, through the power of the Holy Ghost, or through the voice of His servant it was and ever would be the same (see D&C 1:38). Jesus taught the way to heaven in all that He said and did. From His birth to His death, Jesus proved that He indeed had the power to deliver on His promises. When He fed the five thousand, walked on the water, or stepped from the tomb, Jesus gave us the evidence and the reason for all that a man should do with his life—he must follow the Lord in spite of any worldly tradition that teaches otherwise.

After He taught the Pharisees, the Sadducees came next to put their religious arguments to Jesus. While the Pharisees and Sadducees were generally against each other doctrinally, it appears that the two groups teamed up on this occasion. Having found common ground against Jesus, they agreed to work together in order to preserve their position in the eyes of men.

As a complete opposite to these who worked for popularity, Jesus preached in order to increase the faith and the goodness of His hearers, at times alienating the majority in the process. In some instances, what a person truly needed was something unpopular, and learning of it would turn the person against Him. Yet Jesus worked to build a person's faith and not his superficial allegiance. Jesus would hold to the doctrine whatever the personal outcome, because He was more concerned with pleasing His Father than pleasing the world.

After dealing with the Pharisees and Sadducees, Jesus went on to build faith in one who would hear. In the middle of the two groups criticizing Him, a blind man approached Jesus. Leaving those who would not see, Jesus "took the blind man by the hand, and led him out of the town; and when he had spit on his eyes, and put his hands upon him, he asked him if he saw ought" (Mark 8:23). The man answered that he saw the vague outline of men as trees moving along in his line of vision. "After that he put his hands again upon his eyes, and made him look up: and he was restored, and saw every man clearly" (Mark 8:25). On this occasion, as with many others, Jesus told the man not to advertise what was done.

Jesus then departed with His chosen Twelve and went to the headwaters of Galilee near the foot of Mount Hermon. He took His apostles there for a special purpose, to give them that Rock upon which His kingdom on earth would be constructed, even the rock of revelation built upon a foundation of apostles and prophets, Himself being the chief cornerstone. He erected this fortress on the words of testimony, which could only come through revelation. Then He granted the necessary keys of His kingdom to His chief apostle, Peter.

There in a place near Caesarea Philippi, Jesus asked His disciples,

"Whom do men say that I the Son of man am?" (Matthew 16:13). The answers came back reporting the common superstitions regarding the great Healer. Some thought Jesus was a prophet returning from the dead—Elijah, Jeremiah, or John the Baptist being the common examples. As with the majority of religious beliefs, people in Jesus' time would accept the dead prophets and hope for a better future. But they could never accept a living prophet, let alone the Living Christ. Then came the critical question to those who stood before Him: "But whom say ye that I am?" (Matthew 16:15). One can almost sense the silence that followed the question as each examined their deepest feelings regarding the Son of man. Peter then spoke for the Twelve: "Thou art the Christ, the Son of the living God. And Jesus answered and said unto him, Blessed art thou, Simon Bar-jona: for flesh and blood hath not revealed it unto thee, but my Father which is in heaven" (Matthew 16:16–17).

Peter believed in his heart. He had followed with faith. In the process of doing the Lord's will, he had come to know of the doctrine (see John 7:17). It could not be otherwise, for God is faithful to those who act in faith. The same holds true for any who will try an experiment upon the word (see Alma 32) or who will prove God to see if He will not open the windows of heaven (see Malachi 3). In essence, Peter chose early on to act on Andrew's testimony, which was correct; he discovered for himself that which follows seeking, knocking, and asking. He had received that which flesh and blood could not reveal. It had come as the unseen wind gently blows; the knowledge had come to his mind and was confirmed in his heart, or in other words discerned in his spirit. This was in very truth the spirit of revelation (see D&C 8:2–3).

The crucial fact that Peter went to the source to obtain this revelation should not be missed. His brother Andrew reported the good word to Peter as he had heard it from John the Baptist. Peter then went directly to Jesus to hear for himself. Ultimately Peter received his testimony through his Father in Heaven, as Jesus explained. Peter thus provided the pattern for obtaining revelation that those under his leadership would need to follow. He studied it out personally, considered the facts as he heard them, witnessed the works, and then he asked God. Peter came to know through revelation, which he obtained from the living prophet, the scriptures, and the Holy Ghost.

Having so stated that Peter's knowledge came by revelation, Jesus went on to say that it was more than just the wind of faith that Peter had felt in his heart; there was also a rock, even the rock of revelation—the same upon which the Lord would build His church, "And the gates of hell shall not prevail against it" (Matthew 16:18). Jesus then revealed great things to those who stood with Him as His true servants. He told them that He needed to go to Jerusalem, suffer many things of the elders and chief priests and scribes, be killed, and then rise again on the third day. To deny this course would be to embrace the spirit of the adversary. He also told them that if any wished to follow after Him, he also must take up his own cross. Whosoever should save his life would lose it, but he who would lose his life for the sake of Christ would find it. Even obtaining the whole world was nothing compared with the riches of eternity. And some of those present would witness the Son of God coming into His kingdom—a reference to the Resurrection.

Such were the revelations that came that day in Caesarea Philippi as Christ began to establish the rock of revelation, upon which His Church would be constructed. In doing this, Christ also established the necessity of revelators. "And I will give unto thee the keys of the kingdom of heaven," Jesus then told Peter, "and whatsoever thou shalt bind on earth shall be bound in heaven: and whatsoever thou shalt loose on earth shall be loosed in heaven" (Matthew 16:19). "And he began to teach them, that the Son of man must suffer many things, and be rejected of the elders, and of the chief priests, and scribes, and be killed, and after three days rise again" (Mark 8:31).

Peter could not immediately understand when Jesus told of His impending sacrifice. He reacted at the saying and began to rebuke the Lord whereupon Jesus "turned, and said unto Peter, Get thee behind me, Satan: thou art an offence unto me: for thou savourest not the things that be of God, but those that be of men" (Matthew 16:23). All of these things happened in Caesarea Philippi, at the fount of waters that flowed from Mount Hermon into the Sea of Galilee. Jesus revealed great things there. He spoke as the fountain of living waters. On this day He gave His disciples water that would ever sustain them.

A short time later upon "an high mountain apart" (Matthew 17:1), the sealing keys were bestowed according to Jesus' promise. Peter, James, and John came alone with Jesus to witness their Master "transfigured before them: and his face did shine as the sun, and his raiment was white as the light" (Matthew 17:2). "And as he prayed, the fashion of his countenance was altered, and his raiment was white and glistering" (Luke 9:29). Moses and Elias, the revered prophets of old, also appeared. They came "in glory, and spake of his decease which he should accomplish at Jerusalem" (Luke 9:31).

While we do not have the full account of what happened there, we do know that this great and glorious vision was accompanied by the giving of priesthood keys to men on earth. This special occurrence was followed by a personal proclamation of the Father, who appeared in a cloud. "And there came a voice out of the cloud, saying, This is my beloved Son: hear him" (Luke 9:35). From such an event came the prophesied rock upon which Christ's Church would be constructed. This rock of revelation, with the revealed keys of the kingdom, was given to men that they might bring others unto Christ in His Church. Peter, James, and John obtained these keys through the Messiah they loved. They followed after His call and returned from the mount with their authority confirmed.

From that time on, these apostles would continue to accompany Jesus until He reached His final destination: Jerusalem. They would be there when it was time for Him to accomplish the purpose for which He had come. Jesus could now lead the way, reassured by the fact that He had established His Church upon His own rock, even the rock of His revelation, and that it now rested upon the shoulders of His revelators. In this way Jesus could continue to rule His Church as the Living Christ even after His death—the same way He had throughout history, and the same way He still does—through that revelation which comes to prophets.

Modern revelation indicates that these keys still function in the Lord's Church today through His living prophets, seers, and revelators (see D&C 13; 110; 128). As such, the Lord's Church will yet prevail, built upon a foundation of apostles and prophets, Jesus Christ Himself being the Chief Cornerstone. The work still flows from the same Source. Joseph Smith was the prophet of the Restoration and, against the modern religious view which accepts only dead prophets, he became a living modern prophet. Today, the Church is still led by a living prophet. Revelation allows Jesus to function, as He ever has, as our great support. He personally established and still rules and guides His own Church, even The Church of Jesus Christ of Latter-day Saints.

ADDITIONAL COMMENTARY

The Doctrine of Living Revelation: At the time of Christ, the Pharisees could not accept the doctrine of revelation. They believed in dead prophets and waited for a future Deliverer. They could never accept a living prophet, or, in Jesus' case, the Living Christ. They hailed Moses and Abraham, but rejected the Son of Man, even when He stood with them. This is not so different than what occurs in many "Christian" churches today. Many Christians love the scriptures and declare their allegiance to the ancient prophets; they look forward to the future Second Coming of the Savior but cannot accept His present workings with living prophets and apostles.

A Modern Revelatory Experience: Joseph Smith and Oliver Cowdery had an experience similar to what Peter experienced while gaining his testimony. In their words: "While the world was racked and distracted—while millions were groping as the blind for the wall, and while all men were resting upon uncertainty, as a general mass, our eyes beheld, our ears heard, as in the 'blaze of day.' . . . His voice, though mild, pierced to the center."[1]

A Warning of That False Doctrine Which Would Ruin the Entire Structure: Jesus carefully taught His disciples to beware of the leaven, or doctrine, of the Pharisees and Sadducees. The leaven could ruin the whole of the bread that had been presented from heaven.

> They upheld the authority of oral tradition as of equal value with the written law. The tendency of their teaching was to reduce religion to the observance of a multiplicity of ceremonial rules" (see Bible Dictionary: Pharisees). This is not different from what happens with people today who accept the traditions of men or their philosophies as equal or superior to the counsel given of God, even rejecting the revelations which come afresh through living prophets. The Sadducees also were to be warned against: "In their treatment of religious questions they held to the letter of the Mosaic revelation and denied the authority of ancient tradition; . . . Their opposition to our Lord was the result of his action in cleansing the temple, which they regarded as an infringement of their rights. They opposed the work of the apostles because they preached the resurrection (see Bible Dictionary: Sadducees).[2]

The People's Subsequent Misunderstanding When He Came: Elder James E. Talmage noted the seriousness of the people's misunderstanding regarding Jesus the Messiah.

It is significant that among all the conceptions of the people as to the identity of Jesus there was no intimation of belief that He was the Messiah. Neither by word nor deed had He measured up to the popular and traditional standard of the expected Deliverer and King of Israel. Fleeting manifestations of evanescent hope that He might prove to be the looked-for Prophet, like unto Moses, had not been lacking; but all such incipient conceptions had been neutralized by the hostile activity of the Pharisees and their kind. To them it was a matter of supreme though evil determination to maintain in the minds of the people the thought of a yet future, not a present, Messiah.[3]

Upon This Rock, the Rock of Revelation: Elder James E. Talmage also wrote concerning the manner in which Christ would establish His Church:

Through direct revelation from God Peter knew that Jesus was the Christ; and upon revelation, as a rock of secure foundation, the Church of Christ was to be built. Though torrents should fall, floods roll, winds rage, and all beat together upon that structure, it would not, could not, fall, for it was founded upon a rock; and even the powers of hell would be impotent to prevail against it. By revelation alone could or can the Church of Jesus Christ be builded and maintained; and revelation of necessity implies revelators, through whom the will of God may be made known respecting His Church.

Notes
1.   *Messenger and Advocate*, vol. 1 (October 1834), 14–16.
2.   Talmage, *Jesus the Christ*, 360–61.
3.   Ibid., 362.

15

The Prodigal Son and the Father's Enduring Love

Only Begotten Son: Jesus came according to His Father's will, "for God so loved the world, that he gave his only begotten Son (John 3:16). He was one with the Father and came as an expression of the Father's love. To truly understand the nature of such love, look to the actions the Father took to demonstrate His love. The Atonement alone shows a sufficient explanation of what kind of love both the Omniscient and Omnipotent Father and Son have for us, and the kind of love They are willing to share. God's singular purpose is "to bring to pass the immortality and eternal life of man (see Moses 1:39). As the Only Begotten, the Overseer of the souls of men, Christ's perfect love was shown throughout His ministry. Oftentimes, men wonder if the Lord really does care. Then suddenly, He comes.

The Father's love for His children is perfectly expressed in the life and teachings of Jesus Christ and in the Atonement He provided for mankind. The Father reaches out to all His children. He comes to them through His Son and through the servants who are sent under His authority. Jesus worked only through perfect love, even when rebuking those who erred doctrinally. He came to help all of God's children make it back home. And yet with all of the love which He held, He still allowed men to choose for themselves. Jesus walked among the sons of men as their Teacher and Exemplar, but He still allowed men their agency to choose which path they would follow. Because of this, mankind retained the personal responsibility to find the truth. Jesus forced no one to heaven, rather those who truly desired salvation made the necessary effort to obtain it. Men can only rise up in the strength of the Lord if they choose to follow the way that was perfectly exemplified and taught by the Son of God. He truly is the way, the truth, and the life.

Going back into Galilee, Jesus went immediately to a man who sought His help. The man came and knelt down before the Lord and pleaded, "Lord, have mercy on my son: for he is lunatick, and sore vexed: for ofttimes he falleth into the fire, and oft into the water" (Matthew 17:15). The father of the boy then complained to Jesus that His disciples could not cast out the devil at his earlier request. The Savior then lamented His disciples' lack of faith, saying, "O faithless and perverse generation, how long shall I be with you, and suffer you?" (Luke 9:41).

Jesus commanded the men to bring the boy, and "as he was yet a coming, the devil threw him down, and tare him" (Luke 9:42). The boy thrashed on the ground "and wallowed foaming" (Mark 9:20).

> And [Jesus] asked his father, How long is it ago since this came unto him? And he said, Of a child. And ofttimes it hath cast him into the fire, and into the waters, to destroy him: but if thou canst do any thing, have compassion on us, and help us. Jesus said unto him, If thou canst believe, all things are possible to him that believeth. And straightway the father of the child cried out, and said with tears, Lord, I believe; help thou mine unbelief. When Jesus saw that the people came running together, he rebuked the foul spirit, saying unto him, Thou dumb and deaf spirit, I charge thee, come out of him, and enter no more into him. And the spirit cried, and rent him sore, and came out of him: and he was as one dead; insomuch that many said, He is dead. But Jesus took him by the hand, and lifted him up; and he arose. (Mark 9:21–27)

Jesus' disciples witnessed the lad's healing and later asked Jesus privately why they could not heal him. "And Jesus said unto them, Because of your unbelief: for verily I say unto you, If ye have faith as a grain of mustard seed, ye shall say unto this mountain, Remove hence to yonder place; and it shall remove; and nothing shall be impossible unto you. Howbeit this kind goeth not out but by prayer and fasting" (Matthew 17:20–21).

Jesus knew that it was essential for His disciples to have both faith and love. While he was with them, He taught them this by example, providing the help and assistance needed by all men. After His death, they would need to fast and pray to obtain sufficient faith to accomplish their parts in His work.

Some time later Jesus turned to His disciples and said, "The Son of man shall be betrayed into the hands of men: And they shall kill him, and the third day he shall be raised again. And they were exceeding sorry" (Matthew 17:22–23). Though they still did not understand, Jesus taught how with faith all things are possible. And because of His love, all things would be provided for any who would seek Him.

The love of the Savior is incomparable and beyond description. Even a mother's love falls short of the love that brought the Only Begotten Son from His throne above to suffer and die for mankind. "But, behold, Zion hath said: the Lord hath forsaken me, and my Lord hath forgotten me—but he will show that he hath not. For can a woman forget her sucking child, that she should not have compassion on the son of her womb? Yea, they may forget, yet will I not forget thee, O house of Israel. Behold, I have graven thee on the palms of my hands; thy walls are continually before me" (1 Nephi 21:14–16; compare with Isaiah 49). The Lord will always answer those who seek Him. Through Him and under His direction man can also succeed in those things that are expedient for His purposes.

The Lord's miraculous ability to help in any situation was about to be demonstrated again to Peter. After He healed the boy, Jesus was approached by tax collectors, who came demanding tribute to Caesar. Jesus told Peter, "go thou to the sea, and cast an hook, and take up the fish that first cometh up; and when thou hast opened his mouth, thou shalt find a piece of money: that take, and give unto them for me and thee" (Matthew 17:27). So it was and forever would be, the promise of the Lord was fulfilled according to His word.

If the Savior's faith could be compared to a seed that had grown into a tree, and his love with the love of a mother, then perhaps His purity of heart could be equated to the pureness in a child's heart. His answer to the question, "Who is greatest in the kingdom of heaven?" taught the plainness and purity of the gospel of Jesus Christ. He said, "Whosoever therefore shall humble himself as this little child, the same is greatest in the kingdom of heaven" (Matthew 18:4). Jesus did not call one of his great apostles and put him in the midst of the people as the example. He called a child and then told His disciples, "Except ye be converted, and become as little children, ye shall not enter into the kingdom of heaven" (Matthew 18:3).

While the world's heroes are great warriors, athletes, or actors, Jesus set a little child before men to teach them of the true nature of heaven. "For the natural man is an enemy to God, and has been from the fall of Adam, and will be, forever and ever, unless he yields to the enticings of the Holy Spirit, and putteth off the natural man and becometh a saint through the atonement of Christ the Lord, and becometh as a child." The Christlike qualities of a child are to be remembered and lived by those who desire to enter Christ's kingdom and become like Him. Those qualities include being "submissive, meek, humble, patient, full of love, willing to submit to all things which the Lord seeth fit to inflict upon him, even as a child doth submit to his father" (Mosiah 3:19).

Continuing in this same topic of the Savior's love for His children, Jesus went on to teach the parables of the lost sheep, the coin, and the prodigal son. As these teachings indicate, the Lord will go to great lengths to find and recover His lost sheep, whether they become lost by unintentional wandering, irresponsible neglect, or purposeful rebellion. Like the little child who loves and yearns for even an uncaring or abusive parent, Jesus' heart is pure and undefiled even when the love of men waxes cold against Him. Even when the people He came to love were indifferent, irresponsible, or rebellious, He went on in search of His wandering sheep.

The parable of the prodigal son demonstrates the nature of His perfect heart. The story tells of a certain son who left to enjoy his inheritance, having asked for and received all that his father had to give him. The man felt he did not need his father any more. He had what he needed and so he left to experience life as he pleased. His riotous worldly living, which he thought was the true way to live happily, quickly depleted his inheritance until he became entirely destitute, grateful to eat what was left to the pigs.

> And when he came to himself, he said, How many hired servants of my father's have bread enough and to spare, and I perish with hunger! I will arise and go to my father, and will say unto him, Father, I have sinned against heaven, and before thee, And am no more worthy to be called thy son: make me as one of thy hired servants. And he arose, and came to his father. But when he was yet a great way off, his father saw him, and had compassion, and ran, and fell on his neck, and kissed him. And the son said unto him, Father, I have sinned against heaven, and in thy sight, and am no more worthy to be called thy son. But the father said to his servants, Bring forth the best robe and put it on him; and put a ring on his hand, and shoes on his feet: and bring hither the fatted calf, and kill it; and let us eat and be merry: For this my son was dead, and is alive again; he was lost, and is found. (Luke 15:17–24)

As the story tells, there came a point when, after realizing what the world really had to offer, the boy "came to himself." He realized how the world had deceived him into thinking it really had something when all along it really sought to rob him of that which his father had given him. When the boy remembered his father's generosity, he decided to return home to see if he could regain just a small portion of the happiness available through his father's way of living. He knew that even being a hired servant there would be preferable to the situation in which he now found himself. To his great surprise, as he neared his former home, he saw his father running to him to put a ring on his hand, shoes on his feet, and his father's best robe on his body. His father even had the fatted calf prepared for his fill.

In our own efforts to be obedient, perhaps it is this characteristic of our Father's love that can best rekindle our efforts to remain faithful. Just as his father was ready to receive the prodigal son, our Savior waits to embrace all who struggle. It was the prodigal son's memory of his father's love that brought him back, hoping for even a small portion of what he once had with his father. His father had showed him the right way all along, the true way of happiness.

Through his own choices, the prodigal son became separated physically from his father. In the same way each of us will find a time in life when we are distanced spiritually from the Lord. For all, the key to returning is found in remembering. As we remember, we spiritually draw closer to our Father, hoping for a portion of what we once experienced in His love, only to discover that He is running to receive us in His complete embrace. Faith in the Lord Jesus Christ, repentance, baptism by immersion for the remission of sins (or renewing that covenant through the ordinance of the sacrament), and receiving the Holy Ghost are the first principles and ordinances of the gospel. These are the first things that should follow when we remember Christ and His gospel. When we do these things we bring ourselves closer to Him so that we may always have His Spirit to be with us. This Spirit is indeed a complete embrace from a Father who is the only One who has something of any lasting value for His sons and daughters.

ADDITIONAL COMMENTARY

The Way:

There is only one way to happiness and fulfillment. He is the Way.

Every other way, any other way, whatever other way, is foolishness. . . . He is the Savior of the world. Either we accept the blessings of His Atonement and are made clean and pure, worthy to have His Spirit, or we don't and foolishly remain alone and filthy still. . . . Only God can bless us. Only He can sustain us. Only He can cause our hearts to beat and give us breath. Only He can preserve and protect us. Only He can give us strength to bear up the burdens of life. Only He can give us power, knowledge, peace, and joy. Only He can forgive our sins. Only He can heal us. Only He can change us and forge a godly soul. Only He can bring us back into His presence. And He will do all of that and much more if we but remember Him to keep His commandments. What then shall we do? We will remember Him to keep His commandments. It is the only intelligent thing to do.[1]

The Truth:

To that end, Jesus Christ entered a garden called Gethsemane, where He overcame sin for us. He took upon Himself our sins. He suffered the penalty of our wrongs. He paid the price of our education. I don't know how He did what He did. I only know that He did and that because He did, you and I may be forgiven of our sins that we may be endowed with His power. Everything depends on that. What then shall we do? We will "take upon [us] the name of [the] Son, and always remember him and keep his commandments which he has given [us]; that [we] may always have his Spirit to be with [us]." (D&C 20:77). Everything depends on that.[2]

The Life:

We have only two choices. We can either follow the Lord and be endowed with His power and have peace, light, strength, knowledge, confidence, love, and joy, or we can go some other way, any other way, whatever other way, and go it alone—without His support, without His power, without guidance, in darkness, turmoil, doubt, grief, and despair. And I ask, which way is easier? . . . I bear witness of Him, even Jesus Christ, that He is the Son of the living God, He is the Bread of Life, He is the Truth, He is the Resurrection and the Life, He is the Savior and the Light of the World. He is the Way, the only Way. May we have good sense to follow Him.[3]

Notes

1. Lawrence E. Corbridge, "The Way," *Ensign*, Oct. 2008.
2. Ibid.
3. Ibid.

16

⟶ PRINCE OF PEACE ⟵

SPECIAL WITNESSES OF JESUS' NAME

Prince of Peace: The prophet Isaiah established this title through revelation when he wrote that, among so many other names, Jesus would be called the Prince of Peace (see Isaiah 9:6). The people who waited for something more than a peaceful dominion at the Messiah's coming, simply expected a more dramatic display of God's power. They expected the Messiah to do more than heal hearts, restore sight to the blind, cause the lame to walk, and allow the deaf to hear. Only the faithful, those who held to the scriptures over the false oral traditions of the day, recognized Jesus of Nazareth as the Passover Lamb, the Perfecter, the Purifier, the Physician, the High Priest of our profession (Hebrews 3:1), the Power and Right Hand of God. While the Pharisees proclaimed a future Potentate to deliver Israel from the foreign powers that prevailed in Jerusalem, the righteous remembered Isaiah's prophecy of the manner in which Christ would rule and reign as the rightful Propitiator of our sins. He stood with authority as the Prince of Life, yet He came as a servant. "Behold my servant, whom I uphold; mine elect, in whom my soul delighteth . . . He shall not cry, nor lift up, nor cause his voice to be heard in the street. A bruised reed shall he not break, and the smoking flax shall he not quench: he shall bring forth judgment unto truth" (Isaiah 42:1–3). Instead of coming to destroy the oppressor, Jesus came to uplift the downtrodden. He came to help mankind, one soul at a time.

When the time of the feast of tabernacles approached, Jesus' disciples counseled their Lord that He should go into Judaea. They argued that He should demonstrate the power that He held, "that thy disciples also may see the works that thou doest. For there is no man that doeth any thing in secret, and he himself seeketh to be known openly. If thou do these things, shew thyself to the world" (John 7:3–4). The Savior responded that His time had not yet come and therefore He would not go up to the feast. In time He would set His face toward Jerusalem, but for now He still had a private ministry to accomplish in the regions of Perea and Judaea. As mentioned previously, His purpose was to quietly build true faith, not attract ceremonial, superficial, or temporary allegiance.

One way He would accomplish His permanent faith-building was by organizing seventy special witnesses who would go before Him, bearing testimony and teaching truth. These witness were chosen and asked to fully devote themselves to the work, just like the Twelve. Their calling gave them the opportunity to bless mankind and, alongside the apostles, bear witness of His name in all the world. To accomplish this great purpose, these special witnesses would learn to function in the way the Lord had ordained, building the faith of those who were diligently seeking for knowledge.

As they journeyed away from Galilee, Jesus sent messengers into Samaria to prepare the way before Him. The apostles went first to share their witness of the Messiah. But the Samaritans did not receive their testimony, nor would they receive Jesus when He arrived. After this rejection, James and John asked the Savior if they should command fire to come down from heaven and consume the people. Jesus instantly rebuked them, telling that they did not know which spirit they were responding to. He told them that His purpose was not to destroy but to save. He had come to serve, teach, uplift, and bless.

It was at this time that Jesus appointed the seventy other messengers and sent them two by two to prepare the way in the cities He would visit. The Seventy were charged and sent forth with power and authority. The ministry of the Messiah now proceeded through an organized group of the Twelve and the Seventy. Evangelists, pastors, teachers, and so on would also be organized in their own proper time (see Ephesians 4). The scriptures state that the Twelve Apostles are to be "special witnesses of the name of Christ in all the world," and that "The Seventy are also called to preach the gospel, and to be especial witnesses unto the Gentiles and in all the world" (D&C 107:23, 25).

Jesus sent these special messengers of His name to go forth as "lambs among wolves" (Luke 10:3). He then gave them some instructions about how to proceed as they preached the gospel. Just like the Apostles they would have to be "wise as serpents, and harmless as doves" (Matthew 10:16) to survive among the wolves they were sent to convert into sheep. Of course it would not be the wolves in sheep's clothing who would hear. They would need to find the true lost sheep who had forgotten their identity, but who would recognize their Shepherd's voice when He suddenly approached to deliver them from spiritual despair.

In Galilee, Jesus came as the ideal Teacher. He demonstrated perfect faith, hope, and love through everything He did as He went personally with His Twelve and Seventy to teach in His Apostles' hometowns. Offering good will and every good thing to those who would hear, He still left disappointed. Of these towns He said,

> Woe unto thee, Chorazin! Woe unto thee, Bethsaida! For if the mighty works, which were done in you, had been done in Tyre and Sidon, they would have repented long ago in sackcloth and ashes. . . . And thou, Capernaum, which art exalted unto heaven, shalt be brought down to hell: for if the mighty works, which have been done in thee, had been done in Sodom, it would have remained until this day. But I say unto you, That it shall be more tolerable for the land of Sodom in the day of judgment, than for thee. (Matthew 11:21–24)

Jesus had, of course, fulfilled His role perfectly. His miracles and words were perfect examples of what the gospel had to offer. His lamentation came because some of those who witnessed His mighty works still did not repent, and therefore they could not have the Holy Ghost come and truly teach them. They remained as unbelievers, even after all the Savior had done. His miracles did not convert them. The Holy Ghost could not convert them until they acted in faith.

And then there were those who did learn the perfect lesson from the Master. Many did come and follow Him, leaving everything in the world to do so. Consider the Messiah's teaching effectiveness with regard to those who answer, "I will go and do the things which the Lord hath commanded, for I know that the Lord giveth no commandments unto the children of men save he shall prepare a way for them to accomplish the thing which he commandeth them" (1 Nephi 3:7). Imagine what those true disciples learned when they followed their Master, letting the dead bury their dead while they came after Jesus. Imagine what occurred for those who took up their crosses, endured their own Gethsemanes, and went on in whatever path the Lord required of them. Several of these faithful disciples went on to become aids to the Savior throughout the rest of His earthly life.

The Seventy returned, rejoicing over how even the devils were subject unto them through the power of Christ. Jesus confirmed their report; He had indeed given them power over Satan. "Notwithstanding in this rejoice not, that the spirits are subject unto you; but rather rejoice, because your names are written in heaven. In that hour Jesus rejoiced in spirit, and said, I thank thee, O Father, Lord of heaven and earth, that thou hast hid these things from the wise and prudent, and hast revealed them unto babes: even so, Father; for so it seemed good in thy sight" (Luke 10:20–21).

As always, the Lord had much in store for His humble followers. Those who rejected His counsel did so to their eternal detriment. Whereas those who listened had their names written in heaven. As Jesus said, "All things are delivered unto me of my Father: and no man knoweth the Son, but the Father; neither knoweth any man the Father, save the Son, and they to whom the Son will reveal himself; they shall see the Father also" (JST Matthew 11:27).

These words, spoken to the special witnesses of His name, would help them with their own overwhelming and inexhaustible assignments. He continued: "Come unto me, all ye that labour and are heavy laden, and I will give you rest. Take my yoke upon you and learn of me; for I am meek and lowly in heart: and ye shall find rest unto your souls. For my yoke is easy, and my burden is light" (Matthew 11:28–30).

Of the great truths that would help the future leadership of His Church to understand His gospel, one Jesus chose to teach them personally was this: "Come unto me, all ye that labor, and I will give you rest!" Certain tasks in life are simply beyond mortal capacity. The Lord's servants were called to bring salvation to a fallen world, a task that was far beyond their ability to perform. To successfully fulfill their duties, they would have to work in the Lord's way.

This would not mean doing it alone; rather, they would need to rely on the Lord's power, casting their burdens on One who could help them. It would require trusting the Lord, having Him guide the work through revelation, and then allowing those who were under their stewardship to choose whether or not they would heed His voice as it quietly guided them to salvation. Jesus taught that in the work of saving souls, a work that would soon spread to so many, unless men learn to cast their burden upon Him, they will sink under the weight of so great a calling.

Beyond His words, Jesus also lived as a perfect example of how men should work to elevate humanity and bless mankind. He worked one city, one family, one soul at a time, sending forth His word, His power, and His hands to help. He went about doing good (see Acts 10:38). He uplifted, edified, and taught the people. He gave priesthood blessings. He served and assisted wherever He could, whether through His own voice or efforts, or through those of His servants. In this great work Jesus did not sit on His throne ordering His servants from above. He went out and worked with them, reaching out to anyone willing to receive His perfect assistance.

Additional Commentary

Mankind Should Have Been My Business: In Charles Dickens' *A Christmas Carol*, Ebenezer Scrooge is met by the ghost of his long-deceased business partner, Jacob Marley. The spirit begins to teach him the reason for his misery and the purpose of his ponderous chain. He says,

> "My spirit never walked beyond our counting-house—mark me!—in life my spirit never roved beyond the narrow limits of our money-changing hole. . . . Not to know that any Christian spirit working kindly in its little sphere, whatever it may be, will find its mortal life too short for its vast means of usefulness. Not to know that no space of regret can make amends for one life's opportunity misused! Yet such was I! Oh! Such was I!" Ebenezer called back, realizing that he was one just as his partner, "But you were always a good man of business, Jacob." "Business," cried the Ghost, wringing its hands again. "Mankind was my business. The common welfare was my business; charity, mercy, forbearance, and benevolence were, all, my business. The dealings of my trade were but a drop of water in the comprehensive ocean of my business! . . . At this time of the rolling year," the spectre said, "I suffer most. Why did I walk through crowds of fellow-beings with my eyes turned down, and never raise them to that blessed Star which led the Wise Men to a poor abode! Were there no poor homes to which its light would have conducted me!"[1]

Walking in the footsteps of the Prince of Peace, those who serve the Lord will bless mankind in the same manner that He did.

One by One: Those who truly understand the point of this life, that it is an opportunity to work with the Lord in blessing and elevating mankind, will find purpose in their own existence. Jesus set the pattern for this kind of living as He "went about doing good" (Acts 10:38) in mortality and continued to bless His children "one by one" (3 Nephi 17:21) after His Resurrection. Jesus demonstrated how to minister to our fellowmen. In fact, it was the very reason for His life: "For behold," said He, "this is my work and my glory—to bring to pass the immortality and eternal life of man" (Moses 1:39).

One Good Deed at a Time: Deseret Morning News Staff Writer Jerry Johnston described the manner in which President Thomas S. Monson works in the footsteps of the Lord. He wrote,

> No matter how many heads of state he will meet in his new calling as president, no matter how many national interviews he gives or how international his reputation becomes, LDS believers know part of him will forever be the young bishop from 50 years ago—the "ward healer" determined to elevate humanity one good deed at a time. . . . I remembered . . . how he once gave his shoes away to a needy member. I thought of the pleasant notes he sends out by the dozens. And, in a moment of whimsy, I remembered reading Superman comic books as a boy. I could never understand why the Man of Steel spent so much time chasing down cat burglars and tugging babies from the path of speeding cars. He could have cured cancer, fed Africa, found oil on Mars. Now, at age 59, I get the picture. In those early comics, Superman wasn't about pushing life as we know it to new heights. He was about teaching us how to lift others—how to elevate humanity "one good deed at a time." It was, of course, the approach pioneered by the Greatest Teacher of them all. It's also an approach President Thomas S. Monson has modeled over a lifetime.[2]

Sharing the Burden: Jesus often delegated His work, even when He could have done it much more efficiently and with greater power. He understood and closely held to a certain principle of human development. Lee Tom Perry describes this principle:

> We are often asked to do something by leaders who act like we are doing them a favor, when they are doing us a favor. Have you ever thought that when leaders decide to do an assignment themselves, instead of bothering you with it they are doing you harm? I must admit that there have been many times in both my early and recent Church leadership experience when I have chosen to do something I should have delegated. Accordingly, I must plead guilty to many times doing people harm in the process. It was my counselors, who understood this principle far better

than I did, who taught me that we ask people to serve because they need opportunities to serve. Service is the means by which members of the Church become more fully developed. I have been fond of saying that in the Church the only business we are in is the human resources development business. I say this whenever I think someone else is mixing up means and ends, acting like programs are more important than people. People are always more important than programs. Unfortunately, I need to remind myself as often as I remind others of this simple truth, which is perfectly aligned with the plan of salvation.[3]

Notes

1.   Charles Dickens, *A Christmas Carol* (New York City: Macmillan, 1963), 23–25.
2.   Jerry Johnston, "Personal Ministries Have Made President Monson 'Pastoral Leader,'" *Deseret Morning News*, Feb. 7, 2008.
3.   Lee Tom Perry, *Righteous Influence* (Salt Lake City: Deseret Book, 2004), 50.

17

❧ QUICKENER OF THE DEAD ❦

MARY AND MARTHA—THE COST OF ETERNAL LIFE

Quickener of the Dead: The Bible Dictionary defines quick as "living" or "alive," as in Leviticus 13:10. So to quicken is to make alive or to bring to life. Under that definition, Jesus, as the Quickener of those who are dead, is the One who brings life, and the only One who can provide eternal life. The true cost of eternal life is His life. Then, considering the cost paid for our eternal lives, how could any requirement in the gospel ask too much of us?

When teaching the importance of eternal life, Jesus often indicated its value as being far greater than the entire world. "For what is a man profited, if he shall gain the whole world, and lose his own soul?" (Matthew 16:26). The answer could only be understood by the person who understood the true nature of eternal life. Eternal life—"that they might know thee the only true God, and Jesus Christ, whom thou hast sent" (John 17:3); "in my Father's house are many mansions. . . . I go to prepare a place for you" (John 14:2); "ye shall come forth in the first resurrection . . . and shall inherit thrones, kingdoms, principalities, and powers, dominions, all heights and depths . . . and they shall pass by the angels, and the gods, which are set there, to their exaltation and glory in all things, as hath been sealed upon their heads, which glory shall be a fulness and a continuation of the seeds forever and ever" (D&C 132:19). The Lord spent much of His ministry teaching people the importance of their choices while in this short period of their mortal existence and how the consequences of those choices would have a bearing on their eternal life.

He taught this specifically on the day when Jesus went to visit Mary and Martha in Bethany, a village just above Jerusalem. The sisters had a brother named Lazarus. These three devoted disciples of the Master loved Him, and He them. Having come into Bethany, Jesus went immediately to see this family, and "Martha received him into her house" (Luke 10:38). Mary "sat at Jesus' feet, and heard his word," while "Martha was cumbered about much serving" (Luke 10:39–40).

Martha prepared food for her weary guest, finally complaining, "Lord, dost thou not care that my sister hath left me to serve alone? bid her therefore that she help me. And Jesus answered and said unto her, Martha, Martha, thou art careful and troubled about many things: But one thing is needful: and Mary hath chosen that good part, which shall not be taken away from her" (Luke 10:40–42). Martha, though troubled about many things, had missed that one needful thing. She missed the Christ who sat right there in her home. Mary, on the other hand, had found Him. She came to Jesus to worship Him and listen to His words. She held to her testimony of Him over the other worldly things she might have done to impress Him.

Jesus took this opportunity to teach a great lesson about what people choose to do with life and what they consequently end up with. While men often devote their lives to obtaining the trivial things of this world, there is one needful thing, and Mary found it in her home that day and would not leave Him. Those who come to Christ for that One needful thing receive just that. They know how important it is to treasure up a testimony of the Lord over all other things!

Jesus then left Bethany, teaching and serving as He went. "And it came to pass, as he spake these things, a certain woman of the company lifted up her voice, and said unto him, Blessed is the womb that bare thee, and the paps which thou hast sucked. But he said, Yea rather, blessed are they that hear the word of God, and keep it" (Luke 11:27–28). Though many things are necessary in the quest for eternal life, Jesus was teaching the people about the most important principle to help them on their way: hearing and doing the will of God. There would be no other way to obtain that "eternal life which God giveth unto all the obedient" (Moses 5:11). The way to eternal life requires obedience to the commandments and ordinances of God, though thieves and robbers will attempt to go in at some other door (see John 10:1–7).

As He taught these things, a man approached Jesus and said, "Master, speak to my brother, that he divide the inheritance with me. And he said unto him, Man, who made me a judge or a divider over you? And he said unto them, Take heed, and beware of covetousness: for a man's life consisteth not in the abundance of the things which he possesseth" (Luke 12: 13–15).

When speaking to this man, who desired an inheritance, or to Martha, who wanted a perfect home, Jesus' message remained the same: "But seek ye first the kingdom of God and his righteousness, and all these things shall be added unto you" (3 Nephi 13:33). Jesus taught men to place their minds and hearts on the things of eternity over temporary items of worldly value. And yet men would still be foolish with their precious time in mortality. This was the principle the Savior tried to teach the man who wanted his inheritance.

Even so He taught:

> The ground of a certain rich man brought forth plentifully: And he thought within himself, saying, What shall I do, because I have no room where to bestow my fruits? And he said, This will I do: I will pull down my barns, and build greater; and there will I bestow all my fruits and my goods. And I will say to my soul, Soul, thou hast much goods laid up for many years; take thine ease, eat, drink, and be merry. But God said unto him, Thou fool, this night thy soul shall be required of thee: then whose shall those things be, which thou hast provided? So is he that layeth up treasure for himself, and is not rich toward God. (Luke 12:16–21)

Reminiscent of an earlier teaching—that whosoever would save his life should lose it and whosoever would lose his life for His sake should find it (see Matthew 16:25)—Jesus now indicated how important it is to put the Lord before everything else in life. "And there went great multitudes with him: and he turned, and said unto them, If any man come to me, and hate not his father, and mother, and wife, and children, and brethren, and sisters, yea, and his own life also, he cannot be my disciple. And whosoever doth not bear his cross, and come after me, cannot be my disciple" (Luke 14:25–27). At times the choice to follow Jesus would require a temporary sacrifice of the best things in a person's life. How many were easily swayed from their eternal reward by lesser things such as luxury, fun, or sinful, filthy pleasures?

As Jesus next instructed, all disciples should "count the cost" of the things they are doing. Even though it might be enjoyable, how valuable is an activity that detracts from the Holy Sabbath if it comes at the cost of your faith? How much does that job really pay if it costs you your integrity? How priceless is that relationship if it means trading in eternal life? "For which of you, intending to build a tower, sitteth not down first, and counteth the cost, whether he have sufficient to finish it? Lest haply, after he hath laid the foundation, and is not able to finish it, all that behold it begin to mock him, Saying, This man began to build, and was not able to finish" (Luke 14:28–30). When He was teaching of building a tower or a home, those who listened to Jesus understood. But when He began speaking of eternal things, men would often turn away. They could not easily give up their momentary pleasures for the things of eternity.

Yet Jesus would continue to remind His people. He urged them to remember the cost of sin and to remember the price of righteousness. Some choices bring eternal rewards and others eternal losses, He said. For this reason the Savior taught of eternal costs and the need to account for them in all of our choices. He said:

> Lay not up for yourselves treasures upon earth, where moth and rust doth corrupt, and where thieves break through and steal: But lay up for yourselves treasures in heaven, where neither moth nor rust doth corrupt, and where thieves do not break through nor steal: For where your treasure is, there will your heart be also . . . No man can serve two masters: for either he will hate the one, and love the other; or else he will hold to the one, and despise the other. Ye cannot serve God and mammon. (Matthew 6:19–21, 24)

Jesus taught these things in principle and example. What should be placed as most important in this world? Jesus demonstrated the answer in all that He did and said. "And the Pharisees also, who were covetous, heard all these things: and they derided him. And he said unto them, Ye are they which justify yourselves before men; but God knoweth your hearts: for that which is highly esteemed among men is abomination in the sight of God" (Luke 16:14–15).

He went on to teach plainly and with boldness of the kind of results they could expect from the life they so highly esteemed. He said,

> There was a certain rich man, which was clothed in purple and fine linen, and fared sumptuously every day: And there was a certain beggar named Lazarus, which was laid at his gate, full of sores, And desiring to

be fed with the crumbs which fell from the rich man's table: moreover the dogs came and licked his sores. And it came to pass, that the beggar died, and was carried by the angels into Abraham's bosom: the rich man also died, and was buried; And in hell he lift up his eyes, being in torments, and seeth Abraham afar off, and Lazarus in his bosom. And he cried and said, Father Abraham, have mercy on me, and send Lazarus, that he may dip the tip of his finger in water, and cool my tongue; for I am tormented in this flame. But Abraham said, Son, remember that thou in thy lifetime receivedst thy good things, and likewise Lazarus evil things: but now he is comforted, and thou art tormented. And beside all this, between us and you there is a great gulf fixed: so that they which would pass from hence to you cannot; neither can they pass to us, that would come from thence. (Luke 16:19–26)

Those who heard Jesus teach that day were reminded of the importance of heavenly things and the smallness of the things of the world in comparison. In coveting the "drop" while neglecting the weighty matters, many faltered in their ignorance (see D&C 117). Those who did not understand the teachings of eternity missed the spiritual meaning of counting the cost when compared to building a tower.

Even Jesus' disciples asked if those that Pontius Pilate had killed or those upon whom the tower in Siloam fell were sinners above the other Galileans or men of Jerusalem. Jesus answered, "I tell you, Nay: but, except ye repent, ye shall all likewise perish" (Luke 13:5). The importance of repentance in the quest for eternal life was thus established as one of these crucial and weighty matters. Men must repent. Repentance is how those who come unto Christ are able to begin living in the way He has established and how they eventually find life eternal. The only other way is death.

Those Pharisees who listened that day discovered that though they had faithfully observed many ceremonial rules, they had left out the weighty matters of the gospel, such as judgment, mercy, and faith. Similarly, today many omit the required personal practices that encourage devotion to God, even though they diligently involve themselves in the various social functions in the Church. These people think that all is well, yet when they are asked to do something that requires sacrifice instead of simply enjoying the benefits of membership in the Church they will feel inconvenienced and may even refuse to sacrifice. These members have lost sight of that one crucial destination—eternal life.

ADDITIONAL COMMENTARY

Eternal Life: Elder L. Tom Perry of the Quorum of the Twelve Apostles asked the question,

> [When] we think of eternal life, what is the picture that comes to mind? I believe that if we could create in our minds a clear and true picture of eternal life, we would start behaving differently. We would not need to be prodded to do the many things involved with enduring to the end, like doing our home teaching or visiting teaching, attending our meetings, going to the temple, living moral lives, saying our prayers, or reading the scriptures. We would want to do all these things and more because we realize they will prepare us to go somewhere we yearn to go.[1]

The Perceived Drop Versus the Actual More Weighty Matters: Those who heard Jesus teach were reminded of the importance of heavenly things and the smallness of the things of the world in comparison. While coveting the "drop" (see D&C 117) in exchange for the blessings of eternity, many miss the opportunities to serve and grow. For example, Lehi's eldest sons Laman and Lemuel were so focused on worldly things that they failed to prepare for heavenly things. In a similar manner, many people are deceived into thinking they are okay because they have successfully followed those commandments that they enjoy or that they immediately benefit from. Like Laman and Lemuel, they would willingly go to back to Jerusalem for wives but hardly for the brass plates. If they could understand the nature of life's testing and gospel obedience, they would consider both of these types of commandments as equal opportunities to prove valiant to the testimony of Jesus.

Courageous Travelers:

> Life should be an inspiring journey, not a bleak, cheerless path destitute of all that gives color and meaning to it. Some people become discouraged, defeated, beaten in spirit, whipped, and cowed by the lashing winds of adversity until they lose confidence and hope. Everyone who is worth his salt will have opposition to meet. The world needs a stout heart, a brave soul, a smiling face that goes forth in the morning with eagerness for the fray, that sees through the clouds the shining sun. . . . There is an inexpressible joy in the realization of having conquered a personal weakness, in solving a hard problem, in doing faithfully a disagreeable task, in fighting valiantly for the right. Life is a happy and

inspiring journey for courageous travelers.[2]

Not a Little Matter: One poet described how our attitude can affect our obedience to the Lord's will. Those who do not understand this cannot see what is truly weighty in the eyes of the Lord—blessing His children in whatever way He sees fit. Assisting in His work by taking advantage of opportunities to reach out to mankind, no matter how big or small those opportunities may be, is a crucial part of our progression toward eternal life:

> "Father, where shall I work today?"
> And my love flowed warm and free.
> Then he pointed out a tiny spot
> And said, "Tend that for me."
> I answered quickly, "Oh no, not that!
> Why, no one would ever see,
> No matter how well my work was done.
> Not that little place for me."
> And the word he spoke, it was not stern; . . .
> "Art thou working for them or for me?
> "Nazareth was a little place, and so was Galilee."[3]

Notes
1. L. Tom Perry, "The Gospel of Jesus Christ," *Ensign*, May 2008.
2. Bryant S. Hinckley, *Not By Bread Alone* (Salt Lake City: Bookcraft, 1955), 11.
3. Meade MacGuire, "Father, Where Shall I Work Today?" in *Best-Loved Poems of the LDS People*, comp. Jack M. Lyon and others (1996), 152, as quoted by President Thomas S. Monson in "Your Personal Influence," *Ensign*, May 2004, 20.

18

❧ Redeemer ❧

Jesus Enters Jerusalem

Redeemer: The first prophet who recorded this title for Christ was Job, who, under the most trying conditions, testified: "For I know that my redeemer liveth, and that he shall stand at the latter day upon the earth; And though after my skin worms destroy this body, yet in my flesh shall I see God" (Job 19:25–26). For one such as Job, Jesus was the Resurrection and the Life thus fulfilling the word, "he that believeth in me, though he were dead, yet shall he live" (John 11:25). The One that some called Rabbi or Rabboni, the Root of Jesse, and the Rose of Sharon, the One chosen as Ruler of Israel, is the Rock upon which a soul can still find safety and redemption. He is a refuge, providing rest to those who rely on Him. The Righteous One wants to bless His children. As the Ransom provided for men, Jesus truly came for this purpose, not to condemn but to save. His is truly the only name given under heaven whereby men can come unto the Father and be redeemed (see John 14:6). He is the Risen Lord.

Jesus truly came to save those who would believe and follow Him with faith. Salvation would require diligence along the strait and narrow way. He personally walked this path to show the proper way to keep the commandments and fulfill the required ordinances of the gospel. Yet, comparatively speaking, there would be few who would follow this strait and narrow path. Another pathway leading into a great and spacious building was much more appealing. This path's destination was high and lifted up, and so the majority of men were easily swayed in its direction. The scriptures describe this counterfeit pathway with the words "wide is the gate, and broad is the way, that leadeth to destruction, and many there be which go in thereat" (see Matthew 7:13–14). Those who seek only a life of ease and instant gratification, living for the moment while missing that which brings eternal joy, quickly choose this pathway over the Lord's. Unfortunately those who are deceived soon discover nothing at the end of that road but misery and death.

The Lord Jesus came to show the correct way. He provided the necessary evidence of His divinity as he walked along the correct pathway. Some who witnessed Jesus' example reacted negatively to the manner and timing of His actions. Others glorified God. Whatever the reaction, it was still the way of the Lord, the way directed by the Spirit of the Lord, and the way for men to follow if they were interested in salvation.

As Jesus journeyed with His disciples to Jerusalem, He stopped to rest on the Sabbath day. The group entered a synagogue, where they immediately discovered an old woman bowed over with an infirmity so that she could not lift herself up. Jesus came to her and said, "Woman, thou art loosed from thine infirmity. And he laid his hands on her: and immediately she was made straight, and glorified God" (Luke 13:12–13).

The ruler of the synagogue turned on Jesus with "indignation, because that Jesus had healed on the sabbath day, and said unto the people, There are six days in which men ought to work: in them therefore come and be healed, and not on the sabbath day" (Luke 13:14). Jesus answered the ruler with a firm and direct rebuke. "Thou hypocrite, doth not each one of you on the sabbath loose his ox or his ass from the stall, and lead him away to watering? And ought not this woman, being a daughter of Abraham, whom Satan hath bound, lo, these eighteen years, be loosed from this bond on the sabbath day? And when he had said these things, all his adversaries were ashamed: and all the people rejoiced for all the glorious things that were done by him" (Luke 13:15–17).

Jesus then left the synagogue, "And he went through the cities and villages, teaching, and journeying toward Jerusalem" (Luke 13:22). As He traveled, one asked of Him, "Lord, are there few that be saved?" (Luke 13:23). Jesus' answer placed the responsibility for salvation directly on the individual. Though He would do all things necessary that man might be saved and teach men the correct way of salvation, yet each man would have to personally choose to follow His example faithfully, otherwise salvation would remain out of his grasp.

Jesus answered, "Strive to enter in at the strait gate: for many, I say unto you, will seek to enter in, and shall not be able. When once the master of the house is risen up, and hath shut to the door, and ye begin to stand without, and to knock at the door, saying, Lord, Lord, open unto us; and he shall answer and say unto you, I know you not whence ye are" (Luke 13:24–25). Reminiscent of His earlier teaching—"Not every one that saith unto me, Lord, Lord, shall enter into the kingdom of heaven; but he that doeth the will of my Father which is in heaven" (Matthew 7:21)—Jesus again taught the truth concerning the manner of salvation.

Jesus went on to teach those who thought that God's love alone would redeem them without their doing anything to prove their love to Him, or to be worthy of His name.

> But he shall say, I tell you, I know you not whence ye are; depart from me, all ye workers of iniquity. There shall be weeping and gnashing of teeth, when ye shall see Abraham, and Isaac, and Jacob, and all the prophets, in the kingdom of God, and you yourselves thrust out. And they shall come from the east, and from the west, and from the north, and from the south, and shall sit down in the kingdom of God. And, behold, there are last which shall be first, and there are first which shall be last. (Luke 13:27–30)

Moving on toward Jerusalem and the glorious act that awaited Him there, Jesus soon entered Perea. There a group of Pharisees approached Him. With all that we know about the Pharisees and their rejection of the Messiah, one might wonder why they came to Jesus at this time. Yet they came to Jesus in great haste, saying, "Get thee out, and depart hence: for Herod will kill thee" (Luke 13:31). The Pharisees had long been determined to preserve their own power as rulers in the synagogues. Their sudden interest in keeping Jesus alive was questionable at best. "And he said unto them, Go ye, and tell that fox, Behold, I cast out devils, and I do cures to day and to morrow, and the third day I shall be perfected. Nevertheless I must walk to day, and to morrow, and the day following: for it cannot be that a prophet perish out of Jerusalem" (Luke 13:32–33).

Instead of fleeing for safety, Jesus continued to teach. He asked the Pharisees where a man should sit when called to a wedding or to a meeting. These men loved the chief seats in the synagogues where they sat without any authority. Jesus taught that they should choose the lowest seat lest someone greater comes after, and "thou begin with shame to take the lowest room" (Luke 14:9). The lesson was profound from Him who had come as chief over all of these who stood in positions of renown among men: "Whosoever exalteth himself shall be abased; and he that humbleth himself shall be exalted" (Luke 14:10). Jesus went on to teach that when a man makes a dinner, he should not call his friends or rich neighbors, but the poor, the maimed, the lame, and the blind: "And thou shalt be blessed; for they cannot recompense thee: for thou shalt be recompensed at the resurrection of the just" (Luke 14:14).

Jesus next provided an illustration of the narrow way. When many were called by the Lord's servant, they all began to make excuses. One had a piece of ground that he needed to go and see. Another said he had five yoke of oxen that he needed to train. And finally another had married a wife and therefore could not come. Three excuses not to come to the great feast as prepared by the servant of the Lord: personal interests, work, and family. Then came the judgment of the Lord to those who made excuses not to come: "That none of those men which were bidden shall taste of my supper" (Luke 14:24).

Jesus thus taught how men are often called by the servants of the Lord to come and partake of various spiritual feasts as prepared under the inspiration of heaven. Then the excuses begin. As important as family, work, and personal interests are, they are not to be given as excuses when the Lord calls. There may be times when the ox is in the mire on the Sabbath day—the Lord has allowed for such emergencies. The danger comes when men purposefully place things above the Lord. Even the important things of life, things He has given us as blessings, do not serve as an excuse to not do what He requires.

Jesus then left Perea for another visit to Samaria. And when He entered a certain village, ten lepers met Him, standing a distance away, and began to call to Him: "Jesus, Master, have mercy on us." (Luke 17:13). Jesus commanded them to go and show themselves to the priests. "And it came to pass, that, as they went, they were cleansed" (Luke 17:14). One then turned back and glorified God for the act. He "fell down on his face at his feet, giving him thanks: and he was a Samaritan. And Jesus answering said, Were there not ten cleansed? but where are the nine? There are not found that returned to give glory to God, save this stranger. And he said unto him, Arise, go thy way: thy faith hath made thee whole" (Luke 17:16–19). Of the ten, only one walked the strait and narrow way. The others were immediately distracted by other paths, ones that led away from Christ.

Jesus "arose from thence [Samaria], and cometh into the coasts of Judaea by the farther side of Jordan: and the people resort unto him again;

and, as he was wont, he taught them again" (Mark 10:1). "And great multitudes followed him; and he healed them there" (Matthew 19:2). Having gone in this roundabout direction, teaching as He traveled, Jesus eventually arrived in Jerusalem for the Feast of the Tabernacles, which His disciples had long before asked Him to attend.

These who accompanied Jesus had hoped that their Master would go and perform His works before the people in Jerusalem, so that the people there might also see His works and believe. These disciples had spoken with words of persuasion: "For there is no man that doeth any thing in secret, and he himself seeketh to be known openly. If thou do these things, shew thyself to the world (John 7:4)" This Jesus had refused. But He would not decline the opportunity to teach the people in Jerusalem. "But when his brethren were gone up, then went he also up unto the feast, not openly, but as it were in secret. Then the Jews sought him at the feast, and said, Where is he?" (John 7:10–11).

Great murmurings preceded Jesus as the multitudes debated whether Jesus was the foretold Prophet or a deceiver. While they conversed, Jesus made His appearance. "Now about the midst of the feast Jesus went up into the temple, and taught" (John 7:14). The Jews listened with amazement to His teachings, wondering how a carpenter from Nazareth could teach in such a manner, "having never learned" (John 7:15). Jesus told them plainly that what He taught was not His doctrine but the doctrine of His Father. Then He told them how they could know for themselves that He spoke the truth: "If any man will do his will, he shall know of the doctrine, whether it be of God, or whether I speak of myself" (John 7:17).

The people began to question among themselves: "Is not this he, whom they seek to kill? But, lo, he speaketh boldly, and they say nothing unto him. Do the rulers know indeed that this is the very Christ?" (John 7:25–26). The murmurings arose concerning the fact that Jesus of Nazareth could not possibly be the Christ, for they knew Jesus' upbringing, "but when Christ cometh, no man knoweth whence he is. Then cried Jesus in the temple as he taught, saying, Ye both know me, and ye know whence I am: and I am not come of myself, but he that sent me is true, whom ye know not. But I know him: for I am from him, and he hath sent me" (John 7:27–29). The rulers and people listened silently until this blatant declaration of His Messiahship. "Then they sought to take him: but no man laid hands on him, because his hour was not yet come" (John 7:30). Others began to believe Him and asked, "When Christ cometh, will he do more miracles than these which this man hath done?" (John 7:31).

When the Pharisees and chief priests heard of Jesus' words and doings at the temple, they reacted according to their desires and sent officers to take Him. But when the officers came to Jesus, somehow they could only watch and listen. Like the people of Nazareth, who were powerless to pass judgment after His testimony, the officers also found that Jesus stood in authority before them and that they could do nothing. "Jesus stood and cried, saying, If any man thirst, let him come unto me, and drink. He that believeth on me, as the scripture hath said, out of his belly shall flow rivers of living water" (John 7:37–38).

Jesus thus spoke boldly and openly before the congregations that had gathered for the Feast of Tabernacles. Many reacted to His words. Some said, "Of a truth this is the Prophet." Others argued, "Shall Christ come out of Galilee? Hath not the scripture said, That Christ cometh of the seed of David, and out of the town of Bethlehem, where David was?" (John 7:40–42). As for the officers who came to take Him, they returned without fulfilling their assignment. The Pharisees and chief priests asked why they had not brought Jesus according to the order. To this the officers responded, "Never man spake like this man." The Pharisees were enraged at this answer, retorting with offense, "Are ye also deceived? Have any of the rulers or of the Pharisees believed on him? But this people who knoweth not the law are cursed" (John 7:46–49).

How surprised were these knowledgeable Pharisees when suddenly Nicodemus spoke out: "Doth our law judge any man, before it hear him, and know what he doeth?" (John 7:51). What other man among the Sanhedrin could ask such a question? Nicodemus had gone personally to hear Jesus for himself, and he knew that the works Jesus had accomplished were of God. After the many testimonies and evidences given, it is remarkable that so many still rejected the ministry of the Messiah without doing as Nicodemus had done. Did not such a bold, prophetic, and miraculous effort deserve some kind of an investigation by these who knew so much?

These who criticized the Master simply sought to take Jesus and kill Him because their own followers went after Him. To Nicodemus, "They answered and said unto him, Art thou also of Galilee? Search, and look: for out of Galilee ariseth no prophet" (John 7:52). They had already set their minds against Jesus. But Nicodemus had searched. He had looked. He had heard for himself. And now Nicodemus stood to defend the Christ with a simple question that held all sorts of inferences:

- Why are we treating Jesus differently? With all of the others we judge, we begin by hearing their words, examining evidence, and listening to witnesses to discover if there has been any wrongdoing.
- With Jesus we have simply and fearfully jumped to a conclusion that holds a verdict of death. Do we fear the truth?
- Can we not face the facts that have all Israel in commotion?
- Is it possible that the truthful evidences will prove Him as the Messiah to whom we, along with the multitudes who follow Him, should also bow?

Nicodemus was highly respected, and no one had an immediate response for him. "And every man went unto his own house" (John 7:53).

After serious consideration of what had happened that day, the Pharisees came up with a plan to appease Nicodemus' appeal to the law, while at the same time accomplishing their own desires to destroy the Lawgiver whom they knew not. They would seek the downfall of the Messiah by judging Him according to His own words after hearing Him, knowing what He did, and finding an error in it. This plan becomes apparent when on the next day Jesus again taught the people in the temple. Then the scribes and Pharisees brought unto Him a woman "taken in adultery." They had caught her in the very act, and they declared before all that listened: "Now Moses in the law commanded us, that such should be stoned: but what sayest thou?" (John 8:5).

The trap was thus set. If Jesus had compassion on the woman, He would be speaking against Moses, and the rulers would have found an error. If Jesus held to the law of Moses, He would be doing so without compassion—another error in the eyes of the people who expected both a merciful and a just Messiah. If He were truly a defender of the poor and fatherless, He would not be able to witness such a horrible punishment wrought out against this woman, especially at His hand. Whichever the response, Jesus would be destroyed in the eyes of the people who were looking for a blameless Messiah.

The Pharisees and chief priests knew they had what they needed "that they might have to accuse him" (John 8:6). They would now be able to do as Nicodemus had asked—pronounce a judgment after hearing and witnessing Jesus' acts. "But Jesus stooped down, and with his finger wrote on the ground, as though he heard them not. So when they continued asking him, he lifted up himself, and said unto them, He that is without sin among you, let him first cast a stone at her" (John 8:6–7).

Suddenly the tables had turned. What could they say? Jesus held to the law by telling the rulers, whose job it was, to do the task themselves. And by asking that someone who was not guilty of sin carry out the punishment, Jesus showed compassion, for who could cast the first stone? All departed but One—the sinless Son of God. "When Jesus had lifted up himself, and saw none but the woman, he said unto her, Woman, where are those thine accusers? hath no man condemned thee? She said, No man, Lord. And Jesus said unto her, Neither do I condemn thee: go, and sin no more" (John 8:10–11).

With every test given to Jesus, it was the rulers who departed in frustration without any evidence with which to condemn Him. Every time they left with their own consciences pricking them. Jesus declared plainly that their father was the devil, a liar from the beginning. And He said that as children of the devil they were subject to their father's desires, which did not include loving the truth or following it. The single exception was Nicodemus, who did love the truth and sought it. Nicodemus's ability to follow Christ was obviously hindered by his employers, those he would one day have to leave if he were ever to become a true disciple of the Master.

The Pharisees could not understand the Teacher who stood before them declaring only the truth. Such truth He would continue to pronounce when He said, "If a man keep my saying, he shall never see death" (John 8:51). The believers could understand the truth of that saying, but the Pharisees were only looking for ways to find fault with Him.

Jesus went on in Godly rebuke: "Verily, verily, I say unto you, Whosoever committeth sin is the servant of sin. . . . I know that ye are Abraham's seed; but ye seek to kill me because my word hath no place in you" (John 8:34, 37). "Then said Jesus to those Jews which believed on him, If ye continue in my word, then are ye my disciples indeed. . . . If the Son therefore shall make you free, ye shall be free indeed" (John 8:31, 36). The Pharisees could not find this freedom, for instead of following Him, Jesus declared that they followed their "father the devil, and the lusts of your father ye will do" (John 8:44).

The Pharisees now attempted to turn the tables on Him and say that it was He who had a devil, for Abraham was dead and so was Moses. But Jesus simply answered: "Verily, verily, I say unto you, If a man keep my saying, he shall never see death. Then said the Jews unto him, Now we know that thou hast a devil. Abraham is dead, and the prophets; and thou sayest, If a man keep my saying, he shall never taste of death" (John 8:51–52). They then asked if Jesus was greater than Abraham, to which He answered, "Before Abraham was, I AM" (John 8:58). The term I AM used in the Greek translation is identical with the Septuagint usage in Ex. 3:14 which identifies Jehovah (see footnote for John 8:58). The Jews understood His meaning perfectly. "Then took they up stones to cast at him: but Jesus hid himself, and went out of the temple, going through the midst of them, and so passed by" (John 8:59).

In this setting Jesus revealed His true identity. He came as Jehovah in the flesh. To deny Him was to deny the very plan of God. He was the same who was "Beloved and Chosen from the beginning" (Moses 4:2). In premortality He had offered to carry out His Father's plan accordingly. It was He who, when God said, "Whom shall I send?" had first answered, "Here am I, send me." Then another answered, "Here am I, send me. And the Lord said: I will send the first. And the second was angry, and kept not his first estate; and, at that day, many followed after him" (Abraham 3:27–28). It was He, the very Firstborn of the Father, over whom the war in heaven was waged until the "great dragon was cast out, that old serpent, called the Devil, and Satan. . . . And they overcame him by the blood of the Lamb, and by the word of their testimony" (Revelation 12:9, 11). It was He in whom Adam's children would not believe, "For they would not hearken unto his voice, nor believe in his Only Begotten Son, even him whom he declared should come in the meridian of time, who was prepared from before the foundation of the world" (Moses 5:57). It was He who spoke to Moses on the Mount. It was He whom Abraham worshipped when offering up his only son as a similitude of the Only Begotten.

And now the Great Jehovah stood before the people again, this time in the flesh, upon the same Mount Moriah where Abraham had been commanded to offer up Isaac and where Solomon had built the Lord's temple. Here the Jews spoke appropriately of Abraham asking, "Art thou greater than our father Abraham, which is dead?" Jesus answered, "Your father Abraham rejoiced to see my day: and he saw it, and was glad. Then said the Jews unto him, Thou art not yet fifty years old, and hast thou seen Abraham?" (John 8:53–58). Of course He had seen Abraham. He was the Great Jehovah of the Old Testament who had come with an offering of redemption to any who would follow. His way of salvation was indeed narrow to those who heard Him on this day; His offering seemed so at odds with their traditions, which honored the dead patriarchs over the Living Christ.

ADDITIONAL COMMENTARY

The Strait and Narrow Way: There is no better description of the strait and narrow way than that which is symbolically portrayed in Lehi's dream of the tree of life. A rod of iron, symbolic of the word of God, ran along the path to support those who desired to follow. The principles and ordinances of faith, repentance, baptism, and the gift of the Holy Ghost are symbolized by the path. Great temptations and distractions lead many away from the path and the true joy which can only be found at the tree of life, a symbol of the love of God. Those who are deceived by such forbidden pathways, end up either drowning in a river of filthy water or being caught in a great and spacious building which has no foundation and is on the verge of collapse and destruction (see 1 Nephi 8).

Are There Few That Be Saved? Whether the final number of those who are saved will be few or many, one thing we do know for sure: Whoever follows the Lord will be among those who receive eternal life. The Book of Mormon tells of those who followed after the holy order, referring to the priesthood. These people were thus sanctified, having their garments washed white through the blood of the Lamb. "Now they, after being sanctified by the Holy Ghost, having their garments made white, being pure and spotless before God, could not look upon sin save it were with abhorrence; and there were many, exceedingly great many, who were made pure and entered into the rest of the Lord their God" (Alma 13:12).

Art Thou Greater than Abraham Who Is Dead? While Jesus was greater and more intelligent than the Pharisees (see Abraham 3:19), yet He was meek and lowly of heart. When they questioned the Master, the Pharisees showed their allegiance to dead prophets over living ones. Jesus was the Living Christ, standing before His subjects. He was indeed present before Abraham and Moses, the same God whom the revered King David called Lord, and the same with whom Adam, or Michael the Archangel, defeated the rebellious hosts in the war in heaven. He was the One angels bowed to and acknowledged as the King of heaven and earth. And yet these false teachers, who had no authority, felt that they had more to offer the people than He who had come in the express image of the Father. They even tempted Jesus with the same sin of which they were guilty: pride. They asked if He were greater than Abraham. To this Jesus refused an answer, instead stating the doctrine that He was present before Abraham, acting according to His divine position. If the great and spacious building in Lehi's dream represented the pride and vanity of the world, the Pharisees, who resented the Lord and refused His counsel were certainly leaders in that building, actively seeking to lure people away from the meek and lowly pathway that lead to the Lord.

19

⟫ SHEPHERD OF SOULS ⟪

THE BLIND MAN TEACHES THE KNOWLEDGEABLE PHARISEES

Shepherd of Souls: The Savior of mankind, the Stone of Israel, the prophesied Shiloh (see Gen. 49:10), the Stem of Jesse, and the Son of Mary was also the very Son of God. As the Shepherd of souls, Jesus not only knows His sheep by name, but He is also known by His sheep. He can instruct those who receive Him with humility. In all things, Jesus leads His sheep by example. His sheep know His voice and they follow Him. The Good Shepherd stands immovably resolute against any enemy that threatens His followers, and even gave His life to save His sheep. The Savior was no hireling. A hireling comes as a stranger to the sheep. He does not know the sheep, nor do they know him. A hireling only has the ability to drive the sheep along from behind. When the wolf comes, the hireling flees, leaving the sheep to be scattered or killed. Jesus said: "I am the good shepherd: the good shepherd giveth his life for the sheep" (John 10:11). As the Sacrifice which was prepared from the foundation of the world, Jesus willingly came as Savior, making possible the salvation of man. When the hireling would have fled, the Good Shepherd stayed to conquer death at the cost of His own life. Only a God could ultimately accomplish this special role.

In the parable of the Good Shepherd, Jesus proclaimed Himself as the One to show the right way. He also explained the true nature of those

159

who would devise another path and call it the right way. "Verily, verily, I say unto you, He that entereth not by the door into the sheepfold, but climbeth up some other way, the same is a thief and a robber" (John 10:1). Jesus taught the true path by personally walking it first. He said: "But he that entereth in by the door is the shepherd of the sheep. To him the porter openeth; and the sheep hear his voice: and he calleth his own sheep by name, and leadeth them out. And when he putteth forth his own sheep, he goeth before them, and the sheep follow him: for they know his voice" (John 10:2–4).

Along this path, false shepherds would also appear and try to lure the sheep in a different direction. The true sheep would not easily be deceived, for "a stranger will they not follow, but will flee from him: for they know not the voice of strangers" (John 10:5). These faithful sheep would not be interested in the stranger's uncomfortable and foreign voice, especially after the Spirit had warned them that "The thief cometh not, but for to steal, and to kill, and to destroy," whereas the Lord would "come that they might have life, and that they might have it more abundantly" (John 10:10).

Jesus finished His parable by saying, "I am the good shepherd: the good shepherd giveth his life for the sheep" (John 10:11).

He continued, "And other sheep I have, which are not of this fold: them also I must bring, and they shall hear my voice; and there shall be one fold, and one shepherd" (John 10:16). This statement would be fulfilled in the ancient Americas when Jesus appeared among the faithful there after His Resurrection. As He said to the seed of Joseph in the Americas: "But, verily, I say unto you that the Father hath commanded me, and I tell it unto you, that ye were separated from among them because of their iniquity; therefore it is because of their iniquity that they know not of you . . . And verily I say unto you, that ye are they of whom I said: Other sheep I have which are not of this fold; them also I must bring, and they shall hear my voice; and there shall be one fold, and one shepherd" (3 Nephi 15:19, 21). Jesus thus performed His role as Shepherd of the souls of men throughout the world.

Symbolized by the stranger that came to steal the sheep, the Pharisees had long sought to improve their own situation and position among men, sometimes even at the cost of a few sheep or souls. At best the Pharisees could be considered hirelings. But in truth these men sought the Shepherd's very life out of their enmity toward Him. Their pride led them to seek the Messiah's downfall. They were in fact wolves lusting after the blood of the Lamb.

After His testimony at the temple, the rulers and Pharisees continued to seek something against Jesus with which to convince the people of His guilt. But instead of finding what they sought for, they continued to discover evidences of Jesus' power and of their own foolishness. This occurred when Jesus healed a blind man in Jerusalem. The Pharisees immediately went to the man at evening time and asked, "How were thine eyes opened?" (John 9:10). When the man told them, the Pharisees remarked, "This man is not of God, because he keepeth not the Sabbath day. . . . What sayest thou of him, that he hath opened thine eyes?" (John 9:16–17). Getting nothing from the man but a firm witness of the truth, the Pharisees turned to the man's parents and asked them how Jesus had done it. His parents only said, "He is of age; ask him" (John 9:23).

Once again frustrated in their attempt to discredit Jesus and once again disregarding the truth, the Pharisees told the healed blind man, "Give God the praise: we know that this man is a sinner" (John 9:24). It appears that the Pharisees had one goal in mind: to prove that Jesus was not sinless. Doing this would disprove His Messiahship. However, in this case, being unable to find fault, they had to speak about the good Jesus had done on the Sabbath and declare that a sin. It seemed the only sin they could find in Jesus was that he healed the sick, lifted the afflicted, caused the blind to see and the lame to walk, and set the prisoners free—all fulfillments of Messianic prophecies. In the words of the blind man who could now see: "Whether he be a sinner or no, I know not: one thing I know, that, whereas I was blind, now I see" (John 9:25).

"Then said they to him again, What did he to thee? how opened he thine eyes? He answered them, I have told you already, and ye did not hear: wherefore would ye hear it again? will ye also be his disciples? Then they reviled him, and said, Thou art his disciple; but we are Moses' disciples. We know that God spake unto Moses: as for this fellow, we know not from whence he is" (John 9:26–29).

Rejecting the Good Shepherd, these devouring wolves simply could not see the living Messiah when He stood before them. The Pharisees could not understand the voice of God when He called to them. As the Savior had explained, "But ye [the Pharisees] believe not, because ye are not my sheep" (John 10:26). Thus the Pharisees were both blind and deaf, and the formerly blind man wondered at the irony. "The man answered and said unto them, Why herein is a marvellous thing, that ye know not from whence he is, and yet he hath opened mine eyes. Now we know that God heareth not sinners: but if any man be a worshipper of God, and doeth his will, him he heareth. Since the world began was it not heard that any man opened the eyes of one that was born blind. If this man were not of God, he could do nothing" (John 9:30–33).

The Pharisees became instantly offended. They had no way to answer the blind man, so they replied only in accusation. "Thou wast altogether born in sins, and dost thou teach us?" (John 9:34). In reality, the teachers of the law were being taught by a "sinner." The knowledgeable Pharisees were hearing truth from a man who had no learning. All of this came together in such a humorous paradox that only heaven could have produced it. The Pharisees were infuriated.

Jesus would later clarify the principle that He taught to these blind leaders of the people: "If ye were blind, ye should have no sin: but now ye say, We see; therefore your sin remaineth" (John 9:41). Being left once again with guilty consciences, the Pharisees cast the man out of their presence so they could have some peace of mind. Jesus found the man and asked him, "Dost thou believe on the Son of God? He answered and said, Who is he, Lord, that I might believe on him? And Jesus said unto him, Thou hast both seen him, and it is he that talketh with thee. And he said, Lord, I believe. And he worshipped him" (John 9:35–38).

Jesus never let the opportunity pass to teach those who needed instruction. He gave counsel when it was required. He provided the example and showed the way. At times such teaching would come through a call to repentance or a correction in course. In all of this He led His sheep out of love. He worked only to bring His children to the place of true happiness with His Father in Heaven. Thus the Good Shepherd was the one needful Word from heaven. Other teachers from God can only lead as they are inspired by that one true Source.

Jesus' next parable illustrated this very point.

> And he spake this parable unto certain which trusted in themselves that they were righteous, and despised others: "Two men went up into the temple to pray; the one a Pharisee, and the other a publican. The Pharisee stood and prayed thus with himself, God, I thank thee, that I am not as other men are, extortioners, unjust, adulterers, or even as this publican. I fast twice in the week, I give tithes of all that I possess. And the publican, standing afar off, would not lift up so much as his eyes unto heaven, but smote upon his breast, saying, God be merciful to me a sinner. I tell you, this man went down to his house justified rather than

the other: for every one that exalteth himself shall be abased; and he that humbleth himself shall be exalted. (Luke 18:9–14)

Those who thought only of their own position among men while they rejected the Savior of the world could have learned something from this parable, which came from the true Teacher. Instead the Pharisees made it their profession to find fault with the sinless Son of God. Even so the Pharisees came again to test the Savior and prove Him false. "The Pharisees also came unto him, tempting him, and saying unto him, Is it lawful for a man to put away his wife for every cause?" (Matthew 19:3).

Their question was again expertly crafted to destroy the Savior. If Jesus spoke in the negative, they could argue that the Master was going against Moses. Moses truly did allow a writing of divorcement to put an end to marriage, but for "every cause?" Here the Pharisees were manipulating Jesus' answer in order to condemn Him with whatever He said. If Jesus answered in the affirmative then they would have a multitude of causes to put forth as exceptions in order to call Jesus' word into question.

As demonstrated time and time again, Jesus could not be trapped. Instead of simply giving the answer, He quoted the scriptures and let them grapple with the doctrine. Jesus took their malicious questioning as an opportunity to teach them the truth. "And he answered and said unto them, Have ye not read, that he which made them at the beginning made them male and female, And said, For this cause shall a man leave father and mother, and shall cleave to his wife: and they twain shall be one flesh? Wherefore they are no more twain, but one flesh" (Matthew 19:4–6). The Pharisees could not speak against the word of God. At this point Jesus finished with what no man could deny: "What therefore God hath joined together, let not man put asunder" (Matthew 19:6).

The Pharisees did not want the truth. They, like Lucifer, their father, came for something other than the truth. Those with a lying spirit can never understand the truth when it is presented. This is because the first key to righteousness is humility, which implies being teachable. Jesus placed humility first in the Beatitudes for a reason. "Blessed are the poor in spirit: for theirs is the kingdom of heaven" (Matthew 5:3; or as stated to the Nephites "the poor in spirit who come unto me" 3 Nephi 12:3). Moroni teaches that humility is a prerequisite even to faith, hope, and charity, those characteristic elements that bring one to the Lord (see Ether 12:28). "And again, behold I say unto you that he cannot have faith and hope, save he shall be meek, and lowly of heart" (Moroni 7:43).

For this reason the Son of God taught His disciples to become as children and warned them of the leaven of the Pharisees. "Verily I say unto you, Whosoever shall not receive the kingdom of God as a little child, he shall not enter therein" (Mark 10:15). Unfortunately, the Pharisees were not just prideful; they were also dishonest. They would do whatever it took to destroy the Christ, thus proving their own iniquity and priestcraft.

It was when Jesus was teaching these principles in the region of Perea, just beyond Jerusalem, that suddenly "one came and said unto him, Good Master, what good thing shall I do, that I may have eternal life?" (Matthew 19:16). This question came from one who considered himself to be good, as he would soon indicate when answering which commandments he had kept. And yet to this rich and "good" young ruler, the Master would ask, "Why callest thou me good? there is none good but one, that is, God" (Matthew 19:17).

But what good thing should one do to inherit eternal life? Should the man serve incessantly among God's children? Should he build a city or a temple? Should he give his life? Jesus answered, "if thou wilt enter into life, keep the commandments" (Matthew 19:17). And so it was that the one thing the man needed to do in order to be called good were the very things he was already doing. The rich young ruler replied, "All these things have I kept from my youth up: what lack I yet?" (Matthew 19:20).

Jesus answered: "Yet lackest thou one thing: sell all that thou hast, and distribute unto the poor, and thou shalt have treasure in heaven: and come, follow me" (Luke 18:22). The moment of truth arrived for this rich young ruler. What would he do? Would he choose to give up the things of this world and obtain the things of a better? Or would he keep what he presently had on earth but never attain what is prepared above? Along with keeping the commandments, the Savior asks for devotion to Him over the things of the world. He even calls for personal sacrifices of worldly things to obtain heavenly things.

Jesus had long taught: "For what is a man profited, if he shall gain the whole world, and lose his own soul? or what shall a man give in exchange for his soul?" (Matthew 16:26). In this case, with eternal life hanging in the balance, the Savior told the young man exactly what he could do to obtain every blessing of eternity. But what would the man do when the requirement to obtain the riches of eternity was to sacrifice the riches that he presently held? "But when the young man heard that saying, he went away sorrowful: for he had great possessions" (Matthew 19:22).

The rich man left sorrowful, but not nearly as sorry as those with understanding who watched the young man trade the riches of eternity for his temporal possessions. "Then said Jesus unto his disciples, Verily I say unto you, That a rich man shall hardly enter into the kingdom of heaven. And again I say unto you, It is easier for a camel to go through the eye of a needle, than for a rich man to enter into the kingdom of God" (Matthew 19:23–24).

Peter and the other disciples reacted at that saying, knowing that it must then be an almost impossible task for anyone to make it. They "were exceedingly amazed, saying, Who then can be saved? But Jesus beheld their thoughts, and said unto them, With men this is impossible; but if they will forsake all things for my sake, with God whatsoever things I speak are possible" (JST Matthew 19:25–26).

The true disciples of that Shepherd who was sent from above would obtain all that the Father had in store for them by following in their Master's footsteps. They would willingly do as He did. They would be those "who had offered sacrifice in the similitude of the great sacrifice of the Son of God, and had suffered tribulation in their Redeemer's name" (D&C 138:13). How could a man expect to obtain "all that [the] Father hath" (D&C 84:38) if he had not responded when asked to give all that he had to the Father? (see Luke 18:22).

For those who trust in riches, it will be more difficult to reach heaven than for a camel to go through the eye of a needle. But for those who trust in God, it will indeed be possible. As the Savior explained, "With men this is impossible; but with God all things are possible" (Matthew 19:26).

While the rich young ruler could not sacrifice his earthly treasures, the Lord's chosen disciples came offering a sacrifice in similitude of the offering of the Only Begotten. "Then answered Peter and said unto him, Behold, we have forsaken all, and followed thee; what shall we have therefore?" (Matthew 19:27). For these Twelve who had come when they were called, great things were in store—for they had given all things. These chosen representatives of Jesus would be able to take upon themselves Jesus' name with full purpose of heart. They would bear His name to all the earth. They would also be granted the special assignment to be judges of the twelve tribes of Israel. "That ye which have followed me, in the regeneration when the Son of man shall sit in the throne of his glory, ye also shall sit upon twelve thrones, judging the twelve tribes of Israel" (Matthew 19:28). This was an exclusive blessing given to those who truly devoted their lives to serving the Master.

After teaching in Jerusalem and the surrounding areas, Jesus left the multitudes until the next winter when He attended the feast called "Dedication." Arriving back in Jerusalem, He found those who had truly learned from His teachings and become committed in their testimonies. He also discovered others who had not taken His great teachings to heart or who were more devoted to the world. This was manifest when Jesus walked in Solomon's porch at the temple. Certain Jews surrounded Him there and asked, "How long dost thou make us to doubt? If thou be the Christ, tell us plainly" (John 10:24).

Even though Jesus had already told them, they would not believe. He explained to these men that they could not respond to His call "because ye are not of my sheep, as I said unto you. My sheep hear my voice, and I know them, and they follow me" (John 10:26–27).

As it turned out, these men only wanted to hear Jesus plainly declare His Messiahship that they might have something against Him. Future events revealed their true motives, for when Jesus answered plainly, they denounced Him.

> [He said] I and my Father are one. Then the Jews took up stones again to stone him. Jesus answered them, Many good works have I shewed you from my Father; for which of those works do ye stone me? The Jews answered him, saying, For a good work we stone thee not; but for blasphemy; and because that thou, being a man, makest thyself God. Jesus answered them . . . If I do not the works of my Father, believe me not. But if I do, though ye believe not me, believe the works: that ye may know, and believe, that the Father is in me, and I in him" (John 10:30–38).

Again the Jews took up stones to kill Jesus, "but he escaped out of their hand" (John 10:39). "And [Jesus] went away again beyond Jordan into the place where John at first baptized; and there he abode. And many resorted unto him, and said, John did no miracle: but all things that John spake of this man were true. And many believed on him there" (John 10:40–42).

ADDITIONAL COMMENTARY

The Real Problem of the Pharisees: The reason the Pharisees could not see or understand was that they were not sufficiently humble to take counsel and receive the light. Modern revelation tells us, "He that keepeth his commandments receiveth truth and light, until he is glorified in truth and knoweth all things" (D&C 93:28). Light and understanding comes from faith and obedience, with the Holy Spirit confirming the truth of that which is accepted and acted upon. This is why the Lord urges us to "experiment" upon His word and "prove" Him to see if His promises will be fulfilled in our lives (see Alma 32:27 and Malachi 3:10). The Pharisees were always ruled more by tradition than by revelation, preferring to follow the ways of men over the ways of God. For the most part, they rejected the counsel of Jesus; they were not properly baptized nor did they receive the Holy Ghost which would have enabled them to find the correct path to heaven. For the Pharisees and those who similarly will not receive revealed counsel, "that wicked one cometh and taketh away light and truth, through disobedience, from the children of men, and because of the tradition of their fathers" (D&C 93:39).

The Example of Jesus Christ to Show the Way: Jesus followed His Father perfectly. By so doing He also demonstrated the way for man to act. The prophet Nephi explained this by asking the question: "Know ye not that he was holy? But notwithstanding he being holy, he showeth unto the children of men that, according to the flesh he humbleth himself before the Father, and witnesseth unto the Father that he would be obedient unto him in keeping his commandments" (2 Nephi 31:7). Thus He who received light and continued in God received more light until the perfect day (see D&C 50:24). Jesus never failed to follow counsel and thereby He received perfect understanding.

Men and Women of Light: "[Christ is] the true light that is in you" (D&C 88:50). "And if your eye be single to my glory, your whole bodies shall be filled with light, and there shall be no darkness in you; and that body which is filled with light comprehendeth all things" (D&C 88:67).

20

❧ TEACHER ❧

THE RAISING OF LAZARUS

Teacher: Nicodemus said it well when he declared: "Rabbi, we know that thou art a teacher come from God" (John 3:2). Others referred to the Savior as "Master." Even Judas Iscariot on the night he came to betray the Son of Man "came to Jesus, and said, Hail, master" (Matthew 26:49). Whether in life or in death, the Son of God had crucial lessons to share with His Father's children. As the Testator of the right way, Jesus was the Truth as well as the Way and the Life. Even those who would reject Him would come to know through experience that His ways were the only path to happiness. Jesus' words and actions truly taught the things of eternity and the power of God. He showed the way to God in everything He did, from His baptism to the Resurrection. He was, in every sense of the word, a teacher come from God. As He declared his purpose to Pilate: "To this end was I born, and for this cause came I into the world, that I should bear witness unto the truth" (John 18:37).

Jesus was preaching in Perea when a message arrived: Lazarus, the brother of Mary and Martha and a man Jesus loved, was very sick. Jesus remarked that the sickness was not unto death but for the glory of God "that the Son of God might be glorified thereby" (John 11:4). Though He knew of Lazarus's illness, Jesus remained in Perea for two days. "Then after that saith he to his disciples, Let us go into Judaea again. His disciples say unto him, Master, the Jews of late sought to stone thee; and goest thou thither again?" (John 11:7–8). "And they were in the way going up to Jerusalem; and Jesus went before them: and they were amazed; and as they followed, they were afraid. And he took again the twelve, and began to tell them what things should happen unto him" (Mark 10:32).

Jesus had plainly declared His doctrine in Jerusalem, most recently at the temple. As a result the Jews had tried to take Him from the temple and stone Him. For safety, Jesus had gone into the land of Judea, so when He declared His intention to return to danger, His disciples rightly feared the results. Instead of speaking comfort to them, Jesus outlined what would happen in the coming week, "Saying, Behold, we go up to Jerusalem; and the Son of man shall be delivered unto the chief priests, and unto the scribes; and they shall condemn him to death, and shall deliver him to the Gentiles: And they shall mock him, and shall scourge him, and shall spit upon him, and shall kill him: and the third day he shall rise again" (Mark 10:33–34).

While they were traveling into Jericho near Jerusalem, an argument arose between the apostles. It occurred when the mother of James and John approached the Master and asked for a special privilege: that her two sons might sit one on His right hand and the other on His left in His kingdom. Jesus gently rebuked the apostles. He told them that while they would indeed drink of the cup that He should drink of and be baptized with the baptism He would be baptized with, a privilege like a seat beside Him in the kingdom was not His to give. Rather, those positions were to be given only to those whom His Father had prepared.

At that point the other ten disciples were angry with James and John. "But Jesus called them to him, and saith unto them, Ye know that they which are accounted to rule over the Gentiles exercise lordship over them; and their great ones exercise authority upon them. But so shall it not be among you: but whosoever will be great among you, shall be your minister: and whosoever of you will be the chiefest, shall be servant of all. For even the Son of man came not to be ministered unto, but to minister, and to give his life a ransom for many" (Mark 10: 42–45).

They traveled onward, pondering the Lord's words. "And they came to Jericho: and as he went out of Jericho with his disciples and a great number of people, blind Bartimaeus, the son of Timaeus, sat by the highway side begging. And when he heard that it was Jesus of Nazareth, he began to cry out, and say, "Jesus, thou Son of David, have mercy on me" (Mark 10:46–47).

Some of those present told the man to be still, but the more they tried to prevent him, the more he called out. Jesus stopped and asked the men to bring Bartimaeus to Him. When Bartimaeus arrived Jesus asked, "What wilt thou that I should do unto thee? The blind man said unto him, Lord, that I might receive my sight. And Jesus said unto him, Go thy way; thy faith hath made thee whole. And immediately he received his sight, and followed Jesus in the way" (Mark 10:51–52).

As Jesus passed through Jericho with the multitudes thronging about, a certain publican tried to see the Master but could not because he was too short. And so the man ran ahead of the crowd and climbed into a sycamore tree to see him when he passed by that way. When Jesus came to the place where Zacchaeus awaited, Jesus said, "Zacchaeus, make haste, and come down; for to day I must abide at thy house" (Luke 19:5). Zacchaeus obeyed and received the Master joyfully. Those that saw this murmured because Jesus had gone to be a guest of a sinner. Perhaps Jesus' disciples wondered why their pace was so leisurely with Lazarus still so sick. Regardless of how the multitudes or His own apostles responded, Jesus knew the importance of each soul, and in this case He was determined to visit with Zacchaeus.

During dinner Zacchaeus spoke with the Lord, saying, "Behold, Lord, the half of my goods I give to the poor; and if I have taken any thing from any man by false accusation, I restore him fourfold. And Jesus said unto him, This day is salvation come to this house. . . . For the Son of man is come to seek and to save that which was lost" (Luke 19:8–10).

Zacchaeus was thus blessed at the coming of the Lord. He believed, and according to his faith, he was blessed. He had climbed into a tree seeking knowledge and had found the very thing which his soul longed for, a thing he might have missed had he let the opportunity pass unheeded.

As the disciples continued on their journey, Jesus continued to teach them. He, "spake a parable, because he was nigh to Jerusalem, and because they thought that the kingdom of God should immediately appear" (Luke 19:11). He told of the man who received one pound and turned it into ten pounds through wise trading, another that gained five, and another that hid the one pound in a napkin so that he would not lose it. To the first came the words: "Well, thou good servant: because thou hast been faithful in a very little, have thou authority over ten cities" (Luke 19:17, 19). The second man received authority over five cities. But to the man who feared to share his pound, lest someone might criticize how he used it, the master rebuked him and gave his pound to the one who had ten pounds. So it will be for a man who hides his talent carefully because he fears what other men might think, even though these men "will not have [the Master] to reign over them" and are "enemies" to the Lord (see Luke 19:14, 27).

Jesus taught these humble apostles that they still had a great work to perform. If they chose to fear men and hide their talents in the face of adversity, they would fail in their callings. Jesus had given them authority, but they would be required to use it whether the people wanted to hear from the servants of the Lord or not.

Having journeyed fearlessly with His disciples, the Master led the way as they ascended up into Jerusalem. "And it came to pass, when he was come nigh to Bethphage and Bethany" (Luke 19:28–29), He went to take care of that business for which He had purposefully delayed His arrival.

The following story of Lazarus is crucial as it testifies of the power of the Master. He indeed had complete dominion over Satan and his works of darkness, over life and death, over the elements and sickness, and over all things! This story testifies that mankind may capably place confidence in the Son of the Father. Jesus is the Christ. He is perfect. He holds all power. He could bring a man back to life because he held authority over death. He could declare the testimony of His Father and His own divinity without speaking blasphemy. The Master taught all things perfectly in word and in deed. All men should follow Him carefully and devotedly, making any sacrifices necessary to do so.

As the disciples approached their destination, the Savior told them, "Our friend Lazarus sleepeth; but I go, that I may awake him out of sleep. Then said his disciples, Lord, if he sleep, he shall do well. Howbeit Jesus spake of his death: but they thought that he had spoken of taking of rest in sleep. Then said Jesus unto them plainly, Lazarus is dead. And I am glad for your sakes that I was not there, to the intent ye may believe; nevertheless let us go unto him" (John 11:11–15).

When we look at our trials through spiritual eyes, we can often see that they are not necessarily negative. The opposite can actually be true. In this case, even though Lazarus had died, Jesus was "glad" at the report, for He could see how this trial would eventually strengthen His followers' faith.

"Then said Thomas, which is called Didymus, unto his fellow disciples, Let us also go, that we may die with him" (John 11:16). Again, Jesus' apostles feared what might happen in this dangerous region. Of those who worried, it is little wonder that "Doubting Thomas" voiced his fears first.

> Then when Jesus came, he found that [Lazarus] had lain in the grave four days already. Now Bethany was nigh unto Jerusalem, about

fifteen furlongs off: And many of the Jews came to Martha and Mary, to comfort them concerning their brother. Then Martha, as soon as she heard that Jesus was coming, went and met him: but Mary sat still in the house. Then said Martha unto Jesus, Lord, if thou hadst been here, my brother had not died. But I know, that even now, whatsoever thou wilt ask of God, God will give it thee. Jesus saith unto her, Thy brother shall rise again. (John 11:17–23)

Jesus thus declared His purpose. He had come to bring Lazarus from the grave. There was no precedent to explain what Jesus was about to accomplish, and for this reason, Martha could not understand. "Martha saith unto him, I know that he shall rise again in the resurrection at the last day. Jesus said unto her, I am the resurrection, and the life: he that believeth in me, though he were dead, yet shall he live: And whosoever liveth and believeth in me shall never die. Believest thou this? She saith unto him, Yea, Lord: I believe that thou art the Christ, the Son of God, which should come into the world" (John 11:24–27).

The testimony of the Son of God was thus prepared. Martha knew who He was. But she still had no idea how His words would be affirmed in that very hour. While Martha kept her faith in the Son of God, her sister had gone away in bitterness of spirit.

And when she had so said, she went her way, and called Mary her sister secretly, saying, The Master is come, and calleth for thee. As soon as she heard that, she arose quickly, and came unto him. Now Jesus was not yet come into the town, but was in that place where Martha met him. The Jews then which were with her in the house, and comforted her, when they saw Mary, that she rose up hastily and went out, followed her, saying, She goeth unto the grave to weep there. Then when Mary was come where Jesus was, and saw him, she fell down at his feet, saying unto him, Lord, if thou hadst been here, my brother had not died. (John 11:28–32)

This trial of faith for the sisters of Bethany brought them both to grief, and yet each kept her hope in the Lord who had now come. Even with the knowledge he possessed, Jesus did not take their situation lightly. "When Jesus therefore saw her weeping, and the Jews also weeping which came with her, he groaned in the spirit, and was troubled. And said, Where have ye laid him? They said unto him, Lord, come and see. Jesus wept" (John 11:33–35).

Seeing Jesus' emotion, the Jews commented about how much He loved

Lazarus. Some mused, "Could not this man, which opened the eyes of the blind, have caused that even this man should not have died?" (John 11:37). Although those around Him still lacked faith, Jesus went forward to accomplish His design.

> Jesus therefore again groaning in himself cometh to the grave. It was a cave, and a stone lay upon it. Jesus said, Take ye away the stone. Martha, the sister of him that was dead, saith unto him, Lord, by this time he stinketh: for he hath been dead four days. Jesus saith unto her, Said I not unto thee, that, if thou wouldest believe, thou shouldest see the glory of God? Then they took away the stone from the place where the dead was laid. And Jesus lifted up his eyes, and said, Father, I thank thee that thou hast heard me. And I knew that thou hearest me always: but because of the people which stand by I said it, that they may believe that thou hast sent me. And when he thus had spoken, he cried with a loud voice, Lazarus, come forth. And he that was dead came forth, bound hand and foot with graveclothes: and his face was bound about with a napkin. Jesus saith unto them, Loose him, and let him go. (John 11:38–44)

Naturally, the people reacted at the sight of so great a miracle. They who had witnessed His love as He wept and groaned at His friend's grave, now saw His power. "Then many of the Jews which came to Mary, and had seen the things which Jesus did, believed on him. But some of them went their ways to the Pharisees, and told them what things Jesus had done" (John 11:45–46).

Great persecutions followed the raising of Lazarus. The Pharisees gathered in council with the chief priests, saying, "What do we? for this man doeth many miracles. If we let him thus alone, all men will believe on him" (John 11:47–48). They even expressed concern that the Romans would come in response and take away both their "place and nation" (John 11:48). At that statement, the high priest Caiaphas stood and declared: "Ye know nothing at all, Nor consider that it is expedient for us, that one man should die for the people, and that the whole nation perish not" (John 11:49–50). "Then from that day forth they took counsel together for to put him to death" (John 11:53).

Knowing the danger to Him and His followers, after this Jesus "walked no more openly among the Jews; but went thence unto a country near to the wilderness, into a city called Ephraim, and there continued with his disciples" (John 11:54). He taught those who were willing to hear His perfect teachings. In this way, He demonstrated the truth of His earlier teachings; those who are humble will receive, while those who resist the truth will have that which they had taken away.

Additional Commentary

The World Made Accountable for Jesus' Testimony: Elder James E. Talmage notes:

> That the Lord's act of restoring Lazarus to life was of effect in testifying to His Messiahship is explicitly stated. All the circumstances leading up to final culmination in the miracle contributed to its attestation. No question as to the actual death of Lazarus could be raised, for his demise had been witnessed, his body had been prepared and buried in the usual way, and he had lain in the grave four days. At the tomb, when he was called forth, there were many witnesses, some of them prominent Jews, many of whom were unfriendly to Jesus and who would have readily denied the miracle had they been able. God was glorified and the divinity of the Son of Man was vindicated in the result.[1]

Teacher of Gospel Fulness: While men often focus on just a portion of the gospel and declare it to be the way, Jesus insisted on teaching the fulness. Elder Neal A. Maxwell explained the reasons and benefits for teaching in this manner. He said:

> With the enemy combined, it is so vital to keep "in the right way" (Moroni 6:4). Orthodoxy in thought and behavior brings safety and felicity as the storms come, including "every wind of doctrine" (Ephesians 4:14). Happily, amid such winds the Holy Ghost not only helps us recognize plain truth but also plain nonsense!
>
> Orthodoxy ensures balance between the gospel's powerful and correct principles. In the body of gospel doctrine, not only are justice and mercy "fitly joined together [for] effectual working," but so is everything else! (Ephesians 4:16). But the gospel's principles do require synchronization. When pulled apart from each other or isolated, men's interpretations and implementations of these doctrines may be wild. . . .
>
> Thus, the fulness of the gospel of Jesus Christ is greater than any of its parts and larger than any of its programs or principles![2]

The World's Way, the Lord's Way, or My Own Way? Coming unto Christ must be done in the way He has ordained. And yet men still insist on following the Lord in their own way. "They seek not the Lord to establish his righteousness, but every man walketh in his own way, and after the image of his own god, whose image is in the likeness of the world, and whose substance is that of an idol, which waxeth old and shall perish in Babylon, even Babylon the great, which shall fall" (D&C 1:16). Those who journey in their own way may find that the only way that does not end at an impenetrably locked gate is the established path through the door of the Shepherd's flock.

Coming from our Own Sycamore Trees to Accept Jesus into our Lives: Colin B. Douglas shared his own testimony of his figurative journey down from the sycamore tree to receive Christ. He wrote:

> We must be made clean (sanctified), and we must also be declared not guilty of sin (one of the scriptural meanings of justification) in order to return to our Father in glory. The problem is that we have all been guilty. How can we who have been guilty be declared innocent? Only by allowing the innocence of Christ to be put in the place of our guilt; by taking upon us the name of Christ, as we witness in baptism and the sacrament, so that when the Father looks upon us it is, in one sense, as if he looks upon the Son.[3]

Lessons from Zacchaeus: Jesus taught of the blessings available to those who receive Him, whether simple or great, righteous or sinner. In Jericho, many objected to Zacchaeus's status as a "sinner." From them we can learn that many "worthy" people can miss the opportunity to truly let Christ into their lives, being satisfied with their life the way it is or satisfied to observe Jesus and His doings from a distance. Often men seek success through riches, not realizing they are really just lost. Sometimes they think their lives are blessed in all of their conveniences, when they really need Christ to come, and they need to turn their lives to Him. What men justify as okay is often completely wrong.

Letting the Savior into our lives brings about necessary changes as weaknesses are revealed and the Savior's grace makes up for our past inadequacies. The Lord is no respecter of persons. He does not care about physical stature or appearance. He does not worry about nationality or occupation. Any person who fears the Lord and works righteousness is accepted by Him (see 1 Nephi 17:35). When Zacchaeus' heart was converted from the ways of the world to the Lord, though he was still a long way from perfection, he gained salvation.[4]

Notes

1. Talmage, *Jesus the Christ*, 461–62.

2. Neal A. Maxwell, "Behold, the Enemy Is Combined," *Ensign*, May 1993, 76.

3. Colin B. Douglas, "What I've Learned about Grace Since Coming Down from the Sycomore Tree," *Ensign*, Apr. 1989, 13.

4. Ibid.

21

✻ UNCHANGEABLE ✻

THE LAST WEEK

Unchangeable: "For do we not read that God is the same yesterday, today, and forever, and in him there is no variableness neither shadow of changing?" (Mormon 9:9). Those who know God and His ways cannot deny that revelations and gifts have come from Him in every generation of time. They understand why He has communicated the same way in all time periods. They can see why He would reveal His gospel to one nation as well as another. They know He is no respecter of persons, "But in every nation he that feareth him, and worketh righteousness, is accepted with him" (Acts 10:35). "For there is no difference between the Jew and the Greek: for the same Lord over all is rich unto all that call upon him" (Romans 10:12). If He was a God of miracles to Abraham, Isaac, and Jacob, then who could ever imagine Him not remaining so among all of His sons and daughters? In truth, He was the same when He came to the Israelites as He was when He visited the children of Lehi in ancient America and as He still is today.

Everything that the Savior of mankind did from the beginning led up to this final week of His great life. He had fulfilled many purposes in His coming—establishing the gospel among men, teaching His Father's children, setting the example for all to follow, establishing His Church under the authority of His priesthood, bestowing the keys of that priesthood, bearing witness of the truth, and performing many miracles. But the great reason of His coming would be revealed when He went to Jerusalem this last time. His great purpose was to give His life as a ransom for us.

As the time of Passover neared, multitudes went up from their homelands to Jerusalem for the annual sacrifice. Because of Jesus' attendance at the previous feasts and His miraculous doings there, many speculated about the possibility of His coming again. Adding drama to their chatter was the fact that, "the chief priests and the Pharisees had given a commandment, that, if any man knew where he were, he should shew it, that they might take him" (John 11:57).

Six days before Passover, instead of going directly into Jerusalem, Jesus went back to Bethany where He had raised Lazarus from the dead. In that tiny village "they made him a supper; and Martha served: but Lazarus was one of them that sat at the table with him" (John 12:2). Sitting with Lazarus and His chosen Twelve, Jesus received the food Martha had prepared. Mary had also prepared something for Him. "Then took Mary a pound of ointment of spikenard, very costly, and anointed the feet of Jesus, and wiped his feet with her hair: and the house was filled with the odour of the ointment" (John 12:3). Judas Iscariot immediately complained. He pointed out that the wasted oil could have been sold and the money could have been given to the poor. Jesus answered, "Let her alone: against the day of my burying hath she kept this" (John 12:7).

Jesus' presence in Bethany could not be kept a secret for long. Many people came to observe him there, "not for Jesus' sake only, but that they might see Lazarus also, whom he had raised from the dead. But the chief priests consulted that they might put Lazarus also to death; Because that by reason of him many of the Jews went away, and believed on Jesus" (John 12:9–11). Certainly there was an element of danger associated with this special supper on the eve of Jesus' triumphal entry into Jerusalem, but the evening passed peacefully and the disciples' faith grew.

When morning came, with five days to go before the Passover feast, many of the faithful gathered in Jerusalem, anticipating Jesus' arrival into the holy city. They had heard of His presence in Bethany, and many had gone to see Him there. "When they heard that Jesus was coming to Jerusalem" (John 12:12), they prepared for His entrance into the city. They took branches of palm trees and awaited His arrival.

In the morning of His glorious arrival into Jerusalem, Jesus sent two of His disciples, saying, "Go into the village over against you, and straightway ye shall find an ass tied, and a colt with her: loose them, and bring them unto me" (Matthew 21:2). Accordingly, they went to the village and found it as He had said they would. And they also followed his instruction: "if any man say ought unto you, ye shall say, The Lord hath need of them; and straightway he will send them" (Matthew 21:3). They then took the animals "and put on them their clothes, and they set him thereon" (Matthew 21:7).

Throughout history the Lord reached out to His people before they could initiate the process of coming to Him. This triumphal entry into Jerusalem was just such an instance. This time, as always, He came with an offering of eternal life for all who would receive Him. And as always there were many different reactions from the people. There were those who came running and joined with Him in great joy, shouting, "Hosanna, blessed is he that cometh in the name of the Lord. . . . Hosanna in the highest" (Mark 11:9–10). There were some who only observed from a distance, careful to approach too eagerly lest others might see. And there were still others who stood apart, envious, hateful, and bitter because the people were so interested in Him. Whatever their initial reaction, the events of this day would force everyone present to decide if they believed Jesus truly was the Messiah.

As King of Kings and Lord of Lords, Jesus came triumphantly to greet the people over whom He was King. He came in peaceful dominion over the Jews. For the faithful, He entered the city as their invited and long-awaited Messiah, fulfilling the prophecy: "Behold, thy King cometh unto thee, meek, and sitting upon an ass, and a colt the foal of an ass" (Matthew 21:5).

When Jesus rode into Jerusalem on the back of a donkey, His unashamed and faithful followers went with Him to witness Jesus of Nazareth fulfilling that important prophecy of a Messiah who would come, not to dominate on the dark stallion of war, but on a donkey—a symbol of peace. As He rode in, Jesus' disciples spread their coats and robes on the path. They placed branches cut from the surrounding trees over the road before Him. They carpeted the pathway into Jerusalem for its King. The whole procession "cried . . . Hosanna. Blessed is he that cometh in the name of the Lord. . . . Hosanna in the highest" (Mark 11:9–10).

Anyone familiar with the prophecies of the coming Messiah, would have recognized the parallels between Jesus' entry into Jerusalem and Zechariah's prophetic words: "Rejoice greatly, O daughter of Zion; shout, O daughter of Jerusalem: behold, thy King cometh unto thee: he is just, and having salvation; lowly, and riding upon an ass, and upon a colt the foal of an ass" (Zechariah 9:9).

When Jesus of Nazareth suddenly came riding into Jerusalem in this manner, each person present had to decide where he stood in relation to the witnesses that were being offered. Indeed, "all the city was moved, saying, Who is this?" (Matthew 21:10). Those who had long sought to destroy

Him were angry. They thought that if He came at all, He would have to come secretly, for His life was openly threatened. When they instead saw Him coming in such a forthright manner they approached the arriving group and indignantly exclaimed, "Master, rebuke thy disciples" (Luke 19:39). Jesus would never prevent those who followed Him from honoring Him in this way.

The Pharisees were greatly displeased. The Lord's open manifestation of His true identity forced these leaders of the people to consult together as to what they should do. They knew that the entire city was moved to some kind of a response. "The people therefore that was with him when he called Lazarus out of his grave, and raised him from the dead, bare record. For this cause the people also met him, for that they heard that he had done this miracle. The Pharisees therefore said among themselves, Perceive ye how ye prevail nothing? behold, the world is gone after him" (John 12:17–19). After witnessing His entry into Jerusalem, the Pharisees immediately gathered in a secret meeting to plot Jesus' death.

But the work of the Lord could not be prevented by men. Jesus proved to be more powerful than the world that tried to stop Him. On this day, the men of Jerusalem stepped away from their worldly pursuits of their own volition just to see for themselves if indeed Jesus was, as His actions proclaimed Him, the Son of the Father. At that moment a choice was presented to every heart. Who would respond when the Lord swept into their lives unexpectedly and became, for that instant, far more important than anything else they were doing? Would they act upon their feelings? Or, when the moment passed, would they turn back to what they had been doing and forget the incredibly significant thing that had just transpired?

Both of these reactions occurred. Some came and followed Jesus, never to turn back. Others let Jesus pass and went on their own ways, never again to remember the opportunity they had been given. Jesus lamented over these people, "when he was come near, and beheld the city, and wept over it, Saying, If thou hadst known, even thou, at least in this thy day, the things which belong unto thy peace! but now they are hid from thine eyes" (Luke 19:41–42).

Others took offense, knowing it was Jesus, the prophet of Nazareth, who came in the name of the Lord. "And some of the Pharisees from among the multitude said unto him, Master, rebuke thy disciples. And he answered and said unto them, I tell you that, if these should hold their peace, the stones would immediately cry out" (Luke 19:39–40).

The opportunity to respond to the Savior came to the people in Jerusalem, much like it had to Zacchaeus just days earlier. But did they all respond when that stirring in their hearts came? As Jesus looked over the city, he lamented, "thou knewest not the time of thy visitation" (Luke 19:44). However, there were others who did not just let the moment pass unheeded. Certain Greeks, who also worshipped at the feast, came to the disciple Philip and said, "Sir, we would see Jesus" (John 12:21). They, like Zacchaeus the publican, would find that Jesus is no respecter of persons, and that salvation comes when men receive Him.

Arriving in the city where His great sacrifice would be performed, Jesus exclaimed, "The hour is come, that the Son of man should be glorified" (John 12:23). For the last time, Jesus would personally bear witness of His authority under His Father's call. He had been sent by the Father, and in Jerusalem He would reveal that fact plainly in word and in deed. He knew He had been sent to give His perfect life that others might live.

To those who came to listen, including the Greeks who had responded to the events of the day, Jesus declared, "Except a corn of wheat fall into the ground and die, it abideth alone: but if it die, it bringeth forth much fruit" (John 12:24). As He was teaching this important principle regarding His purpose in the coming days, Jesus suddenly began to pray, "Now is my soul troubled; and what shall I say? Father, save me from this hour: but for this cause came I unto this hour. Father, glorify thy name. Then came there a voice from heaven, saying, I have both glorified it, and will glorify it again. The people therefore, that stood by, and heard it, said that it thundered: others said, An angel spake to him. Jesus answered and said, This voice came not because of me, but for your sakes" (John 12:27–30).

The purpose for which Jesus had come now approached, an hour that would demand the attention of all men. Even as He pondered the enormity of this time, He explained, "Now is the judgment of this world: now shall the prince of this world be cast out. And I, if I be lifted up from the earth, will draw all men unto me" (John 12:31–32).

Jesus knew He had come to die that men might live. He explained to the people what He had come to do and how no one could take this commission from Him. He had come to provide deliverance from the devil who tried to blind and deceive men. To those who had followed Him into Jerusalem for whatever reason, He declared: "He that believeth on me, believeth not on me, but on him that sent me. And he that seeth me seeth him that sent me. . . . For I have not spoken of myself; but the Father which sent me, he gave me a commandment, what I should say, and what I should speak" (John 12:44–45, 49).

Following Jesus' renewed declaration of His divinity, He went up to the temple and cleansed His Father's house for the second time. His actions again testified of His authority to act in His Father's name. Following His cleansing of the temple, the blind and the lame of the city came to Him to be healed. "And when the chief priests and scribes saw the wonderful things that he did, and the children crying in the temple, and saying, Hosanna to the Son of David; they were sore displeased, And said unto him, Hearest thou what these say? And Jesus saith unto them, Yea; have ye never read, Out of the mouth of babes and sucklings thou hast perfected praise? And he left them, and went out of the city into Bethany; and he lodged there" (Matthew 21:15–17).

On the morning of the following day, the fourth day before Passover, Jesus left his lodging in Bethany and went near a fig tree for food. "And when he saw a fig tree in the way, he came to it, and found nothing thereon, but leaves only, and said unto it, Let no fruit grow on thee henceforward for ever. And presently the fig tree withered away" (Matthew 21:19). Jesus often taught in symbols. This fruitless tree in Jerusalem was a prototype of what would soon occur in this spiritually desolate land that had rejected its Savior when they might have shared in the fruits of His salvation. The Creator and giver of life had come to them as the Living Water. But when "He came unto his own. . . . His own received him not" (John 1:11). "I am come," Jesus would teach, "a light into the world, that whosoever believeth on me should not abide in darkness. And if any man hear my words, and believe not, I judge him not: for I came not to judge the world, but to save the world. He that rejecteth me, and receiveth not my words, hath one that judgeth him: the word that I have spoken, the same shall judge him in the last day" (John 12:46–48).

On this fourth day, He returned to Jerusalem and taught in His temple. While He was there many of the rulers who now sought His life came seeking a word from Jesus that could justify their actions in the eyes of the people. They asked Him by what authority He acted. Jesus turned the question back to them:

> I also will ask you one thing, which if ye tell me, I in like wise will tell you by what authority I do these things. The baptism of John, whence was it? from heaven, or of men? And they reasoned with themselves, saying, If we shall say, From heaven; he will say unto us, Why did

ye not then believe him? But if we shall say, Of men, we fear the people; for all hold John as a prophet. And they answered Jesus, and said, We cannot tell. And he said unto them, Neither tell I you by what authority I do these things. (Matthew 21: 24–27)

To those who came to trap Him, Jesus then taught a parable which served as a firm rebuke. He spoke of two sons whose father had asked them to work in the vineyard. The first refused to go but afterward repented and went. The second accepted the call but never went. Of the two, Jesus asked, which did the will of the father? The Pharisees who heard the parable answered, "The first." Jesus then spoke plainly: "Verily I say unto you, That the publicans and the harlots go into the kingdom of God before you. For John came unto you in righteousness, and ye believed him not: but the publicans and the harlots believed him: and ye, when ye had seen it, repented not afterward, that ye might believe him" (Matthew 21:31–32).

Then came an even more harsh rebuke. "Hear another parable," Jesus said to those who were gathered at the temple. He went on to tell of a certain householder who had planted a vineyard, hedged it round about, digged a winepress in it, built a tower, and then let it out to husbandmen while he went into a far country. When the time of the harvest arrived, the householder sent servants to the husbandmen to collect the portion of fruit that belonged to him as owner. But when the servants arrived, the husbandmen killed and kept the fruit for themselves. The householder then sent other servants who were also beaten and killed. Finally he sent his son, saying, "They will reverence my son" (Matthew 21:37). But when the husbandmen saw the son they said: "This is the heir; come, let us kill him, and let us seize on his inheritance" (Matthew 21:38). And this they did.

Jesus then asked the Pharisees, "When the lord therefore of the vineyard cometh, what will he do unto those husbandmen? They say unto him, He will miserably destroy those wicked men, and will let out his vineyard unto other husbandmen, which shall render him the fruits in their season" (Matthew 21:40–41). In Jesus' typical style he allowed the guilty to condemn themselves with their own words. Then He told them that indeed they were the ones who had rejected the Son and that because of this, the kingdom of God would be taken from them and given to others. These men, like the fig tree in Jerusalem which had withered at the Master's word, were to be cast out where they would wither without the Living Water that would have sustained them.

Jesus then said, "The stone which the builders rejected, the same is become the head of the corner" (Matthew 21: 42). This statement referred to one of Isaiah's great Messianic prophecies: "And he shall be for a sanctuary; but for a stone of stumbling and for a rock of offence to both the houses of Israel, for a gin and for a snare to the inhabitants of Jerusalem. And many among them shall stumble, and fall, and be broken, and be snared, and be taken" (Isaiah 8:14–15). Indeed the Messiah had come to the Jews. He came as their Rock of safety. But for some He became a rock of offence upon which they stumbled.

Realizing what Jesus meant, the Pharisees sought to lay hands on him, but fearing the multitudes they held back for the moment. Later, Jesus' disciples came to Him separately and He taught them the meaning of His words.

> Verily, I say unto you, I am the stone, and those wicked ones reject me. I am the head of the corner. These Jews shall fall upon me, and shall be broken. And the kingdom of God shall be taken from them, and shall be given to a nation bringing forth the fruits thereof; (meaning the Gentiles.) Wherefore, on whomsoever this stone shall fall, it shall grind him to powder. And when the Lord therefore of the vineyard cometh, he will destroy those miserable, wicked men, and will let again his vineyard unto other husbandmen, even in the last days, who shall render him the fruits in their seasons. (JST Matthew 21:51–55)

The Pharisees were offended at the parables which denounced their authority and established Jesus as the Son of God. "Then went the Pharisees, and took counsel how they might entangle him in his talk" (Matthew 22:15). They devised a plan. They would send their disciples along with some Herodians to Jesus. These people would profess that they believed Him, flatter Him, and then tempt Him to speak in such a way as to condemn Himself before the people. Even so they came to Jesus and said, "Master, we know that thou art true, and teachest the way of God in truth, neither carest thou for any man: for thou regardest not the person of men. Tell us therefore, What thinkest thou? Is it lawful to give tribute unto Caesar, or not?" (Matthew 22:17).

Jesus perceived their plan. He knew that if He were to denounce Caesar, the Pharisees would have something against Him with which to justify their murderous desires. He responded, "Why tempt ye me, ye hypocrites? Shew me the tribute money. And they brought unto him a penny. And he saith unto them, Whose is this image and superscription? They say unto him, Caesar's. Then saith he unto them, Render therefore unto Caesar the things which are Caesar's; and unto God the things that are God's. When they had heard these words, they marvelled, and left him, and went their way" (Matthew 22: 18–22).

In this case, the Pharisees tempted Jesus with pride, a sin that they themselves obviously struggled with. Because of their great skill in the law and their desire to teach among men, Satan often tempted them to use their gospel knowledge contentiously, pridefully, for their own benefit, or for other wrongful purposes, like priestcraft or seeking positions of renown among men. In these cases their strength—an extraordinary knowledge of the scriptures—could be twisted against the Lord and His purposes.

The Sadducees came next, asking Jesus about the doctrine of marriage. They were simply told, as they had been before, "Ye do err, not knowing the scriptures, nor the power of God" (Matthew 22:29). Lacking a knowledge of these two things, they could not understand the Resurrection nor the Father's ability to fulfill His word: "What therefore God hath joined together, let not man put asunder" (Matthew 19:6).

Finding the Sadducees silenced by the Savior's word, the Pharisees stepped forward once again and asked concerning the great commandment in the law. Jesus answered: "Thou shalt love the Lord thy God with all thy heart, and with all thy soul, and with all thy mind. This is the first and great commandment. And the second is like unto it, Thou shalt love thy neighbour as thyself. On these two commandments hang all the law and the prophets" (Matthew 22:37–40).

Finding his tempters silenced, Jesus asked them, "What think ye of Christ? whose son is he? They say unto him, The Son of David. He saith unto them, How then doth David in spirit call him Lord . . . If David call him Lord, how is he his son?" (Matthew 22: 42–45). Jesus thus referred to the fact that David could not call his son Lord unless Christ somehow also preceded him as the premortal Firstborn. Even David, the revered king, would give deference to the Messiah. While others would draw attention only to Christ's earthly lineage, the king Himself would call Him Lord. And now Jehovah stood in the flesh before these who disrespected the Son of David, but none of them could argue with his lineage. For this reason "no man was able to answer him a word, neither durst any man from that day forth ask him any more questions" (Matthew 22:46).

All of these things happened in Jerusalem, where Jesus had come to proclaim that He was the promised Messiah who would save His people.

The reactions that accompanied Jesus' coming revealed the true nature of those He came to help. Jesus' final word at the temple spoke against such wicked men as the Pharisees and other hypocrites. He concluded His testimony by speaking against certain sins that prevailed in Jerusalem: hypocrisy; doing things for the glory of men and to exalt oneself (like worshipping with long prayers and publicly offered tithes) while omitting the more important private matters of judgment, mercy, and faith. Having thus spoken, Jesus then concluded His words at the temple by saying, "Ye shall not see me henceforth, till ye shall say, Blessed is he that cometh in the name of the Lord" (Matthew 23:39).

After He had spoken to the people, Jesus lamented, "O Jerusalem, Jerusalem, thou that killest the prophets, and stonest them which are sent unto thee, how often would I have gathered thy children together, even as a hen gathereth her chickens under her wings, and ye would not! Behold, your house is left unto you desolate" (Matthew 23:37–38).

From the temple Jesus and His disciples went to the Mount of Olives, where Jesus proceeded to tell them what would happen to the great city of Jerusalem. His disciples began to wonder and asked, "Tell us, when shall these things be? and what shall be the sign of thy coming, and of the end of the world?" (Matthew 24:3). Jesus answered: "Take heed that no man deceive you" (Matthew 24:4). Following the warning, the Savior went on to give a list of those things that Satan would use to deceive and blind men before the Savior made His appearance. Jesus gave a great prophecy of His Second Coming and many of the signs that would precede it. He gave them the parable of the ten virgins, which taught them the importance of preparing for His coming. He also gave the parable of the talents, which emphasized the manner in which they should use their God-given abilities to work for the Kingdom, and not just for themselves. All of these things would prepare them for the wonderful time of His Second Coming.

Jesus ended His teachings on the Mount of Olives with a final parable of the sheep and the goats. In the day of Jesus' coming, all nations would be gathered unto Him. There He would separate the sheep from the goats. The sheep would be those who fed the hungry, gave drink to the thirsty, took in the stranger, clothed the naked, and visited the imprisoned. Whereas the goats would be those who served themselves, the world, and Lucifer. "Inasmuch as ye have done it unto one of the least of these my brethren," the Master concluded, "ye have done it unto me" (Matthew 25:40).

When Jesus finished His teachings upon the Mount of Olives, the disciples departed with Him. As they were leaving, Jesus turned to them and said, "Ye know that after two days is the feast of the passover, and the Son of man is betrayed to be crucified" (Matthew 26:2). Mark's narrative describes how at the very time of this prophecy, the chief priests and the scribes were gathered in discussion concerning how they might overtake Jesus and put him to death. "But they said, Not on the feast day, lest there be an uproar of the people" (Mark 14:2).

Caiaphas had already reacted to the fact that many people thought Jesus was the Son of God. He and his council had recently taken great offense to the raising of Lazarus as an irrefutable proof that they just simply could not answer. And now, after observing Jesus' blatant arrival in the city, Caiaphas set his murderous intention into place. "Then assembled together the chief priests, and the scribes, and the elders of the people, unto the palace of the high priest, who was called Caiaphas. And consulted that they might take Jesus by subtilty, and kill him" (Matthew 26:3–4).

In the meantime, Jesus went back to Bethany where He dined with Simon the Pharisee, who was also a leper. During the feast a woman approached Jesus, weeping, and began to wash his feet with her tears and then dry them with her hair. While so doing she kissed His feet and anointed them with ointment. She had an alabaster box, a valuable treasure in its own right, which was filled with an ointment called spikenard. She broke this box and poured the ointment on Jesus' head. This brought criticism on several accounts. The Master's disciples thought it was a great waste, declaring it could have been sold for three hundred pence and the money given to the poor. The Pharisees present complained that Jesus allowed a sinner to anoint Him, and that if He had come as a true prophet He would have known and prevented the action.

To His disciples Jesus answered: "Let her alone; why trouble ye her? she hath wrought a good work on me. . . . She is come aforehand to anoint my body to the burying" (Mark 14:6, 8). And to the Pharisees He answered with a parable: "Simon, I have somewhat to say unto thee. And he saith, Master, say on. There was a certain creditor which had two debtors: the one owed five hundred pence, and the other fifty. And when they had nothing to pay, he frankly forgave them both. Tell me therefore, which of them will love him most?" (Luke 7:40–42). Simon the Pharisee answered that the one he forgave the most would love him the most. Jesus then went on to tell those around Him that the woman who anointed Him wasn't the only sinner in the room that owed much to the creditor. But since she came to

Him to repent, her love was thus greater than Simon's who had done no such thing. "And he said to the woman, Thy faith hath saved thee; go in peace" (Luke 7:50).

ADDITIONAL COMMENTARY

The Opportunity When Presented: President Spencer W. Kimball pondered the scenario of Jesus' triumphal arrival and the choice each soul was presented with on that day. He quoted Percy Adams Hutchinson who gave this verse in his "Wordless Christ" (Vicisti Galilee, stanza 1):

> Ay, down the years, behold he rides,
> The lowly Christ, upon an ass;
> But conquering? Ten shall heed the call,
> A thousand idly watch him pass.

"And I wondered," commented President Kimball, "how many tens of thousands did hear his voice, felt an inner twinge of heart, felt impelled to follow, but lingered and procrastinated . . . How many felt the stir that comes in human breasts when truth, pressed in upon them but pressured by minor exigencies, moves far away from their eternal destiny? And then I think: Procrastination—thou wretched thief of time and opportunity!"[1]

Evidence of the Rightful King: Many scholars have explained the significance of the Lord's arrival. Jackson and Millet noted: "'To ride upon white asses or ass-colts was the privilege of persons of high rank, princes, judges, and prophets.' Christ's doing so attested that he entered the Holy City as its rightful king."[2] And Edersheim stated: "The waving of the palm-branches was the welcome of visitors or kings, and not distinctive of the Feast of Tabernacles."[3]

Witnessing Their Understanding of Jesus' Fulfillment of the Prophecies: Elder Bruce R. McConkie describes the influential testimony given by the believers on this day who cried "Hosanna!" He says,

> Hosanna means literally, save now, or save we pray, or save we beseech thee, and is taken from the Messianic prophecy which foretold that such would be the entreaty of Israel to their Messiah in the day of his coming. For more than a thousand years the Jewish people had studied and considered the inspired utterance that the promised Lord

of Israel would be 'the stone which the builders refused,' that he would 'become the head stone of the corner,' and that the cries of the people of him would include the expressions, 'Save now, I beseech thee, O lord: O lord, I beseech thee, send now prosperity. Blessed be he that cometh in the name of the Lord' (Psalms 118: 22–26). What more could the people have said to testify of their belief that Jesus was the Christ than to go back to this famous Messianic utterance and announce that it was fulfilled in him![4]

Those Who Fell that Should Have Followed: Jesus taught how the adversary tempts men in the area of their own strength. This was true for the Pharisees and Sadducees, and for the Lord Himself. In a discourse entitled "Our Strengths Can Become our Downfall," Elder Dallin H. Oaks warns of this kind of temptation: "But our weaknesses are not the only areas where we are vulnerable. Satan can also attack us where we think we are strong—in the very areas where we are proud of our strengths. He will approach us through the greatest talents and spiritual gifts we possess. If we are not wary, Satan can cause our spiritual downfall by corrupting us through our strengths as well as by exploiting our weaknesses."[5]

Notes

1. Spencer W. Kimball, in Conference Report, Apr. 1966, 74–75, as quoted with commentary by Pinegar, Bassett, and Earl in *Latter-Day Commentary*, 284.
2. *Studies in Scripture, Volume 5: The Gospels*, ed. Kent P. Jackson and Robert L. Millet, 374, as quoted with commentary by Pinegar, Bassett, and Earl in *Latter-Day Commentary*, 283.
3. Edersheim, *The Life and Times of Jesus the Messiah*, 2:372, as quoted with commentary by Pinegar, Bassett, and Earl in *Latter-Day Commentary*, 283.
4. McConkie, *Doctrinal New Testament Commentary*, 1:579.
5. Dallin H. Oaks, "Our Strengths Can Become our Downfall," Speech given to Brigham Young University, 7 June 1992.

22

❧ VINE ❧

THE LAST SUPPER AND A BETRAYER

Vine: "I am the vine, ye are the branches: He that abideth in me, and I in him, the same bringeth forth much fruit: for without me ye can do nothing" (John 15:5). Any branch detached from this Vine only withers before it is cast into the fire to be burned. Those who are attached to the Lord are fruitful. The specific way in which to make this attachment has been given through revelation. The Lord said: "Verily I say unto you, all among them who know their hearts are honest, and are broken, and their spirits contrite, and are willing to observe their covenants by sacrifice—yea, every sacrifice which I, the Lord, shall command—they are accepted of me. For I, the Lord, will cause them to bring forth as a very fruitful tree which is planted in a goodly land, by a pure stream, that yieldeth much precious fruit" (D&C 97:8–9).

Jesus desired that His disciples be connected to the strength of His power. He provided all things to them for that purpose—the teachings, the ordinances, and the covenants. Men could bind themselves to Him by following His counsel. Unfortunately, some rebelled against Jesus' way and lost that opportunity to be bound to Him. Near the end of the Savior's life, Judas Iscariot had begun to criticize the actions of the Master. It was he who complained when the costly ointment was "wasted" on Jesus. At some point along the way Judas began to consult with the Pharisees and chief priests. In time, he even honored them and began to be ashamed of the Lord.

Jesus knew the thoughts of Judas's heart all along. He once declared:

"Have not I chosen you twelve, and one of you is a devil? He spake of Judas Iscariot the son of Simon: for he it was that should betray him, being one of the twelve" (John 6:70–71). Judas thus allowed this sin in his heart, until "entered Satan into Judas" (Luke 22:3). As Judas's story illustrates, the adversary often works by tempting men with doubt and worldly pressures until he can convince them to give in and deny the Lord. When Judas gave in to this temptation he detached himself from the One through whom he might have received life and salvation.

Finally, the thoughts in Judas's heart could be hidden no longer. Judas spoke evil and conspired with men. "And he went his way, and communed with the chief priests and captains, how he might betray him unto them. And they were glad, and covenanted to give him money. And he promised, and sought opportunity to betray him unto them in the absence of the multitude" (Luke 22:4–6).

At the same time some other members of the Twelve went to a certain man, and said, "The Master saith, My time is at hand; I will keep the passover at thy house with my disciples" (Matthew 26: 18). The man gave over his house according to the Master's word, and the disciples made ready the Passover. At evening time, "when Jesus knew that his hour was come that he should depart out of this world unto the Father, having loved his own which were in the world, he loved them unto the end" (John 13: 1), Jesus sat down in that house with His Twelve Apostles. The Master truly loved those He taught, even with the pressures of that great sacrifice which was soon to follow. He loved them to the end, regardless of the fact that one of them would soon betray Him.

Only Jesus recognized Judas's treachery. The others might have noticed Judas's erroneous or foolish sayings, but only the Master could tell where such a course was leading him. When Jesus declared the betrayal as they sat around the Passover table, saying, "one of you shall betray me. Then the disciples looked one on another, doubting of whom he spake" (John 13:21–22). But it would come to pass as He had declared it. One of them who ate bread with Him would betray Jesus' innocent blood according to prophecy: "He that eateth bread with me hath lifted up his heel against me" (John 13:18). They all began to be very sorry at the saying and one by one asked, "Lord, is it I?" (Matthew 26:22).

Jesus answered, "The Son of man goeth as it is written of him: but woe unto that man by whom the Son of man is betrayed! it had been good for that man if he had not been born" (Matthew 26:24). Simon Peter beckoned to John the Beloved, who sat closest to Jesus "leaning on Jesus' bosom" (John 13:23) whom it should be that would betray Him. Jesus answered, "He it is, to whom I shall give a sop, when I have dipped it. And when he had dipped the sop, he gave it to Judas Iscariot, the son of Simon. And after the sop Satan entered into him. Then said Jesus unto him, That thou doest, do quickly. . . . He then having received the sop went immediately out: and it was night" (John 13: 26–27, 30).

Jesus then turned to those who remained faithful. "And he said unto them, With desire I have desired to eat this passover with you before I suffer: For I say unto you, I will not any more eat thereof, until it be fulfilled in the kingdom of God" (Luke 22:15–16). Jesus then took the cup, gave thanks, and told the disciples to take and divide amongst themselves, saying, "I will not drink of the fruit of the vine, until the kingdom of God shall come" (Luke 22:18).

Then He took bread, gave thanks, and brake it, and said, "This is my body which is given for you: this do in remembrance of me. Likewise also the cup after supper, saying, This cup is the new testament in my blood, which is shed for you" (Luke 22: 19–20). The sacrament was instituted, initiating the renewal of the baptismal covenant which Jesus had earlier given, the way to witness acceptance of Jesus' offering for man. In this way Jesus gave His disciples the very ordinance they would need to observe in order to remain attached to Him and continually produce fruit worthy of the Lord.

But before any of this happened around that Passover table, Jesus Christ had washed His disciples' feet. Simon had protested the event. Not realizing the symbolism of the ordinance, he said, "Thou shalt never wash my feet. Jesus answered him, If I wash thee not, thou hast no part with me" (John 13:8). Peter's understanding began to open with that saying, and he responded, "Lord, not my feet only, but also my hands and my head" (John 13:9).

Some cannot easily understand the importance of physical ordinances in the gospel plan, but their import was established from the beginning. "And thus all things were confirmed unto Adam, by an holy ordinance, and the Gospel preached, and a decree sent forth, that it should be in the world, until the end thereof; and thus it was" (Moses 5:59). Jesus then asked His disciples, "Know ye what I have done to you? Ye call me Master and Lord: and ye say well; for so I am. If I then, your Lord and Master, have washed your feet; ye also ought to wash one another's feet. For I have given you an example, that ye should do as I have done to you" (John 13:12–15).

The scriptures had expressed the great commandment for centuries: "Thou shalt love thy neighbour as thyself" (Matthew 22:39). Following His demonstration of washing His disciples feet, He now said to them: "A new commandment I give unto you, That ye love one another; as I have loved you, that ye also love one another. By this shall all men know that ye are my disciples, if ye have love one to another" (John 13:34–35). In fact, this commandment was not so new. They had always been commanded to love one another as they loved themselves. Now the Lord said that they should love as He had loved them, a greater love than that for self as they would soon see in His great offering.

As much as Christ loved His disciples, He would now have to leave them. He said, "whither I go, ye cannot come" (John 13:33). His disciples reacted to the saying. Peter asked, "whither goest thou? Jesus answered him, Whither I go, thou canst not follow me now; but thou shalt follow me afterwards. Peter said unto him, Lord, why cannot I follow thee now? I will lay down my life for thy sake" (John 13:36–37). Peter spoke from his heart, but he did not know that when the pressure mounted against him, his flesh would yet prove weak. He would thrice deny the Christ whom he loved.

The depth of the apostles' love for the Savior is evident in both Peter's question, and Thomas's response to Jesus' next words. Jesus said, "In my Father's house are many mansions: if it were not so, I would have told you. . . . And if I go and prepare a place for you, I will come again, and receive you unto myself; that where I am, there ye may be also. And whither I go ye know, and the way ye know" (John 14:2–4). Thomas responded, "Lord, we know not whither thou goest; and how can we know the way?" Thomas's fear of losing His Lord, whom he had only recently found, could not be hidden in his response.

The fact that the Savior spent the next hour comforting His disciples, tells what they were experiencing at this time. The Lord's strengthening words would also reveal what these apostles would have to endure for Him in the near future. They loved Him. They trusted Him. Yet they feared the world. Jesus recognized these feelings and would identify them by saying, "But because I have said these things unto you, sorrow hath filled your heart" (John 16:6).

Jesus' words of comfort to his apostles in John 14 can be applied to all disciples of the Master. In reading them, it should be noted how, as always, Christ was trying to strengthen His apostles, even though it was He who would shortly be going through the Atonement. The words He used at this time reveal how the Son of God still strengthens His disciples. He strengthens them through faith in His word. On the eve of Jesus' great sacrifice, he said, as recorded by John:

1. Let not your heart be troubled; ye believe in God, believe also in me (John 14:1).
2. In my Father's house are many mansions. . . . I go to prepare a place for you (John 14:2).
3. I will come again, and receive you unto myself (John 14:3).
4. Whither I go ye know, and the way ye know (John 14:4).
5. I am the way, the truth, and the life (John 14:5).
6. He that hath seen me hath seen the Father (John 14:9).
7. If ye shall ask anything in my name, I will do it (John 14:14).
8. If ye love me, keep my commandments (John 14:15).

Jesus also told them, "And I will pray the Father, and he shall give you another Comforter, that he may abide with you for ever. . . . I will not leave you comfortless: I will come to you. . . . He that hath my commandments, and keepeth them, he it is that loveth me: and he that loveth me shall be loved of my Father, and I will love him, and will manifest myself to him. . . . If a man love me, he will keep my words: and my Father will love him, and we will come unto him, and make our abode with him" (John 14:16–23).

Jesus is indeed the true vine. And men are the branches that can bear life and fruit, but only when they are attached to Him. When severed, the branch withers and cannot bear fruit of itself. Jesus is the Source while mankind serves as the vessels of His light. As the Savior would later teach His other sheep, "Therefore, hold up your light that it may shine unto the world. Behold I am the light which ye shall hold up" (3 Nephi 18:24).

Again Jesus reiterated the need to love one another, even as He loved them. "Greater love hath no man than this, that a man lay down his life for his friends" (John 15:13). As the Savior taught in word and in deed, love of God and fellowman is essential in the course of salvation. Love for the Lord is demonstrated in the keeping of His commandments (see John 14:15). "Ye are my friends," He would teach, "if ye do whatsoever I command you. . . . Ye have not chosen me, but I have chosen you, and ordained you, that ye should go and bring forth fruit, and that your fruit should remain: that whatsoever ye should ask of the Father in my name, he may give it you. These things I command you, that ye love one another" (John 15:14–17).

Yet with all of the love the Lord and these chosen witnesses would show mankind, the world would still hate them. "If ye were of the world," Jesus explained, "the world would love his own: but because ye are not of the world, but I have chosen you out of the world, therefore the world hateth you" (John 15:19). Jesus declared this doctrine before telling of the importance of His servant, the prophet. He said: "He that receiveth whomsoever I send receiveth me" (John 13:20). Just as there is no way to the Father but through Christ, neither is there any other way to follow Christ but through the word of His servants (see D&C 84:35–38 and D&C 1:37–38). Even the prophet Isaiah asked the question, "Who is among you that feareth the Lord, that obeyeth the voice of his servant . . . ?" (Isaiah 50:10).

Along with the witnesses from His servants, Jesus' promise of a Comforter, referring to the Holy Ghost, would add to their testimonies. For in addition to comforting, Jesus explained, "he shall testify of me" (John 15:26). At this point the Savior also warned the apostles that men would try to kill them. These wicked men would think they were doing God a service by mistreating His servants. When such persecutions would come, He would send them the Comforter to help them through it all. He explained, "It is expedient for you that I go away: for if I go not away, the Comforter will not come unto you; but if I depart, I will send him unto you" (John 16:7).

Jesus continued to teach about the Holy Ghost, who, in addition to His main purpose of testifying, would also reprove the world of sin, inspire righteousness, and render a perfect judgment. He would guide into all truth. He would show of things to come. He would glorify the Son of God. And He would show the things of God unto those who belonged to God.

Jesus also taught that while His disciples would weep and lament over what would befall their Master, the world would rejoice. But the sorrow of those who loved Him would ultimately be turned into joy. "For the Father himself loveth you, because ye have loved me, and have believed that I came out from God" (John 16:27). Jesus then declared that He would leave them and go to the Father. After this they would be scattered. Great tribulations would beset them. Apostasy would occur throughout His established Church. Yet, with all of these problems that would follow Jesus' departure, these who were faithful would not need to despair. "These things I have spoken unto you, that in me ye might have peace. In the world ye shall have tribulation: but be of good cheer; I have overcome the world" (John 16:33).

Jesus then offered that great intercessory prayer, before going up to Gethsemane to begin His great Atonement. His final words in the upper room were as follows:

"Father, the hour is come; glorify thy Son, that thy Son also may glorify thee:

"As thou hast given him power over all flesh, that he should give eternal life to as many as thou hast given him.

"And this is life eternal, that they might know thee the only true God, and Jesus Christ, whom thou hast sent.

"I have glorified thee on the earth: I have finished the work which thou gavest me to do.

"And now, O Father, glorify thou me with thine own self with the glory which I had with thee before the world was.

"I have manifested thy name unto the men which thou gavest me out of the world: thine they were, and thou gavest them me; and they have kept thy word.

"Now they have known that all things whatsoever thou hast given me are of thee.

"For I have given unto them the words which thou gavest me; and they have received them, and have known surely that I came out from thee, and they have believed that thou didst send me.

"I pray for them: I pray not for the world, but for them which thou hast given me; for they are thine.

"And all mine are thine, and thine are mine; and I am glorified in them.

"And now I am no more in the world, but these are in the world, and I come to thee. Holy Father, keep through thine own name those whom thou hast given me, that they may be one, as we are.

"While I was with them in the world, I kept them in thy name: those that thou gavest me I have kept, and none of them is lost, but the son of perdition; that the scripture might be fulfilled.

"And now come I to thee; and these things I speak in the world, that they might have joy fulfilled in themselves.

"I have given them thy word; and the world hath hated them, because they are not of the world, even as I am not of the world.

"I pray not that thou shouldest take them out of the world, but that thou shouldest keep them from the evil.

"They are not of the world, even as I am not of the world.

"Sanctify them through thy truth: thy word is truth.

"As thou hast sent me into the world, even so have I also sent them into the world.

"And for their sakes I sanctify myself, that they also might be sanctified through the truth.

"Neither pray I for these alone, but for them also which shall believe on me through their word;

"That they all may be one; as thou, Father, art in me, and I in thee, that they also may be one in us: that the world may believe that thou hast sent me.

"And the glory which thou gavest me I have given them; that they may be one, even as we are one:

"I in them, and thou in me, that they may be made perfect in one; and that the world may know that thou hast sent me, and hast loved them, as thou hast loved me.

"Father, I will that they also, whom thou hast given me, be with me where I am; that they may behold my glory, which thou hast given me: for thou lovedst me before the foundation of the world.

"O righteous Father, the world hath not known thee: but I have known thee, and these have known that thou hast sent me.

"And I have declared unto them thy name, and will declare it: that the love wherewith thou hast loved me may be in them, and I in them." (John 17:1–26).

ADDITIONAL COMMENTARY

The Role of Ordinances in Connecting Us with Christ: Jesus established a permanent connection with these disciples, in whom the fruits of His salvation would be established throughout the earth. These men had remained with Him through every trial and temptation that had already come. They would now be kept safely in His power until the end of the earth and into eternity. At His departure this same blessing became available to all His disciples. Men can be connected to Him through covenants. The ordinances of the sacrament and the promises made in temples would continue as they were established on the eve of the Savior's great Atonement.

23

➤ WELLSPRING OF ETERNAL LIFE ⬅

THE ATONEMENT

IN THE GARDEN OF GETHSEMANE

Wellspring of Eternal Life: Jesus, who would be called Wonderful, the Word, the Way, the Truth, and the Life, would also, as the Living Water, be the Wellspring of Eternal Life. The Well of Water would flow freely from the Garden of Gethsemane into the lives of all who loved Him and kept His commandments. Jesus told the woman at the well, "But whosoever drinketh of the water that I shall give him shall never thirst; but the water that I shall give him shall be in him a well of water springing up into everlasting life" (John 4:14). In the modern dispensation, the Savior said, "But unto him that keepeth my commandments I will give the mysteries of my kingdom, and the same shall be in him a well of living water, springing up unto everlasting life" (D&C 63:23). On the day of His mediation between men and God, what seemed then to be a horrible separation was in reality a reuniting of man to his God. What appeared to be the cause of such sadness would in actuality be the only thing that could ever bring eternal happiness. Jesus went through the ultimate sorrow to bring mankind the highest joy.

Of all of the events in the Savior's life, what He accomplished in the glorious Atonement must be remembered most often. As He worked out the Infinite Atonement, He entered into every life. In this act He descended below all things, went through all things, and rose above all things. He felt every anxiety, pain, temptation, infirmity, sin, and sorrow of every situation faced by each of God's children. Somehow, when He entered into that sacred garden to offer His own life, Jesus became the most important part of every life. When any difficulties arise in life, you can turn to Christ. Not only is He completely familiar with the situation, but He is also the solution. He truly is the way, the truth, and the life.

Gethsemane literally means "the press of oil." The inherent metaphor is profound in how it illustrates what Jesus did for all mankind. In Gethsemane Jesus was like an olive pressed down under the weight of the world's sins. He described it thus: "Which suffering caused myself, even God, the greatest of all, to tremble because of pain, and to bleed at every pore, and to suffer both body and spirit—and would that I might not drink the bitter cup, and shrink—Nevertheless, glory be to the Father, and I partook and finished my preparations unto the children of men" (D&C 19:18–19).

The Savior had lived a perfect life, and, as the Son of the Immortal Father, He could not be killed by the devices of men. Nor would He die as a result of mankind's sins. Rather He was crushed by them, His blood oozing from every pore. Great was the burden, but still greater was the Son of God. To Him death, the wage of sin, was not due. Our only basis of comparison might be the heaviness inflicted by our own sins "which in the smallest, yea, even in the least degree you have tasted at the time I withdrew my Spirit" (D&C 19:20). That Jesus could take such a load for all mankind is the highest monument to His goodness. He who knew no sin took upon Himself all the sins of the world.

Going up toward the Garden of Gethsemane, Jesus turned to Peter and said, "Simon, Simon, behold, Satan hath desired to have you, that he may sift you as wheat: But I have prayed for thee, that thy faith fail not; and when thou art converted, strengthen thy brethren" (Luke 22:31–32). Peter would deny Christ that same night, fearing what might follow. But later Peter stood boldly for Jesus, in spite of the consequences. Peter's change occurred after he received the gift of the Holy Ghost. It was then that Peter became completely converted and could strengthen his brethren in word and deed, being filled with the Holy Ghost himself.

Peter answered the Savior's warning by saying that he was ever willing to go with Him, "both into prison, and to death. And he said, I tell thee, Peter, the cock shall not crow this day, before that thou shalt thrice deny that thou knowest me" (Luke 22:33–34).

Jesus then turned to the rest of His disciples and taught them. Indeed He taught as He loved, unto the end, for "when Jesus knew that his hour was come that he should depart out of this world unto the Father, having loved his own which were in the world, he loved them unto the end" (John 13:1). He asked His disciples if they had ever lacked, even when He sent them without purse or scrip. They testified that they had lacked nothing. Then He said, "But now, he that hath a purse, let him take it, and likewise his scrip: and he that hath no sword, let him sell his garment and buy one. For I say unto you, that this that is written must yet be accomplished in me, And he was reckoned among the transgressors: for the things concerning me have an end" (Luke 22:36–37).

Jesus led His disciples onward through Jerusalem, over a brook called Cedron, and up to the Mount of Olives, where there was a garden. He took them to the place where He "ofttimes resorted . . . with his disciples" (John 18:2). Jesus' chosen followed until he said, "Sit ye here, while I go and pray yonder" (Matthew 26:36). He also encouraged them with the words, "Pray that ye enter not into temptation" (Luke 22:40). As always He thought of the needs of those He had come to strengthen, even as He approached the Garden of Gethsemane.

Then He took Peter, James, and John a little farther, and as He walked He began to feel "sore amazed, and to be very heavy" (Mark 14:33). Such a weight began to settle upon His soul that it amazed even Him, with his great knowledge and capacity to understand. He remarked, "My soul is exceeding sorrowful, even unto death: tarry ye here, and watch with me" (Matthew 26:38). Jesus then proceeded alone until "he was withdrawn from them about a stone's cast, and kneeled down, and prayed" (Luke 22:41). Matthew adds that as "he went a little further, [He] fell on his face" (Matthew 26:39).

His words poured out to the Father: "If thou be willing, remove this cup from me: nevertheless not my will, but thine be done" (Luke 22:42). From there He treaded the winepress alone. Luke recorded that "being in an agony he prayed more earnestly: and his sweat was as it were great drops of blood falling down to the ground" (Luke 22:44). At this moment Jesus "prayed more earnestly" or in other words, more intently, so that He could accomplish the work He had come to do.

He had come to take upon Himself every sin, every difficulty brought about by men—the wickedness, iniquity, depravity, immorality, violence, destruction—every improper deed, word, or thought. Having never felt the ravages of a single sin before, He now had "laid on Him the iniquity of us all" (see Isaiah 53:6). He "poured out his soul unto death" (Isaiah 53:12). Neither did He "shrink" (D&C 19:18), nor pull back in the giving of His life for the sins of the world. He did not resist, hesitate, surrender, or break in this offering. Instead of retreating from the task, He approached it head on and conquered it.

He did so according to the prophecy that in those anguishing hours of His offering "he [should] see his seed" (see Mosiah 15:10–12), identified in the scriptures as those who have heard the words of the prophets and hearkened unto their words, the true disciples of the Lord Jesus Christ. On this most sacred of all occasions, those who would seek redemption and receive this sacred offering appeared. The atoning Lord blessed those who came to Him on this night. And He blessed them in the same way He had always done His work—one by one.

After the first period of prolonged suffering, Jesus came out to find His chosen apostles sleeping. With a mild rebuke He gently exhorted them again to "Watch and pray, that ye enter not into temptation: the spirit indeed is willing, but the flesh is weak" (Matthew 26:41). Even in the hour of His greatest agony, He continued to act as their Teacher.

He went back a second time and offered up His heart to His Father as only a Son could do, saying, "O my Father, if this cup may not pass away from me, except I drink it, thy will be done" (Matthew 26:42). With this Jesus advanced into His second hour of suffering, but this time He was not "sore amazed." Now He knew by experience what He was going into. In addition to His earlier worry that He "might not drink the bitter cup, and shrink" (D&C 19:19), now Jesus knew what He was facing. He alone perfectly understood the pain He would have to endure in order to bring about the Atonement.

After that second hour, Jesus returned again to give His sleeping disciples another reminder. In His anguish, He still came to serve them, even though they offered nothing in return.

Going into the third hour, with now both the experience and the kind of fatigue that only He could know, He "prayed the third time, saying the same words" (Matthew 26:44). Who can fathom the extraordinary hour that necessitated for the Creator of the world the appearance of "an angel unto him from heaven, strengthening him" (Luke 22:43)?

After three hours of pain that pen cannot describe, Jesus went back to His sleeping disciples. The noise from the approaching chief priests and their officers broke the stillness of the night, and the apostles stood to face their opponents. Within moments the party arrived to confront the Savior of the world. His chosen Twelve were all present, including the betrayer who stood on the opposite ground.

Christ's atoning sufferings were thus begun, coming upon our Savior according to the prophecies of thousands of years. On this occasion Jesus overcame all that the adversary could ever inflict upon all mankind. There, in that darkest hour, Jesus conquered Satan. He accomplished His great Atonement for each of us in a deep and profoundly personal way, so that He could help us to overcome Satan. He descended alone into that dreadful vat of the winepress to rescue us—one by one.

ADDITIONAL COMMENTARY

He Prayed More Earnestly: Elder Bruce R. McConkie explained this "more earnest" prayer:

> The Son of God who did all things well—whose every thought and act and deed was perfect; whose every prayer pierced the firmament and ascended to his Father—the Son of God himself (note it well) "prayed more earnestly." Even he reached a pinnacle of perfection in prayer that had not always been his. And as to the blood that oozed from his pores, we cannot do better than recall the words of the angelic ministrant, spoken to the Nephite Hebrew, Benjamin: "And lo, he shall suffer temptations, and pain of body, . . . even more than man can suffer, except it be unto death; for behold, blood cometh from every pore, so great shall be his anguish for the wickedness and the abominations of his people." (Mosiah 3:7)[1]

The Most Bitter Cup: Elder Neal A. Maxwell explains what happened during the Savior's defining moment in Gethsemane in the following words: "At the end, meek and lowly Jesus partook of the most bitter cup without becoming the least bitter. . . . The Most Innocent suffered the most. Yet the King of Kings did not break. . . . You and I are so much more brittle. For instance, we forget that, by their very nature, tests are unfair."[2]

He Took It All Upon Himself: President Boyd K. Packer explained: "He, by choice, accepted the penalty for all mankind for the sum total of all wickedness and depravity; for brutality, immorality, perversion, and corruption; for addiction; for the killings and torture and terror—for all of it that ever had been or all that ever would be enacted upon this earth."[3]

When He Went Into the Garden to Pray: Elder Merrill J. Bateman explained what occurred when Jesus went into the garden to pray. He said,

> The prophet Abinadi further states that "when his soul has been made an offering for sin he shall see his seed" (Mosiah 15:10). Abinadi then identifies the Savior's seed as the prophets and those who follow them. For many years I thought of the Savior's experience in the garden and on the cross as places where a large mass of sin was heaped upon Him. Through the words of Alma, Abinadi, Isaiah, and other prophets, however, my view has changed. Instead of an impersonal mass of sin, there was a long line of people, as Jesus felt "our infirmities" (Heb. 4:15), "[bore] our griefs, . . . carried our sorrows . . . [and] was bruised for our iniquities" (Isaiah 53:4–5). The Atonement was an intimate, personal experience in which Jesus came to know how to help each of us. The Pearl of Great Price teaches that Moses was shown all the inhabitants of the earth, which were "numberless as the sand upon the sea shore" (Moses 1:28). If Moses beheld every soul, then it seems reasonable that the Creator of the universe has the power to become intimately acquainted with each of us.[4]

In the Garden of Gethsemane: Elder Orson F. Whitney (1855–1931), who served in the Quorum of the Twelve Apostles, had a dream as a young missionary that changed his life forever:

> One night I dreamed . . . that I was in the Garden of Gethsemane, a witness of the Savior's agony. . . . I stood behind a tree in the foreground. . . . Jesus, with Peter, James, and John, came through a little wicket gate at my right. Leaving the three Apostles there, after telling them to kneel and pray, He passed over to the other side, where He also knelt and prayed. . . . "Oh my Father, if it be possible, let this cup pass from me; nevertheless not as I will but as Thou wilt."
>
> As He prayed the tears streamed down His face, which was [turned] toward me. I was so moved at the sight that I wept also, out of pure sympathy with His great sorrow. My whole heart went out to Him. I loved Him with all my soul and longed to be with Him as I longed for nothing else.
>
> Presently He arose and walked to where those Apostles were kneeling—fast asleep! He shook them gently, awoke them, and in a tone of tender reproach, untinctured by the least show of anger or scolding, asked them if they could not watch with Him one hour. . . .
>
> Returning to His place, He prayed again and then went back and found them again sleeping. Again He awoke them, admonished them,

and returned and prayed as before. Three times this happened, until I was perfectly familiar with His appearance—face, form, and movements. He was of noble stature and of majestic mien . . . the very God that He was and is, yet as meek and lowly as a little child.

All at once the circumstance seemed to change. . . . Instead of before, it was after the Crucifixion, and the Savior, with those three Apostles, now stood together in a group at my left. They were about to depart and ascend into heaven. I could endure it no longer. I ran from behind the tree, fell at His feet, clasped Him around the knees, and begged Him to take me with Him.

I shall never forget the kind and gentle manner in which He stooped and raised me up and embraced me. It was so vivid, so real that I felt the very warmth of His bosom against which I rested. Then He said: "No, my son; these have finished their work, and they may go with me; but you must stay and finish yours." Still I clung to Him. Gazing up into His face—for He was taller than I—I besought Him most earnestly: "Well, promise me that I will come to You at the last." He smiled sweetly and tenderly and replied: "That will depend entirely upon yourself." I awoke with a sob in my throat, and it was morning.[5]

Of this story, Elder Jeffrey R. Holland of the Quorum of the Twelve Apostles explained:

This tender, personal glimpse of the Savior's loving sacrifice is a fitting introduction to the significance of the Atonement of Jesus Christ. Indeed the Atonement of the Only Begotten Son of God in the flesh is the crucial foundation upon which all Christian doctrine rests and the greatest expression of divine love this world has ever been given. Its importance in The Church of Jesus Christ of Latter-day Saints cannot be overstated. Every other principle, commandment, and virtue of the restored gospel draws its significance from this pivotal event.[6]

Notes

1. Bruce R. McConkie, *The Mortal Messiah, From Bethlehem to Calvary*, Book IV (Salt Lake City: Deseret Book, 1970), 125.

2. Neal A. Maxwell, "Irony: The Crust on the Bread of Adversity," *Ensign*, May 1989, 62–63.

3. Boyd K. Packer, "Who Is Jesus Christ?," *Liahona*, Mar. 2008, 12–19.

4. Merrill J. Bateman, "A Pattern for All," *Liahona*, Nov. 2005, 74–76.

5. Jeffrey R. Holland, "The Atonement of Jesus Christ," *Ensign*, Mar. 2008, 32–38.
6. Ibid.

24

❧ The Atonement Continued ❧

The Lord's Reactions to the Judgments and Punishments of Men

"[Jesus] struggled with and overcame the powers of men and devils, of earth and hell combined; and aided by this superior power of the Godhead, He vanquished death, hell and the grave, and arose triumphant as the Son of God, the very eternal Father, the Messiah, the Prince of Peace, the Redeemer, the Savior of the world; having finished and completed the work pertaining to the atonement, which His Father had given Him to do as the Son of God and the Son of man."[1]

—*John Taylor*

Now that Jesus had initiated the workings of His great offering, Lucifer would come, seeking to avert His course. All that followed on that night stemmed from the works of the adversary and his minions, who would try to overthrow the great plan of God. Jesus proved greater, not succumbing in a single instance to the devices of the devil. Instead of destroying the plan, Satan only fulfilled it, bringing about the very last sacrifice of the Son of God, who came to give His innocent life for man.

Hearing before chief priests
+ Location: Caiaphas' palace.

◆   References: Matthew 26:57–68; Mark 14:53–65; Luke 22:54; John 18:13, 19–24.

As he had secretly promised to do, Judas stepped forward to where Jesus stood with the eleven apostles near the Garden of Gethsemane, and "forthwith he came to Jesus, and said, Hail, master; and kissed him" (Matthew 26:49). Jesus answered, "Friend, wherefore art thou come?" (Matthew 26:50). "Judas, betrayest thou the Son of man with a kiss?" (Luke 22:48). "Jesus therefore, knowing all things that should come upon him, went forth, and said unto them, Whom seek ye?" Those officers and chief priests who had arrived to take the Master answered, "Jesus of Nazareth." Without hesitancy, deception, or fear, Jesus answered only, "I am he" (John 18:4–5).

Great power accompanied His simple declaration, and his would-be captors "went backward, and fell to the ground" (John 18:6). He who had created the world still stood as its Master, even as He was being arrested and judged by men. Jesus continued, "I have told you that I am he: if therefore ye seek me, let these go their way" (John 18:8).

Peter instantly drew his sword and smote off the ear of the high priest's servant, Malchus, Jesus rebuked His chief apostle and said, "the cup which my Father hath given me, shall I not drink it?" (John 18:11). Then he touched the man's ear and healed him. Turning to the company of "the chief priests, and captains of the temple, and the elders, which were come to him," He said, "Be ye come out, as against a thief, with swords and staves? When I was daily with you in the temple, ye stretched forth no hands against me: but this is your hour, and the power of darkness" (Luke 22: 52–53).

Jesus had come to them during the day, many times, but now they came to take Him to an illegal midnight trial. Symbolically, Jesus came as the Light of the World, while His enemies were the children of darkness. With the Master's determination to go back into Jerusalem, the fear that had long prevailed among His disciples overpowered even those who had declared their desires to go with Jesus unto death. Then "all the disciples forsook him, and fled" (Matthew 26:56).

The officers then took Jesus and led Him to Caiaphas' palace, where the high priests, scribes, and elders awaited. Although initially the disciples reacted by taking flight, Peter actually followed Jesus to the palace, "and went in, and sat with the servants, to see the end" (Matthew 26:58). John's record states that "Simon Peter followed Jesus, and so did another disciple: that disciple was known unto the high priest, and went in with Jesus into the palace of the high priest. But Peter stood at the door without" (John 18:15–16).

Several things are apparent in this account. First, the disciples felt that their lives were in jeopardy when their Master was taken to be judged by men. Second, at least two of them, Peter and John, followed the Master into this "den of thieves" as Jesus had often titled such places (see Matthew 21:13, 38). We can sense the danger these disciples felt, considering Peter's response to those who soon asked him of his connection with Jesus of Nazareth. And yet there stood Peter at the very jaws of hell, wherein they had taken the King of heaven. While many remember Peter's failure in handling the temptations which quickly followed, the love he must have had to go against such fears and come to the palace in the first place is often overlooked.

Two false witnesses were found and brought before the midnight council to testify against Jesus. They testified, using the words the Savior had spoken at the temple during His first visit to Jerusalem: "This fellow said, I am able to destroy the temple of God, and to build it in three days" (Matthew 26:61). That charge would bring the council to consider the only thing they could hold against Jesus—blasphemy. Only the Son of God could make such a claim and be guiltless of the alleged crime, but this court's intention was to prove His blasphemy.

To do this they needed Him to declare His Godhood or divinity before those present. They also needed something to disprove His word. After the two witnesses verified that He had personally proclaimed who He was, "the high priest arose, and said unto him, Answerest thou nothing? what is it which these witness against thee? But Jesus held his peace. And the high priest answered and said unto him, I adjure thee by the living God, that thou tell us whether thou be the Christ, the Son of God" (Matthew 26:62–63).

Many had asked this question of Jesus before, and each time the Master had left the hearer to discover the answer through His words, His works, or through the signs and prophecies given about Him. This time was different. "Again the high priest asked him, and said unto him, Art thou the Christ, the Son of the Blessed? And Jesus said, I am: and ye shall see the Son of man sitting on the right hand of power, and coming in the clouds of heaven. Then the high priest rent his clothes, and saith, What need we any further witnesses? Ye have heard the blasphemy: what think ye? And they all condemned him to be guilty of death" (Mark 14:61–64).

As before in Nazareth, the evidence of Jesus' blasphemy was His works: healing the sick, lifting the afflicted, causing the blind to see, the lame to walk, and setting the prisoners free—and these were all fulfillments of Messianic prophecies. Adding to that the Messiah's own words, the council only proved that Jesus was the Messiah, even providing witnesses that supplied evidence to prove His word.

Peter's denial

+ Location: Caiaphas' palace.
+ References: Matthew 26:69–75; Mark 14:66–72; Luke 22:55–62; John 18:15–18, 25–27.

While Peter stood outside of the proceedings, one of the women servants at the door recognized him and asked, "Art not thou also one of this man's disciples?" (John 18:17). "And he denied [Jesus], saying, Woman, I know him not" (Luke 22:57). Other servants who stood without the palace also asked Peter, "Art not thou also one of his disciples? He denied it, and said, I am not" (John 18:25). Finally one of the servants of the high priest said, "Did not I see thee in the garden with him?" (John 18:26). "Then began he to curse and to swear, saying, I know not the man. And immediately the cock crew" (Matthew 26:74). "And the Lord turned, and looked upon Peter. And Peter remembered the word of the Lord, how he had said unto him, Before the cock crow, thou shalt deny me thrice. And Peter went out, and wept bitterly" (Luke 22:61–62).

Perhaps the best example of repentance in recorded history comes from Peter. He not only slept through the suffering in Gethsemane, which he had been personally invited to witness, but on that very same night, he also thrice denied Christ, of whom Peter was supposed to be a special witness. The story of Peter's repentance begins with the recognition that occurred when the "cock crew" (Matthew 26:74). Suddenly Peter "remembered the words of Jesus, which said unto him, Before the cock crow, thou shalt deny me thrice" (Matthew 26:75). How important it is to remember the Savior and His words in the process of repenting. Some call recognition the first step of repentance.

Godly sorrow will follow this recognition. Peter understood his error and "he went out, and wept bitterly" (Matthew 26:75). The scriptures refer to this kind of sorrow. "For godly sorrow worketh repentance to salvation not to be repented of: but the sorrow of the world worketh death. For behold this selfsame thing, that ye sorrowed after a godly sort, what carefulness it wrought in you, yea, what clearing of yourselves, yea what indignation, yea, what fear, yea, what vehement desire, yea, what zeal, yea, what revenge! In all things ye have approved yourselves to be clear in this matter" (2 Corinthians 7:10–11).

What did this do for Peter? Peter would yet become the chief Apostle. While he would not be perfect in the flesh, like his Master, yet "learned he obedience by the things which he suffered" (Hebrews 5:8). We can only imagine the way in which Peter rent his heart when he realized his error. Did Peter confess his sin? Did he forsake it? Did he turn to the Lord with all of his heart and give the rest of his life to the work? Was he forgiven? We see the atoning grace of forgiveness in Peter's life when, only a short time later, he reunited with the other faithful apostles, and "with great power gave . . . witness of the resurrection of the Lord Jesus: and great grace was upon them all" (Acts 4:33).

Soldiers mock Jesus
+ Location: Caiaphas' palace.
+ Reference: Luke 22:63–65.

Though they had no evidence against Him, the court declared Jesus guilty of blasphemy. If anything could be proved in the council that gathered that evening it would be that Satan, the source of darkness, prevailed among those that surrounded the Light of the World. Those present began to spit upon Jesus of Nazareth. Then they covered His face while they struck Him with the palms of their hands, saying, "Prophesy unto us, thou Christ, Who is he that smote thee?" (Matthew 26:68). "And many other things blasphemously spake they against him" (Luke 22:65). In marked irony those who cried blasphemy were the ones guilty of the crime.

The next morning
+ Location: Jerusalem.
+ References: Matthew 27:1; Mark 15:1; Luke 22:66; John 18:28.

After such a night of which we have only the briefest account, the morning did not bring relief. Punishment and judgment were the order of the day. Jesus would still have to endure with perfection to complete His sacrifice.

Hearing before Caiaphas
+ Location: Jerusalem.
+ References: Matthew 27:1; Mark 15:1; Luke 22:66–71; John 18:24, 28.

Before sending Jesus before Pilate, the complete council of the Sanhedrin had to rule on the matter. The Sanhedrin had power over civil and
ecclesiastical judgments, and while being the supreme court in such cases,
with power to arrest and pass sentence, power over life and death remained
with the Romans (see Bible Dictionary, Sanhedrin). Accordingly, Jesus was
brought before Caiaphas and the rest of the members of the Sanhedrin.
There He was again asked the same questions related to blasphemy. And
again He was pronounced guilty by men.

Hearing before Pilate

+ Location: Jerusalem.
+ References: Matthew 27:2, 11–14; Mark 15:1–5; Luke 23:1–6;
  John 18:28–38.

After the Savior's judgement before Caiaphas, "the whole multitude
of them arose, and led him unto Pilate" (Luke 23:1). The Sanhedrin had
still found no evidence against Him, but now they sought to validate themselves by continuing to charge Him falsely. "And they began to accuse him,
saying, We found this fellow perverting the nation, and forbidding to give
tribute to Caesar, saying that he himself is Christ a King" (Luke 23:2).

Finding the people in an uproar and the religious leaders so affected,
Pilate regarded Jesus carefully. He began to ask questions, such as "What
accusation bring ye against this man?" (John 18:29). The chief priests
answered only that if Jesus were not a malefactor they would not have
brought Him. "Then said Pilate unto them, Take ye him, and judge him
according to your law. The Jews therefore said, It is not lawful for us to
put any man to death" (John 18:31), revealing their true intentions toward
Jesus. But Pilate "knew that for envy they had delivered him" (Matthew
27:18).

Pontius Pilate then entered into the judgment hall and called Jesus
forth to ask Him plainly,

> Art thou the King of the Jews? Jesus answered him, Sayest thou
> this of thyself, or did others tell it thee of me? Pilate answered, Am I
> a Jew? Thine own nation and the chief priest have delivered thee unto
> me: what hast thou done? Jesus answered, My kingdom is not of this
> world: if my kingdom were of this world, then would my servants fight,
> that I should not be delivered to the Jews: but now is my kingdom not
> from hence. Pilate therefore said unto him, Art thou a king then? Jesus
> answered, Thou sayest that I am a king. To this end was I born, and for
> this cause came I into the world, that I should bear witness unto the

truth. Every one that is of the truth heareth my voice (John 18: 33–37).

Pilate then returned to those who accused Jesus and said that he had found no fault in the man. This saying brought an even greater reaction from those who had delivered Jesus to be judged. "And they were the more fierce, saying, He stirreth up the people, teaching throughout all Jewry, beginning from Galilee to this place" (Luke 23:5).

By the mention of Jesus teaching in Galilee, Pilate asked if perchance Jesus were a Galilaean. When hearing the declaration that Jesus came from Nazareth, Pilate sighed a breath of relief. This meant that the decision was no longer his to make. "And as soon as he knew that he belonged unto Herod's jurisdiction, he sent him to Herod, who himself also was at Jerusalem at that time" (Luke 23:7).

Judas's remorse and death
+ Location: Temple.
+ Reference: Matthew 27:3–10.

The consequence of sin is death. For this reason Jesus alone held power over life. After betraying such "innocent blood," Judas Iscariot felt unbearable remorse of conscience (Matthew 27:4). He was experiencing the consequences of his deliberate actions. Soon he could no longer endure the pain of his choices. He went out and hanged himself on a tree (see also Acts 1:18).

Hearing before Herod
+ Location: Jerusalem.
+ Reference: Luke 23:7–10.

Jesus the Messiah had words for the scribes, Pharisees, and hypocrites. He spoke comfort to the adulterous woman. He talked to children, widows, publicans, centurions, rich young rulers, rabbis, and heathens alike. But to Herod, "he answered him nothing" (Luke 23:9).

This offended Herod who had long desired to see Jesus, having heard many great things and having hoped to see some great miracle done by Him. Herod asked many questions, and the chief priest and scribes accused Jesus to the king's face. Then "Herod with his men of war set him at nought, and mocked him, and arrayed him in a gorgeous robe" (Luke 23:11). For the man who had beheaded John the Baptist, Jesus had no words. Perhaps His silence speaks volumes, an eloquent and profound discourse emanating through His sealed lips.

215

Second hearing before Pilate

- Location: Antonia.
- References: Matthew 27:15–31; Mark 15:6–15; Luke 23:11–17.

Herod sent Jesus back to Pontius Pilate. But Pilate's wife had a warning for him this time: "When he was set down on the judgment seat, his wife sent unto him, saying, Have thou nothing to do with that just man: for I have suffered many things this day in a dream because of him" (Matthew 27:19). Pilate then called the chief priests and rulers together and said, "behold, I, having examined him before you, have found no fault in this man touching those things whereof ye accuse him: No, nor yet Herod: for I sent you to him; and, lo, nothing worthy of death is done unto him. I will therefore chastise him, and release him" (Luke 23:14–16).

Those who sought only Jesus' death cried out at once for Pilate to release Barabbus instead, a known murderer, knowing that, according to tradition, one prisoner would be released at the Passover Feast. Pilate then asked what he should do with Jesus which is called Christ? They all answered that Jesus should be crucified. "And the governor said, Why, what evil hath he done? But they cried out the more, saying, Let him be crucified. When Pilate saw that he could prevail nothing, but that rather a tumult was made, he took water, and washed his hands before the multitude, saying, I am innocent of the blood of this just person: see ye to it" (Matthew 27:23–24). His comment referred back to the dream his wife had that he should have nothing to do with that "just man."

A murderer released

- Location: Jerusalem.
- References: Matthew 27:15–21, 26; Mark 15:6–15; Luke 23:18–25; John 18:39–40.

The sharp contrast between Barabbus and Christ provides a sad commentary on those who chose the evil murderer over the Lord. Ironically those who Jesus came to deliver from spiritual captivity repaid Him by crying out, "Crucify him, crucify him. And [Pilate] said unto them the third time, Why, what evil hath he done? I have found no cause of death in him: I will therefore chastise him, and let him go. And they were instant with loud voices, requiring that he might be crucified. And the voices of them and of the chief priests prevailed" (Luke 23:21–23).

The vile murderer Barabbus was pardoned while the Holy One, the very Judge and Deliverer, was made captive by the judgment of men. Jesus' greatness is seen at this moment. There was no word of condemnation from Jesus. Instead he maintained perfect dignity, self-control, and self-restraint. As ever before, the Savior of mankind did not cry out for justice. Neither did He send an earthquake to destroy, nor a bolt of lightning with a legion of angels. Jesus simply closed His mouth and received the judgment.

In all of Jesus' silence, even while Pilate sought to be free and clean of the situation, the people cried out, "His blood be on us, and on our children" (Matthew 27:25).

Jesus scourged and mocked

+ Location: Jerusalem.
+ References: Matthew 27:27–31; Mark 15:15–20; John 19:1–12.

Finally giving in, "Pilate, willing to content the people, released Barabbas unto them, and delivered Jesus, when he had scourged him, to be crucified. And the soldiers led him away into the hall, called Praetorium; and they call together the whole band. And they clothed him with purple, and platted a crown of thorns, and put it about his head, And began to salute him, Hail, King of the Jews! And they smote him on the head with a reed, and did spit upon him, and bowing their knees worshipped him" (Mark 15:15–19).

Jesus' scourging was done according to the Roman torture associated with crucifixion. First He was whipped with leather straps that had pieces of metal and bone embedded into its ends, "forty times save one." This torture alone prevented many from even reaching the cross as the incurring shock would frequently bring about a premature death. Again a prophecy was fulfilled in this part of Jesus' offering, as Isaiah said: "Surely he hath borne our griefs, and carried our sorrows: yet we did esteem him stricken, smitten of God, and afflicted. But he was wounded for our transgressions, he was bruised for our iniquities: the chastisement of our peace was upon him; and with his stripes we are healed" (Isaiah 53:4–5).

At this point Pilate went out again and cried to the people, "Behold, I bring him forth to you, that ye may know that I find no fault in him" (John 19:4). Jesus then came out wearing the crown of thorns and purple robe. Pilate called out to the multitude, "Behold the man!" (John 19:5).

The chief priests answered, crying back, "Crucify him, crucify him. Pilate saith unto them, Take ye him, and crucify him: for I find no fault in him. The Jews answered him, We have a law, and by our law he ought to die, because he made himself the Son of God" (John 19:6–7). Herein lies the case for Jesus of Nazareth: He had indeed declared Himself the Son of God, but there was no fault found in Him. For the chief priests to prove blasphemy they needed to find a fault, not just a declaration of divinity. Yet they found only the testimony of the Son of God, in word and deed.

While the chief priests seemed to miss this point because of their blind hatred and sole purpose in destroying Jesus, Pilate started to consider the facts. "When Pilate therefore heard that saying, he was the more afraid; And went again into the judgment hall, and saith unto Jesus, Whence art thou?" (John 19:8–9).

Throughout the Messiah's ministry, He gave ample proof of His authenticity. The honest in heart were not lacking in evidence concerning the Messiah. Jesus had fulfilled the many given prophecies, provided the works of the Christ, and lived a fault-free life. "But because of priestcrafts and iniquities, they at Jerusalem [would] stiffen their necks against him, that he be crucified" (2 Nephi 10:5).

Pilate, being a reasonable man, considered the many things that testified of Him. "Then saith Pilate unto him, Speakest thou not unto me? Knowest thou not that I have power to crucify thee, and have power to release thee? Jesus answered, Thou couldest have no power at all against me, except it were give thee from above: therefore he that delivered me unto thee hath the greater sin. And from thenceforth Pilate sought to release him" (John 19:10–12).

Jesus taken to Golgotha

+ Location: Near Jerusalem.
+ References: Matthew 27:32–34; Mark 15:20–23; Luke 23:26–31; John 19:13–17.

When the Jews noticed that Pilate was reconsidering the situation, they instantly "cried out, saying, If thou let this man go, thou art not Caesar's friend: whosoever maketh himself a king speaketh against Caesar" (John 19:12). Hearing those words, Pilate feared the people and brought Jesus forth and answered, "Behold your King! But they cried out, Away with him, away with him, crucify him. Pilate saith unto them, Shall I crucify your king? The chief priest answered, We have no king but Caesar. Then delivered he him therefore unto them to be crucified. And they took Jesus, and led him away" (John 19:14–16).

The crowd took Jesus away to Golgotha, where He, "bearing his cross went forth into a place called the place of a skull, which is called in the Hebrew Golgotha" (John 19:17). Matthew, Mark, and Luke tell how, at a certain point along the way, Simon, a Cyrenian who had come to Jerusalem for Passover, bore the Savior's cross. A great company of people followed after Him, "and of women, which also bewailed and lamented him" (Luke 23:27).

The crucifixion

+ Location: Calvary.
+ References: Matthew 27:35–44; Mark 15:24–33; Luke 23:32–43; John 19:18–22.

Fulfilling prophecy, the Jews crucified the Son of God with a sign over His head provided by Pilate: "THIS IS JESUS THE KING OF THE JEWS" (Matthew 27:37). The words spoken by each person and group who came to see Jesus at the cross reveal their hearts. Though the power of darkness was present, tempting Jesus to falter, the Lord remained perfect unto the end.

Several people came and spoke to Jesus while He was on the cross:

+ Mockers who passed by to revile, wagging their heads: "Thou that destroyest the temple, and buildest it in three days, save thyself. If thou be the Son of God, come down from the cross" (Matthew 27:40).
+ Chief priests, scribes, and elders: "He saved others; himself he cannot save" (Matthew 27:42). "Let him save himself, if he be Christ, the chosen of God" (Luke 23:35). "If he be the King of Israel, let him now come down from the cross, and we will believe him. He trusted in God; let him deliver him now, if he will have him; for he said, I am the Son of God" (Matthew 27:42–43). "Let Christ the King of Israel descend now from the cross, that we may see and believe" (Mark 15:32).
+ The soldiers: "If thou be the king of the Jews, save thyself" (Luke 23:37).
+ One of the thieves: "If thou be Christ, save thyself and us" (Luke 23:39).
+ The other thief, speaking first to rebuke his counterpart, and second to honor the Lord: "This man hath done nothing amiss. . . . Lord, remember me when thou comest into thy kingdom" (Luke 23:41, 42).
+ Centurion: "Certainly this was a righteous man" (Luke 23:47).
+ His disciples: Of all the words spoken at the cross, not one word was recorded from His disciples. Their silent reverence during

His offering far exceeded anything they could have said. Truly there were no words to express their feelings at this time.

The words Jesus spoke while on the cross:

- "Father, forgive them; for they know not what they do" (Luke 23:34).
- "Verily I say unto thee [speaking to the second thief], To day shalt thou be with me in paradise" (Luke 23:43).
- To Mary: "Woman, behold thy son!"
- To John: "Behold thy mother!" (John 19:26–27).
- "I thirst" (John 19:28).
- "My God, my God, why hast thou forsaken me?" (Matthew 27:46).
- "It is finished" (John 19:30).
- "Father, into thy hands I commend my spirit" (Luke 23:46).

Over the course of Jesus' suffering, a three-hour period of darkness had come over the land. An earthquake shook the world when the Savior "bowed his head, and gave up the ghost" (see Matthew 27:50–51). This earthquake rent the veil of the temple, exposing its inner, most holy court to the eyes of men. Symbolic of the people's defiling the sacred Son, the holy temple lay open and disgraced for all to see. His flesh was torn, and His blood was spilt. The world will forever remember the sacrifice He gave, a sacrifice that still moves honest men across the earth to faith and repentance, and then on to baptism and receiving the Holy Ghost. "For, behold, the Lord your Redeemer suffered death in the flesh; wherefore he suffered the pain of all men, that all men might repent and come unto him. And he hath risen again from the dead, that he might bring all men unto him, on conditions of repentance. And how great is his joy in the soul that repenteth!" (D&C 18:11–13).

Soldiers cast lots for Jesus' robe
- Location: Calvary near Jerusalem.
- References: Matthew 27:35; Mark 15:24; Luke 23:34; John 19:23–24.

Many who were present did not understand the significance of Jesus' death. "Then the soldiers, when they had crucified Jesus, took his garments, and made four parts, to every soldier a part; and also his coat: now the coat was without seam, woven from the top throughout. They said therefore among themselves, Let us not rend it, but cast lots for it, whose it shall be: that the scripture might be fulfilled, which saith, They parted my raiment among them, and for my vesture they did cast lots. These things therefore the soldiers did" (John 19:23–24).

The sign: King of the Jews
+ Location: Calvary near Jerusalem.
+ References: Matthew 27:37; Mark 15:26; Luke 23:38; John 19:19–22.

Others who were there acted with knowledge and learned to reverence the Son of God. Even Pilate who wrote the saying over the cross felt impressed to honor Jesus. John records that the inscription read: "Jesus of Nazareth the King of the Jews." This title was written in Hebrew, Greek, and Latin, so it could be read by all who passed the cross on their way into the city. Calvary stood above the main thoroughfare into Jerusalem where many would pass. "Then said the chief priests of the Jews to Pilate, Write not, The King of the Jews; but that he said, I am the King of the Jews. Pilate answered, What I have written I have written" (John 19:21–22).

Darkness: sixth to ninth hour
+ Location: Jerusalem.
+ References: Matthew 27:45; Mark 15:33–36; Luke 23:44–45.

The New Testament record of the Jews (the stick of Judah) records that the darkness over the earth went from the sixth hour until the ninth hour. "The sun was darkened, and the veil of the temple was rent in the midst" (Luke 23:45), and an earthquake shook (see Matthew 27:51). The Book of Mormon, Another Testament of Jesus Christ (the stick of Joseph), records: "And it came to pass that when the thunderings, and the lightnings, and the storm, and the tempest, and the quakings of the earth did cease—for behold, they did last for about the space of three hours; and it was said by some that the time was greater; nevertheless, all these great and terrible things were done in about the space of three hours—and then behold, there was darkness upon the face of the land" (3 Nephi 8:19). These two records have become one in our hand (see Ezekiel 37:16–17) to establish the witness that Jesus is the Christ, and that even the God of all men suffered when He beheld His great Son suffering.

Jesus' mother put in John's care
+ Location: Calvary.
+ Reference: John 19:25–27.

As He was suffering on the cross, Jesus told Mary that John would be her son, and then He told John that Mary would be his mother. The event was significant. Even in His suffering, Jesus still provided for those around Him. He continued to put the needs of others before His own, even then. It was a similar act to that which occurred the night before when Jesus healed the ear of one of the men who had come to take Him captive. To the end, Jesus rendered good for evil. He never stopped helping, teaching, or serving others, even in His extremity.

Death of Jesus Christ
+ Location: Calvary.
+ References: Matthew 27:46–50; Mark 15:37; Luke 23:46; John 19:28–30.

As Jesus had long instructed the people, no man could take His life from Him. He gave His life voluntarily to ransom the sinner. "Therefore doth my Father love me, because I lay down my life, that I might take it again. No man taketh it from me, but I lay it down of myself. I have power to lay it down, and I have power to take it again. This commandment have I received of my Father" (John 10:17–18). Even so, when Jesus bowed His head, He gave up the ghost. He did so only after He personally declared the work finished.

Earthquake: Veil of Temple rent
+ Location: Jerusalem.
+ References: Matthew 27:51–53; Mark 15:38; Luke 23:45.

The earthquake that occurred at Jesus' death provided an additional witness of who it was that was crucified: the Creator of the earth and all things in it, even the very ground that supported mankind.

Pierced by a spear
+ Location: Calvary.
+ Reference: John 19:31–34.

When evening approached, the Jews worried about the approaching Sabbath, not wanting the bodies to remain on the cross during the Sabbath day. They asked Pilate for permission to break the legs of those being crucified in order to hasten their deaths. The soldiers then came and broke the legs of the thieves. When they found Jesus already dead, "one of the soldiers with a spear pierced his side, and forthwith came there out blood and water" (John 19:34).

From the time of Simeon's early prophecy in the temple, Mary knew what awaited Jesus, and how she would also suffer when He died. As he took the baby Jesus in his arms, Simeon declared: "Behold, this child is set for the fall and rising again of many in Israel; and for a sign which shall be spoken against; (Yea, a sword shall pierce through thine own soul also)" (Luke 2:34–35). On that night when a spear pierced Jesus' side to ensure His death, His was not the only soul that was pierced. Jesus was not the only one whose heart was utterly broken by the sins of men.

Passover scripture fulfilled
+ Location: Calvary.
+ Reference: John 19:35–37.

Only a few truly recognized the Christ when He came, though He came as prophesied "for the fall and rising of many in Israel" (Luke 2:34). Every word written in the law and the prophets concerning Christ was fulfilled, including the Passover scripture: "A bone of him shall not be broken" (John 19:36). Surely the prophecies that accompanied the Savior were sufficient to convince those who sought, asked, and knocked. Those who rejected the Messiah also had to reject the many prophecies about Him. Especially after witnessing His offering, many would come to understand that He truly was the Messiah.

On this culminating occasion, the Messianic prophecies contained in the scriptures provided overwhelming evidence of Jesus' divinity: "Out of Egypt have I called my son" (Matthew 2:15); "to open the blind eyes, to bring out the prisoners" (Isaiah 42:7); "They pierced my hands and my feet" (Psalms 22:16); "In my thirst they gave me vinegar to drink" (Psalms 69:21); "I gave my back to the smiters" (Isaiah 50:6); "he was wounded for our transgressions" (Isaiah 53:5); "I was prised at . . . thirty pieces of silver" (Zechariah 11:13); "I was wounded in the house of my friends" (Zechariah 13:6); "He poured out his soul unto death" (Isaiah 53:12); "They shall look on him whom they pierced" (John 19:37).

Adding to these the previously mentioned prophecies that a virgin should conceive; that the stone which the builders refused is become the head of the corner; that a prophet would come before Him as a voice of one crying in the wilderness, saying, "Prepare ye the way of the Lord;" that He would indeed come out of Bethlehem; and "He shall be called a Nazarene" (Matthew 2:23; lost Old Testament scripture), it becomes even more obvious that the people surely had sufficient reason to believe. But just as He had prophesied, many would only come to know after they had lifted Him up on the cross.

In those days, believing in the Messiah required one to act in faith with a testimony based on the prophecies of old. Is it any different now? The prophecies and commandments that we have at our fingertips still require faith. To follow them takes diligence. Living the gospel requires walking faithfully into the darkness at times. Sometimes there are things in the gospel that we can't see plainly or understand immediately. Those who proceeded forward with faith during Jesus' life beheld that Light which burst forth upon them just as He had prophesied.

Watchers near the cross
+ References: Matthew 27:54–56; Mark 15:39–41; Luke 23:47–49.

Though many forsook Him, there were several women in Jesus' life who remained faithful to the end. "And many women were there beholding afar off, which followed Jesus from Galilee, ministering unto him: Among which was Mary Magdalene, and Mary the mother of James and Joses, and the mother of Zebedee's children" (Matthew 27:55–56). "And all his acquaintance, and the women that followed him from Galilee, stood afar off, beholding these things" (Luke 23:49).

Jesus' burial
+ Location: Near Jerusalem.
+ References: Matthew 27:57–61; Mark 15:42–47; Luke 23:50–56; John 19:38–42.

Two counselors from the Sanhedrin worked together to bring Jesus' body from the place of common burial to that reserved for royalty—Joseph of Arimathaea and Nicodemus. The record describes Joseph as a disciple of Jesus and a good, just man. Though he was a member of the council, he "had not consented to the counsel and deed of them" (Luke 23:51). As a rich man of Arimathaea (Matthew 27:57), he "waited for the kingdom of God" (Mark 15:43) "but secretly for fear of the Jews" (John 19:38).

Nicodemus also came at the risk of his reputation. Both of these men sacrificed personally and professionally in order to accomplish this task. They probably were not able to keep their allegiance to Christ secret after they helped to honor Him in His burial. Their sacrifice in burying Jesus likely cost them their reputations, if not their lives.

Joseph of Arimathaea plead with Pilate for the body of Jesus. Nicodemus brought a mixture of myrrh and aloes to prepare the burial. "Then took they the body of Jesus, and wound it in linen clothes with the spices, as the manner of the Jews is to bury" (John 19:40). They took Jesus to a place in a garden with a new sepulchre "wherein was never man yet laid" (John 19:41) and buried Jesus there.

After this, the story of Nicodemus, as recorded in the Bible, ends. But this much is clear: after going secretly to Jesus by night, testifying in His behalf, and risking his very reputation in Jesus' burial, Nicodemus had become a true disciple, along with his fellow counselor, Joseph of Arimathaea.

Chief priests and Pharisees seal the tomb
+ Location: Near Jerusalem.
+ Reference: Matthew 27:62–66.

The chief priests and Pharisees learned of Jesus' entombment and also went to Pilate. "Sir," they said, "we remember that that deceiver said, while he was yet alive, After three days I will rise again. Command therefore that the sepulchre be made sure until the third day, lest his disciples come by night, and steal him away, and say unto the people, He is risen from the dead: so the last error shall be worse than the first. Pilate said unto them, Ye have a watch: go your way, make it as sure as ye can. So they went, and made the sepulchre sure, sealing the stone, and setting a watch" (Matthew 27:63–66).

Like Lazarus had not many days earlier, Jesus now lay in a tomb. When Jesus had gone to raise Lazarus, He had wept, all the while knowing that He would bring Lazarus back to the world of the living. In Lazarus's story He had seen a type of the path he would take only days later.

When Jesus was buried, there were many who came to witness with Joseph of Arimathaea and Nicodemus. "And Mary Magdalene and Mary the mother of Joses beheld where he was laid" (Mark 15:47). All who came did so at great personal risk, but those who had watched at the cross would certainly not forsake Him now. The Savior's family would have been there. Contemplating the similarity to Lazarus provides a reminder that Jesus had many friends in the vicinity who cared for Him much more than they worried about the world's retribution. Mary and Martha would certainly have been there, along with their brother. In addition to Mary Magdalene, who never would have left Him, Joanna (the wife of Chuza, Herod's steward) was probably there, as she had been throughout His ministry (Luke 8:3). Joanna had ministered to Him from the start, along with Susanna. Salome, the mother of James and John, was surely there at His burial and at the cross if it was at all possible.

Perhaps the friends Jesus made along the way also came, such as Jairus, the ruler of Capernaum's synagogue. Maybe the centurion from Capernaum was there. Was he the same centurion who, when he saw the earthquake at Jesus' death, declared, "Truly this was the Son of God" (Matthew 27:54)? What about the woman at the well from Samaria? Would she have missed the sacrifice given for her after the Savior had made a personal effort in her behalf? What about the widow from Nain? Or Peter's mother-in-law? Would the woman taken in adultery or the man held captive by the legion of devils, both of whom were rescued by Christ, have come for Him in His hour of need? What about the woman whose issue of blood was healed, or of the leper who implored, "Lord, if thou wilt, thou canst make me clean" (Matthew 8:2)? Would any of Jesus' neighbors from Nazareth have come? Would any of the disciples of John the Baptist? Of the five thousand fed, how many came to witness Jesus' offering of the Bread that would never run out and that Living Water that would never go dry?

Peter was there. After having wept bitterly, the chief Apostle would surely have come back to witness and stand forever faithful. If the mother of James and John had come, then surely her sons accompanied her. Thomas would have been there. Matthew, Mark, and Luke would have been there too, with all of the remaining Apostles. What of Jesus' earthly guardian, his father the carpenter? No mention of Joseph is made even at the cross, but surely if he was still alive he would have been there, along with many others.

Of all those who likely came, the only ones mentioned at the burial are Joseph of Arimathaea, Nicodemus, and the two Marys. Like those who loved Jesus in days of old, we still remember His offering today. We do so each time we partake of the sacramental emblems of His sacrifice. We still figuratively bow before His tomb and remember the flesh that was torn for us and the blood that was spilt. He is our Exemplar; His great offering tells the true importance of the gospel. And For this reason He has asked that we always remember Him.

ADDITIONAL COMMENTARY

A Testimony of Jesus Christ from a Contemporary: Flavius Josephus recorded:

> Now, there was about this time, Jesus, a wise man, if it be lawful

to call him a man, for he was a doer of wonderful works,—a teacher of such men as receive the truth with pleasure. He drew over to him both many of the Jews, and many of the Gentiles. He was [the] Christ; and when Pilate, at the suggestion of the principal men amongst us, had condemned him to the cross, those that loved him at the first did not forsake him, for he appeared to them alive again the third day, as the divine prophets had foretold these and ten thousand other wonderful things concerning him; and the tribe of Christians, so named from him, are not extinct at this day.[2]

On the Physical Death of Jesus Christ:

Jesus of Nazareth underwent Jewish and Roman trials, was flogged, and was sentenced to death by crucifixion. The scourging produced deep stripelike lacerations and appreciable blood loss, and it probably set the stage for hypovolemic shock, as evidenced by the fact that Jesus was too weakened to carry the crossbar (patibulum) to Golgotha. At the site of crucifixion, his wrists were nailed to the patibulum and, after the patibulum was lifted onto the upright posts (stipes), his feet were nailed to the stipes. The major pathophysiologic effect of crucifixion was an interference with normal respirations. Accordingly, death resulted primarily from hypovolemic shock and exhaustion asphyxia. Jesus' death was ensured by the thrust of a soldier's spear into his side. Modern medical interpretation of the historical evidence indicates that Jesus was dead when taken down from the cross.[3]

Beyond the Physical Aspect: Anyone who has experienced something that takes them to the extreme of what they can endure physically and emotionally will realize that Jesus' suffering must have been increased dramatically by the empathy He felt for those around Him. He must have felt such sorrow as He watched them prepare for Him to leave them. And He was even moved to sorrow in thinking of those who betrayed Him.

The Sacrifice of the Father in the Giving of His Son: Imagine a father and mother with a young son who is sick. These parents are forced to watch as their son suffers from a disease which eventually takes his life. Their son suffers greatly, but not nearly as much as his parents, who so love their son, and who faithfully watch over him until his untimely departure.

As Simeon had prophesied, when the spear penetrated Jesus' side to ensure His death, it was Mary whose heart was also broken beyond repair. When Jesus from the Cross cried out, "My God, my God, why hast thou forsaken me?" (Mark 15:34). Father in Heaven, who had suffered with His Son through everything had withdrawn to allow Jesus the personal victory. What a great sacrifice was made by all of His parents when Jesus was given for the sins of men.

Notes

1. John Taylor, "He Lives! The Witness of Latter-day Prophets, *Ensign*, Mar. 2008, 8–11; and http://JesusChrist.lds.org, under the heading "Testimonies of Him" and "He Lives! The Witness of Latter-day Prophets."
2. Flavius Josephus, *Josephus Complete Works* (Grand Rapids, Michigan: Kregel Publications, 1960), 379.
3. William D. Edwards, Wesley J. Gabel, and Floyd E. Hosmer, "On the Physical Death of Jesus Christ," *JAMA*, 21 Mar., 1986, 1456.

25

❧ The Atonement Continued ❧

The Resurrection of the Lord Jesus Christ

"I give you my testimony: The resurrection of Jesus Christ is the greatest historical event in the world to date. He lives! He lives with a resurrected body. There is no truth or fact of which I am more assured than the truth of the literal resurrection of our Lord."[1]

—*Ezra Taft Benson*

The Resurrection is the greatest miracle of all time! It is the means by which all mortals will eventually be delivered from Satan and escape the bondage of sin and death. Its power comes through the Son of God, the Redeemer of the world who personally conquered every temptation the adversary could ever inflict, and did it without committing a single sin. Jesus is the Resurrection and the Life. The wonder of His glorious miracle, the Resurrection, will be documented below as it was revealed to chosen witnesses, ancient and modern, who shared what they received from the Lord Himself:

First day: Earthquake, angels open tomb
- Location: Near Jerusalem.
- References: Matthew 28:1–2; Luke 24:1–2.

On the third day after the Lord was entombed, "In the end of the Sabbath, as it began to dawn toward the first day of the week" (Matthew 28:1), a great earthquake occurred in the morning and an angel of the Lord descended and rolled back the stone from the door (see Matthew 28:2). "His countenance was like lightning, and his raiment white as snow; And for fear of him the keepers did shake, and became as dead men" (Matthew 28:3–4).

Mary Magdalene comes to the open tomb

- Location: Near Jerusalem.
- Reference: John 20:1–2.

Mary Magdalene came first to see the open tomb. She came when it was still early and dark. And when she saw "the stone taken away from the sepulchre and two angels sitting thereon" (JST John 20:1), she departed hastily and ran to find Peter and John. When she found them, she wept, saying, "They have taken away the Lord out of the sepulchre, and we know not where they have laid him" (John 20:2).

Mary's actions tell so much concerning her faith in the Lord. She went early to the tomb and was the first to arrive that morning. She departed from there hastily and went directly to the Apostles. She wept at His absence. Mary is an example of the believers who put their trust in Him.

Peter and John run to the tomb

- Location: Near Jerusalem.
- References: Luke 24:12, 24; John 20:3–10.

Peter and John ran together to the tomb. John arrived first and "stooping down, and looking in, saw the linen clothes lying; yet went he not in. Then cometh Simon Peter following him, and went into the sepulchre, and seeth the linen clothes lie, And the napkin, that was about his head, not lying with the linen clothes, but wrapped together in a place by itself. Then went in also that other disciple, which came first to the sepulchre, and he saw, and believed" (John 20:5–8).

"Woman, why weepest thou?"

- Location: Near Jerusalem.
- Reference: John 20:11–13.

With our faith, our great hope is in Jesus Christ who broke the bands of death that man might also live again. We have the assurance of His Resurrection from those who know. Among those who have become witnesses of Jesus' Resurrection, Peter and John were first. But even while they began to understand, Mary did not. While these two went into the tomb, Mary still stood without weeping for grief. She cried, "They have taken away the Lord" (John 20:2). After they saw, Peter and John went away, leaving Mary alone with her grief.

Again Mary looked into the tomb. This time she saw two angels, one at the head and the other at the feet where Jesus had lain. "Woman, why weepest thou?" they asked. "She saith unto them, Because they have taken away my Lord, and I know not where they have laid him" (John 20:13).

Even with witnessing angels, Mary could not be comforted. She loved her Master above all things. Still weeping for grief, Mary turned away "and saw Jesus standing, and knew not that it was Jesus. Jesus saith unto her, Woman, why weepest thou? whom seekest thou? She, supposing him to be the gardener, saith unto him, Sir, if thou have borne him hence, tell me where thou hast laid him, and I will take him away" (John 20:15).

Then, in recorded simplicity, a single word changed everything: "Mary" (John 20:16). Mary turned at the familiar voice, and all suddenly came into focus. She responded, "Rabboni; which is to say, Master" (John 20:16). Jesus answered, "Touch me not; for I am not yet ascended to my Father: but go to my brethren, and say unto them, I ascend unto my Father, and your Father; and to my God, and your God" (John 20:17).

Disciples told but disbelieve
+ Location: Near Jerusalem.
+ References: Mark 16:10–11; Luke 24:9–11; John 20:18.

Mary Magdalene went immediately as her Master had commanded and told the disciples what she had seen and heard. "And [her] words seemed to them as idle tales, and they believed them not" (Luke 24:11). The reader may wonder at their disbelief after all of the prophecies. Even at this point "they knew not the scripture, that he must rise again from the dead" (John 20:9). Even so, "when they had heard that he was alive, and had been seen of her, believed not" (Mark 16:11). This is in contrast to Peter and John who did believe (see John 20:8). Now three witnesses stood to testify of their understanding and build the faith of those who were soon to witness His coming to all men.

Two Marys come to the tomb
+ Location: Near Jerusalem.
+ References: Matthew 28:1; Mark 16:1–4; Luke 23:55; 24:3.

In returning to the tomb, the two Marys witnessed the angels and heard the heaven-sent testimony of the risen Lord as delivered below.

Angels: "He is risen"
+ Location: Near Jerusalem.

- References: Matthew 28:2–8; Mark 16:5–8; Luke 24:4–8.

"And the angel answered and said unto the women, Fear not ye: for I know that ye seek Jesus, which was crucified. He is not here: for he is risen, as he said. Come, see the place where the Lord lay" (Matthew 28:5–6).

Women meet Jesus

- Location: Near Jerusalem.
- References: Matthew 28:9–10; Mark 16:9.

"As they went to tell his disciples, behold, Jesus met them, saying, All hail. And they came and held him by the feet, and worshipped him. Then said Jesus unto them, Be not afraid: go tell my brethren that they go into Galilee, and there shall they see me" (Matthew 28:9–10).

Officials bribe soldiers

- Location: Near Jerusalem.
- Reference: Matthew 28:11–15.

As for the guards sent by Caiaphas to watch the tomb, they eventually awoke, and "behold, some of the watch came into the city, and shewed unto the chief priests all the things that were done. And when they were assembled with the elders, and had taken counsel, they gave large money unto the soldiers, Saying, Say ye, His disciples came by night, and stole him away while we slept. And if this come to the governor's ears, we will persuade him, and secure you. So they took the money, and did as they were taught" (Matthew 28:11–15).

The testimony of Jesus never would go forth by those who were unworthy, be it spoken by devils or men. Even with the knowledge that proceeded to the council from the words of the guards, the chief priests continued to consult against the testimony of Jesus.

Jesus appears to two disciples

- Location: Emmaus.
- References: Mark 16:12; Luke 24:13–32.

Mark records that Jesus appeared to two others who went and told their report unto the disciples and "neither believed they them" (Mark 16:13). Luke's account provides a few more details. Traveling on the road to Emmaus, these two disciples were walking together and conversing of the things that had happened and affected them so. As they communed and reasoned about what they had heard "Jesus himself drew near, and went with them" (Luke 24:15).

They continued walking and conversed with the stranger, but the two men did not recognize their fellow traveler. The stranger asked what they talked about and why they were sad. The first disciple answered, wondering how this stranger could not know of the mysterious things that had been happening in Jerusalem. "What things?" He asked. "And they said unto him, Concerning Jesus of Nazareth, which was a prophet mighty in deed and word before God and all the people: And how the chief priests and our rulers delivered him to be condemned to death, and have crucified him" (Luke 24:19–20).

The two men went on to tell how they knew Jesus "had been he which should have redeemed Israel" (Luke 24:21). They explained how all of these other things that had happened were not what they had been expecting. Like the other disciples, "they thought that the kingdom of God should immediately appear" (Luke 19:11), but to their surprise, it appeared instead like the Son of man had no power over the kingdoms of the world.

And yet, they went on to explain, a report had emerged from certain women that He lived again. "Then he said unto them, O fools, and slow of heart to believe all that the prophets have spoken: Ought not Christ to have suffered these things, and to enter into his glory?" (Luke 24:25–26).

The stranger then began to expound the scriptures to their understanding, from Moses on through all the prophets, concerning the Messiah. When they arrived at the house to which they journeyed, they asked their fellow journeyer to abide with them, for the day was far spent. There He took bread, blessed it, brake it in their presence, and gave it to them to partake of. "And their eyes were opened, and they knew him; and he vanished out of their sight" (Luke 24:31). They instantly began to marvel at the unusual event and remarked, "Did not our heart burn within us, while he talked with us by the way, and while he opened to us the scriptures?" (Luke 24:32).

The two travelers returned to Jerusalem to report their findings to the eleven remaining apostles. Those who gathered under Peter responded, according to Luke's account, "Saying, The Lord is risen indeed, and hath appeared to Simon. And they told what things were done in the way, and how he was known of them in breaking of bread" (Luke 24:34–35).

The indication here is that Jesus had also now appeared to Simon Peter. This is verified later by Paul. "And that he was buried, and that he rose again the third day according to the scriptures: And that he was seen of Cephas, then of the twelve" (1 Cor. 15:4–5). Cephas is the name Jesus first called Peter (see John 2:42).

Jesus appears to disciples

+ Location: Jerusalem.
+ References: Mark 16:14; Luke 24:36–49; John 20:19–23.

That evening, "when the doors were shut where the disciples were assembled for fear of the Jews, came Jesus and stood in the midst, and saith unto them, Peace be unto you" (John 20:19). Yet they were "terrified" and "affrighted," and supposed that they were seeing a spirit. "And he said unto them, Why are ye troubled? and why do thoughts arise in your hearts? Behold my hands and my feet, that it is I myself: handle me and see; for a spirit hath not flesh and bones, as ye see me have" (Luke 24:38–39).

Jesus thus appeared in His resurrected body to those who would go forth as His special witnesses. He showed them His hands and His feet, and then He asked if they had any meat. They gave Him a piece of broiled fish and honeycomb, which He took and ate before them. He also opened the scriptures to their understanding, teaching them "that repentance and remission of sins should be preached in his name among all nations, beginning at Jerusalem" (Luke 24:47). "Then said Jesus unto them again, Peace be unto you: as my Father hath sent me, even so send I you. And when he had said this, he breathed on them, and saith unto them, Receive ye the Holy Ghost" (John 20:21–22).

Thomas does not believe

+ Location: Jerusalem.
+ Reference: John 20:24–25.

After their initial reactions of shock and terror, "Then were the disciples glad, when they saw the Lord" (John 20:20). Thomas was absent when the Savior first appeared. He missed the witness of the greatest miracle ever recorded. When the others told Thomas about it, He still doubted. They said, "We have seen the Lord. But he said unto them, Except I shall see in his hands the print of the nails, and put my finger into the print of the nails, and thrust my hand into his side, I will not believe" (John 20:25). Even with ten special witnesses declaring the testimony, along with others who had also seen, Thomas still would not believe.

Eight days later: With Thomas

+ Location: Jerusalem.
+ Reference: John 20:26–29.

Jesus would return to this group with a special lesson for His doubting disciple. At Jesus' second arrival, He confirmed to them that He indeed lived, that His promises were true, that He had power to keep those promises, and that men would be blessed for relying in faith upon Him.

> And after eight days again his disciples were within, and Thomas with them: then came Jesus, the doors being shut, and stood in the midst, and said, Peace be unto you. Then saith he to Thomas, Reach hither thy finger, and behold my hands; and reach hither thy hand, and thrust it into my side: and be not faithless, but believing. And Thomas answered and said unto him, My Lord and my God. Jesus saith unto him, Thomas, because thou hast seen me, thou hast believed: blessed are they that have not seen, and yet have believed. (John 20:26–29)

Peter: "I go a fishing"
- Location: Sea of Galilee.
- Reference: John 21:1–19.

After obtaining that special witness, Peter returned to the Sea of Galilee with James and John, Nathanael, Thomas, and two other disciples, saying, "I go a fishing" (John 21:3). His friends said they would also go, but even with all of them fishing, they caught nothing. After Jesus' departure the first inclination of these disciples was to return to the things they had done before Jesus called them.

In the morning they saw Jesus on the shore but did not recognize Him. He called out, "Children, have ye any meat? They answered him, No" (John 21:5). He called back, "Cast the net on the right side of the ship, and ye shall find. They cast therefore, and now they were not able to draw it for the multitude of fishes" (John 21:6).

John said, "It is the Lord." (John 21:7).

Peter thrust himself into the sea to swim to the Lord he loved, coming first to Jesus as he had often done. He wouldn't wait for the ship to drag the fishes slowly into shore. When they all came to the land they found a fire with coals heating up some fishes and bread. Jesus then called for the disciples to bring in the fish they had caught, which they did without the net breaking.

After they had dined, Jesus turned to Peter, and said, "Simon, son of Jonas, lovest thou me more than these?"

"Yea, Lord; thou knowest that I love thee."

"Feed my lambs."

Then He turned a second time to Peter, and said, "Simon, son of Jonas, lovest thou me?"

"Yea, Lord; thou knowest that I love thee."

"Feed my sheep."

Jesus turned yet a third time to Peter, and said, "Simon, son of Jonas, lovest thou me?"

At this point Peter was grieved that the Savior would ask the same thing again. "Lord, thou knowest all things; thou knowest that I love thee."

"Feed my sheep" the Savior responded (see John 21:15–17).

Peter inquires about John

+ Location: Jerusalem.
+ Reference: John 21:20–22.

Jesus next told Peter that his ministry would take him to places he would not want to go and that eventually in "death he should glorify God" (John 21:19). Jesus concluded with, "Follow me" (John 21:19).

Having so heard what would befall his own discipleship, Peter asked about John. Jesus answered, "If I will that he tarry till I come, what is that to thee? follow thou me" (John 21:22).

The great commission to the Twelve

+ Location: A mountain of Galilee.
+ References: Matthew 28:16–20; Mark 16:15–18.

The eleven apostles then went to a mountain in Galilee where Jesus had said to go. There He appeared to them again. "And Jesus came and spake unto them, saying, All power is given unto me in heaven and in earth" (Matthew 28:18). With this comforting thought, all mankind can rest assured that the plan is in effect and that Jesus has indeed overcome the world as He said He would.

In fact the Savior has accomplished all things for man, but that doesn't remove our personal responsibility to obtain salvation. Men are still "free to choose liberty and eternal life, through the great Mediator of all men, or to choose captivity and death, according to the captivity and power of the devil; for he seeketh that all men might be miserable like unto himself" (2 Nephi 2:27).

Because men were still free to choose, there was still a great work for Jesus' true disciples to perform. Jesus therefore commissioned His apostles, gave them authority, and sent them forth as His Father had first sent Him. Even today, authorized servants on earth are called in the same manner and told: "Go ye therefore, and teach all nations, baptizing them in the name of the Father, and of the Son, and of the Holy Ghost: Teaching them to observe all things whatsoever I have commanded you: and, lo, I am with you alway, even unto the end of the world. Amen" (Matthew 28:19–20).

Ascension, proclamation
+ Location: Near Jerusalem.
+ References: Mark 16:19–20; Luke 24:50–53.

The graves of other saints were opened after Jesus was Resurrected, and many of the righteous dead were seen. Great rejoicing spread among the believers at this time. On one occasion the Savior of mankind led His disciples "out as far as to Bethany, and he lifted up his hands, and blessed them. And it came to pass, while he blessed them, he was parted from them, and carried up into heaven. And they worshipped him, and returned to Jerusalem with great joy" (Luke 24:50–52).

The book of Acts tells how the Savior taught among His disciples, "To whom also he shewed himself alive after his passion by many infallible proofs, being seen of them forty days, and speaking of the things pertaining to the kingdom of God" (Acts 1:3). The disciples asked if Jesus would at that time restore the kingdom again to Israel as many had expected all along. The Savior answered that it was not for them to know the times or seasons which the Father put in his own power.

> But ye shall receive power, after that the Holy Ghost is come upon you: and ye shall be witnesses unto me both in Jerusalem, and in all Judaea, and in Samaria, and unto the uttermost part of the earth. And when he had spoken these things, while they beheld, he was taken up; and a cloud received him out of their sight. And while they looked stedfastly toward heaven as he went up, behold, two men stood by them in white apparel; Which also said, Ye men of Galilee, why stand ye gazing up into heaven? this same Jesus, which is taken up from you into heaven, shall so come in like manner as ye have seen him go into heaven. (Acts 1:8–11)

Mark records: "So then after the Lord had spoken unto them, he was received up into heaven, and sat down on the right hand of God. And they went forth, and preached every where, the Lord working with them, and confirming the word with signs following" (Mark 16:20).

The importance of the Resurrection is without comparison in all of the doctrines that surround the Atonement. Jesus is indeed risen. He is alive again. And if He lives, then so shall we. Death is conquered. Man has been set free. Eternal life is possible. Immortality is assured. With faith in this testimony, we can look forward to that which awaits us. As Ether taught: "Wherefore, whoso believeth in God might with surety hope for a better world, yea, even a place at the right hand of God, which hope cometh of faith, maketh an anchor to the souls of men, which would make them sure and steadfast, always abounding in good works, being led to glorify God" (Ether 12:4).

ADDITIONAL COMMENTARY

The following testimonies of the living Christ are given by the latter-day prophets, "for the testimony of Jesus is the spirit of prophecy" (Revelation 19:10).[2]

Thomas S. Monson: "With all my heart and the fervency of my soul, I lift up my voice in testimony as a special witness and declare that God does live. Jesus is His Son, the Only Begotten of the Father in the flesh. He is our Redeemer; He is our Mediator with the Father. He it was who died on the cross to atone for our sins. He became the firstfruits of the Resurrection. Because He died, all shall live again. 'Oh, sweet the joy this sentence gives: "I know that my Redeemer lives!" ' May the whole world know it and live by that knowledge, I humbly pray, in the name of Jesus Christ, the Lord and Savior, amen.

Gordon B. Hinckley: "I know that I am not the head of this Church. The Lord Jesus Christ is its head. My mission, my chief responsibility, my greatest honor comes in bearing solemn testimony of His living reality. Jesus Christ is the Son of God, who condescended to come into this world of misery, struggle, and pain, to touch men's hearts for good, to teach the way of eternal life, and to give Himself as a sacrifice for the sins of all mankind. He is 'King of Kings and Lord of Lords, and He shall reign forever and ever' (Handel's Messiah). . . . I bear solemn witness that He lives and stands on the right hand of His Father."

Howard W. Hunter: "I am grateful . . . for my affiliation with a people who have a firm conviction that God lives, that Jesus is the Christ; and I bear witness to you that the story of the babe born in the manger at Bethlehem is not a myth of the past, but that Jesus, the Son of God was born of Mary into mortality; that he lived among men; that he died upon the cross and was resurrected; that he actually and truly lives today; and that he is a personal being and is the Savior of the world."

Ezra Taft Benson: "The question is sometimes asked, 'Are Mormons Christians?' We declare the divinity of Jesus Christ. We look to Him as the only source of our salvation. We strive to live His teachings, and we look forward to the time that He shall come again on this earth to rule and reign as King of Kings and Lord of Lords. In the words of a Book of Mormon prophet, we say to men today, 'There [is] no other name given nor any other way nor means whereby salvation can come unto the children of men, only in and through the name of Christ, the Lord Omnipotent' (Mosiah 3:17)."

Spencer W. Kimball: "We place [Jesus Christ] on a pedestal as no other group I know of. To us he is not only the Son of God, he is also a God and we are subject to him. . . . No matter how much we say of him, it is still too little. He is not only the Carpenter, the Nazarene, the Galilean, but Jesus Christ, the God of this earth, the Son of God, but most importantly, our Savior, our Redeemer. . . . I add my own testimony. I know that Jesus Christ is the Son of the living God and that he was crucified for the sins of the world. He is my friend, my Savior, my Lord, my God."

Harold B. Lee: "After a long night of searching and days of spiritual preparation that followed, I came to know as a witness more powerful than sight, until I could testify with a surety that defied all doubt, that I knew with every fiber of my soul that Jesus is the Christ, the Son of the living God, that He lived, He died, He was resurrected, and today He presides in the heavens, directing the affairs of this church, which bears His name because it preaches His doctrine. I bear that testimony humbly and leave you my witness."

Joseph Fielding Smith: "Salvation is in Christ. It comes because of the infinite and eternal atonement which he wrought by the shedding of his blood. He is the Son of God, and he came into the world to ransom men from the temporal and spiritual death that came because of what we call the fall. Through his goodness and grace all men will come forth from the grave, to be judged according to the deeds done in the flesh. . . . I know that he lives, that he rules in the heavens above and in the earth beneath, and that his purposes shall prevail. He is our Lord and our God. As he himself said to Joseph Smith: 'The Lord is God, and beside him there is no Savior' (D&C 76:1)."

David O. McKay: "'How can we know the way?' asked Thomas, as he sat with his fellow apostles and their Lord at the table after the supper on the memorable night of betrayal; and Christ's divine answer was: 'I am the way, the truth, and the life.' (John 14:5–6.) And so he is! He is the source of our comfort, the inspiration of our life, the author of our salvation. If we want to know our relationship to God, we go to Jesus Christ. If we would know the truth of the immortality of the soul, we have it exemplified in the Savior's resurrection. . . . He is the one Perfect Being who ever walked the earth; the sublimest example of nobility; Godlike in nature; perfect in his love; our Redeemer; our Savior; the immaculate Son of our Eternal Father; the Light, the Life, the Way."

George Albert Smith: "The Savior died that we might live. He overcame death and the grave and holds out to all who obey His teachings the hope of a glorious resurrection. I have found many in the world who have not known that we believe in the divine mission of our Lord, and I have been led to say upon more than one occasion that there are no people in the world who so well understand the divine mission of Jesus Christ, who so thoroughly believe him to have been the Son of God, who are so sanguine [confident] that at the present time he is enthroned in glory at the right hand of his Father, as the Latter-day Saints."

Heber J. Grant: "To members of the Church throughout the world, and to peace-lovers everywhere, we say, behold in this Man of Galilee not merely a great Teacher, not merely a peerless Leader, but the Prince of Peace, the Author of Salvation, here and now, literally and truly the Savior of the World! . . . Jesus is the Redeemer of the world, the Savior of mankind, who came to the earth with a divinely appointed mission to die for the redemption of mankind. Jesus Christ is literally the Son of God, the Only Begotten in the flesh. He is our Redeemer, and we worship him."

Joseph F. Smith: "The Holy Spirit of God has spoken to me—not through the ear, not through the eye, but to my spirit, to my living and eternal part,—and has revealed unto me that Jesus is the Christ, the Son of the living God. I testify to you that I know that my Redeemer lives. Furthermore, I know that I shall see Him on this earth, and that I shall see Him as He is. . . . The Lord has revealed this to me. He has filled my whole spirit with this testimony, until there is no room for doubt."

Lorenzo Snow: "That Being who dwelt in Heaven, who reigned there before the world was, who created the earth, and who, in the meridian of time, came down to perfect and save that which He had created, has appeared to men in this age. We testify to the whole world that we know, by divine revelation, even through the manifestations of the Holy Ghost, that Jesus is the Christ, the Son of the Living God, and that he revealed himself to Joseph Smith as personally as he did to his apostles anciently, after he arose from the tomb, and that he made known unto him [the] heavenly truths by which alone mankind can be saved."

Wilford Woodruff: "The object of Christ's mission to the earth was to offer himself as a sacrifice to redeem mankind from eternal death. . . . He acted strictly in obedience to his Father's will in all things from the beginning, and drank of the bitter cup given him. Herein is brought to light, glory, honour, immortality, and eternal life, with that charity which is greater than faith or hope, for the Lamb of God has hereby performed that for man which [man] could not accomplish for himself. . . . There is no being that has power to save the souls of men and give them eternal life, except the Lord Jesus Christ, under the command of His Father."

John Taylor: "Anointed, indeed, with the oil of gladness above His fellows, He struggled with and overcame the powers of men and devils, of earth and hell combined; and aided by this superior power of the God-head, He vanquished death, hell and the grave, and arose triumphant as the Son of God, the very eternal Father, the Messiah, the Prince of peace, the Redeemer, the Savior of the world; having finished and completed the work pertaining to the atonement, which His Father had given Him to do as the Son of God and the Son of man."

Brigham Young: "I testify that Jesus is the Christ, the Savior and Redeemer of the world; I have obeyed his sayings, and realized his prom-ise, and the knowledge I have of him, the wisdom of this world cannot give, neither can it take away. . . . Our Lord Jesus Christ—the Savior, who has redeemed the world and all things pertaining to it, is the Only Begotten of the Father pertaining to the flesh. . . . He has tasted death for every man, and has paid the debt contracted by our first parents."

Joseph Smith: "And this is the gospel, the glad tidings, which the voice out of the heavens bore record unto us—That he came into the world, even Jesus, to be crucified for the world, and to bear the sins of the world, and to sanctify the world, and to cleanse it from all unrighteousness; That through him all might be saved whom the Father had put into his power and made by him . . . 'And now, after the many testimonies which have been given of him, this is the testimony, last of all, which we give of him: That he lives! For we saw him, even on the right hand of God; and we heard the voice bearing record that he is the Only Begotten of the Father—That by him, and through him, and of him, the worlds are and were created, and the inhabitants thereof are begotten sons and daughters unto God'" (D&C 76:22–24).

Notes

1. Benson, *The Teachings of Ezra Taft Benson*, 17–18.
2. "He Lives! The Witness of Latter-day Prophets, *Ensign*, Mar. 2008, 8–11; and http://JesusChrist.lds.org, under the heading "Testimonies of Him" and "He Lives! The Witness of Latter-day Prophets."

26

⇝ ΧΡΙΡΣΤΟΣ, CRISTOS ⇜

THE BOOK OF MORMON— ANOTHER TESTAMENT OF JESUS CHRIST

ΧΡΙΡΣΤΟΣ, Cristos—Cristos means Christ in Greek, which is the language of the New Testament. Along with the New Testament record, The Book of Mormon is a special witness of Christ (or Cristos) to all the world. It was written with this special testimony as its main message: "And also to the convincing of the Jew and Gentile that JESUS is the CHRIST, the ETERNAL GOD, manifesting himself unto all nations" (title page of the Book of Mormon). This scriptural record tells of a people separated from Jerusalem at the time of the Babylonian takeover because of the wickedness there. It provides a needed second witness of Jesus' name from a nation outside of Israel. It also provides further testimony of the Lord's physical Resurrection, with His appearance in the ancient America's as the resurrected Christ. This second scriptural witness provides evidence of continuing revelation and the Lord's love for all of His children.

By the time Jesus appeared to the faithful sons of Lehi, after His Resurrection, many great prophecies and signs had preceded His coming. The people in the land Bountiful had gone up to the temple amidst great destructions. There they heard a voice. The first time they heard it, they could not recognize its meaning, nor could they the second time. But the third time they understood the words of God the Father: "Behold, my Beloved Son, in whom I am well pleased, in whom I have glorified my name—hear ye him" (3 Nephi 11:7). Jesus then appeared and bore witness: "Behold, I am Jesus Christ, whom the prophets testified shall come into the world" (3 Nephi 11:10).

The resurrected Lord stood before the people, and they in turn fell to the earth, recognizing His glory. He stretched forth His hand and said, "behold, I am the light and the life of the world; and I have drunk out of that bitter cup which the Father hath given me, and have glorified the Father in taking upon me the sins of the world, in the which I have suffered the will of the Father in all things from the beginning" (3 Nephi 11:11). He then invited His people to arise and thrust their hands into His side, feel the prints of the nails in His hands and feet, and know for themselves "that I am the God of Israel, and the God of the whole earth, and have been slain for the sins of the world" (3 Nephi 11:14).

The witness of the Lord Jesus Christ in ancient America thus came from the Father, the Son, and the Holy Ghost. It proceeded from Bountiful throughout the land through many chosen witnesses who saw with their own eyes and felt with their own hands His physical Resurrection. "And when they had all gone forth and had witnessed for themselves, they did cry out with one accord, saying: Hosanna! Blessed be the name of the Most High God! And they did fall down at the feet of Jesus, and did worship him" (3 Nephi 11:16–17). This appearance served as an indisputable testimony to all who would later hear the account. Everyone present became responsible for spreading the testimony that proceeded from there. For on this day, as the record stands, "the multitude did see and hear and bear record; and they know that their record is true for they all of them did see and hear, every man for himself; and they were in number about two thousand and five hundred souls; and they did consist of men, women, and children" (3 Nephi 17:25).

The record from ancient America serves as another proof that God does not change. Jesus' words in that land, along with the doctrines and ordinances He revealed, were the same as those He taught his disciples in Jerusalem. In this way the Book of Mormon establishes a second scriptural witness of the Lord, "Proving to the world that the holy scriptures are true, and that God does inspire men and call them to his holy work in this age and generation, as well as in generations of old; Thereby showing that he is the same God yesterday, today, and forever. . . . Therefore, having so great witnesses, by them shall the world be judged. . . . And those who receive it in faith, and work righteousness, shall receive a crown of eternal life" (D&C 20:11–14). In our day, two separate accounts of the gospel have come together from different nations so that the interpretation of the doctrine is one. These two witnesses together provide everything a soul needs to be truly accountable before God. With the Lord speaking His gospel to two nations, where is there room for doubt? For "What greater witness can you have than from God?" (D&C 6:23).

In addition to the Old and New Testament, the Book of Mormon is another Testament of Jesus Christ. It is written for the express purpose of "the convincing of the Jew and Gentile that JESUS is the CHRIST, the ETERNAL GOD, manifesting himself unto all nations" (title page to the Book of Mormon, paragraph 2). After He had finished His work among the Jews, the testimony of the Lord was completed with this second scriptural witness from a nation beyond Israel.

The Book of Mormon tells of God's dealings with His people in ancient America. It contains the fulness of the restored Gospel of Jesus Christ. The book was written by prophets of ancient time by the spirit of prophecy and revelation. It tells of Jesus' personal appearance among His "other sheep" (see John 10:16) in ancient America and of His setting forth His doctrine to His people there. It also tells of the downfall of those who ultimately rejected the prophets and the Lord's teachings.

After the prophet Mormon had compiled all of the records and prophecies into one account and added his own witness, his son Moroni finished the record by adding his own prophecies. Moroni then buried the gold plates in a hill called Cumorah.

> On September 21, 1823, the same Moroni, then a glorified, resurrected being, appeared to the Prophet Joseph Smith and instructed him relative to the ancient record and its destined translation into the English language. In due course the plates were delivered to Joseph Smith, who translated them by the gift and power of God. The record is now published in many languages as a new and additional witness that Jesus Christ is the Son of the living God and that all who will come unto him and obey the laws and ordinances of the gospel may be saved. (Introduction to the Book of Mormon, paragraphs 4–5)

The coming forth of the Book of Mormon has fulfilled the prophecy of John concerning the way in which the gospel of Jesus Christ would be restored to the earth in the latter days. "And I saw another angel fly in the midst of heaven, having the everlasting gospel to preach unto them that dwell on the earth, and to every nation, and kindred, and tongue, and people" (Revelation 14:6). The Book of Mormon was given to the boy Joseph Smith by an angel and was translated by heaven's power. The record it contains of the everlasting gospel was thereby fully restored to every nation, kindred, tongue, and people before the Second Coming of the Lord Jesus Christ. This record was preserved so that it could be taken to all people in the way the Lord desired, through the efforts of His ordained servants.

As Joseph translated the record, he learned that it held an account of a people from Jerusalem. These were worthy descendants of the same Joseph who was sold into Egypt. They left Jerusalem after prophetic warnings told them of its impending destruction and the period of Babylonian captivity that would follow. Under the direction of their prophet and patriarch Lehi, and guided by the Lord, this group came across many waters to reach the promised land. They settled in the land of ancient America, where after the death of Lehi their families divided into two groups. The first were called Nephites after their leader Nephi, Lehi's obedient son who followed the Lord. The second were called Lamanites after their leader Laman, Lehi's disobedient son who rebelled against the teachings of his father. Many important lessons can be learned from this account. From the Book of Mormon we learn that those who followed the prophets received great blessings, while those who rejected the prophets and fell into great errors were not blessed. In every case, those who honored God, regardless of their heritage, were prosperous.

At the beginning of this record, Lehi prophesied that the Son of God would come to earth in six hundred years to fulfill the prophecies that had been revealed through all the holy prophets. At the very time of His coming six hundred years later, a new star would be seen by Lehi's people, just as it would be seen in Jerusalem. This star would signify His birth. Thirty-three years later great destructions would mark the time of His death. The resurrected Jesus would then appear among the people of ancient America.

This all happened, just as Lehi prophesied. Christ came to fulfill His word to the seed of Joseph. Those who followed the Lord in that land became a delightsome people, fulfilling Jesus' prophecy as given in Jerusalem: "And other sheep I have, which are not of this fold: them also I must bring, and they shall hear my voice; and there shall be one fold, and one shepherd" (John 10:16).

After generations of peace, following the Savior's appearance, the people in the Book of Mormon eventually rejected the gospel and cursed themselves with utter annihilation. Concerning this destruction and the record that would be preserved, Isaiah prophesied,

> And thou shalt be brought down, and shalt speak out of the ground, and thy speech shall be low out of the dust, and thy voice shall be, as of one that hath a familiar spirit, out of the ground, and thy speech shall whisper out of the dust. . . . And the vision of all is become unto you as the words of a book that is sealed, which men deliver to one that is learned, saying, Read this, I pray thee: and he saith, I cannot; for it is sealed: And the book is delivered to him that is not learned, saying, Read this, I pray thee: and he saith, I am not learned. . . . Therefore, behold, I will proceed to do a marvellous work among this people, even a marvellous work and a wonder: for the wisdom of their wise men shall perish, and the understanding of their prudent men shall be hid. . . . And in that day shall the deaf hear the words of the book, and the eyes of the blind shall see out of obscurity, and out of darkness. . . . They also that erred in spirit shall come to understanding, and they that murmured shall learn doctrine. (Isaiah 29:4, 11–12, 14, 18, 24)

This special witness stemming from the people of ancient America stands next to the Bible as another Testament of Jesus Christ. It speaks of the reality of His life, sacrifice, and physical Resurrection from the tomb. And it tells of the gospel that all men must follow to come unto Him and be saved. The Book of Mormon was given to us through the ministration of an angel who came to a boy prophet, thus beginning this special time in the history of the world when the Lord has proceeded "to do a marvelous work among them, that I may remember my covenants which I have made unto the children of men, that I may set my hand again the second time to recover my people, which are of the house of Israel" (2 Nephi 29:1). The gospel has been restored to the earth, like a stone cut out of a mountain without hands (see Daniel 2). And this is the book that, as prophesied, will gather scattered Israel home and prepare the world for the Second Coming of the Lord Jesus Christ.

ADDITIONAL COMMENTARY

ΧΡΙΡΣΤΟΣ: This word does not really begin with the English letter X. Rather it is a Greek word beginning with the Greek letters chi (X) and then rho (P), which correspond with the English C then R.

A Testimony Out of the Dust to Sweep the Earth: "And righteousness will I send down out of heaven; and truth will I send forth out of the earth, to bear testimony of mine Only Begotten; his resurrection from the dead; yea, and also the resurrection of all men; and righteousness and truth will I cause to sweep the earth as with a flood, to gather out mine elect from the four quarters of the earth, unto a place which I shall prepare" (Moses 7:62).

As One Testimony in Our Hand: Ezekiel prophesied concerning the record of the Nephites, saying, "Moreover, thou son of man, take thee one stick, and write upon it, For Judah, and for the children of Israel his companions: then take another stick, and write upon it, For Joseph, the stick of Ephraim, and for all the house of Israel his companions: And join them one to another into one stick; and they shall become one in thine hand" (Ezekiel 37:16–17). The Bible, also termed the stick of Judah, is a testament of Jesus Christ, written by the people of Judah and his companions. The Book of Mormon, termed the stick of Joseph, is another testament of Jesus Christ, written by the descendants of Joseph—Lehi's family.

The Lord Testifies That the Book of Mormon Is True: In the words of Jesus Christ: "And he [Joseph Smith] has translated the book, even that part which I have commanded him, and as your Lord and your God liveth it is true" (D&C 17:6). The resurrected Jesus spoke about this record when He appeared in ancient America: "And now behold, I say unto you that when the Lord shall see fit, in his wisdom, that these sayings shall come unto the Gentiles according to his word, then ye may know . . . that the words of the Lord, which have been spoken by the holy prophets, shall all be fulfilled; and ye need not say that the Lord delays his coming unto the children of Israel" (3 Nephi 29:1–2).

If You Believe in Christ, Believe in His Words:

> And now, my beloved brethren, and also Jew, and all ye ends of the earth, hearken unto these words and believe in Christ; and if ye believe not in these words believe in Christ. And if ye shall believe in Christ ye will believe in these words, for they are the words of Christ, and he hath given them unto me; and they teach all men that they should do good. And if they are not the words of Christ, judge ye—for Christ will show unto you, with power and great glory, that they are his words, at

the last day; and you and I shall stand face to face before his bar; and ye shall know that I have been commanded of him to write these things, notwithstanding my weakness. (2 Nephi 33:10–11)

The Testimony of Two Nations:

Know ye not that there are more nations than one? Know ye not that I, the Lord your God, have created all men, and that I remember those who are upon the isles of the sea; and that I rule in the heavens above and in the earth beneath; and I bring forth my word unto the children of men, yea, even upon all the nations of the earth? Wherefore murmur ye, because that ye shall receive more of my word? Know ye not that the testimony of two nations is a witness unto you that I am God, that I remember one nation like unto another? Wherefore, I speak the same words unto one nation like unto another. And when the two nations shall run together the testimony of the two nations shall run together also. And I do this that I may prove unto many that I am the same yesterday, today, and forever; and that I speak forth my words according to mine own pleasure. And because that I have spoken one word ye need not suppose that I cannot speak another; for my work is not yet finished; neither shall it be until the end of man, neither from that time henceforth and forever. Wherefore, because that ye have a Bible ye need not suppose that it contains all my words; neither need ye suppose that I have not caused more to be written. (2 Nephi 29:7–10)

The Testimony of Three Witnesses:
To prove to the world that this holy record is true, the Lord called upon three witnesses: Oliver Cowdery, David Whitmer, and Martin Harris. These bore solemn testimony of the Book of Mormon, which they never denied. They held to this testimony throughout their lives, whether in the Church or out. Their words are recorded in the beginning pages of the Book of Mormon:

BE IT KNOWN unto all nations, kindreds, tongues, and people, unto whom this work shall come: That we, through the grace of God the Father, and our Lord Jesus Christ, have seen the plates which contain this record, which is a record of the people of Nephi, and also of the Lamanites, their brethren, and also of the people of Jared, who came from the tower of which hath been spoken. And we also know that they have been translated by the gift and power of God, for his voice hath declared it unto us; wherefore we know of a surety that the work is true. And we also testify that we have seen the engravings which are upon the plates; and they have been shown unto us by the power of God, and not of man. And we declare with words of soberness, that an angel of God came down from heaven, and he brought and laid before our eyes, that we beheld and saw the plates, and the engravings thereon; and we know that it is by the grace of God the Father, and our Lord Jesus Christ, that we beheld and bear record that these things are true. And it is marvelous in our eyes. Nevertheless, the voice of the Lord commanded us that we should bear record of it; wherefore, to be obedient unto the commandments of God, we bear testimony of these things. And we know that if we are faithful in Christ, we shall rid our garments of the blood of all men, and be found spotless before the judgment-seat of Christ, and shall dwell with him eternally in the heavens. And the honor be to the Father, and to the Son, and to the Holy Ghost, which is one God. Amen.

The Testimony of Eight Witnesses: Christian Whitmer; Jacob Whitmer; Peter Whitmer, Jun.; John Whitmer; Hiram Page; Joseph Smith, Sen.; Hyrum Smith; and Samuel H. Smith.

> BE IT KNOWN unto all nations, kindreds, tongues, and people, unto whom this work shall come: That Joseph Smith, Jun., the translator of this work, has shown unto us the plates of which hath been spoken, which have the appearance of gold; and as many of the leaves as the said Smith has translated we did handle with our hands; and we also saw the engravings thereon, all of which has the appearance of ancient work, and of curious workmanship. And this we bear record with words of soberness, that the said Smith has shown unto us, for we have seen and hefted, and know of a surety that the said Smith has got the plates of which we have spoken. And we give our names unto the world, to witness unto the world that which we have seen. And we lie not, God bearing witness of it.

"What Greater Witness Can You Have than from God?" (D&C 6:23): As the last prophet to write in the Book of Mormon, Moroni left a challenge for any honest seeker of truth to obtain a personal witness of the Book of Mormon's truthfulness. Moroni stated that this witness will be given from God Himself if one will read the book, ponder its words and promises, and finally ask God to reveal its truthfulness through the power of the Holy Ghost (see Moroni 10:3–5). "Those who gain this divine witness from the Holy Spirit will also come to know by the same power that Jesus Christ is the Savior of the world, that Joseph Smith is his revelator and prophet in these last days, and that The Church of Jesus Christ of Latter-day Saints is the Lord's kingdom once again established on the earth, preparatory to the second coming of the Messiah" (Intro-duction to the Book of Mormon, Another Testament of Jesus Christ, paragraphs 6, 8–9).

27

✤ YAH'WEH, JEHOVAH ✤

JESUS' APPEARANCE IN MODERN TIMES

Yah'weh: This word is also rendered "YHWH" or "JHVH," and is a modern transliteration of the Hebrew word translated Jehovah in the Bible.[1] Jesus was the long foretold Messiah, the mortal Christ of the New Testament. But in the Old Testament He was also known as Jehovah, the "Unchangeable One," or "the eternal I AM" (see Ex. 6:3; Psalms 83:18; Isaiah 12:2; 26:4), who came to the prophets of old and established His laws among His Father's children. As arranged from the foundation of the world, Jesus would be the One to govern in Heavenly Father's work. Simply speaking, Jehovah is the premortal Christ. He came to earth as Jesus to receive His tabernacle of clay and to act as a Savior for the people of the earth. Before His birth, He declared "I, even I, am the LORD; and beside me there is no saviour" (Isaiah 43:11). Isaiah praised His saving power: "Behold, God is my salvation; I will trust, and not be afraid; for the Lord JEHOVAH is my strength and my song; he also is become my salvation" (Isaiah 12:2; see also 2 Nephi 22:2). Of all of the things He told the Jews, perhaps one reference carried the greatest offence, when He said, "Your father Abraham rejoiced to see my day: and he saw it, and was glad. Then said the Jews unto him, Thou art not yet fifty years old, and hast thou seen Abraham? Jesus said unto them, Verily, verily, I say unto you, Before Abraham was, I am" (John 8:56–58). The Jews understood His meaning perfectly. "Then took they up stones to cast at him" (John 8:59).

God does not change. He is "the same yesterday, today, and forever, and in him there is no variableness neither shadow of changing"

(Mormon 9:9). This doctrine is often attacked and challenged by modern-day "believers." Many contend that while God once spoke, He no longer needs to today. But how could a God who once loved and assisted His children with the voice from heaven, who has spoken in the same manner in every previous dispensation, no longer feel the need to speak to us? Could He who once voiced His will through prophets, revelation, and the ministration of angels no longer be needed in such a day as this? The restoring of the gospel of Jesus Christ began with the restoration of the doctrine of revelation. Most notably it began with a revelation of the Living God and the Living Christ. Today revelation flows from heaven as it did in the days when Peter received his testimony that Jesus was the Christ, the Son of the Living God (see Matthew 16:16).

In 1820 a religious excitement had stirred up the area around Joseph Smith's home. This movement was an attempt to have "everybody converted, as they were pleased to call it" (Joseph Smith—History 1:6), but it generated feelings of animosity between the various sects as proselytes filed off to one church or another. It also created questions in Joseph's young mind. One day, when reading in the Epistle of James in the Bible, he found some direction: "If any of you lack wisdom, let him ask of God, that giveth to all men liberally, and upbraideth not; and it shall be given him" (James 1:5). The passage made a firm impression upon the feelings in Joseph's heart, and he decided to follow the counsel.

Going into a grove of trees on the edge of his family's property, Joseph knelt and began to offer up the desires of his heart. Suddenly he was "seized upon," as he described it, by "some power which entirely overcame me, and had such an astonishing influence over me as to bind my tongue so that I could not speak. Thick darkness gathered around me, and it seemed to me for a time as if I were doomed to sudden destruction" (Joseph Smith—History 1:15). Exerting his powers to call upon God to deliver him from his enemy, Joseph saw a pillar of light. He testified:

"I saw a pillar of light exactly over my head, above the brightness of the sun, which descended gradually until it fell upon me . . . When the light rested upon me I saw two Personages, whose brightness and glory defy all description, standing above me in the air. One of them spake unto me, calling me by name and said, pointing to the other—"This is my Beloved Son. Hear Him!" (Joseph Smith—History 1:16–17).

The insights available from this experience came through pure revelation. They are specific for the current dispensation, now known as the fulness of times, and include the following: God is a glorified, exalted, res-urrected personage of flesh and bones. His body is as tangible as man's. He is a literal Person as the Biblical prophets declared Him to be, and He can speak face to face with His children today as in times of old (see Exodus 33:11). The heavens are not closed. God is not an absentee Master, but a concerned, helpful, loving Father. His Son Jesus Christ is also a res-urrected personage who ascended to His Father to sit with Him on His throne in heaven as the ancients prophecied (see Acts 7:55–56). Simply put, God is still able to communicate with His children. His kingdom is still rolling forth to fill the whole earth.

This vision, followed by subsequent ministrations from angels over the ensuing years, facilitated the Restoration of the gospel of Jesus Christ. The translation of the Book of Mormon—Another Testament of Jesus Christ, brought about a restoration of the true doctrine. Other revelations became the Doctrine and Covenants and helped organize the fledgling Church of Jesus Christ of Latter-day Saints. The fact remains that everything brought forth through the Prophet Joseph Smith was given to testify that Jesus is the Christ, that the Lord does not change, that He lives, that His work continues today as in former times, and that men must act in accordance with the ways He has established in order to be saved. The Church of Jesus Christ of Latter-day Saints is the kingdom of God restored with priest-hood authority on the earth today.

As Joseph learned, Christ stands today on the right hand of His Father. His work goes on in preparation for His glorious and not too dis-tant Second Coming when "the glory of the Lord shall be revealed, and all flesh shall see it together" (Isaiah 40:5). He reveals His secrets unto His prophets today as He did in times of old (see Amos 3:7). A prophet of the Lord still guides this work through revelation, with the Lord remaining as Head of the Church. And His work continues: temples adorn the earth as a result of the restored sealing power given to the Prophet; missionaries with priesthood authority travel the earth, seeking out the elect of God; the Book of Mormon is sweeping the earth like a flood; the Church welfare system is blessing the poor over the earth; ordinances that were once lost to the earth are now restored; disciples today are baptized by immersion and receive the gift of the Holy Ghost through the laying on of hands. In all corners of the earth, faith in the Lord has increased, and repentance, bap-tism, and all of the gifts of the Spirit are again available. The visions and blessings of old are returning, and angels are coming to visit the earth.[2]

When Peter first declared, "Thou art the Christ, the Son of the living God" (Matthew 16:16), he spoke of something flesh and blood had not revealed to him (see Matthew 16:17). This knowledge had come through revelation, "for the testimony of Jesus is the spirit of prophecy" (Revelation 19:10). Jesus spoke of the power of this revelation when He said to Peter, "upon this rock I will build my church; and the gates of hell shall not prevail against it" (Matthew 16:18).

James and John also received this witness and the keys of His ministry upon the Mount of Transfiguration. The other Apostles obtained the same witness by revelation either from the Lord Himself, from angels sent to declare it, or through the living prophet and the incomparable gift of the Holy Ghost. The Apostle Paul declared His testimony before men and kings, ultimately giving his life for it. All of the apostles and prophets lived, and many died, for this testimony.

Joseph Smith established the testimony of the Living Christ in this dispensation when he received what we now refer to as the First Vision (so called in reference to the veil parting for the first time in the modern dispensation). After his initial vision, other important experiences would strengthen Joseph's witness of Christ to the world. One such event occurred while Joseph was working on the translation of the Bible and Sidney Rigdon was serving as scribe. When they translated John 5:29, describing the resurrection of the dead, a vision opened and both were allowed to see and converse with the Savior. Now two men stood with this special knowledge of the Living Christ that they would declare before the world.

The results of this revelation are recorded in the Doctrine and Covenants, with specific testimony regarding the Lord and His ways: "After the many testimonies which have been given of him, this is the testimony, last of all which we give of him: That he lives! For we saw him, even on the right hand of God; and we heard the voice bearing record that he is the Only Begotten of the Father" (D&C 76:22–23).

The Lord also revealed Himself to the Prophet Joseph on April 3, 1836. Again Joseph did not stand alone as a witness of this remarkable occurrence. Oliver Cowdery accompanied him into the Kirtland Temple after its completion and dedication, and there the Prophet and his scribe retired to the west pulpit and bowed themselves in humble prayer. The details of this appearance are also recorded in the Doctrine and Covenants.

> The veil was taken from our minds, and the eyes of our understanding were opened. We saw the Lord standing upon the breastwork of the

pulpit, before us; and under his feet was a paved work of pure gold, in color like amber. His eyes were as a flame of fire; the hair of his head was white like the pure snow; his countenance shone above the brightness of the sun; and his voice was as the sound of the rushing of great waters, even the voice of Jehovah, saying: I am the first and the last; I am he who liveth, I am he who was slain; I am your advocate with the Father. (D&C 110:1–4)

The strength and impact of Joseph's testimony of the Living Christ was increased with the translation of the Book of Mormon, which would send this witness to all the world. This book testifies of Jesus in several ways:

1. Many prophets testify within the pages of the book in an effort to convince both "Jew and Gentile that JESUS is the CHRIST, the ETERNAL GOD, manifesting himself unto all nations" (title page of the Book of Mormon);
2. The book's very existence testifies of Christ, "Proving to the world that the holy scriptures are true, and that God does inspire men and call them to his holy work in this age and generation, as well as in generations of old; Thereby showing that he is the same God yesterday, today, and forever" (D&C 20:11–12);
3. With the Book of Mormon came the organizing of The Church of Jesus Christ of Latter-day Saints. The Church has fulfilled many prophecies, including that the gospel would roll forth like a great stone cut out of a mountain without hands to fill the earth before the end should come (see Daniel chapter 2);
4. The Book of Mormon prepares a person's heart to receive a personal manifestation of the divinity of Christ from the Holy Ghost (see Moroni 10:3–5).

In the end, the testimony of the Prophet Joseph Smith would be sealed with his own blood and with the blood of his brother, who stood with him unfailingly. After all that the Prophet had given the world, the enemy combined against him and his brother, Hyrum, taking them to Carthage Jail with other faithful men. Then on June 27, 1844, a mob approached the jail. They shot both Joseph and Hyrum to death. The Prophet's witness of Christ, his specially prepared testimony was thus sealed with his own blood. Joseph's testimony remains unequaled by any other man.

In this profound manner, the Prophet Joseph became the paramount witness of Christ. The strength of the Prophet's testimony was evidenced in his life, work, sacrifice, and death. His words now remain forever established to testify that Jesus is the Living Christ who still stands at the head of His kingdom, guiding and ruling from above. The revelations of the Prophet Joseph Smith and his successors have brought a fulness of testimony to the world.

Through the workings of Joseph Smith and subsequent servants of the Lord, the true believers are being prepared to receive their King at His glorious Second Coming. This was the Prophet's special role, and this calling has continued from Joseph to the living prophet in the present day, with the priesthood guiding the work. In the special manner only Heaven can provide, the Lord's voice will indeed come "unto all men, and there is none to escape; and there is no eye that shall not see, neither ear that shall not hear, neither heart that shall not be penetrated" (D&C 1:2). Such is the nature of this marvelous work that will reach all men. All the earth shall be affected. Such wonderful and glorious events will ultimately bring every knee to bend and every tongue to confess that Jesus is the Christ.

ADDITIONAL COMMENTARY

A Living God That Changes Not: Ralph Waldo Emerson shattered the bedrock of New England ecclesiastical orthodoxy when he spoke at the Divinity School at Harvard, saying: "It is my duty to say to you that the need was never greater [for] new revelation than now." He also said, "The doctrine of inspiration is lost. . . . Miracles, prophecy, . . . the holy life, exist as ancient history [only]. . . . Men have come to speak of . . . revelation as somewhat long ago given and done, as if God were dead. . . . It is the office of a true teacher to show us that God is, not was; that He speaketh, not spake."[2] The Quaker mystic Rufus Jones similarly noted that "God is a living, revealing, communicating God—the Great I Am, not a great He Was."[3]

A God Who Once Loved and Assisted His Children: One of the best known religious reformers from New England, Jonathan Edwards, said, "It seems to me a[n] . . . unreasonable thing, to suppose that there should be a God . . . that has so much concern [for us], . . . and yet that he should never speak, . . . that there should be no word [from him]."[4]

The Principle of Present Revelation: John Taylor said,

> Whoever heard of true religion without communication with God? To me the thing is the most absurd that the human mind could conceive of. I do not wonder [that] when the people generally reject the principle of present revelation, skepticism and infidelity prevail to such an alarming extent. I do not wonder that so many men treat religion with contempt, and regard it as something not worth the attention of intelligent beings, for without revelation religion is a mockery and a farce. . . . *The principle of present revelation . . . is the very foundation of our religion.*[5]

God Is Not Dead, Nor Doth He Sleep: "Then pealed the bells more loud and deep: 'God is not dead, nor doth he sleep; The wrong shall fail, the right prevail, With peace on earth, good will to men.'"[6]

Restoration of the Doctrine of Revelation: Jeffrey R. Holland declared, "At a time when the origins of Christianity were under assault by the forces of Enlightenment rationality, Joseph Smith [unequivocally and single-handedly] returned modern Christianity to its origins in revelation."[7]

The Preeminent Revelator of Jesus Christ: Elder D. Todd Christofferson said, "I love and bear witness of the Prophet Joseph Smith. Through his personal association with the Lord, his translation and publication of the Book of Mormon, and the sealing of his testimony with his martyr's blood, Joseph has become the preeminent revelator of Jesus Christ in His true character as divine Redeemer. Jesus has had no greater witness nor more devoted friend than Joseph Smith."[8]

Reasons to Rejoice in the Restoration: Today the Lord is preparing His children for His coming as He did in days of old. He has already made His appearance to chosen witnesses and brought His priesthood power to the earth through angels who have bestowed their priesthood keys. Moses, Elias, and Elijah have committed to men the keys of gathering, the keys of the dispensation of the gospel of Abraham, and the keys of the sealing power before the great and dreadful day of the Lord (see D&C 110:11–16). Visions and blessings, angels and temples, commandments and ordinances, the priesthood and its sealing powers are had again today as they were in the days of old. Those who desire to follow the Lord and walk in His ways are able to receive His gospel again as it has been given from heaven.

Rejoice, the Lord Is King:

> Let the mountains shout for joy, and all ye valleys cry aloud; and all ye seas and dry lands tell the wonders of your Eternal King! And ye rivers, and brooks, and rills, flow down with gladness. Let the woods and all the trees of the field praise the Lord; and ye solid rocks weep for joy! And let the sun, moon, and the morning stars sing together, and let all the sons of God shout for joy! And let the eternal creations declare his name forever and ever! And again I say, how glorious is the voice we hear from heaven, proclaiming in our ears, glory, and salvation, and honor, and immortality, and eternal life; kingdoms, principalities, and powers! (D&C 128:23)

Notes

1. Merriam-Webster's Collegiate Dictionary: Tenth Edition (Springfield, Massachusetts: Merriam-Webster's, 1998).
2. Ralph Waldo Emerson, *The Complete Essays and Other Writings of Ralph Waldo Emerson*, ed. Brooks Atkinson (New York: Modern Library [Random House Publishing], 1940), 75, 71, 80.
3. Hugh B. Brown, speech given to Brigham Young University, 8 Mar. 1950, as quoted by Leonard J. Arrington and Davis Bitton in *The Mormon Experience: A History of the Latter-day Saints* (New York: Alfred A. Knopf, 1979), 5.
4. *The Works of Jonathan Edwards*, vol. 18, *The "Miscellanies" 501–832*, ed. Ava Chamberlain (2000), 89–90, as quoted by Jeffrey R. Holland in "Prophets, Seers, and Revelators," *Liahona*, Nov. 2004, 6–9.
5. John Taylor, "Discourse by John Taylor," *Deseret News*, 4 Mar. 1874, 68, as quoted by Holland in "Prophets, Seers, and Revelators," 6–9.
6. Henry Wadsworth Longfellow, "I Heard the Bells on Christmas Day," *Hymns*, no. 214.
7. See Richard L. Bushman's essay "A Joseph Smith for the Twenty-First Century, in *Believing History* (2004), 274, as quoted by Holland in "Prophets, Seers, and Revelators," 6–9.
8. D. Todd Christofferson, "Born Again," *Ensign*, May 2008, 76–79.

28

❖ ZION'S KING ❖

THE APOSTOLIC WITNESS PREPARING THE WORLD FOR THE MILLENNIAL KING

Zion's King: "I am Messiah, the King of Zion, the Rock of Heaven, which is broad as eternity; whoso cometh in at the gate and climbeth up by me shall never fall" (Moses 7:53). Defined as the Lord's people who are of one heart and one mind, dwelling in righteousness with no poor among them (see Moses 7:18), Zion gladly received its King when He came the first time. The pure in heart will do so again when Jesus stands a second time on Mount Zion according to the scripture: "And I looked, and, lo, a Lamb stood on the mount Sion, and with him a hundred forty and four thousand, having his Father's name written in their foreheads" (Revelation 14:1).

In preparation for the Lord's Second Coming, and following the prophesied Restoration of His gospel, His work now proceeds in His own established and ordained way. Signs will warn of His coming, and even now the gospel is being preached in all the world as a witness and a warning that the Lord will soon make His appearance. He will come to rule and reign as King of Kings and Lord of Lords. The King of Zion will come to all who will receive Him as their Lord.

The Twelve Apostles of the Lamb have the responsibility of bearing testimony of the Son of God in all the world (see D&C 107:23). They are "sent out, holding the keys, to open the door by the proclamation of the gospel of Jesus Christ, and first unto the Gentiles and then unto the Jews" (D&C 107:35). These disciples are they "who shall desire to take upon them my name with full purpose of heart. And if they desire to take upon them my name with full purpose of heart, they are called to go into all the world to preach my gospel unto every creature" (D&C 18:27–28).

In a marvelous vision, recorded at the beginning of the Book of Mormon, Lehi witnessed the Son of God, and directly after this he saw a vision of the Twelve Apostles. For "he also saw twelve others following him, and their brightness did exceed that of the stars in the firmament. And they came down and went forth upon the face of the earth" (1 Nephi 1:10–11). The mission of the Twelve Apostles has been declared from the beginning: to open the door of salvation in all the world by proclaiming the name of Christ. How great is their calling!

Nephi also saw the Twelve Apostles and how they went forth. He saw that the world gathered to fight against them, and the great and spacious building, representing the pride of the world, fell before them.

> Behold, the world and the wisdom thereof; yea, behold the house of Israel hath gathered together to fight against the twelve apostles of the Lamb. And it came to pass that I saw and bear record, that the great and spacious building was the pride of the world; and it fell, and the fall thereof was exceedingly great. And the angel of the Lord spake unto me again, saying: thus shall be the destruction of all nations, kindreds, tongues, and people that shall fight against the twelve apostles of the Lamb. (see 1 Nephi 11:35–36)

These apostles and those ordained under their direction have great power and a special influence for good upon the world.

> And they shall go forth and none shall stay them, for I the Lord have commanded them. Behold, this is mine authority, and the authority of my servants. . . . And verily I say unto you, that they who go forth, bearing these tidings unto the inhabitants of the earth, to them is power given to seal both on earth and in heaven, the unbelieving and rebellious. . . . Wherefore the voice of the Lord is unto the ends of the earth, that all that will hear may hear. . . . And the arm of the Lord shall be revealed; and the day cometh that they who will not hear the voice of the Lord . . . neither give heed to the words of the prophets and apostles, shall be cut off from among the people (D&C 1:5–6, 8, 11, 14).

Ultimately the prophets and apostles of the Lord will successfully bear record of the Lamb in all the world (see 1 Nephi 13:24). The record of the gospel will go forth by their humble yet majestic efforts (see 1 Nephi 13:26, 39–41). And they will work mighty miracles (see Mormon 9:18). In addition to this they will:

- baptize (D&C 18:29)
- ordain other priesthood officers (D&C 18:32)
- administer the sacrament (D&C 20:40)
- confirm baptized members (D&C 20:41, 43)
- teach and watch over the Church (D&C 20:42)
- take the lead in meetings, wherever they go (D&C 20:44)
- act as special witnesses of Christ's name (D&C 27:12; 107:23)
- bestow the Holy Ghost by the laying on of hands (D&C 35:6)
- preach the Resurrection (D&C 63:52)
- build up the Church (D&C 84:108)
- prune the Lord's vineyard (D&C 95:4)
- direct the work of the seventy (D&C 107:34; 124:139)
- hold the keys to proclaim the gospel (D&C 107:45; 124:128) and the power to send missionaries to every nation (D&C 112:21).

They will also testify in Jerusalem among the Jews in a manifestation of the Lord's power (see Revelation 11). And, as in times of old, they will send forth their written testimony of Jesus Christ (see Ether 12:41, the New Testament record, the Book of Mormon, and "The Living Christ" as a few examples).

The Twelve Apostles of the Lamb will thus prepare the world for the Second Coming of the Lord Jesus Christ through their own testimony and through the work that is directed under their authority.

And then the Lord will come. He will stand upon Mount Zion. His voice will be heard and His face will be seen. He will come with all His holy angels in the clouds of heaven. He will reveal His glory to all mankind upon the earth, and every knee shall bow and every tongue confess that Jesus is the Christ. When He comes again, He will come to reign as King of Kings and Lord of Lords. "And the glory of the LORD shall be revealed, and all flesh shall see it together. . . . O Zion, that bringest good tidings, get thee up into the high mountain; O Jerusalem, that bringest good tidings, lift up thy voice with strength; lift it up, be not afraid; say unto the cities of Judah, Behold your God" (Isaiah 40:5, 9).

The Millennium will thus be ushered in, and the Lord will return to reign among His people. Then the government will truly be upon His shoulder (see Isaiah 9:6). Peace will prevail under the Prince of Peace. Great blessings will flow to all who have loved the Lord. As prophesied, "the Son of man shall come in his glory, and all the holy angels with him, then shall he sit upon the throne of his glory: And before him shall be gathered all nations: and he shall separate them one from another, as a shepherd divideth his sheep from the goats" (Matthew 25:31–32).

For those who are faithful there shall be a place prepared to live with the King. This place will be called Zion.

> And it shall be called the New Jerusalem, a land of peace, a city of refuge, a place of safety for the saints of the Most High God; And the glory of the Lord shall be there, and the terror of the Lord also shall be there, insomuch that the wicked will not come unto it, and it shall be called Zion. And it shall come to pass among the wicked, that every man that will not take his sword against his neighbor must needs flee unto Zion for safety. And there shall be gathered unto it out of every nation under heaven; and it shall be the only people that shall not be at war one with another. And it shall be said among the wicked: Let us not go up to battle against Zion, for the inhabitants of Zion are terrible; wherefore we cannot stand. (D&C 45:66–70)

A great wedding feast will take place as part of the grand Millennium. This feast is mentioned throughout the scriptures. The marriage supper of the Lamb will be made ready, the Church will come prepared as the bride, "arrayed in fine linen, clean and white: for the fine linen is the righteousness of saints" (Revelation 19:8). The Saints will be called to this special marriage feast, and they will rejoice, for "Blessed are they which are called unto the marriage supper of the Lamb" (Revelation 19:9).

Jesus will then "reign personally upon the earth," and "the earth will be renewed and receive its paradisiacal glory" (tenth article of faith). Temptation will be abolished. Wickedness will be thrown down. Every corruptible thing will be consumed. "And also that of element shall melt with fervent heat; and all things shall become new, that my knowledge and glory may dwell upon the earth" (D&C 101:25). "For the great Millennium of which I have spoken by the mouth of my servants, shall come. For Satan shall be bound, and when he is loosed again he shall only reign for a little season, and then cometh the end of the earth. And he that liveth in righteousness shall be changed in the twinkling of an eye, and the earth shall pass away so as by fire" (D&C 43:30–32).

Jesus alone will be exalted in that day. The Eternal Messiah will stand to rule as King of Kings. Every knee will bend before Him. Every tongue will speak in worship. As He was lifted up, even so shall He raise every soul to stand before Him and be judged of Him according to the works and the desires of that soul's heart (see D&C 137:9).

A season of peace and joy will follow.

> And in that day the enmity of man, and the enmity of beasts, yea, the enmity of all flesh, shall cease from before my face. And in that day whatsoever any man shall ask, it shall be given unto him. And in that day Satan shall not have power to tempt any man. And there shall be no sorrow because there is no death. And in that day an infant shall not die until he is old; and his life shall be as the age of a tree; And when he dies he shall not sleep, that is to say in the earth, but shall be changed in the twinkling of an eye, and shall be caught up, and his rest shall be glorious. (D&C 101:26–31)

For a thousand years there will be no war, pain, or sorrow.

> And it shall come to pass, that every one that is left of all the nations which came against Jerusalem shall even go up from year to year to worship the King, the Lord of hosts, and to keep the feast of tabernacles. . . . In that day there shall be upon the bells of the horses, HOLINESS UNTO THE LORD; and the pots in the Lord's house shall be like the bowls before the altar. Yea, every pot in Jerusalem and in Judah shall be holiness unto the Lord of hosts. (Zechariah 14:16, 20–21)

Many things will change during this peaceful reign of Christ. As Isaiah has prophesied,

> The wolf also shall dwell with the lamb, and the leopard shall lie down with the kid; and the calf and the young lion and the fatling together; and a little child shall lead them. And the cow and the bear shall feed; their young ones shall lie down together: and the lion shall eat straw like the ox. And the sucking child shall play on the hole of the asp, and the weaned child shall put his hand on the cockatrice's den. And they shall not hurt nor destroy in all my holy mountain: for the earth shall be full of the knowledge of the Lord, as the waters cover the sea. (Isaiah 11:6–9)

The Lord will reign supreme. He will sit upon His throne, and all nations will flow unto Him to worship. "And he shall judge among the nations, and shall rebuke many people: and they shall beat their swords into plowshares, and their spears into pruninghooks: nation shall not lift up sword against nation, neither shall they learn war any more" (Isaiah 2:4). Those who are allowed to remain will come to know the Lord and His ways, for He will teach them. "Then shall they know that I am the Lord their God. . . . Neither will I hide my face any more from them: for I have poured out my spirit upon the house of Israel, saith the Lord God" (Ezekiel 39:28–29).

Not only will those who are privileged to remain on the earth come into subjection under the Prince of Peace, but the blessings will flow to all who seek the Lord. "In that day shall the branch of the Lord be beautiful and glorious, and the fruit of the earth shall be excellent and comely for them that are escaped of Israel" (Isaiah 4:2). All men will praise the Lord when Israel will be completely gathered home and enjoy Millennial rest from its cares, sorrows, fears, and bondage (see Isaiah 14). And "the Lord of hosts shall reign in Mount Zion, and in Jerusalem, and before his ancients gloriously" (Isaiah 24:23).

During this time the earth will become such a wonderful place to live. "For, behold, I create new heavens and a new earth: and the former shall not be remembered, nor come into mind. . . . And I will rejoice in Jerusalem, and joy in my people: and the voice of weeping shall be no more heard in her, nor the voice of crying. There shall be no more thence an infant of days, nor an old man that hath not filled his days: for the child shall die an hundred years old" (Isaiah 65:17, 19–20). "For as the new heavens and the new earth, which I will make, shall remain before me, saith the Lord, so shall your seed and your name remain" (Isaiah 66:22).

This will be a day of life and resurrection. Those who are redeemed of the Lord will come unto Him to remain forever. It will be a day of rejoicing and a day of thanksgiving. There will be singing and praising of the Lord.

> And now the year of my redeemed is come; and they shall mention the loving kindness of the Lord, and all that he has bestowed upon them according to his goodness, and according to his loving kindness, forever and ever. In all their afflictions he was afflicted. And the angel of his presence saved them; and in his love, and in his pity, he redeemed them, and bore them, and carried them all the days of old. . . . And the graves of the saints shall be opened; and they shall come forth and stand on the right hand of the Lamb, when he shall stand upon Mount Zion, and upon the holy city, the New Jerusalem; and they shall sing the song of

the Lamb, day and night forever and ever. (D&C 133:52–53, 56)

Such are the blessings that will flow under the Millennial Messiah. For this reason the Twelve Apostles of the Lamb are now sent forth to prepare the world for His coming as the King of Zion. The testimony of the apostles and prophets will prepare the way before Him, as with John the Baptist at His first coming.

The One for whom all praise is due, the One that we adore, our Beloved Christ, shall come. And every knee shall voluntarily bow. Every tongue shall with rejoicing confess that Jesus is the Christ, the Almighty. He who rules in the heaven shall rule on earth, and all will come to know, even as we already know: Jesus is the Living Christ, the Son of the Eternal Father. We praise our God for the perfect gift of salvation, given to us in the form of His Son, Jesus Christ, who is and always will be the way, the truth, and the life.

ADDITIONAL COMMENTARY

The Responsibility as a Witness of Christ: The Twelve Apostles are already doing all of the things mentioned in this chapter that will bear witness of the Lord Jesus Christ and prepare the world for His coming. But they should not be alone in bearing their witness of the Son of God. Elder D. Todd Christofferson confirms:

> Apostles, by virtue of their priesthood office, are commissioned as special witnesses of Christ in all the world (see D&C 107:23). Their testimony is vital in the Lord's work of salvation. Yet the Apostles must not and do not stand alone. All of us who are baptized and confirmed have taken upon us the name of Jesus Christ with a commitment "to stand as witnesses of God at all times and in all things, and in all places" (Mosiah 18:9). It is within the capacity of each of us to become His witness. Indeed, the Lord relies on "the weak and the simple" to declare His gospel (see D&C 1:19, 23), and it is His desire "that every man might speak in the name of God the Lord, even the Savior of the world" (D&C 1:20).[1]

Biblical Prophesies of the Latter-day Restoration of the Gospel Preceding the Savior's Second Coming: The following scriptures contain prophesies of the Restoration.

+ Isaiah 2:2–3; Isaiah 11:11–12; Isaiah 29:14; Jeremiah 31:31;

Ezekiel 37:26–28; Daniel 2:44–45; Joel 2:28–32; Malachi 3:1,
6–7, 17; Malachi 4:5–6;

+ Matthew 17:10–11; John 1:19–25; Matthew 24:14; Acts 3:20–21;
Ephesians 1:10; James 1:5–6 (included here as the scripture that
helped bring about the Restoration); Revelation 14:6–7.

Notes

1. D. Todd Christofferson, "Becoming a Witness of Christ," *Ensign*,
Mar. 2008, 59.

✦ APPENDIX ✦

THE BEATITUDES— A PROGRESSION TO GODHOOD

Step one: Blessed are the poor in spirit (poor in pride or humble in spirit).

The beginning of this journey requires humility. If a man is not humble he will not be able to progress any further along this pathway, for it requires an attitude of listening, learning, and following. After the Savior's great and last sacrifice ended animal sacrifice, it was the sacrifice of a broken heart and a contrite spirit that became acceptable before the Father (see 3 Nephi 9:19–20). As the Lord Himself demonstrated, it takes humility to begin on this pathway. Many of Jesus' other teachings elaborated upon this first step, such as the one in which the Lord set a child in the midst of the people and taught that unless men become as little children they can never enter into the kingdom of heaven (see Matthew 18:1–6).

Step two: Blessed are those that mourn.

This step follows humility. Those who are humble are not light-minded, especially when it comes to such serious matters as spiritual life and death. Humility leads to an understanding that the cost of this gospel was the very life of Jesus Christ. This mourning is a direct reference to the broken heart and contrite spirit that characterize those who understand Christ's Atonement. Only the humble will proceed on to this second step. Alma the Younger was humbled by an angel, and then found that he was "racked with eternal torment, for my soul was harrowed up to the greatest degree and racked with all my sins" (Alma 36:12). Alma could not have taken this step without humility. In his case the angel had to help him along. When we learn of the Lord, as did Alma, we find that God will have

269

a humble people. Humility is what makes the very thought of coming into the presence of God unworthily rack the soul with inexpressible horror (see Alma 36:14). After coming to this step Alma stated, "And it came to pass that as I was thus racked with torment, while I was harrowed up by the memory of my many sins, behold, I remembered also to have heard my father prophesy unto the people concerning the coming of one Jesus Christ, a Son of God, to atone for the sins of the world" (Alma 36:17). This step leads a person to Christ and in time the desire to follow in His ways supersedes all else.

Step three: Blessed are the meek.

Meekness is not weakness. It is obedience. It is power under control. Meekness is self-mastery. A meek person does not act out of a need to impress others, but out of a determination to do what is right regardless of what others might think. The Creator of the Universe described Himself as meek and lowly of heart. If a person is lacking in self-control, perhaps it is because he is still on level one and first needs to become humble. Or perhaps he is on level two and still needs to have a broken heart and a contrite spirit. Those who have a broken heart and contrite spirit, come to remember Christ. Those who know Him and understand His sacrifice on their behalf can do nothing but what He would have them do. For this reason He said, "If ye love me, keep my commandments" (John 14:15).

Step four: Blessed are they which do hunger and thirst after righteousness.

If on the previous levels a man has obeyed only by exercising self-discipline, this is the step in which he now comes to Christ because he wants to. On this level he hungers for righteousness. He thirsts for it. On this level parents and leaders stop worrying about him, because he has become self-motivated. He obeys the truth of his own volition because he loves it. He loves the Lord. He seeks the word of the Lord in the same way that a famished man seeks for food and water or a drowning man seeks a breath of fresh air. For those who so seek, the promise follows that they shall find. For those who knock, it shall be opened. For those who ask, it shall be given.

Step five: Blessed are the merciful.

Those who have progressed to this step and discovered righteousness become less critical of others and more merciful. They become more kind and forgiving. A person simply cannot take this step if he has not previously hungered after Christ and progressed through the previous levels. This step requires faith and repentance, hope, and charity or the pure love of Christ all of which result from progressing through the previous levels.

Step six: Blessed are the pure in heart.

At this point, a person becomes pure. His motives become pure. The gospel is a part of him because of his love for God the Father and Jesus Christ. A great blessing follows this step. On this level the pure in heart will obtain the promise that they will see God.

Step seven: Blessed are the peacemakers.

At some point along the way, all of these preparations turn from a focus on oneself to blessing others beyond oneself. Certainly on this step men and women can be called "peacemakers" as they become the children of Christ.

Step eight: Blessed are the persecuted

This is an interesting and challenging step. Those who become peacemakers often become targets for the problem-makers. Certainly Satan's plan is to incite the enemies of God, for "he stirreth them up to iniquity against that which is good" (D&C 10:20). But there is an eternal reward for those who endure persecutions. Those who progress to this step become like the Savior, rendering good for evil in the face of adversity. The only way do this is to forget oneself and focus instead on blessing others. Those who can do this are true peacemakers in every sense of the word.

ABOUT THE AUTHOR

Brett D. Benson is a seminary instructor and a principal for the seminaries and institutes of religion program of The Church of Jesus Christ of Latter-day Saints. He earned a BA from the University of Utah in Biology and an MA in education, with an emphasis in curriculum and instruction, from the University of Phoenix. He coauthored *How to Remember Everything in the New Testament.*

Brother Benson has served in the Church as a bishop, branch president, ward young men president, and a missionary in the Portugal Lisbon mission. Brett and his wife, Jodi, live in Layton, Utah, and are the parents of eight children: Tyler, Rachel, Matthew, Joseph, Hannah, Hyrum, Sarah, and Katelyn.

0 26575 53009 4